DAVID LIBERTO

RETURN OF THE LOST ONES

Book One of the BlueSteel Series

Book One of the Teresan Saga

In memory of my mother, Rose R. Liberto.

Before she traveled to the next realm, she told me she would read my book.

This one's for you, Mom.

CONTINENT OF ANTHIL

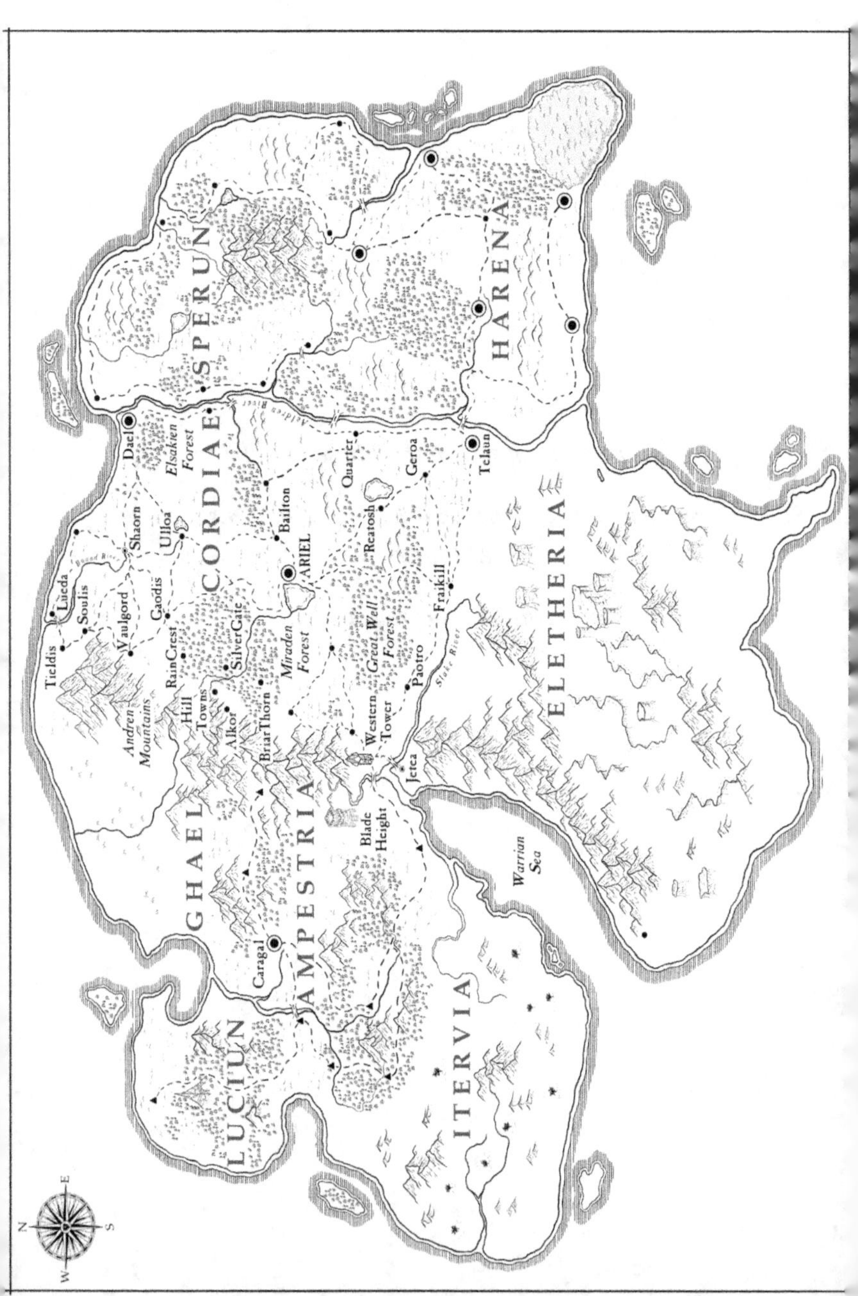

NATION OF CORDIAE

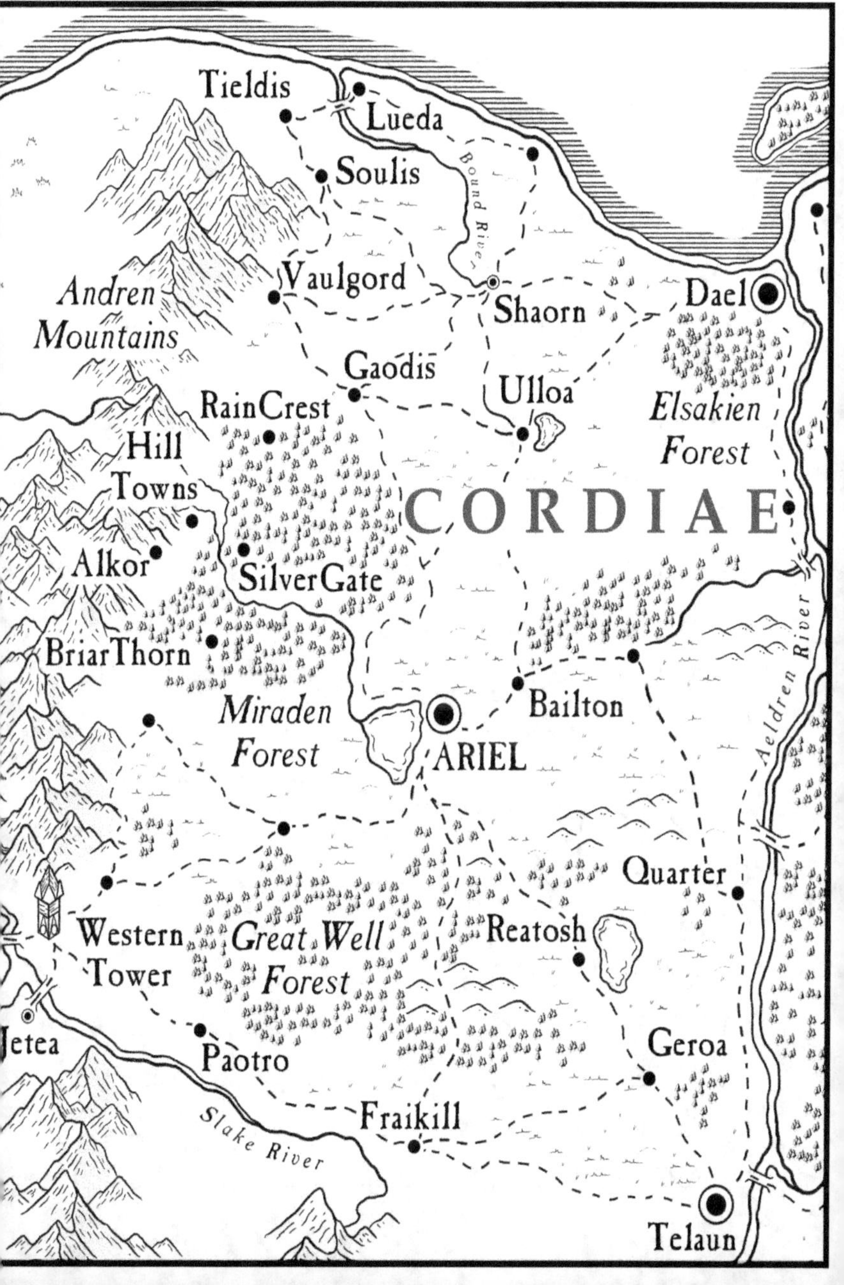

RETURN OF THE LOST ONES

(BlueSteel Series, Book 1)

Contents

PROLOGUE

With a heavy limp, Fenric eagerly advanced down the long hallway without a soul in sight. His left sandal broke the unusual silence as it scuffed against the cold slate imported from another continent. The central palace tower had been cleared under the pretense of releasing a new research project. Mandrate innovation often resulted in casualties, and the local populace would opt to take a brief vacation instead of risking an obscure death.

The fabricated announcement had a purpose; the most advanced mandrates in the world wanted this meeting to be a secret. Normally, sycophants would be crawling all over the central palace tower like ants, desperate for an ounce of attention from a master, but quiet reigned in the empty halls today. Fenric's worn shoe scuffed the ground, breaking the silence. Fenric was about to have the attention of the entire Ampestrian High Council.

Centuries. He had waited centuries for this opportunity. Obstacles, adversaries, and failures had been removed, overcome by sheer will—except for one last hurdle.

The High Council. They would decide his fate. His master had informed him there were a few council members who opposed his will, as they sought to promote their own disciples for such an infamous quest.

No. It was his and his alone.

Not wanting to miss his chance, Fenric increased his pace. He rarely minded his limp, acquired a few hundred years before, but he was determined to arrive exactly on time. Fenric's body wasn't as horribly deformed as those of advanced power, the archmandrates. Mandra had its costs. The more you use it, the harder on the body. You could tell a lot about a mandrate by how deformed they were.

He entered a dark circular hall, giant bronzed columns buttressing a vaulted ceiling that funneled into the main tower above. Resting in the exact center of the dark, enclosed rotunda, a circular steel platform with nine wedges waited. Each wedge held sculpted images representing the nine main disciplines of mandra. Wrought iron sigils formed a perimeter around the circle.

Fenric mounted the steel platform, the focal center of the palace. In turn, the palace was the center of Caragal, the capital city of Ampestria, the cradle of mandra for the entire continent. If you wanted to advance, this was where a mandrate had to be.

He only waited a moment. As expected, the circular platform separated from the ground with a smooth levitation, and Fenric ascended to the pinnacle of his career. He marveled at the unseen energy flawlessly maneuvering him to the top. Invisible beauty.

Fenric rose through the council chamber's floor opening as the platform slowly decelerated to a halt, drawing flush with the floor and aligning each of the nine wedges with its respective triangle, which lined up with one of nine thrones.

The archmandrates. Horribly deformed masters of mandra, the most feared beings on the continent, sat in almost complete darkness around him.

ArchMandrate Koen, the Head of the High Council and Prime Minister of Ampestria, ignited the yellow globe under his black-scaled right hand, illuminating a metal wedge under Fenric's feet.

"We have already called the session to order. Fenric, disciple of Jenter, and Stacia, my disciple, have been called."

To his right, a shimmer in midair coalesced into a large flat oval revealing a female, lithe and seemingly untouched by mandra. Stacia was on assignment in Cordiae and had been a longtime rival of Fenric's. Her mission was crucial to the High Council, but his quest could do more, much more, for the Council.

But there were risks. Cordiae was hostile to mandrates. Greater risk, greater reward.

Fenric scanned the thrones. He was among great beings, and this was his opening to join their ranks.

Prime Minister Koen continued. "We have already heard the arguments for the mission. Fenric, ArchMandrate Jenter has recommended you, and the Council has agreed that you have the required skill-set to complete the mission. Do you accept?"

Fenric bowed. "Oh yes, Prime Minister Koen. I accept."

"Any further objections?" Koen asked.

From the oval, Stacia said, "I ask the High Council to consider my petition to secure the target for Fenric's mission. I am better suited, and I believe the chance of success will be higher."

Fenric barely contained his mandra from the instant rage. If anyone had escaped his reach and had the experience to challenge him, it was Stacia.

The orange wedge lit up, and Fenric's master, ArchMandrate Jenter, spoke. "Stacia has her own target, and we don't want to compromise her years of work. Fenric's competency in this matter has already been established."

The green wedge lit up, and from the dark came a dry, craggy voice. "There is no certainty in either case. Nothing should change."

Prime Minister Koen said, "The ArchMandrate of Divination has spoken. Stacia, your objection is valid, but keep to your own task. Both are crucial pieces."

"Yes, Master."

Fenric's tension evaporated, but he would not forget her objection.

"Fenric, you will depart immediately for the Cordiaen border. Your supplies have already been transferred. Travel by conventional means from there, and, yes, your requests for compensation have been approved…if you succeed."

Fenric couldn't suppress his smile. "Thank you, Prime Minister and High Council."

Prime Minister Koen's black-scaled hand tapped the globe once more. "Do not underestimate the Tainted One. We will be watching."

"Excellent," Fenric replied, bowing.

Koen added, "Stacia, the Council has ruled that you will begin the next phase."

"Yes, Master."

The clock was now ticking. Their missions had connected pieces that required sensitive timing. Fenric would ensure his part did not falter, and he grudgingly conceded that she would most likely also perform well. Success was imminent.

"You may go. May Karak, in his benevolence, grant you success," Koen finished.

Stacia's image faded, and the oval disintegrated into an ethereal green mist.

Fenric bowed as a black oval bordered by ropes of green-and-purple light materialized to his right. His chance had finally come. Adrenaline surged through his body like the first time he had used mandra. All the pieces had aligned. Now, he had to execute.

Fenric stepped into the darkness.

CHAPTER 1

"There are two types of soldiers: the ones who want to fight and the ones who have to fight."
—Cleric Joern, *Advanced Cordiaen Military Tactics, Volume 2.*

Pol rubbed his light-brown face with both hands as he sat up. His sixteen-year-old body had woken without difficulty, as it did every morning before dawn, but it always took a moment to clear his head. Daytime naps required a longer wake up period and his sisters would often play pranks, taking advantage of his post-sleep confusion.

Sitting on the floor of the dark bedroom, his hands brushed the still-warm crimson blanket laid out beneath him that had served as his bed for years. His grandmother, who had passed a few years before, had sewn it and gifted it to him for Festival. Pol treasured the blanket and its connection to the woman who had been so kind. His grandfather had built the bedroom and second floor living quarters atop their family store years ago. Pol didn't mind sleeping on the floor his family had crafted with love

Some mornings he wondered if a cot or bed might provide a better night's sleep, but those luxuries would not fit in the dark single room above his family's cobbler shop, where his parents and two sisters continued sleeping with soft breathing. The blanket would do.

As Pol's thoughts cleared, he felt the wood floor for his garments he had laid out the night before. Where most young men his age might wake past dawn, Pol had a legacy to fulfill. Maybe not the legacy his father wanted, but each morning he set out for Dael Keep to make his grandparents and uncle proud.

Occasionally, when he pushed himself up off the floor to begin his day, Pol sometimes paused for a second and wondered what might happen if he laid back down to get a little more sleep. Uncle Eash had told him many times not to ignore the distracting thoughts but, instead, own them and embrace them. He said when you conquer those moments, you conquer yourself.

In the dark, Pol quietly changed into the clothes, his brown training tunic and leather training shoes with padded soles, his favorite pair. He couldn't remember how many times he had repaired those shoes, but there were some benefits to being a cobbler's son.

Pounding on the front door jarred Pol from his thoughts. He jumped off the warm blanket, hoping the loud percussion wouldn't wake the rest of the family as early as it was.

Maybe a neighbor in trouble? Pol raced down the stairs, across his father's cobbler's shop, and to the familiar green-painted front door. He deftly unbolted the three locks, and when the door opened, a pair of muddy leather shoes smacked his face.

Surprised, Pol fell back a step. He couldn't see past the mud covering the left side of his face, but he mustered his discipline and clamped his mouth upon recognizing the culprit.

Emerald velvet robes clung to an obese man, standing in the threshold with flushed cheeks. He leaned forward and pointed a chubby finger at Pol, who cast his gaze down, as was expected of a commoner. Pol had recognized the jeweled silver brooch on the doublet lapel, signifying a dal, a son of a daum, a nobleman of Cordiae. Pol specifically remembered fixing this man's shoes a week ago.

"Do you know who I am, boy? No, no. If you knew who I was, I wouldn't have garbage for shoes. You helped your father fix my shoes. If you knew who I was, then you would've done a better job."

Wincing at the fetid alcohol breath, Pol lifted his hand to wipe the mud that was covering his left eye.

The drunk noble, Dal Marwin, caught Pol's wrist before his hand could reach his face. Again, Pol drew upon the discipline he had spent six years perfecting with his uncle and didn't move. But a spark of anger flared. Pol fought back the instinct to fling the dal onto his back, begging for mercy.

"I didn't tell you to wipe that, boy. Now pick up my shoes."

He released Pol's wrist, and Pol exhaled slowly, quietly, and retrieved the muddy shoes. The plush soft leather had separated from the sole with obvious tears and damage to the toe. It seemed likely that the dal had been kicking some innocent object during the previous evening's drunken revelry. It also seemed likely that the dal didn't want to pay a new repair bill.

"I paid your father good money to have these repaired, and now look at them. Look at them!"

The spark of anger ignited into a small whisper of flame hovering above the coals within Pol's soul. Only the discipline contained the heat.

"I have to meet with Vair Einreg for lunch today. These shoes better be ready by then. If they are not, every noble in this city will hear of your father's failure."

Pol would not dishonor his father. "Yes, Dal Marwin."

The dal slapped Pol across the face, mud flinging to the floor. Pol did not budge. He did not trust his natural instincts, which might seriously injure the man before him.

Dal Marwin wiped his hand over Pol's tunic. "So you remember me. That was a lesson to never let this happen again. Your father should have taught you better."

Pol kept his eyes cast down. *Holding your tongue takes more effort than speaking your mind, but sometimes, it's the best answer.* His father's words flowed through his mind, but the angry flame in his soul flared.

The noble sneered and made a wobbly about-face. His servant opened the door to his black carriage and had to assist the fat dal back into his vehicle. Pol remained still, watching the carriage lurch forward as if more inebriated than its owner.

One more year. One more year and Pol could leave. He wondered if the anger in his heart would burn the mud off his tunic and face.

He heard footsteps behind him and recognized his father's approach. Pol still didn't move. Laor stepped around and faced his son with a towel in hand. He said nothing, and Pol refused to look him in the eye as his father gently wiped the mud away.

When Pol could open his eye, he released his fists.

"Sorry, Pol."

He didn't respond. His father had allowed him to endure worse. Pol heard someone come down the stairs and turned to find his mother with tears coursing down her cheeks, waiting on the bottom stair.

The soul flame blossomed into a fire. He did not want to see his mother troubled. Pol had to leave. He said to her, "I'm okay." She nodded, and he left, pushing the door open past his father who followed him outside.

Everything in Pol's heart told him to run and leave his father behind, but he knew better.

"Let it out, Pol."

No. He had unleashed a fiery tirade upon his father before and had regretted it. While Pol appreciated his father's insight into his heart, he did not approve of his father's motives. Pol kept his head down and followed the street to Dael Keep, where he went every morning before sunrise.

No. This wouldn't work. If he didn't vent a little, he would explode. "You let it happen," Pol said softly, not trusting himself to speak louder.

"Yeah, that was a tough one. Proud of how you handled it."

The fire within raged. Is that all he was going to say? Pol kept his voice low. "Proud? For taking another hit?"

"We both know you're strong enough to have leveled Dal Marwin to the ground. It takes a true man to resist violence, even when it's most deserved."

"But he'll do it again. And again."

"I'll take care of the shoes and talk to him when he's sober, Pol. Thank you for considering our family."

The flames burst into a bonfire. "We're at *their* mercy."

"*Their* business feeds us. You don't slap the hand that feeds you."

Pol let a bit of rage slip. "I'd rather starve." He balled his hands into fists. "I can't fight back. You won't even let me fight anyone besides Uncle Eash…even to help."

Silence. In the early morning dark, their footfalls on the dirt road made the only sound. Pol did not care if he had overstepped his place.

Laor said, "When you're on your own, you can make that choice, just like our ancestors did, just like my father did. Until then, I need your help to feed your sisters."

Pol wanted to wrestle his father to the ground and shout in his face, "*You're wrong!*" but Pol did not want to disrespect his father or hear another lecture about Grandfather's poor choices, so he clamped his lips together.

Uncle Eash's words flashed from memory. *You gonna let that anger control you?* Discipline tempered the rage and reined in the heat. Pol focused on his surroundings out of habit because an emotional fighter loses sight of the goal.

This close to Dael Keep, near the city's center, the muddy road ended and the cobblestone streets began. Their footfalls sounded louder on the stone, but the well-fitting stones and smooth footing attested to Cordiaen engineering and attention to detail. Footsteps echoed nearby from a scattering of apprentice bakers commuting to their shops. Servants also scurried about, acquiring last-minute ingredients for their master's breakfast. Few others had a reason to be up this early.

Pol did. Every quiet morning, except PointDay, he traveled the barely lit dirt roads to the QuonGuard garrison nestled inside Dael Keep, where Quon Daoringer, the ruler of Dael, lived.

Pol made that trip every morning to fulfill his mission, his purpose. He was not about to let his anger slip any further and risk his father canceling his training. If he had hurt that dal, he would have been barred from training. Pol could not have that.

As if the God of Cordiae, Lohem, desired to calm his rage, cold, fat raindrops assaulted Pol's head as he approached the gates to Dael Keep. He ran a hand through his dark-brown hair and removed a few more chunks of mud. At least the muddy remnants on his face would wash off easier.

Stars faded in the predawn firmament when Pol and his father reached the immense gate. Thirty feet of expertly crafted stone, wood, and iron rose before him in a constructed bastion of defense with six QuonGuards at attention. The rain had drenched their red-and-white checkered tunics, and as Pol and his quiet father approached, a few gave a nod of recognition, but the rest ignored them. Almost every day for the last six years, Pol had passed through the imposing gates before dawn on his way to the QuonGuard garrison. Most citizens would not be permitted inside Dael Keep that early without reason, but Uncle Eash served on the QuonGuard, and Pol was well known.

The subset of aging stone buildings comprising the garrison sat within the inner bailey against the keep's outer wall. With his rage smoldering, Pol found little comfort in the familiar smithy's iron hammer ringing out amidst a sporadic horse's whinny as the front bailey became alive with morning chores. Even the scent of morning bread didn't bring the usual satisfaction.

Deeper within the inner bailey, they approached the garrison entrance. Miltou stood guard by himself in the torchlight and waved to Pol as he approached. "Morning, Pol. Laor, good to see you escorting the lad. Wet one, isn't it?"

Pol's anger wavered a smidge. Miltou had said good morning to him for years.

"Yes, sir. Business going well?" Laor asked. The guard had a small wooden toy business on the side. Pol's father had even agreed to host a display in his shop.

"Of course! Won't retire anytime soon, but it's fun! Eash has been up for a while. Says he's got a surprise for Pol today. Wonder if he's trying to make you quit training with those surprises."

Pol almost let a smile slip, but held onto his anger. "They'll prepare me for the King's Army."

Miltou chuckled. "Eash hasn't converted you to the QuonGuard yet?"

"Not yet."

Miltou inspected Pol. "You okay, Pol? What happened to your face?"

His father said, "Run-in with one of my customers. Thanks for asking."

"Gotcha. One of those mornings, huh? Get you going. Eash'll work it out of you."

Pol nodded to the older QuonGuard as he trekked across the muddy garrison courtyard. The garrison armory sat in the west wall and faint candlelight flickered from the room onto the muddy courtyard. Pol wiped his leather shoes on the outside mat and stepped inside, finding his uncle Eash burnishing a shield.

His uncle paused midstroke, looked Pol up and down, and asked, "That bad?"

Laor entered behind Pol.

"That bad," Eash answered himself. He returned the gleaming kite shield to a rack. "Was going to wait for the rain to pass, but you look like a spring that's about to pop off. Go get ready."

Pol stepped around his father without a look and pulled a wooden sword from a barrel outside the armory. He hung back, waiting under the armory awning for his uncle.

"Thanks, Eash," his father said.

"What happened?"

"Pol answered the door."

Eash shook his head and said, "One of these days… one of these days, he might not hold back."

"That's the day we end up on the streets."

"It's not that bad, Laor."

"How can you say that? Cousin Akrin's family is homeless. No one has heard from Felter in years. Why? Because of a legend." He held up a finger. "No lectures. You're here. You're keeping the family tradition, and I support you, and that's what Father wanted. I'm doing the best I can with what he didn't give me."

"That was your choice—" Eash dropped his head and held up his hands. "Let's not do this now. Father loved you too, Laor. He would have been proud to see Pol train."

"I hear the words. I'm trying to believe."

Eash patted his brother's shoulder. "I'll send him home at the usual time."

"Thank you." Laor left the armory and joined Pol outside. "Work hard. See you later."

"Yes, sir," Pol replied. With his head down, his father trod out the garrison in the rain. Pol wanted to say more but didn't trust his mouth. He loved his father, but he was ashamed of him.

Eash brushed past him, taking a position in the center of the courtyard and holding his own sword and wooden shield. "Get it out. Don't hold the anger in; it'll poison you."

Eash saluted Pol, holding up his sword.

Pol returned the salute and held it as he allowed all the frustration, the anger, the words, the humiliation, and the things unsaid to build into a roaring, fiery torrent inside him. Gripping his wooden sword until his fingers blanched, Pol charged his uncle. The young man poured his anger, frustration, and disappointment into the overhead swing.

His wooden sword splintered, and his uncle's wooden shield cracked on the first contact.

Eash laughed. "Now that's what I call letting it out. Again."

Pol grunted and took the shield from his uncle and laid the broken weapons by the armory before retrieving new ones.

"There's plenty more. Let's go," his uncle said.

Some of the fire had been released, but not all. Pol charged again and instead of a colossal blow, he directed his energy into speed. He had to be faster without a shield, a natural disadvantage Eash had placed on him a year before. The clack of the wood on wood was cathartic. Sparring with someone who could take his hits invigorated him. Pol's wooden sword blurred.

But he couldn't land a hit.

Eash defended well and had the advantage. As they continued, Pol felt the anger release from him like vapor from the dew-covered ground. They sparred for a half hour, back and forth. Pol knew all of Eash's moves, patterns, and techniques, but his excessive use of speed placed him at a disadvantage. He would tire first.

Seeking an advantage, Pol advanced with two quick swipes, meeting both sword and shield. Then, Pol feinted a swing at the shield before kicking it at an angle. The shield flew from Eash's grasp and when the expected counter sword thrust came, Pol stepped inside the thrust and held Eash's offending arm. He plowed his right fist, holding his sword hilt, into his uncle's stomach. A grunt rewarded his effort, but Pol's feet flew out from under him. The back of his head cracked against the muddy courtyard stone. The tip of a heavy wooden sword pressed against his chest.

Breathing hard, Eash lifted his sword. "Excellent work disarming and pressing into the attack. With limited space, it's smart to improvise with your fist." A wry grin spread across Uncle Eash's face. "You might want to take a crack at the face instead." He held out his hand.

Pol let his uncle haul him to his feet. "Didn't want to explain to Father that I broke your nose."

Eash grimaced. "Thank you. Good job releasing your anger, but you left yourself open."

"Hard to let it go. Gives me strength."

Eash held up a finger. "If you ever want a chance at achieving the full potential of the Vroshen line—"

"I must remove all limitations, especially anger."

"Knowing it and doing it are two different things. Lohem gives you strength; anger weakens you. Emotions are fleeting; you can't rely on them. Discipline will never fail. Lohem will never fail you."

"Yes, sir." Pol did not fully understand, but he trusted his uncle.

Eash gave him a tentative glance. "The fire you described, inside yourself; is it raging right now?"

"It was. It's smaller now. Why?" Pol didn't hide his eagerness. Uncle Eash rarely wanted to discuss the inner fire.

"Another time. We have more work to do." Uncle Eash walked over to the armory.

Pol scraped the excess mud off his soaking tunic and ragged dark-brown pants. At least his clothes matched his face. He caught Miltou laughing from the gate.

His uncle shelved his shield and pulled out three more swords from the training barrel. "Surprise!"

They both now had two swords. This was Pol's favorite style. He smiled on the inside. His uncle could always make him smile.

"Now, focus. Don't allow anger to overwhelm you. And don't break my nose." Eash smirked as he advanced. He must enjoy this as much as Pol did.

Pol brought six years of training to bear. Their swords flew, and as usual, Pol did his best to match his uncle's speed, but when Eash's sword rapped his undefended left wrist, the sword almost dropped, and Pol had the tip of another sword at his throat.

"Good. It's nice to know I still have something to teach you."

"Always, Uncle."

"Then learn one more thing: just as your father allows you to learn our ancestral way of fighting, allow him to follow his own path."

The fatigue took the edge off Pol's emotions. "But it's not what he was made for. He knows it."

"Doesn't matter. It's his choice."

"When his choice allows a dal to throw muddy shoes in my face, I take issue. Do you know how many times I've had to hold back, even against thieves?"

"Well said, but you're Cordiaen. Obedience—"

"Is life," Pol finished.

"Which is why having that choice, ordered to truth, is important. Respect it. Without it, we live under tyranny." He held up a finger. "Don't even think it. He allows you a choice or you wouldn't be here. That's him obeying his father."

Uncle Eash knew Pol well. "I am grateful. I just know what he could have been."

"That's not for you to decide or grieve. As long as it's ordered to truth, accept his choice just as he accepts yours." He clapped Pol on the back. "Enough. Let's finish before you have to go peek at Quel Adeel."

Pol sputtered.

"What? Didn't think I knew why you leave just after sunrise, take the same route, and always arrive home a touch late? For someone who dislikes nobles as much as you do, you sure seem to have a crush on one."

Pol hung his head. "I'm defeated, but you're a stalker."

"No, I'm a QuonGuard who is well-informed about everything regarding the quon's family, including his daughter. Now, let's finish up."

After another hour with pants covered in mud, Pol could weave a proper defense, but the forearm welts would bruise the next day.

Eash held up a sword. "I know you could do this all day, but it's time."

With a small bow, Pol replied, "Thank you, Uncle, for training in the rain."

"Rain, sun, snow…you must be ready. Now, go work hard for your father so he doesn't give me any grief."

"Yes, sir."

Eash ruffled Pol's close-cropped dark-brown hair. At six foot five, Eash stood an inch taller than Pol and towered over most other guards. "I know you will. You landed a fist to my gut. Not many guards can boast of that."

The right corner of Pol's mouth turned up slightly. He was proud of that hit.

"That's all the smile I'm gonna see. If you change your mind about the QuonGuard, you can start right away. Age limit is sixteen; you're already there."

Pol said, "Thank you, but no. King's Army for me. That's what Grandfather and you did."

Eash said, "Captain wanted me to try."

Yelling from the garrison entrance interrupted them. Pol turned to find the QuonGuard captain, Uertel, storming toward them with a flushed face and a slew of hissed curses dropping from his lips. Miltou received the captain's helmet as the officer barged past.

"Pol, get going. He's in a mood," his uncle said.

Pol nodded, handing off his wooden swords before retreating toward the far wall. He had witnessed the captain's temper before and had no desire to remain.

Captain Uertel marched right up to Eash. "He just wanted a ride, Eash. He just wanted a ride without being bothered!"

His uncle kept a passive face and didn't respond.

"Do you think I'm a bother, Eash?"

"No, Captain."

"That's right." The captain looked around, found Pol, and pointed. "Let me tell you something, boy. If you want to join us, learn here and now that the safety of the quon goes before your own life, even if we are a *bother*."

Pol nodded but continued to move to the gate as the captain turned back to Eash. "But we have to obey, Eash."

"Yes, Captain."

"Get cleaned up and have a detail prepared to meet the quon's carriage when he returns." The captain plowed his fist into his palm. "At least he'll see we remain prepared to serve."

"Yes, Captain." Eash stood to the side as the captain pushed past him. Pol scooted out the garrison gate, waving to Miltou standing at attention and holding the captain's helmet.

The inner bailey buzzed with more activity, and the rain had passed. After a quick glance at the morning sun's position, Pol returned his vision to the muddy ground. He would have plenty of time to make it to his father's shop before it opened.

Pol considered the captain's words to him. Yes, as a QuonGuard, placing the quon before your own life made sense. That was the job. But guarding nobles didn't appeal to Pol at all.

No. He wanted the King's Army grunt uniform, the first step to becoming an officer, just like his grandfather and uncle, and nothing would stop him.

CHAPTER 2

"If you are not two steps ahead of your enemy, you are one step behind."

–Cleric Joern, Advanced Cordiaen Military Tactics, Volume 2.

Qual Stefan, fifth son of Quon Daoringer, entered the grand foyer of the restaurant, annoyed with the typical rainy weather found in Dael. Inside, warm candlelight illuminated curved walls framing the spacious antechamber. Young minor nobles leaned against the walls in clusters, and members of each clique made a point of extending their necks to catch glimpses of Stefan, with some trying to snatch his attention.

Stefan removed his rain-drenched cloak and handed it to a waiting servant. The tall man made a point of inspecting the gold brooch over Stefan's left breast as he received the dripping garment with a bow. Stefan's gold shield brooch had five sets of small round rubies at the edges and a ship with three masts crashing through golden waves in the middle; his family emblem mirrored the naval power found in Dael, situated on the North Sea coastline in northwest Cordiae. Stefan allowed the servant to inspect the brooch, understanding that it served as a prerequisite for admission to the foyer. The Eagle's Nest served the elite nobility in Dael. Anyone not wearing a noble's brooch could not gain entrance, and progressing beyond the antechamber required a certain reputation, something Stefan had fought for and earned. .

Even in a private establishment, the servant's red-and-white tunic acknowledged Stefan's father, Quon Daoringer, ruler of Dael.

The servant remained bowed as he addressed Stefan. "Good morning, Qual Stefan. Allow me to show you to your seat. I understand it is not your usual balcony table."

Stefan gave the briefest nod and reminded himself to ask for the servant's name; the pleasant man had been showing him to his seat for more than a year and had not failed to impress. He followed the servant and ignored the throat clearing and timid waves from the various minor nobles who could not gain admittance beyond the foyer. He ignored them. No shortcuts. They would have to earn entrance, as he had.

Past the guards, an arched hallway led to a dining room. Candlelight from bronze sconces illuminated lavishly dressed patrons lounging on plush divans to either side.

Stefan recognized sons and daughters of local noble families, but he avoided direct looks as conversations quieted with his passing. Stefan smiled to himself. Few seventeen-year-olds could gain entrance past the door, but his bypassing the hallway entirely always raised a few eyebrows.

Two moonlighting King's Army soldiers stood before the entrance to the dining area, but the guards remained impassive as the servant led Stefan across the threshold. The expansive dining room ceiling soared above him, with murals portraying the various angel choirs. Drawing upon years with private tutors, Stefan could prattle off the angel choir names and their significance, but the theology was not as important to him as the rank. Some ranked higher than others, even though they were all angels. This restaurant had been founded on that hierarchical principle, which reflected Cordiaen social structure. Stefan was near the top, and that was all he needed.

Two balconies flanked the upper hall on the mezzanine level, and while Stefan typically preferred the quiet of the balcony, he expected more vulgar company than usual today and thus followed the servant to the requested table.

Elegant mahogany tables dotted the dining room, along with crimson-cushioned cedar chairs. As the servant guided him to a booth on the far wall, Stefan nodded to a few of the patrons dining on poached eggs, fruit, and assorted breakfast dishes. These men and women were worth acknowledging.

Stefan was pleased to see a separate table with empty chairs and a steaming breakfast already served near his awaiting booth. Stefan positioned himself in the booth so he could see the entrance. The servant began removing the adjacent silver dinnerware at his table, but Stefan held up a hand.

"I know it's early, but lunch for two. Steak and house vegetables with a side of the spiced potatoes."

"Excellent, Qual," the servant replied, bowing, and retreated. Twenty feet away, behind the serving counter at the bar, a brown-skinned man with a trim black goatee and mustache watched over the room. He wore the traditional attire for a chef in Cordiae, a long-sleeved, double-breasted black jacket and a red-and-white caldana around his forehead. The wide silk cloth designated him as the head chef, and when Stefan met his gaze, he gave a small bow. Stefan knew him as Chef Illiat, though he went by many names in Dael's darker corners. With Illiat appearing relaxed, Stefan assumed all the morning's preparations were in place. Stefan relaxed and replied with a single nod before turning to survey the patrons.

Polite banter filled the room, but Stefan could not make out any conversations. The servant returned with a small wineglass filled with apple cider. "If I may, Qual Stefan, Master Chef Illiat would like to remind you it's not too late to withdraw."

Stefan smirked. They had gone through this, and while he appreciated Illiat's concern, Stefan had committed to his plan. Based on the available information, all of Stefan's calculations resulted in him as the victor today, even if there might be some collateral damage.

"Inform the Master Chef that I appreciate his concern, but I must move forward."

The servant placed the glass of cider before Stefan. "I will do so, Qual Stefan. Master Chef Illiat would also like to remind the qual to remain hydrated."

Illiat didn't like it when Stefan drank wine before lunch. Stefan lifted the cup to Illiat and sipped the cider. Illiat smirked in response before returning to the kitchen.

Stefan had dozens of acquaintances but few friends, and among them, Illiat seemed to actually care, which was why Stefan entertained his concerns. But too much depended on today. After two years of positioning, strategizing, and hard decisions, Stefan was about to eliminate the last obstacle to his glorious financial ascension.

A commotion started at the dining room entrance. Slightly earlier than expected, that obstacle, Cal Geraul, burst into the dining hall from the hallway.

Stefan had never met Cal Geraul, but his reputation matched his entrance. Wearing a short red cape and with his chin tilted up, the first son of Couv Broon paused momentarily at the entrance, ostentatiously scanning the dining hall. Four armed personal guards flanked the noble, which spoke to his reputation, as a cal would rarely have a retinue. Ignoring the polite—but firm—pleas of the servants, Geraul locked on to Stefan. He plowed between tables and patrons without regard. Seated patrons protested the disruption. Illiat would never have allowed such behavior, and the establishment guards would have forcibly prevented entrance to the cal and his entourage if Stefan had not informed them he was expecting such an intrusion. Two of the restaurant servants continued to follow the cal and guards, begging them to leave. When one guard paused and turned toward the servants, pulling the hilt of his sword from its scabbard, the servants backed away.

Geraul abruptly stopped at Stefan's table.

Stefan sipped his cider.

"Qual Stefan. There's no escape." The cal's menacing tone sounded rehearsed, and Stefan restrained himself from snorting his cider through his nose. "Let's have a chat, shall we?"

Stefan placed his cup on the table and examined Geraul's bronze brooch. A single sapphire adorned the base with the cal's family emblem of a cornfield in the brooch's center. "Cal Geraul, how unexpected. Have a seat. There's a table right there for your men."

Geraul frowned and turned to the nearby table with four empty chairs. He jerked his thumb to the table, and his guards sat down. They shared a look with one another and the breakfast laid out before them.

Stefan held back a smile. "The food here is excellent, Cal. Your men are welcome to eat."

The guards didn't wait for further permission as they dove into the meal before them. Nearby patrons conversed with urgent, though hushed, tones. Geraul slid into the seat across from Stefan. The servant promptly delivered two plates of the steak and vegetables.

"Cal Geraul, what would you care to drink?" the servant asked.

Geraul didn't respond as he studied the meal. He frowned at the cup before him. "I'm not thirsty." The servant bowed and left while Geraul studied the meal and the young qual. "You must know why I've come if you've made these preparations."

He adapted well. As Stefan cut into his steak, he reassessed the cal. "Yes. You've come to bully a little kid."

"Don't patronize me and don't waste my time. I know your portfolio. You've conquered the wine market here in Dael and ruined a score of merchants who didn't cooperate. Now you've entered the military supply chain, and you're on the verge of ruining me."

Yes, the cal understood more than Stefan had expected. "Didn't realize I was so threatening."

Geraul let out a slow exhalation. "I'm employing as much patience as I can. I have enough evidence to bring the matter to your father. Does he know how ruthless you can be to his merchants? Does he know they call you 'the Bear'?"

"Quon Daoringer is aware of my work, though he doesn't like to be bothered about little details. Most nobles and merchants won't do business with a kid, but they respect 'a bear.' Who wouldn't?" Stefan took another sip of cider. "So you came here with threats and swords to do what, exactly? You know of my connection to the quon. Wouldn't threatening me be a dangerous move for business if the quon doesn't like what you're doing?"

"You've pushed me to an uncomfortable point, quon or not. Supplying the King's Army is *my* ticket, and I'm here to weed out threats. I'm not afraid of Quon Daoringer."

That wasn't true. Everyone was afraid of Quon Daoringer, including Stefan. He swallowed a bite of spiced potatoes. "Hmm. That means you have some powerful connections that support you. Excellent. Would you like to be my partner?"

Geraul frowned. "What?"

"I have no desire for my father to get involved, and I really want to spread my wings beyond Dael. You have contacts in the central regions of Cordiae that would be nice to engage. So, I'm willing to offer you five percent of my profits for the next three years on anything— anything—I make supplying the King's Army."

Geraul tightened his lips.

Seeing him waver, Stefan pointed to Geraul with a piece of steak on his fork. "It's a no-lose situation. If I fail, there's no risk. If I succeed, I share the profit."

Geraul folded his arms. "No. I risk losing those contacts to you, and I don't want to be associated with you. I do my own work."

Stefan paused as he swallowed the piece of steak. "I have no desire to steal anything from you, and I don't want a trade war. It lowers prices, reduces profit, and attracts attention. Are you sure you're not going to eat?"

The vein in Geraul's forehead throbbed noticeably. "You're smart for a kid. I get it. You're trying to make a name for yourself as the fifth son of a quon, but I'm giving you one chance to back away from my routes, contacts, and holdings. I don't believe you're serious about this 'offer.'"

"I'm very serious. I wanted to give you an opportunity before I upended the market," Stefan replied.

"Do you think I'm going to let you gain a foothold in central Cordiae? I'm going to warn everyone. You'll be lucky to convince a peddler to sell you water."

The offer had been a long shot, but Geraul had acted as expected. "So, that's a no?"

Geraul's fists clenched atop the table. "You don't seem to understand. If you don't submit—first, I'm going to have my men educate you, right here, right now. Then, I'll make it my life's goal to crush your livelihood."

Stefan didn't look away. Now, he could cut the act. "I'm sorry you're not interested in joining me. When you took it upon yourself to show up in Dael, I assumed you would jump at the opportunity to join my business, but you have made your point clear. Now, let me make myself clear. I'm a qual. I'm already deep into central Cordiae. I'll have a majority of your contacts switch over to me within a week. You will be lucky to have anything to sell to the King's Army in a month. Without me, you're nothing. You had your chance."

Geraul got to his feet. "I will crush you."

The cal's four guards stood. Forks clattered to the ground, and napkins clung to their laps at awkward angles as they reached for their swords.

In response, twenty men and women sitting at tables around the guards leapt to their feet, drawing previously hidden blades.

Stefan held back a smile.

A broad-shouldered man from the next table commanded the guards, "Sit down."

The four exchanged quick, wide-eyed glances, re-sheathed their weapons, and dropped back onto their seats. The armed "patrons" sat down, resuming their conversations and hiding their weapons.

"Threats don't bother me, Geraul," Stefan said.

Geraul scanned the room. "You set me up?"

"You were poised to be the leading supplier to the King's Army, but you don't have the same financial backing or access to the same selection of materials that I have. I thought a partnership would be beneficial to both of us."

"Still keeping to your story? You play a dangerous game."

"It is a game. You got in my way. You lost."

Geraul stood, and twenty heads turned to him. "Game's not over." He looked around. "Will you allow me to leave?"

"Of course. I just have some friends here to make sure you didn't get on the quon's wrong side. Father has a temper, you see."

Two more veins on Geraul's forehead pulsated as his face flushed. He stormed toward the exit. His four guards followed, slowly at first, and then trotting to keep up. The twenty well-dressed men and women quietly left through various exits, leaving a few patrons in their seats, looking around.

As Geraul left, a flutter of concern flew through Stefan's chest. His informants would keep an eye on cal, but the interaction had confirmed Stefan's suspicion. The man was dangerous.

Chef Illiat approached Stefan's table, clapping. "That was worth clearing out most of my restaurant for the morning. But I will have to make amends to Cal Geraul's father, Couv Broon. I want to stay on his good side. That will come out of your generosity."

Stefan took another bite of his steak. "Generosity? You think I'm capable of generosity?"

"You've got a point." Illiat sat down. "Just to clarify, couldn't you have just sent the man a letter?"

"I did. That's why he's here." Stefan savored the spiced potatoes. "Geraul is a huge player in the market and a formidable obstacle. I wanted to size him up and try to get on his good side. The letter was an invitation to join me. Geraul didn't write back. He just showed up."

"You undercut his business and bullied him just like you did to a dozen other merchants in Dael. He had every right to show up here to pick a fight." Illiat devoured the potatoes Geraul had ignored.

"I have a reputation to uphold. Not everyone will take a kid seriously."

Illiat pointed to the door with his fork. "He does. He's not stupid. He has something to prove as well, being the son of a minor couv."

Stefan wiped his mouth with a napkin. "Yes, he will go to great lengths to protect what he has made. I've been through this before. Not worried." He tried to keep the concern from his showing on his face.

"I couldn't keep the hall completely clear. Your father will probably get wind of this."

Stefan paused to recalculate his father's response. "Quon Daoringer is well-informed about my dealings. I am confident he uses the Pulse to monitor me. It's all a game. I know how to play." Stefan knew the Pulse, the Cordiaen king's national spy network, would work fast, though.

"Well, I hope you don't lose any pieces as you play. I appreciate all you've done for me. Your attendance and wine have brought in some excellent business. If Geraul doesn't have you killed by the end of today, we should have a special dinner here for you."

Stefan lifted the glass of cider. "Until then."

CHAPTER 3

"Cordiaen Commanders who rely on their eyes alone will fail. You must use all your faculties to plan, assess, and execute, even your dreams."

–Cleric Joern, Advanced Cordiaen Military Tactics, Volume 2.

Stacia kept one eye on the Eagle's Nest as she hid in the alley across the street. The rain had just stopped, leaving a musty smell that mingled with the refuse littering the street. The avenue bustled before her as hawkers yelled, urchins begged, and nobles passed through with the typical morning traffic found in a major city.

Sheep. They had no concept of what existed beyond their borders, just as she had not understood centuries ago.

Stacia monitored the area in her hooded and tattered gray tunic and thread bare pants, which provided scant protection, but rendered her almost invisible in this part of Dael. Her mission required low visibility, but she also had no desire to attract the unwanted attention that poor women on the street often encountered. She could handle it, but killing Cordiaens was more hassle than it was worth. Scanning the street and alley, she felt confident no one had marked her as she waited.

Two years. She had spent two years back in her home country to complete this mission. Gaining trust was essential, and finding the right target had been tedious. Thankfully, Geraul had found her in Ulloa, and she had served him without fault. At some point in her life, she might have felt shame at what she was about to do, but not today.

When Geraul emerged from the restaurant, he found her in the prearranged spot and barely nodded. That was all she needed.

She sprinted away down the alley. Three blocks, right turn, four more blocks, left turn. She hugged the walls, moving silent and quick before turning down one last alley.

A broad-shouldered figure rested against a tavern's back wall. He had not bothered to conceal himself or display any legitimate reason to be there. Stacia rolled her eyes at his incompetence; the "assassin" shouted his amateur ability with his dark-green cloak over a black leather jerkin and pants. The guy was trying too hard.

Stacia refrained from frowning, as she still needed him. His demeanor and stance didn't impress her, but he should be able to get the job done.

"Anvil, is it?"

He nodded.

"Geraul approved. The girl should be in the carriage. Take her. The quon may be with her. Kill him."

Anvil pulled back his green hood, revealing pockmarked olive skin, a Telaunian from southwestern Cordiae. A hesitant scratchy voice responded, "Only supposed to be the girl. Message said nothing about the quon. Geraul wanted this?"

"Yes, his meeting went worse than expected."

"He never mentioned it. Why should I believe you?" He pulled his hood back up, turned back down the alley, and walked away.

She removed a small purse from beneath her tattered tunic. She unwound the leather binding and jingled the coins. "This is necessary to Geraul."

The man stopped and turned back. After a moment, he stepped forward and placed his hand under the purse. Stacia dropped it.

Gold Cordiaen crowns spilled into his hand. He hefted the purse a few times. "For a quon, I want this doubled when I complete the job."

"I will triple this if you are successful."

The purse disappeared under his cloak. "Triple it is." He pulled his hood around his head and left down the alley.

Stacia scoffed, waiting a moment to follow the "assassin." If he could be bought, he was not to be trusted.

She froze, sensing movement half a block away. Not surprised, Stacia sighed again, as she would have to cover for Anvil's carelessness. Sliding quietly down the alley, she noted that her mark had retreated. They were careful and quick.

At least she would get to play a little.

Using her mandra, she dashed through the alleyways like a shadow and halted face-to-face with the snoop. A young girl, who couldn't be more than twelve, with dirt covering her face and short black hair, froze before her.

Stacia paused.

The girl reminded Stacia of herself, and normally Stacia would have scared the girl and let her go, but unfortunately, the girl had been in the wrong place with the wrong information. A faint echo of concern, or what should have been concern, crossed her chest. Her heart no longer carried such worries, but Stacia snorted at her the remaining vestiges of her conscience.

The girl's eyes widened in fear while the rest of her body remained frozen. Stacia would have to make her death appear natural. It wasn't malicious. Stacia couldn't risk exposure yet.

A second mark retreated a few blocks away. Stacia kept the girl in place while she bounded away. Five seconds later, she captured a mud-splotched youth and brought him back to the girl.

"Let's make this quick. Who do you work for?" Stacia asked.

The girl tightened her lips, but the pale boy said, "The Bear."

How appropriate.

CHAPTER 4

After negotiating a shipping deal with Vair Einrig, Stefan waved to Illiat as he departed a half hour after Geraul. In the hallway connecting the dining room to the foyer, all talking ceased among the clusters of nobles as he passed, and he met the same silence as he strode into the foyer and out the door held open by the head servant. It must have been quite the show for everyone. Word about the encounter would spread quickly, but that was to his advantage. Reputation was everything.

Even after spewing hours of rain, the clouds retained their ominous gray as they hovered over the city, but having endured Dael's torrential storms his entire life, Stefan did not worry. Instead, he took advantage of the reprieve and strolled down the bleached cobblestone main street to return to his home, Dael Keep. His father refused to provide him with his own carriage or horse, and he did not want to waste his money that could be better spent investing. Besides, he enjoyed walking, which afforded easier access to his less reputable contacts and transactions.

His father did not completely neglect Stefan's needs. The young man lived at Dael Keep, ate well, and received an allowance for his clothing. Stefan brushed a few errant rain drops from his long-sleeved velvet doublet with red-and-white trim. He maintained the latest fashion while not attracting attention to himself. The gold brooch bearing his father's crest glinted in the midmorning sun at his left lapel and served as his only accessory. Other trinkets were a waste.

As Stefan continued down the street, considering expenditures he could eliminate, he heard something out of place. The wind? No, it sounded like a bird. He looked down the alley to his left, and halfway down the narrow street, a small, emphatic hand waved at him. The sound had been a faint whistle. Stefan usually ignored such encounters since he received network updates via written notes at the keep. Ambitious "cubs," members of his little spy network, sometimes wanted to make a name for themselves and attract his attention with a personal meeting, but even from this distance, Stefan wondered if something was wrong.

He casually turned down the alley and kept scanning entrances and exits, wary of the unexpected summons. When he approached, Stefan found a boy, shaking, with wide eyes and a pale, dirty face.

"What's wrong?" Stefan asked.

"I'm…Dirt. I…I know it's against the rules to talk to you." He jerked his head up and down the alley. "But you have to know."

Stefan crouched down to the kid's level. The boy couldn't have been more than ten years old. "What do I have to know, Dirt?"

The kid scanned the alley again. "Something's wrong. Something's *really* wrong. I was tailing Eanna and Frac's patrol when they found something strange off Ariel Lane. I kept back like I's supposed to, but something got ahold of them." Dirt's eyes blinked. "They're lying on the ground. They're not moving. They're not breathing."

Stefan furrowed his brow as his mind raced. "What had they found?"

"I don't know, but whatever it is, seems no one else is supposed to know. I'm going to be canned for it, but you should know," Dirt replied.

Stefan stood and scanned the alley again. The kid could be lying. These street urchins were consummate actors. Still, Geraul could be causing trouble, and it was better to be safe than sorry.

Stefan handed the kid a half silver crown. "Pass the word to the leaders: hibernate. Got it?"

Dirt nodded emphatically. Every cub should know what that meant.

"Take the main street and go," Stefan said.

Dirt pocketed the coin and bolted without any further prompting. Stefan's mind continued to race through possibilities as he marched back up the alley. There wasn't much of anything by Ariel Lane except a few low-end shops pretending to offer high-end goods.

Would Geraul have had two of his cubs killed to send a message? Stefan had expected some retaliation from the cal, which was why his network was on high alert, but if Geraul was targeting his network, then Stefan should protect them. He had a soft spot in his heart for the young urchins, but they had been counseled on the dangers when they signed up. Would it be enough if they laid low? Sure, the cubs should be protected as long as they remained out of sight. Stefan expected to receive further updates when he returned to the keep.

Should he tell the King's Army garrison fall commander?

Stefan stopped just as the keep wall came into view. If Geraul was targeting anything related to Stefan, shouldn't he try to stop it? But how did he know if the incident actually involved Geraul?

"No," he said aloud to himself as he continued on the main street to the keep. He would have to explain more than he wanted to. Once he returned to the keep, he could have an anonymous tip sent to the local fall commander.

That assuaged his conscience. He had already spent enough resources organizing the morning, and his father probably would not appreciate what he had done to Geraul. Not that his father should care, as Geraul's father, Couv Broon, lived in Shaorn's protectorate, not Dael's, but Stefan did not want to risk it. His father's wrath was something to fear, so it was best not to draw attention to himself today.

Five QuonGuards bowed to him at the gate, and Stefan maintained a brisk pace through the bailey. A small force of ten QuonGuards stood at attention just inside the gate, and Stefan recognized the same formation when his father had previously left without his guard. Stefan had criticized the guard's petulant behavior before, but he recognized its significance now. He considered where his father might have gone when he stopped short before the stables. The carriage was gone. He checked the muted sun's position. The pieces clicked into place.

He froze.

Maybe he was overthinking. He had done that many times before. Suppressing his intuition, Stefan argued that he needed more information before running around making assumptions.

Scurrying through the halls of the keep and up the grand central stairs, Stefan angled around corners with familiar ease as he headed to his quarters. His sister's door stood open, confirming she was not inside.

Stefan ripped out the small key from his inner shirt pocket and threw open his door after fiddling with the lock for a second. From the door, Stefan could see the empty desk top.

No message.

At his desk, he began rifling through the drawers and scanning the ground, hopeful for any misplaced parchment. Nothing.

He should have at least gotten a report on Geraul. Had his network been paralyzed?

Stefan ran toward his open bedroom door. He had to tell the captain and the fall commander.

I have to do something. Stefan halted at the door. *Do I, though?*

Again, did he have all the information he needed to make a correct assessment? Maybe it was coincidental. If he was wrong, he might lose a lot of money. If he was right, his family could be in trouble. No, Geraul would not go that far. It made little sense for Geraul to go after the quon.

Quon Daoringer of Dael had a reputation of his own that had kept the Sperunese on the other side of the Aeldren River for years. If Geraul attacked the quon, it would ruin him more than Stefan ever could.

Stefan closed the door to his room. He just had to let the day play out and hope everyone, including Dirt, was safe.

～

Pol strode past small stores on his way back to his father's cobbler shop and his home. Ariel Lane merchants boasted some of the best quality and wares in the city even though they were not next to the high-end stores on Dael's main street. Pol may be ashamed of his father's abandonment of the family's legacy, but his father's diligent attention to detail and quality work made Pol proud to work beside him and learn from him.

The rain had stopped, and Pol navigated around mud puddles in the street not wanting to ruin his training shoes. Even though he had left the keep grounds, Pol kept his head down out of habit. He'd received enough lessons from his father and indignant nobles to risk offending someone on the street. Everyone in Dael learned how to recognize the different brooches signifying status throughout the country. The nobles prided themselves on their status.

Pol said, "You can have it," to no one. The only status symbol he wanted was a grunt tunic from the King's Army. He would have preferred to start as an officer, but he couldn't afford entry into the Officer Academy in Ariel, the capital city.

He could still make officer one day, and when he did, he would earn enough to help take care of his family.

A few blocks away from his home on Ariel Lane, Pol spied a carriage farther down the street. Only wealthy merchants or nobles owned carriages, which often rolled past the house in search of particular wares. Sometimes, his father would have Pol set up displays to entice riders in those carriages. While Pol had never ridden in a carriage, he told himself that he never needed to…except, there was one person he imagined he would be willing to ride with.

The approaching carriage was larger than most; it had to be the one. Pol could make out the red with white trim, signifying the Quon of Dael's personal carriage. She would be in it. Quel Adeel had never talked to him, but ever since he'd spied her through the carriage window one day as he returned from the keep, Pol rarely missed an opportunity to see her.

Sure, she was a noble, and one of the highest ranked as a daughter of Quon Daoringer. Only a princess would rank higher. But Pol wondered if her interior was as beautiful as the exterior.

Thoughts of Adeel curbed his irritation of having to step off the street to accommodate the carriage. He had a momentary thought to remain in the street and make the carriage go around him. *Why do I always have to get out of the way?*

When horses drawing the carriage came closer with their hooves clopping, he remembered what his father had said before. *Living with nobles is not always fair, but it's the way things are. Are you going to let your anger rule you?* Pol often had to repeat that to himself. He stepped off the street as usual and watched the carriage approach. At least he would get to see her.

Through the passenger window, a beautiful young maiden stared out with her chin on her hand. When their eyes met, Pol froze; she rarely looked at him, but he rarely looked up either. Her smooth brown skin and long brown hair framed a delicate face with high cheekbones. Her deep-brown eyes caused him to catch his breath. Quel Adeel, daughter of Quon Daoringer, had a beauty that did not disappoint. Given her status, Pol should have lowered his eyes to avoid being too forward.

But he didn't, and she tilted her head at him. She did not look like a noble to Pol. Nobles were not beautiful like her. But as the carriage continued, the red and white colors reminded him of the quon, and Pol thought he glimpsed the local ruler in the carriage as well.

Suddenly, Pol crashed forward to the ground from a sharp crack to his head. He landed on his hands and knees and his vision swam, but he did not black out.

Pol raised his head to see what hit him. A figure in a dark-green hood rushed the carriage. The image took a few seconds to register.

The figure reached the carriage and ripped open the side door.

The girl's scream pierced Pol's brain. He jumped to his feet and barreled toward the carriage. Noble or not, this was wrong. The assailant threw Quel Adeel to the ground while retaining a fistful of her dark hair. The carriage driver yanked on the reins, and the carriage skidded to a stop with the horses rearing.

Pol closed the distance to the assailant, who had pivoted toward the carriage with his back turned to Pol. The assailant reached for something underneath his tunic and hurled it into the carriage as Pol rammed his shoulder into the assailant's back.

Pol rolled through the muddy street and came to his feet, having picked up a mud-covered rock during the roll. Adeel had been thrown to the side. The assailant tore off his green cloak and revealed a black leather jerkin and several sheathed daggers.

Years of training with his uncle screamed at Pol to take the offensive at such a disadvantage. Reacting, Pol hurled the stone he had picked up at the enemy's head and charged. A left arm parried the stone, giving Pol an opportunity to strike the left flank. A hidden leather cuirass met his fist, and the attacker's right fist aimed for Pol's face. Pol leaned back, but the right hook caught his right lower jaw. Grunting as he took the hit, Pol kept his balance and kicked the man's legs out from under him just as Eash had done to him earlier. Pol jumped on the man's chest, but not before a dagger plunged into his right thigh. The assailant tried to wrestle Pol off, but the enemy's boots kept slipping in the mud.

Pol roared in pain as the leg injury registered, but he maintained his position atop the man while pinning the enemy's right hand with his left. Gritting his teeth, Pol deflected a punch and pummeled the man's face with Eash's words burning in his mind: *you might want to take a crack at the face.*

Pol didn't stop even when the man went limp underneath him. A hand pulled his right shoulder. Pol whipped his head around and cocked his fist to face Quon Daoringer. The quon placed his hand on Pol's fist.

"It's done, boy. It's done." The noble had dark-brown skin, a chiseled face, and short gray hair. A gold brooch with a small crown on top, rubies, and what looked like a ship adorned his red coat and glinted in the morning sun.

Pol dropped his fist and turned back, realizing the enemy lay unconscious. Blood seeped from the assailant's deformed nose, and both eyes were swollen and closed, but the man still drew breath.

Pol held up his hands. Blood covered his lacerated knuckles. He inhaled sharply as he sat back. Pain seared his right leg, and a wave of dizziness threatened to knock him out. The dagger still protruded from his right thigh. Unsure if it was wise, Pol gritted his teeth and pulled out the dagger. He groaned with the pain. Seeing the blood gush from the wound, he swallowed back bile and tore his brown tunic off his chest, feeling lightheaded.

The quon took the tunic from Pol's hands, ripped it further, and began tightly wrapping Pol's leg. "Should have left it for the cleric. Here, apply pressure."

With a deep breath, Pol pushed on the wound with two hands and leaned into the next wave of dizziness. He fought to remain upright.

Sobs from behind him pierced Pol's awareness. Once Quon Daoringer finished the dressing, he went to Adeel and placed his arms around her. She had a bloody scrape over her left temple but didn't seem to have serious injuries.

"It's okay, dear," the quon said to her as he knelt down. Adeel hugged her father, who turned to Pol and asked, "What's your name?"

"Pol," he replied with gritted teeth.

"Pol, thank you for saving us."

Pol gave a single nod and, out of instinct, asked, "Is she okay?"

"She'll be sore, but otherwise fine."

Even with her hair disheveled and her face blotchy from crying, Pol couldn't help but appreciate her beauty and her dark-brown eyes. He felt a small constraint on his heart as he noted the gold brooch on her now muddy green dress. As the next wave of dizziness hit, he became self-conscious that he was shirtless and covered in blood and mud.

Two dozen soldiers with hard, fast footfalls came around the corner, led by the quon's carriage driver.

Eash broke formation upon seeing Pol. "Pol, what did you do?" There was alarm in his eyes as he looked from Pol's hands to Adeel.

Quon Daoringer stood and held out a hand. "Peace. He just saved our lives, but how do you know this boy?"

Eash bowed his head and avoided the quon's eyes. "My liege, he is my nephew."

"How is it that this boy saved my life from an assassin?" The quon's change to a harsh tone surprised Pol. Was he wrong to have helped?

Eash shot a quick glance to his captain, standing beside him. The officer nodded to Eash, who then replied, "My liege, he is trained in combat."

"Did you train him?"

"Yes, my liege."

"Peace be with you. I'm not angry with you or anyone here. I'm angry at myself. My daughter is injured, and I did not have the chance to protect her because this boy did everything for me. What's your name?"

Eash stood up straight, and Pol held his breath even amidst the pain. Would he say it?

"Second Sergeant Eash Vroshen."

Pol's eyes widened. He'd said it—out loud—with people around.

The quon froze. "Vroshen? Is this boy also a Vroshen?"

Eash nodded slowly. "Yes, my liege."

Pol's eyes widened. The quon knew. What would happen to their family now?

The quon took his time as he assisted his daughter to her feet. "This boy has brought great honor to that infamous name." He turned to Pol. "But given that name, it is to be expected. You are safe here." The quon looked at the QuonGuards. "Is that clear, Captain?"

"Yes, my Quon!"

Even through the pain, Pol's heart lifted in hope.

The quon looked around. A crowd had started gathering. "We have taken too much time. Secure the assassin. I want answers within the hour."

The captain saluted with his right fist held over his heart. "Yes, my Quon. Are you hurt?"

"No. Lohem's Hand protected me, but this young man sustained a knife wound. Get him to the infirmary." He turned to Eash as if he wanted to say something more but addressed the captain instead. "I should have accepted your offer this morning."

"When you declined an escort, I'm sorry that I didn't insist."

"No, this is my fault. I put my daughter in harm's way." He assisted Adeel into the carriage.

Pol tore his eyes away from Adeel and focused on his bleeding hands. The pain overwhelmed his adrenaline, and nausea assaulted him. He made it to his feet, but more blood seeped from under the makeshift bandage. As he took a half step forward, his right thigh wouldn't support his weight, and he went down on his right knee.

Eash lunged forward, taking Pol's arm and putting it around his shoulder. Slowly, Eash stood up with him. The captain took Pol's other arm over his shoulder.

Quon Daoringer motioned. "Come. Put him in the carriage. Send someone for Cleric Rian."

Pol shook his head. He didn't want any favors from a nobleman. His uncle gently elbowed him in the ribs and guided him to the carriage seat. Pol grunted as he sat down on the plush velvet blue bench. If his mother saw how he was getting blood and mud on that velvet, she would have finished the assassin's job.

"I'll catch up to you, Pol," Eash whispered. "Glad you're okay. Lohem protects you, but don't do anything stupid." Pol cocked his head slightly, and Eash chuckled. "Don't do anything *else* stupid."

As Eash left, Pol realized Quel Adeel sat across from him. She held her hand to her temple but didn't take her eyes off him. He wanted to say anything, even a simple "hello," but the pain overwhelmed any attempt. He focused on staying upright.

Quon Daoringer entered the carriage on the other side. When he closed the door, Pol noticed the dagger lodged in the wooden rail above the quon's head. The quon wrenched it out. "That could have been my head. If you hadn't hit him, Pol, I might be dead."

The reality hit Pol hard as he held his leg, but he kept silent and simply nodded.

The quon called out, "To the keep!"

As the carriage pulled away, the captain shouted to his soldiers, "Bring that man to the dungeon! Sweep the area. He may not have been alone."

Pol grimaced as the carriage lurched forward. This was not how he had envisioned his first carriage ride.

—⁊⁊⁊—

Stacia backed away from the roof's edge. The attempt had failed, but the effect would be the same. The High Council would be pleased as Fenric's target should be delivered as divined.

She shivered in glee. Each success was a step forward, a step up.

Anvil, the worthless "assassin," would betray Geraul in the dungeons as expected; money rarely purchased loyalty, and she would be one step closer to completing her mission. Another win.

The unexpected surprise was locating the Vroshen line. Koen, her master, would be very pleased. He was in the business of finding heroes.

CHAPTER 5

"Many mistakenly believe that there is a winner and a loser when the battle ends. Often, the outcome is decided long before the first sword is drawn."

–Cleric Joern. Advanced Cordiaen Military Tactics,
Volume 2.

In his quarters, Stefan stopped pacing when he realized lunch had not been served. In the keep, he did not need the sundial, oil lamp, candle clock, or the weak attempts at mechanical devices to measure the day; appointments, meetings, or any scheduled event occurred according to meals. Dael chefs had mastered quality and service just as efficiently as the King's Army. So when lunchtime came and passed with no one knocking on his door, Stefan sat on the side of his bed with a sinking weight in the pit of his stomach.

"Something happened."

No one had delivered a missive, a letter, or even a whisper. His entire network had gone silent. Even after the hibernation command, he had expected to receive some word.

Taking a deep breath and slowly releasing it through his mouth, Stefan pivoted his strategies for the worst scenario.

He never thought he would have to put these plans into motion, but at least he had plans.

Stefan walked to his desk and squatted before it. Reaching his hand underneath and along the left side, he found the tiny knob. With a series of turns, a panel loosened under the knob, and Stefan removed the panel and extracted the papers from the hidden compartment. Stefan carefully replaced the panel and secured it before taking his seat and reviewing his previous work. Concerned for lost time, he quickly added a few extra notes with his quill and sealed the letters.

Stefan stepped over to the cold fireplace in his quarters. A wrinkle creased his forehead as he sought the correct spot, with fingers surveying the gritty and soot-covered wall. When a piece wiggled, Stefan pressed harder, and a rectangular metal chute opened. He deposited the letters, closed the chute lid, and washed his hands at the wash bowl near his bed. His servants would assume he had been messy with his inkpot, which would explain the residual black water. He always tried to be one step ahead.

An easy breath flowed from him, and Stefan took a seat in his leather-cushioned chair by the window. His hands trembled at having to take such measures to protect his holdings, but he rejoiced in having prepared such measures. Nothing short of the God of Cordiae, Lohem, could tear down his little empire.

A quarter of an hour later, his door burst open. Six QuonGuards piled into the room, and Stefan held up his hands. Relief filled his heart. His father was alive; no one else would take such measures against him.

"Qual Stefan, Quon Daoringer demands your presence," said a guard.

"Excellent, I just have to make a quick stop to the toilet—"

"Now."

"Okay then," Stefan replied while they flanked him and proceeded to the exit.

In the halls, servants milled about, but they hushed as he passed, escorted by the guards. The entire keep already knew more than he did. The guards led him down the main staircase to the third floor. Peeking over the banister, dozens of nobles ran about to various small groups in the foyer. Stefan corrected himself: most of the city knew more than he did.

Upon reaching his father's office, a guard rapped on the door, and a muffled "Enter" responded.

Stefan swallowed and took a deep breath before stepping into the room.

Quon Daoringer, in his chain mail cuirass with a blood-red tabard bordered with white trim, did not look up as he signed a parchment at his desk. The lead guard—Stefan didn't bother with their inferior titles—pointed to a cushioned chair before his father's desk. Stefan sat. No matter what trouble he found himself in, the guards would not dare touch him.

The quon looked up at the guards and then the door after he finished signing a document. The soldiers hurried out, carefully closing the door. Stefan could hear them shuffle into formation outside.

They did not leave.

In a flowing dark-red velvet dress, Stefan's mother, Quoness Esrealda, sat on a cushioned wooden bench against the wall. Her folded arms and pressed lips confirmed the severity of his situation.

Quon Daoringer finally looked up at him. Stefan knew better than to stare back and cast his gaze down.

The quon asked, "Why did you threaten Cal Geraul?"

Stefan never tried to manipulate his father; nothing ever got past the man. "He was competing against my supply venture for the King's Army."

"Wine wasn't enough?" The quon's hand curled into a fist. "You have thousands in gold. Thousands. Why is that not good enough for a seventeen-year-old who hasn't finished his basic studies?"

Stefan held back his quick retort. Every word would fashion his punishment. "Should I respond, my liege?"

"Oh, yes."

Stefan didn't cringe, but he wanted to. "Quon, I have finished basic studies. I haven't had a tutor in over two years."

Quon Daoringer glanced at his wife.

She spoke with an even tone. "He completed the program three years ago. The tutors barely did anything for him. You gave him permission to pursue the business."

"He finished with the military history tutor as well?"

Every single war since the first cleric, Jeitoh, founded the country. So…many…books. "Completely."

Daoringer turned on his son. "Impressive, but answer the question. Why isn't being rich good enough? Are you that consumed by greed?"

Stefan tried to keep his face passive but failed. "Do you really have to ask why the fifth son of a quon needs to fight for his future?"

"I decide your future."

Stefan bit his tongue, which was about to get him in worse trouble.

"I know you're smart. Up to this point, your exploits impressed me. My son, 'the Bear.' You're the smartest kid I've got. But if you're so smart, why did you threaten this noble?"

Stefan looked down at his hands. Honesty was the only route here. "I wanted more."

The quon stood and began pacing behind his desk. "I won't thank you for being honest; I know you've calculated your odds here. What you don't know is that your sister was almost abducted this morning by one of Geraul's lackeys."

Stefan's eyebrows shot up.

Daoringer's voice simmered with anger. "He tried to assassinate me, Stefan." The quon slammed his hands down on the desk and yelled, "I have the cal and the assassin in my dungeon right now, spilling every single detail. The only reason I'm not dead and your mother isn't paying ransom for your sister is because a boy, a peasant, saved our lives." The quon stalked around his desk and to Stefan's chair, lowering his voice. "The dagger hit two inches above my head." The quon leaned over and whispered, "He tried to kill me, boy. Now, do you think your stunt was wise?"

"No, my Quon," Stefan whispered.

"What was that?"

Stefan cleared his throat and repeated, "No, my Quon."

Quon Daoringer straightened. "Geraul sobbed that his intention was only to capture the girl to use against you." He paused. "He begged for mercy and said that he didn't know I would be riding with her."

Stefan couldn't swallow past the lump in his throat.

His father continued, "Of course, I do not believe him, and he will stand trial. The assassin claims there was a female messenger who informed him of Geraul's orders. Without explicit evidence, I cannot hang the son of a couv. I cannot even hang this Anvil without the king's permission." He sat down, tapping his desk. "Do you understand the position I am in? Do you understand the ramifications of what's happened? Do you know what you have *done?*"

Stefan kept his eyes down. He had never seen his father this angry. He knew better than to say a word.

"What do you have to say?"

Stefan cringed. "I'm sorry. I didn't—"

"Didn't what? Consider the possibilities? You are smart when you have the right information. You are unbeatable at that Chain game you play with your brother. But with people and emotions, books will only help you so much."

Stefan kept his head down. This was going to be brutal.

"This is not how we raised you. I may not be a holy man, but you know the faith. You know right from wrong. You failed." The quon paused for an entire minute as he shared a look with m the quoness. "I am stripping it all away. The wine, the gold, the investments."

Stefan caught his breath. *Everything?*

"As for what to do with you, I want to discuss it with your mother." The quon leaned back in his chair. "Well?"

Stefan waited a moment to ensure he didn't sound impertinent. "I'm very sorry. I would never want anything bad to happen to you or the family. You have said it well. I didn't understand. I would beg your permission to settle the businesses personally as there are men and women whose livelihood and families depend on those jobs."

"That is impressive. I want to believe your sincerity, but I also know what you, the Bear, did to hardworking wine merchants in my city behind my back. I will let you close things up, but you will not leave the keep."

Stefan nodded. He expected that much.

"No, no. You do not understand. I know of your little network. I have rounded them all up. The older ones are being kicked out of Dael as we speak, and your 'cubs' have been returned to the orphanages. You will not fart without me knowing. Now, what do you have to say?"

Stefan swallowed the lump. He wanted to know. "How is Adeel?"

"Impressive, Esrealda. He actually thought of someone other than himself. Adeel's head hurts, and she is scared. You could learn a lot from this Pol who saved her. He put both her and me before himself."

"Very good, my Quon." *A peasant saved them?*

"I won't send you to the dungeon this time. Go to your new quarters and await instruction."

New quarters? The dungeon might be better. Stefan stood and approached his mother. "I'm sorry, Mother." He presented his face to her with eyes closed. After an interminable moment, the crack of her hand against his cheek almost sent him to the floor. With his cheek stinging, he gave a small bow to each parent and opened the door.

The guards guided him up the stairs to the sixth and top floor. Voices from the foyer below continued to follow him as he ascended. The lead guard did not even open the door for him. Stefan entered, and they slammed the door behind him.

The simple guest bedroom usually housed a lesser visiting noble, but Stefan pushed aside the inconvenience.

The guilt of putting his family in danger humiliated him. He had underestimated Geraul, and the consequences had almost cost lives. The worst was that he owed a peasant for those lives.

〰

Quoness Esrealda unfolded her arms. "What will you do?"

Quon Daoringer sighed. "I cannot fault the kid for wanting to get ahead. Lohem knows how smart he is. There is no way I could have done what he has done by seventeen. But he crossed a line, and I have no choice but to make an example of him."

"So…"

"Military."

"No. Daoringer, our son?"

The quon reached down and opened a low drawer in his desk. He pulled out a crimson envelope and blew the dust off it. King Surtian, the previous king of Cordiae, had signed these documents six years before, and his son, King Sraung, had also signed the orders a few years ago. "Stefan would have made a great quon." He gently laid the envelope on his desk. "There must be consequences. His current path will lead to destruction…and not just his."

"I know. This could have been much worse. Still."

"Yes, he is my son, and I have a responsibility to guide him that I have been neglecting. I thought allowing him the freedom to run his business would bring maturity with responsibility. I have failed him." He began writing on special yellow parchment. "I do not trust Stefan to the Academy. He would own that weak establishment in a year. I have an acquaintance who will educate the boy in ways I cannot."

"Who? Someone here in Dael? Ariel?"

He stopped writing. "No. Do you remember General Granite?"

"The one who publicly defied King Surtian. Wasn't he decommissioned?"

"No. He was reassigned."

"Reassigned? The military is bad enough, but apprenticed to a disgraced officer? Why?" the quoness asked.

"Because Granite owes me a favor."

〰〰

Pol pushed himself up in his infirmary bed, careful to move slowly and avoid aggravating his injuries. His hands and right leg burned from the dressings placed by the nurse when he first arrived. The bleeding had stopped, but his wounds ached.

He had never had such fine treatment in his life. A bed. A real bed. The nurse had explained the infirmary served anyone in the keep from the quon to the stable boy. A row of beds, not just linens on the ground or cots, ran along either wall of the long room. Reaching the ceiling, oak cabinets with medical supplies lined the far wall to his left, and the only entrance lay to his right. Afternoon sunlight streamed in through the open windows with white, billowing curtains. The fine furnishings were surreal but beautiful, and he could enjoy them alone, which itself was a luxury. No one else shared the infirmary. For a moment, he had peace.

Wincing from soreness, Pol swung his feet over the bedside. A tray of food on a raised wooden table beside his bed had motivated him to risk aggravating his wounds. Slowly lifting the gleaming silver cover, Pol's jaw dropped.

Pork tenderloin with rich brown gravy bordered mashed blue tubers. A small house constructed from asparagus with carrot shreds forming the roof adorned the plate.

Pol gave thanks to Lohem, and with the same skill required to use a sword, he focused on keeping the fork in his bandaged right hand. The pork tenderloin melted in his mouth, and he did not even care about the gravy running down his chin from the mashed blue tubers. He paused before picking apart the small house constructed from vegetables, wondering if he should eat the creation. The rumors that the Dael Quon Chef was one of the best in the country were to be believed. He regretted the pain in his jaw with each bite, but the rush of flavor made up for the discomfort.

After savoring the last bite, Pol pushed the small wooden table to the side and tested his right leg. Pain seared up his thigh and into his hip. He eased back down on the bedside and shook his head. *Why did I do this again? Why did I fight for a noble and his daughter?*

Pol snorted. Status had nothing to do with a young woman being assaulted. Pol wouldn't have let that happen to anyone. His father had taught him better. His uncle had taught him better. But a poor kid who had received more than one beating at the hand of a noble had some reservations.

Pol was eight years old when a noble gave him his first beating. His father had had a longtime client, Lear Latian, who had a son the same age as Pol. Father would bring Pol to their residence while he worked on the Learess's shoes. Pol would play with Lan Yultian while his father worked. The boys had played ball and had many adventures throughout the lear's home, but Yultian never came to Pol's home. During one visit at the lear's residence, Yultian had wanted to play servant and noble. Pol had to be the servant. When Pol had failed to cook some imaginary food that Yultian liked, Yultian had slapped him across the face. Pol had thought they were playing a game and punched Yultian.

Lear Latian, Yultian's father, taught Pol the difference between noble and commoner for the black eye Yultian had received. The lear beat Pol almost unconscious before his father intervened and rescued Pol. Laor had lost the lear's business. Then, the lear's friends dropped his father's business as well. His father had saved him, but his father had been punished. That had always stuck with Pol.

The infirmary door creaked open, and his father and Uncle Eash pushed through. Eash smiled at seeing Pol. "There's the boy!"

They entered and strolled past the other beds, stopping at Pol's. His father lifted Pol's right hand. "Well?"

Pol winced at the movement. "Cut up pretty good. I can move my fingers and they still have feeling, but my hands are swollen. Don't know if I broke my right hand," Pol said.

Eash said, "You were pounding on a leather cuirass, boy. And that man's face wasn't a pillow." Laor and Pol smiled. Uncle had a point.

Eash continued, "How's the leg?"

"Having trouble putting weight on it. Bleeding stopped when I got here."

His father examined the bandage. "Someone cleaned these up real nice."

"There was a nurse who did that, but I'm waiting for the cleric to return." Why did his father seem more concerned now? What about earlier that morning?

"I see. Feeling better? Eat well?" Laor asked.

Pol held back a retort and told himself he should be grateful for his father's concern. "Yes, sir. I've never eaten food like that before."

"Pol, your father is just asking after you. We're all concerned. You don't have to be suspicious."

Eash always could read him better than his father, but to be fair, Eash had spent more time with Pol.

"Yes, sir." Speaking of family—"Will the quon really protect our family?"

Laor whipped his head to Eash with an uneasy look. Eash said, "All we can do is trust. You protected his family. Maybe this is what we've been waiting for."

"The quon knows?" His father's face flushed, and Pol winced, having only seen his father react like that once before. They had repaired furniture in the shop for months afterward.

Laor found his voice. "Why? Why would you ruin my family?"

Anger building, Pol spoke up. "Quon Daoringer said we were safe. He said that. Told the QuonGuard to make sure of it."

"How many people did you tell, Eash?" His father's voice raised.

"Pol did a great thing. The family should get the credit. Quon Daoringer is a hard man, but he's just. This is what we've been waiting for, Laor."

"That's up for debate, but I wasn't included." Laor paced down the line of beds. "This is my family, Eash."

Pol held his breath. He couldn't believe this conversation was happening within his hearing.

Eash drew himself up. "It's *our* family. Centuries of *our* family. It's not about you. How many Vroshen have suffered? How many of our ancestors died to keep the traditions, protecting a country that hates us?" He dropped his hands. "Vroshen had the foresight. His predictions came true. The noble class has failed the country; they failed us. I won't bury our name. I won't bury the blood, sweat, and tears our ancestors poured into this family."

Pol had heard that argument many times from his uncle, and it resonated with his heart.

Laor responded with an even tone. "It's a choice we're all given. Vroshen gave that choice to both of his sons. Father gave me the choice. I gave Pol the choice. It's a gift, not a command. I chose to keep the name out of respect for our father. I chose to let my son train with you. If I'm going to reveal our name and face the risks, that's my choice, not yours, no matter how noble."

Eash stared Laor down, but after a moment, Eash released his clenched fists. Pol's father had a good point, and Pol allowed the thought to sink into his heart. His father had allowed him to make choices. He didn't have to.

"You're right." Eash sighed. "You're right. I apologize, Laor. I should have given Pol the chance to reveal it. In my defense, how else was I going to explain how a sixteen-year-old took down an assassin—a bad one, but still?"

"Doesn't matter. Apology accepted. I just hope Quon Daoringer meant what he said."

Pol exhaled. Previous arguments about their blessed heritage had not ended so peacefully.

A small knock at the door interrupted, and Eash called out, "Come in."

Quel Adeel entered and stole Pol's breath. Her fine brown hair had been redone with a blue ribbon. A large bruise had developed over her left cheek. She wore a light-blue dress with matching shoes and carried herself with more grace than any other girl Pol knew. He glanced down at his chest and silently thanked the nurse who had given him a white tunic.

Adeel must have caught the glance as a small pink bloom filled her cheeks, but she recovered quickly as she stopped by his bed. "Good afternoon. I came down to see how you're doing."

"Hi. I'm, uh, fine." His brain suddenly did not function.

Adeel said, "Oh. Well, I wanted to thank you. I'm scared to think what might have happened if you had not been there today."

Pol hadn't thought that far ahead. Someone had wanted to steal this girl for a reason. A nobleman's daughter was a valuable commodity. Why did he get mixed up in this? Was he taking a long time to respond?

Eash stepped in. "We are so glad you are safe, Quel."

Pol nodded emphatically.

Quel Adeel said, "Thank you. You're Pol's uncle? It is Pol, right?"

Pol needed to talk and not just nod. "Yes…this is my uncle, Eash, and my father, Laor."

Adeel gave each a slight nod before returning her attention to Pol. He considered that facing another assassin might be easier.

Talking. More talking. "Um, how's the quon?"

"Thank you for asking. He is doing well. He is angry at my brother, but he was not injured," Adeel said.

"Your brother?" Pol asked.

"I don't know the details, but my older brother Stefan is partially responsible for the attack. Quite embarrassing. Papa will take care of him." She stepped forward. "Pol, I also came to ask you a favor."

Pol swallowed past his dry throat. "Okay."

Adeel said, "My father will host a small dinner tomorrow night in your honor. Would you be willing to return to Dael Keep?"

Eash smiled, and his father's eyes widened.

Pol checked his mouth. His immediate reaction was to say yes. But come back to Quon Keep, filled with lords and ladies? He would prefer to go another round with the assassin. Still, he would get to see Adeel again. He was taking too long again. "I'd enjoy that. Thank you for offering." Eash elbowed his arm. "Quel."

She smiled. "Excellent." Pol's heart steeled itself against that beautiful smile for two full seconds before returning a lopsided smile. She was beautiful, even if she was a noble. Adeel grinned.

In embarrassment, Pol shifted his position, and the pain in his thigh flared.

Adeel's face softened at his grimace. "I'm so sorry Cleric Rian is late. He was on the other side of the city."

With a bow, his father said, "The Quel is most kind."

Pol refrained from rolling his eyes. His father did not need to pander.

The infirmary door burst open, and a portly cleric rolled down the aisle. "Who's talking about me?" he asked, scanning each person. After a bow to Quel Adeel, he fixed his attention on Pol. "Ah, the hero."

Without preamble, the cleric took off the leg dressing with fresh bright-red blood oozing. Pol winced at the rough handling. Weren't clerics supposed to be gentle? He pulled the edges of the puncture open and examined the wound. "Cleaned out well. No bone involvement. You'll have to come back in a few days to have the dressing changed. Have you ever been healed by Lohem before?"

"No, sir."

"I'm Cleric Rian, not an officer. You say, 'No, Master Rian' or 'Cleric Rian.' "

"Yes, sir, uh, Cleric Rian." He wasn't about to say "master."

"Let me explain how this works because some people think it's mandra or my own special powers, but that's not the case." Cleric Rian rolled up his sleeves. "I'm going to pray and ask Lohem to heal you. With this blessing, you may heal quicker depending upon Lohem's will. I have no control in that regard. Understand?"

"Yes, Cleric Rian."

"Don't be upset if it doesn't heal as quickly as you expect. Lohem's will is not our own." Cleric Rian placed both hands over the wound and pressed. Pol gritted his teeth. Did the man need to push on his wound to pray?

His father, uncle, and Adeel bowed their heads.

Cleric Rian began the traditional healing prayer, then he not so gently grabbed Pol's hands and repeated the prayer. Pol considered himself faithful, and while he had heard of the power of clerics, he questioned the man's abilities. There was no golden light or strange visions like he had expected from his uncle's war stories. Still seated, his wounds did not feel different. Pol sighed. He assumed Lohem wanted him to hurt for a bit.

Cleric clapped him on the back. "You're ready now, son."

"Not quite," replied Quel Daoringer as he entered and approached. Everyone except Pol bowed. Pol dipped his head a little when he noticed the others. The quon had changed into a chain mail cuirass with a red tabard bordered with white trim. Stern black eyes held Pol's gaze as Cleric Rian stepped aside for the quon, who asked, "So what can I do to repay you, young man?"

How do you feel about your daughter's hand in marriage? "Thank you for the healing and the food. Nothing more, Quon."

The quon examined Pol's bandages. "Is that so?" He looked at Laor. "So you're the young man's father?"

"Laor, Your Grace," his father replied with a bow.

"Is it true your surname is Vroshen?"

Laor glanced at Pol and then Eash. "Yes, Your Grace."

"I understand why you are concerned. Be not afraid. I have only respect for your blessed lineage."

Cleric Rian lifted his eyebrows. "Vroshen? The Vroshen family? Well, that explains things."

Laor dipped his head. "Without offending Master Rian, Quel Adeel, or Your Grace, we beg secrecy in this matter. While those present may be accommodating, others may not."

"Well said. I give you my word that your family will be under my protection. That brings me to why I'm here," Quon Daoringer replied. "Pol, you provided a great service to us today. How can I repay you?"

Pol's mind went blank again.

Uncle Eash chuckled. "C'mon, boy. Speak up."

The quon added, "Just ask, Pol."

Laor's gaze bored into Pol, and he knew what his father would ask for. Pol glanced at Adeel for a second, and his heart fluttered as their eyes met. His uncle chuckled again. No. Pol knew what he wanted to ask for.

"Sir, I just want to be an officer in the King's Army. That's what my ancestors aspired to. That's our duty."

"Pol!" his father exclaimed with a glance at the quon.

"Pol," Uncle Eash said softly, "I was going to keep it a surprise, but I was going to pay for you to go to the Academy. Ask for something else."

"Let me understand," Quon Daoringer said. "You could ask for anything, and you want to become an officer in the King's Army?"

Pol did not have to reconsider. "You know about my ancestors. You know I have an obligation to this country. I've wanted it for years, but not with my uncle's money."

"I'm willing to offer you more, Pol. Crowns or a title?" Quon Daoringer pried.

"Pol, consider your family," his father pleaded.

"I am. Vroshen himself chose the same. He never wanted the title or money. He only wanted to serve. Why do you think I've been training all this time? Why did you let me train?"

Laor closed his eyes. "Because my father would have wanted it." He dropped his head and sighed. "It's your choice."

Quon Daoringer regarded Pol silently for a moment. "You are a credit to your parents and uncle. I will not forget this." He folded his hands together. "I respect your choice, Pol, but I can't send you to the Academy."

"But you—"

The quon raised a hand. "You will receive training, but it will be with someone I trust. You're too valuable to send to the Academy."

It took Pol a second to register the response. Too valuable?

"Your Grace?" Eash asked.

The quon grinned at Uncle Eash. "Adeel, did Pol accept the invitation?"

"Yes, Papa."

"Splendid. Son, I'll see you tomorrow night. Would you bring your family?"

Pol took a turn being surprised. "Yes, sir. Thank you."

Laor beamed and bowed. "Your Grace is most kind."

"No. This boy was kind in sacrificing himself. This is the least I can do. For now." He held an arm out to his daughter, who took it gracefully and gave Pol a quick glance. Pol returned the look with a smile. After she left through the door, the cleric secured the bandage around his leg. Pol's limb screamed in agony, and he brought his hand down to push the man away.

Cleric Rian caught his arm. "Pol, when you come tomorrow, address the quon as 'Quon' or 'Your Grace.' Got it?"

"Yes, sir."

Cleric Rian smacked the side of his head. Pol rubbed his scalp. He had little interaction with clerics, but this one was brutal. "Yes, Cleric Rian."

Eash chuckled and helped Pol to his feet. "Obey the cleric, Pol."

"Yes, sir."

Pol could stand. The leg still hurt, but he could put weight on it. Maybe Lohem had healed him? Pol decided that any help was appreciated, and he would take time to thank Lohem.

Cleric Rian said, "Time to go. Carriage is waiting." Pol was about to shake his head, and the cleric caught the pause. "The quon won't take no for an answer."

Pol resigned himself to another reason to owe the quon. With his uncle's assistance, he limped out of the infirmary and into the keep proper. Pol couldn't help but notice all the people in the hallway and foyer who had stopped to stare at him. Some looked to be servants, and others had gleaming brooches, but they all stared at him and whispered.

"Uncle, what's wrong?" Pol asked, nodding to the crowd.

"Word gets around. It's not every day a kid prevents the assassination of the quon."

"Am I in trouble?" Pol didn't enjoy drawing this kind of attention.

"No, you're popular, but some consider that to be trouble."

CHAPTER 6

Through his window, Stefan stared at the world moving outside the keep. The inner bailey bustled with activity as teams of horses moved supplies, courtiers traveled to and from his father's hall, and QuonGuards patrolled. The microcosm reflected the city, the region, and the rest of the country. Was he really removed from it? Seemed surreal. He did not doubt his father's intent and authority to fulfill the punishment, but how far did his father's reach extend?

His oldest brother, Qual Heir Cyprian, cleared his throat, pulling Stefan's attention from the window and back to the game board his brother had set up. A traditional ebony board with silver hexagonal spaces contained silverwood and pearlwood pieces comprising their respective armies. After three seconds of consideration, Stefan moved his pearlwood trell piece.

Cyprian shook his head. "You could at least pretend to take the game seriously."

"It's been a rough day." Stefan lifted his chin off his hand and reclined in his chair. He drew his hands onto his lap when they brushed the chair's coarse wooden edges. He already missed his leather chair.

Cyprian touched a smooth pearlwood cleric game piece with his index finger. "That's why I'm spending it with you."

Stefan snorted. "Don't lie. Father wants you to keep an eye on me."

"Of course he does." Cyprian moved his cleric piece, waiting a moment before removing his hand.

In Chain, players controlled armies with various power units represented by detailed images. The unit image faced the controlling player, inscribed on an oval-shaped piece held up with a sturdy hexagonal base, smaller than the demarcated section that contained it. The opposing player only saw an army of ovals on stands in the beginning, unaware of how their opponent had arranged their forces. Cheap sets contained pieces made of oak with images painted on them, but Stefan had a special set, as he was particularly fond of the game. His brother controlled the Cordiaen forces and their allies made from the rare silverwood of Miraden Forest, while Stefan used "enemy" pieces composed of lost ones, reyuul, and other evil units made from aromatic pearlwood found in GreatWell Forest. Stefan couldn't see what Cyprian just moved, but he knew.

"The Vinsh maneuver with the cleric won't work if you advance it too soon."

"I'm pretending not to hear that," Cyprian said as he continued studying the board. "So, if you're always one step ahead, why didn't you know Geraul would attack like that?"

"I have been grilled enough today." Stefan leaned forward, moved his reyuul piece with a resounding thud, and folded his arms.

"Don't lose that often, do you?" asked Cyprian.

"I have never lost until today. Absolutely horrible. Truth is, I did not think Geraul would move against the quon. It's suicide for his business, and yesterday the cal seemed very interested in fighting for his business."

Cyprian continued to pour over the board. "Father said Geraul confessed he wanted to abduct Adeel. Why?"

"Intimidation, money, or both? Geraul would have planned it so that someone else took the fall. He gets the money, and then later he might have tipped me off that he 'may have been involved.' Theoretically, I would then be intimidated. Instead, he messed up, and I'm ruined."

Cyprian toyed with one of his silverwood pieces on the board. "Father has the impression that your greed outweighed your reason. Is that why you pushed Geraul so hard? Was this about money or something else?"

"You really have to ask that? You know how hard Father drilled self-sufficiency into us. Those 'opportunities' when I had been thrown into a dungeon were eye-openers. Even now, where is my family? Where are my brothers? They're out making a name for themselves."

"Actually, they're all returning today to show support." Cyprian sighed. "I'm sorry you can't be the quon. You may be the most talented of us sons, but you're not the oldest."

Stefan refrained from upending the game board. "I don't want it. You can have it. I mean it. I never wanted to be quon."

"Then what do you want?"

Stefan said, "I told you already: I want a future. No one is going to give it to me."

Cyprian moved a voltai piece to support his cleric. "No. You want your own future. You don't want anyone telling you what your future should be."

The truth hit Stefan so hard in the gut, he took a moment to catch his breath. This was why he spent time with Cyprian, whose wisdom always caught him off guard even if his Chain moves did not. Still, Cyprian's future was already set. "Don't patronize me, Qual Heir. I have my doubts you could appreciate my situation."

"Maybe. Maybe not. Try me." Cyprian stood.

Stefan's mouth was getting him into even more trouble. Cyprian was the only family member he could really talk to, and Stefan had taken it too far. "No, I am sorry. I do not mean to snap at you. You are not wrong. I have got—I had plans. I told you. It has been a rough day."

Sympathy filled Cyprian's face, and he took his seat, examining the Chain board. "What will you do now?"

Stefan wanted to spill everything. He wanted to reveal his contingency plans and explain how he was going to make Father proud through his perseverance, but he didn't want to compromise Cyprian's position. "As you say, whatever Father wants. I do not have a choice."

"Not to be a jerk, but Father almost died, and Adeel almost got kidnapped. I would say you deserve it."

"Rub it in, why don't you?" No. Stefan should not take that tone with Cyprian. "I am sorry. I might deserve this, but it does not mean I have to like it." Stefan moved a moltengore piece and stared at the exquisite detail of the monster.

Cyprian frowned at the move. "Sure you will not consider my offer to be my QuonGuard captain?"

"Okay. I have bigger plans no matter what Father does to me. Besides, I do not fight as well as you."

"At least not sword to sword." Cyprian moved his cleric back a space.

A knock sounded at the door. Stefan advanced his archreyuul piece, captured Cyprian's king, and stood. "You might have been able to stall me if you had kept moving your cleric forward. Next time, pay attention to the *move* order."

Cyprian's face flushed. "Really? Stefan."

Stefan grinned at his brother's loss of emotional control as Illiat entered with a guard. Stefan's shoulders relaxed as the master chef bowed first to Cyprian and then gave a head nod to Stefan.

"Cyprian, this is Master Chef Illiat from the Eagle's Nest."

Cyprian exhaled loudly and swatted at the cleric piece. "Good day to you, Master Chef Illiat."

"And to you, Qual Heir Cyprian. Qual Stefan, it's still raining outside."

Stefan understood that to mean his network remained compromised, and everyone was in hiding.

Cyprian glanced out the window. The sun was shining. "Stefan, I'm standing right here. Don't patronize me."

Stefan ignored his brother and replied, "Thank you, Illiat, but I am not allowed to leave. I trust you brought an umbrella just in case."

Illiat said, "I did, my Qual, but I did not bring two."

Illiat was safe but may be suspected of involvement with Stefan. No one had tried taking him into custody. Illiat did not have immediate means to rescue Stefan.

Cyprian leaned over and whispered. "If you keep this up, I'll have you thrown in the dungeon."

Stefan needed to let Illiat know he had a plan in place. "I assume you were in a rush. Do not be troubled. If I step out with Lord Cyprian, I can always ask for one."

"Excellent, Qual. I'm glad to see that you're okay. Many are concerned."

His business contacts have asked if everything would fall through. Stefan was not about to give up so easily. "The quon is not pleased, Illiat, but he is merciful. I'll miss eating at the Nest, but I'd ask that you tell everyone that I'm thinking of them."

"I'll do more than that, Qual. Again, I'm glad you're okay."

Illiat will help keep things running for now and assist with the contingency plan. Stefan gave a head bow to the chef. "Thanks for coming by."

Illiat returned a deeper bow to Stefan and Cyprian before leaving with the guard.

Cyprian shook his head. "Do you really think you can defy Father?"

"Who said anything about that? We were just talking about the weather, and Illiat was concerned about me."

"A chef?"

"He owns the Eagle's Nest, and, well, he's the only one who I trust."

"Lonely at the top?"

Stefan clenched his fist but remembered it was Cyprian. "I'm not at the top…yet. I have found that trust is more important than status in some cases."

Cyprian feigned chest pain. "Did I just hear that? Does Stefan actually see past a brooch? Or do you only care about those who can help you?"

Again, his brother's accusation knocked the wind out of his sails, and Stefan did not have a witty retort. Instead, he picked up the pieces of his Chain game and placed them neatly in their case, which his father had gifted to him when he was eight. "The social circles I keep are necessary to move ahead, but I would not trust those nobles with my life. Illiat has saved me many times."

"He cannot save you now," Cyprian said.

"I can take care of myself. Always one step ahead."

"If you defy Father, he will put you in the dungeon. For longer than one night this time," Cyprian said with a grave tone.

"Listen, Illiat's going to take over things. Honest."

"You know he will be watched," Cyprian said.

"I am counting on it."

<hr>

Pol's third carriage ride took them back through the streets of Dael to Dael Keep. As the daylight waned, Pol looked out the window to find lamplighters beginning their work. Dusk slowly gave way to evening, and the lampposts ignited in a rhythmic fashion. With his self-imposed schedule, Pol rarely stayed out past sundown, and he had not seen the lamps lit in months. The mesmerizing globes, which slowly ignited, reinforced the foreign sensation of the evening, and tension crept into his shoulders. With deliberate concentration, he relaxed his posture as if assuming his sword stance. The thought of seeing Adeel so soon threatened to reclaim some anxiety, but just as he would when facing an opponent, Pol refused to let anxiety overwhelm him. Adeel was a girl just like his sisters, right?

Pol tugged at the starched collared shirt chafing his neck and adding to his discomfort. The round collar hugged his neck, and the stiff brown leather jerkin forced him to sit up straight. New black pants pressed against his injured leg, but his mother said he looked handsome. Not wanting to upset the woman who had scrambled to find the new outfit for him, Pol refrained from grimacing, but he had not expected to be so uncomfortable in the borrowed clothes.

The change in the carriage speed caught his attention as they slowed to pass a creeping line of carriages waiting to enter the keep. Pol had expected only his family to be dining with the quon.

Jenieve, his sister, pointed out the carriages. "Look at them all."

Laor leaned over to look out the window. "Yep. Looks like it's going to be a big party of fancy people. Posey, you all right?"

Pol's mother fanned herself with a hand holding a cotton handkerchief. "I've never been to something like this. There's no chance of avoiding embarrassment. Would you take off that hat now?"

Laor pulled his cap tighter on his head. "Leave me be, woman."

The carriage slowed to a halt before the keep, and Pol noted the other carriages had created a bottleneck at the gate. When the carriage door opened, Pol started as the unexpected servant, who had introduced himself as Dwoat, stuck his head inside. "My apologies, but we'll have to walk the rest of the way. I have explicit instructions to make sure you arrive on time. Please."

Laor waved for Pol to go. "Our pleasure. Let's not disappoint Quon Daoringer."

Pol eased himself down the steps, wincing with each movement. Once everyone had disembarked, Dwoat led them past a line of carriages waiting to enter the keep's main gate. Miltou stood guard at the entrance with five other soldiers, and he called out to the other guards as Pol's family approached. The six soldiers at the gate stood at attention, and together they began singing the quon's anthem, "The Act of Valor." Soon, guards all over the walls took up the song. Pol scanned the area for the quon as the song usually announced his presence.

Eash leaned over. "They do this for you. You're a bit if a celebrity among the QuonGuard now."

Pol let his jaw drop a little. "They shouldn't. They would have done a better job."

"Maybe. But when it mattered, you acted and gave what you could. That is the core of our mission. Much appreciated, Pol."

"Uncle…" For six years, Pol had passed under the gates with his own respect for the soldiers who guarded the quon. Hearing them sing brought a lump to his throat.

Laor repositioned his cap with a slight tilt. "Son, it takes a humble man to receive gratitude well. I know you might not like these nobles, but be gracious here. No matter what. The quon serves the city and the king well. You saved his life yesterday. Allow him to return the gratitude. Make our family proud."

"Yes, Father."

Nobles, tradesmen, and servants within the bailey stopped as Dwoat escorted Pol's family. Some cheered, and some just stood watching them pass. Pol felt his face flush as he limped behind Dwoat. He didn't think he could last long if this kept up the entire night.

Dwoat led them through the keep's thick steel-reinforced doors, reaching twenty feet high, into a grand foyer. Ever since the Expulsion centuries before, Cordiaen architecture reflected a functional approach. Steel and mortar replaced fancy materials like soft and expensive metals, glass, and weak wood. Inside, spiral red stone columns marched through the foyer toward the great hall. The smooth stone floor held the occasional embedded red marble tile, repelling sound. Voices echoed through the foyer, and myriad perfumes and colognes mingled on the air drafts from the entrance. Well-dressed lords and ladies clumped in groups, laughing and conversing.

Pol's mouth went dry as some gave his family quizzical looks. He did not have any fashion sense, and his family stood out like a scuff on polished shoes. Pol's mother and sisters must have picked up on the attention and huddled closer to Laor. His father stood tall, even when a large, well-dressed noble stopped before them. It was Dal Marwin.

"Laor? What do you think you're doing here? Do you know what kind of disgrace this is?"

His father stepped forward. "The quon invited us, Dal."

The obese man was about to respond when Dwoat said, "If you please, Mr. Pol and family are here by personal invitation from the quon. Excuse us, Dal."

Passing the noble, Pol held back a smirk and the desire to dance as Dal Marwin sputtered, "Personal invitation?"

Dwoat had them quickly bypass the rest of the foyer and enter the Quon Hall. The arched ceiling soared above them with supporting giant stone pillars. Guests and servants bustled about, but some stopped and stared at the family passing through. It took a few minutes to traverse the hall to find tables covered with either red or white cloths situated on either side of a central aisle. The aisle ended with a twenty-foot-wide crescent-shaped table before a wide dais. The dais had multiple red cushioned seats but no thrones. The red-and-white Dael crest hung below the crimson-and-gold Cordiaen crest on the red stone wall.

Dwoat led Pol's family to the left and stopped at a table near the front. Pol helped his sisters sit before he pulled out his own chair, as his mother had taught him. As he sat down, Dwoat touched his shoulder. "Excuse me, Mr. Pol, but the quon has requested your presence at his table tonight."

Pol looked at his father, hoping he might say no, as Pol had no desire to sit before all the other tables.

Laor nodded emphatically. "It'll be fine." Eash just smiled while Posey held both of her hands to her mouth.

Pol remembered his father's words from earlier and pushed his chair back under the table. *For the family.* Trying to minimize his limp, he followed Dwoat across the aisle toward the crescent-shaped head table. Dwoat guided him to the far edge of the empty table. Grunting with soreness, Pol sat down in the heavy oak chair with an impeccably glossy finish.

Dwoat leaned over. "If you need anything, Mr. Pol, just ask."

"Thanks, Dwoat." Pol looked around to make sure no one could hear him. "If I hide under the table, come rescue me."

Confusion flashed across the servant's face, followed by a small smile. "Mr. Pol, if I may, if you can defeat an assassin, I'm sure you can handle a dinner with us." He bowed, waved over a servant with a water pitcher, and whispered in the servant's ear. "But, actually, Mr. Pol, this is Yuir. He will serve you tonight."

Yuir bowed and filled a wooden cup with water for Pol.

"Thank you, Yuir. Nice to meet you," Pol said.

The servant must not have been used to being greeted, as he almost dropped the flagon, recovered, and then bowed to Pol. "Most welcome, sir." Yuir and Dwoat bowed together, retreated from the table, and began conversing in hushed tones.

Over the next half hour, Pol watched the hall and the tables slowly filled with lords and ladies. Servants ran from table to table and group to group, offering wine, ale, and appetizers. More than one noble deliberately stared at him as he sat alone. Pol flashed his eyes down when he found a noble boring into him with their gaze. The situation was already awkward; he did not need to provoke any further trouble.

Instead, Pol distracted himself with a mental rehearsing of sword drills and combat positions. The drills helped him focus and reinforced his confidence as long as he didn't look toward the crowd. Every few minutes, he would glance over at his family, who also appeared isolated, but at least they had each other.

Finally, a bell rang, and everyone in the hall stood. Pol refrained from groaning as he placed weight on his right leg.

A thin, elderly man in red-and-white robes that appeared too large and wearing a shiny gold necklace stepped out from a hallway near the dais. "Good evening, and welcome to Dael Keep!" he called in a loud, firm voice that seemed out of place for his size. "I have the pleasure of presenting to you the Quon Family of Dael: Quel Adeel,

Qual Stefan"—gasps and murmurs—"Qual Escuar, Qual Oniat, Qual Wearth, and Qual Heir Cyprian."

The QuonGuard escorted Adeel and her brothers forward to the table. Quel Adeel held the arm of one of the older brothers, and Pol thought it might be Qual Heir Cyprian. He guided the quel to the chair next to Pol and then with a nod, graciously acknowledged Pol, who returned a bow. The qual heir then moved to a seat closer to the middle. Coming to stand on the other side of Adeel was a young man who looked the same age as Pol. Light brown skin framed a wide face and black hair, styled short. Pol recognized Stefan as the brother Adeel had mentioned the day before. His presence among this crowd must be a scandal. Under his red long-sleeved doublet with white trim, Stefan's slender build and arms pronounced his lack of physical training. Pol knew all nobles received arms training on some level, as combat readiness permeated all levels of the Cordiaen culture, but Pol understood some took it more seriously than others.

The young man's eyes raked over Pol with unveiled contempt. Disconcerted, Pol looked away, not wanting to stoke any anger.

"And finally, I present Quon Daoringer and Quoness Esrealda."

The quoness entered on the arm of the quon. With bows, curtsies, and light applause, the congregated hall paid its respect. Pol remembered conversations with his father about Quon Daoringer being well-liked due to his firm policies that kept Dael safe and prosperous.

Quon Daoringer lifted his voice to the hall. "Thank you, Chamberlain Hiuken and all present tonight. We give thanks to Lohem for delivering our family from danger. Please enjoy your dinner."

The quon family took their seats, and Pol felt a gentle tug downward on his arm as Adeel guided him to his chair.

Pol felt his face flush. Taking deep breaths, he focused on the grain of the polished table. The elite quality of the oak with its seamless lines was just as imposing upon close inspection. Everything around him seemed to be of the highest quality. Pol refocused on the sword drills and traced his finger on the wood. After a moment, his shoulders relaxed, and he found Adeel quietly waiting.

Feeling even more awkward at her composure with his delay, Pol stopped moving his finger and ventured, "Quel, how are you feeling?"

"I'm much better than yesterday. My headache is mostly gone, but my neck is still sore even with small movements."

Talking. Yes, he could keep talking. "Makes sense. I have experienced the same with hard training, and yesterday was brutal."

"Yes. Yes, it was." She brushed a meticulously perfect black curl of hair off her shoulder. "And you? How are you feeling?"

"Leg's not bleeding, but it still aches when I put weight on it."

The brother, Qual Stefan, leaned over. "Too bad you had to come with such an injury. If it's too much, I can have a servant carry you home."

Pol looked sharply at Adeel's brother. Did he really just say that? Pol caught himself and lowered his gaze back to the table.

Adeel rolled her eyes. "Pol, this is Qual Stefan, my older brother who should learn to be nice, especially after yesterday."

Stefan did not reply.

Pol did not know anyone could talk to a noble like that. He wanted to reply with something polite as his mother had instructed him, or maybe even witty to compliment Adeel's introduction, but he floundered to find anything to say. Instead, Pol stood, providing the qual with a small bow as expected of his station.

Stefan snorted. Pol fought the flush creeping up his face as he sat back down. Adeel turned on her brother. "Stefan, he saved my life from the danger you created. Be nice."

Pol didn't understand what was going on. He whispered to Adeel, "My lady, did you tell him about my family?"

"No, Pol. I would not do that." Her voice carried sincerity, and he believed her.

"Then how did I upset Qual Stefan?"

"You got involved, peasant," Stefan barked.

Adeel whirled on her brother. "Stefan! You were placed here to thank Pol."

"Thank him for what? Doing my shoes? He's a cobbler's kid."

Adeel's face flushed a little. "What part of 'saved my life' do you fail to understand? I don't care if he sweeps the chimney, he's a hero."

"He's a disgrace to the table. It doesn't matter what he did."

Pol kept still. Any visible emotion or words could make the situation erupt. If it came to blows, he figured Stefan wouldn't stand a chance. Pol envisioned how he would gently guide Adeel safely to the side before he yanked Stefan out of his seat and to the ground without seriously injuring him. Fighting with the quon's son in front of a hall filled with nobles might not go well for the quon's family, and he remembered how important the evening was to his family, to his parents. Pol was just going to have to stomach whatever Qual Stefan dished out. His heart softened, considering Adeel's defense, but it was only making the lordling angrier.

Adeel took a breath to talk, but Pol placed a hand on hers. "Quel, it's not necessary."

"Get your hand off my sister," came the loud response.

The quon and the qual heir were already moving to flank Stefan. Most of the hall quieted at the interaction. The quon placed his hand on Stefan's shoulder. "I realize it may be disconcerting to sit near the hero who prevented your sister from being abducted and your father from being murdered." He leaned down. "I realize he's not our usual guest, and I also realize you are humiliated. But I swear, if you continue in this manner, I will make you spend a full day in the stocks after I have you flogged right here in the hall. Try that for humiliation." Quon Daoringer said to Pol. "Pol, if he says anything else rude to you, just let me know."

"Yes…Your Grace."

The quon smiled and gently kissed his daughter on the temple before returning to his seat. The quon heir said to Pol, "I'm Cyprian, the oldest. Wanted to say thanks for what you did."

"My pleasure, Qual Heir." Pol could see Cyprian's resemblance to the quon. The qual heir also kissed Adeel's head before advancing toward the congregated mass of nobles.

Based on what just happened, Pol assumed that Stefan's family was using the opportunity to teach him a lesson. Pol's father had given him worse scoldings. Pol dismissed his anxiety, knowing he would be safe tonight.

Adeel excused herself, and Pol stood as she left the table. He ventured a look to his own family and found Dal Marwin with a small party of nobles pointing at his father. Cyprian approached the dal and got so close their noses almost touched.

The dal retreated, bowing to the qual heir who waited as the dal's crew departed before turning to Laor.

After a moment of conversing, Cyprian held out his hand and received Laor's cap. He tried it on. Men and women from nearby tables who had previously ignored Pol's family were now offering praise for the hat. Cyprian returned the cap and shook hands with Laor.

Adeel returned. She had applied something to her left temple that further masked the bruise, but Pol could see the outline. She smiled and was about to talk when the quon stood. The hall quieted.

"I will invite Cleric Rian to say the blessing."

Cleric Rian stood and went to the open area before the main table. After waiting for the crowd to settle, Cleric Rian brought his hands together, folding his fingers except for the index fingers, as tradition instructed. The cleric provided a simple Cordiaen blessing, invoking Lohem and health upon the king, country, quon, and city.

As soon as he finished, dinner entered in waves. For the appetizer, Yuir placed a small red and white porcelain cup before him. A solitary egg with a smooth, cream-colored shell and covered in small brown dots nestled securely in the cup's flared sides.

Pol froze, unsure of what to do, but thankfully, Yuir leaned over and whispered, "Gently tap the shell from the side and remove it. Eat the yolk. It's delicious." Yuir slipped away before Pol could thank him.

Without hesitation, Adeel used a spoon to open her egg and scoop out the contents. Pol followed suit, with less finesse, and became pleasantly surprised after a small taste. As he moved through the different courses, his mouth exploded with flavor at the vegetable, an eggplant variant with tomato sauce and cheese. He used all the skill he could muster to avoid getting a single drop of sauce on himself. With a refreshing politeness, Yuir and Adeel coached him on the various utensils and how to hold his cup. The meal finished as Yuir served lamb with mint sauce, followed by chicken covered with garlic, lemons, and rosemary. Pol beamed at Adeel's small compliments throughout, and he caught himself staring at her a few times.

Adeel placed her fork down. "Pol, tell me about your family."

Pol followed her example and placed his fork down but didn't know if he could speak over the loud beating of his heart. "What do you want to know?"

"What are your sisters like?"

Pol looked over at his family's table. More nobles were talking with his father and asking to see his hat. "Jenieve and Fait work hard with my mother at the seamstress's. They are skilled and very patient. Of course, they can be annoying, but I love them."

"They work? I have never worked. Is it hard?"

Pol held back laughter. "Yes, Quel. Work is hard, but you get used to it."

"You must think me a fool, but I've never had to worry about money."

"Then you're blessed, as my father would say. I hope you use your time for something good."

An expression of what might have been dismay crossed Adeel's face, though it quickly faded. "I am tutored as a daughter of a quon. Other than that, I usually enjoy my carriage rides in the morning, except for yesterday, of course. I also spend time with my friends." She paused. "Do you have friends?"

"Yes, Quel. After I've done my work at my father's shop for the day, sometimes I play felball with my friends in the street."

Adeel clasped her hands together. "I've seen it from my carriage. You run and kick a ball. It looks so fun. I've tried to get Stefan to do it, but he's always too busy."

Thoughts of running through streets with Adeel made his heart smile. "One day, I could show you."

Adeel brought her hands down. "That might be nice." There was an awkward pause, but it looked like she might have something else to say. Pol realized he did not have good conversational skills. "So…are you by any chance courting a young lady, Pol?"

Pol couldn't hold back the flush. He looked past her at Stefan, who did not appear to be listening. "No, Quel. Between training, working, and my family, I haven't met anyone."

"Oh. I see."

Quon Daoringer stood and gently struck his pewter mug with his spoon. As Adeel's attention focused on her father, Pol sighed in gratitude for the break in the conversation.

After the hall quieted, Quon Daoringer raised his voice. "Before dessert arrives, I wish to take a moment to introduce our guest here at the table. I'm sure there are a few who might be interested." Light laughter from around the hall. Pol sat up straight, heart pounding at the attention.

"This young man is Pol, son of Laor, the cobbler whose shop is off Ariel Street for those who might need his services."

Pol allowed a small smile. Father should be quite busy starting tomorrow.

The quon continued, "Yesterday morning, my carriage was attacked by an assassin targeting my daughter and me."

Murmurs erupted throughout the hall.

"Pol, here, single-handedly thwarted the attack and captured the assassin."

Gasps.

The quon explained the fight in detail with some embellishment. "Pol is being trained by his uncle, our very own QuonGuard, Sergeant Eash. Please stand, Sergeant."

Dressed in a new QuonGuard uniform, Eash stood and bowed low to the quon. Applause rippled through the hall before he resumed his seat.

"Now, I thought Pol might have aspirations to join the QuonGuard, but he clearly informed me that he wants to enlist with the King's Army. I guess I will defer to His Majesty."

Polite laughter.

"But I could not help being concerned that his heroism might be lost in the lower ranks of the King's Army." Quon Daoringer paused for a second. "I will send Pol to Gaodis for special officer training." The quon turned to Pol. "If you approve?"

It took a second to register to Pol that he was supposed to vocalize his resounding yes. "Yes, Your Grace. Most kind, Your Grace."

The quon continued, "Excellent. You shall leave within the week. But I must add that you won't be going alone."

Pol failed at any decorum as his head snapped up. The quon eyed Stefan. "Yes, after much consideration, my wife and I believe it to be in the best interest of our son, Stefan, to join you in this training."

Pol's heart dropped into his stomach. Stefan's face drained of color, but he remained absolutely still.

"We announce this, hoping our son will learn the discipline to order his gifts." He paused. "Stefan, this is my will for you."

Stefan nodded once.

Quon Daoringer raised his glass. "To Pol. Thank you for being a hero for this country."

A chorus of "hear, hear" followed, and Pol lifted his own cup in return.

Pol's family had their cups raised as well. Servants emerged from doors, carting out desserts.

After taking a sip from her own cup, Adeel said, "I guess you'll be leaving soon. I won't get to talk with you again for some time."

Pol almost choked on his wine. "I'm sorry for that, but I'm excited for the opportunity."

"Of course. But if we can't talk, maybe we can write?"

Pol was having difficulty keeping up with the pace of events. The first reaction blurted from his lips. "But I'm a commoner."

"No, you're training to be an officer, and you hail from a legendary family. There is a difference."

What just happened? She wanted to get to know him? Pol glanced at Qual Stefan and then the quon. He probably should say no, given the circumstances, but this was Quel Adeel asking him. "I'd be honored to write to you, Quel Adeel."

"Good. Now, tell me the story of how you saved me."

"My pleasure, Quel."

CHAPTER 7

"Many who seek power crave control. Feed them control."

*–ArchMandrate Koen. Journal of Mandrate
Recruitment, Volume 1873, issue 3.*

An ethereal film encased the country farmhouse like a thin aura. Against the moonless night, the protective shield shimmered a lilac hue, but Fenric doubted the residents knew of its existence. Only in Cordiae would a farmhouse have that kind of security. Only in Cordiae would a cleric waste time protecting something so trivial, so worthless.

The black-cloaked figure chuckled softly. Nothing made sense in this part of the world, but that is why he had come. That is why he had traveled hundreds of miles across the Andren Mountains and through Miraden Forest. Cordiae needed him.

The hooded figure scoffed at the dirt road he stood upon. Fenric hoped the provincial stink of the nearby silverberry fields would not cling to him when he returned home, but he had work to do, and it required that he wade in the pigsty.

There were a few gems to be found, though. A quick glance confirmed the departure of the soldier called

"Stone" down the road, heading back toward the village. The black-cloaked figure had wasted hours waiting for Stone to leave. He specifically wished to avoid that one, that liar. The coward.

How could anyone not know who the soldier really was? One look was enough. What a farce! How could the most infamous mind of Cordiae, hated but respected by so many Ampestrians, stand to humiliate himself by taking a meal with the squealing pigs in the farmhouse?

It was beyond comprehension. The worthless humans huddled together in the farmhouse must be ignorant. Stone had helped them pick berries earlier, eaten dinner with them, and held the squirming baby for the mother as if he were one of them. Why?

Irrelevant. Master Jenric would be pleased. The bounty would be most pleasant with the mission already a success.

But there was more, so much more, to accomplish.

A half mile to the south, the dark canopy of Miraden Forest outlined the night sky. This farm stood on the outskirts, miles from the village center. No one else threatened to interfere with his work. He had chosen well.

He slowly bent over and picked up a small, rough stone covered in grit. How appropriate. The "stone" would grant him entry.

Carefully placing his deformed feet so as not to make a sound, the black-cloaked figure approached the farmhouse. In response, lilac spikes erupted from the protective shield covering the farmhouse. Irritating. He just needed to be cautious. One step at a time.

The annoying sounds of after-dinner playtime grew louder as he drew closer. Children squealing with full bellies and playing with their indulgent father grated on his nerves, but he couldn't rush. Every step had to be played out with care.

He froze when the mother turned her head toward the window as she patted her infant on the back. The close candlelight would obscure her view of the darkness, but he waited quietly until her attention returned to the baby. The infant would be worthless for what needed to be done. The others would be given a gift, a purpose.

Stopping just beyond the range of the ethereal spikes, the black-cloaked figure ignored the burning pain, as if he were drawing close to flames. He flicked his hand, and the rock hit the wooden door.

A slight commotion took place. Behind the door, the father's muffled voice said, "It must be Stone. He must have forgotten something."

No. Not your beloved Stone.

The door opened, and the spiked shield parted. The fool didn't understand the rules. Opening the door was an invitation.

The father stepped back, his face contorting in fear. Good. Fear would make this easier.

The farmer found his voice. "What do you want?"

"You."

〰〰

The drip of water hit the small puddle in perfect cadence. Geraul had memorized the timing overnight. The ripples of the puddle reflected the dim luminescence in the dungeon cell. The only light in the cell danced on the sidewall as it passed through the grated door hole. It had taken hours before his eyes grew accustomed enough to discern the cell's outline. Every few minutes, he waited for the drop. He barely slept. The drop would not let him. The pain in his jaw, stomach, back, arms, or legs had not kept him awake. The guards had beaten him as soon as they had thrown him into the cell. He had told them everything. Everything. He had told the quon everything as well, but Daoringer didn't believe him. He said a dagger had almost impaled his face. Geraul wished it had.

Then Geraul would be dead. Just like Anvil.

He wouldn't be sad that he had lost everything. He wouldn't have to count down until the next drop hit the puddle. He wouldn't have to wait for the king's representative to pronounce judgment. A simple and quick execution would be nice.

Geraul's internal timing recognized he had a few moments until the next drip. Why did he have to come to Dael? Geraul snorted. Half of his business contacts dried up in a week, and it didn't take a chamberlain to recognize the danger he faced. Placing his face in his hands, Geraul shook his head at the loss. He had underestimated the snot-nosed kid who must have known Geraul had come into town, hired guards, and planned on showing up at the restaurant. He had never come across any competitor as cutthroat and prepared.

Geraul took some comfort in the unintended consequences. Stefan would bear some responsibility for the assassination attempt.

A great weight dropped into the pit of his stomach. He was an accomplice to the attempted assassination of a quon. Each time he considered it, Geraul couldn't believe it. Anvil should have only scared the girl. Kidnapping had been ruled out as too aggressive, but Geraul had considered it.

The drip would come soon.

He had chosen to use Stacia to help layer the culpability and prevent implication. Something had gone wrong. The guards had said some kid had beaten Anvil, who, for some reason, tried to assassinate the quon. It didn't matter. The snot would hopefully be punished, but who knew?

The drip was late.

Geraul looked over at the puddle. He couldn't frown. It hurt too much from the beatings. He glanced up at the ceiling. Halfway up, he thought he saw something shimmer. He relaxed his eyes.

The droplet hung in midair.

Ignoring the soreness in his extremities, Geraul stood. He limped a few feet to the drop and lifted his hand to the suspended drop of water. Before his hand came into contact with the water, a familiar voice behind him said, "Fascinating, isn't it?"

Geraul whirled. In the faint light, it took him a moment to adjust to the figure in front of him. It was Stacia.

"Stacia! What's going on? What are you doing here? What happened?"

Stacia still wore her tattered gray tunic. "Hello, Geraul. That's a lot of questions. Sit down. Let's talk."

"No. Answer my questions."

Geraul's eyes widened as his arms locked at his sides, and an unseen force lifted him off the ground.

Stacia stepped forward. "You're not in a position to demand anything right now."

His mind reeled. That was how she got inside the cell. "Reyuul," he whispered.

"What are you going to do about it?"

Geraul looked at his feet hovering above the ground. Against this kind of power? "Nothing," he conceded.

"What? No smart remark? No yelling? Is this my Geraul?"

Her words cut deep, but he refused to rise to the bait. "You're obviously not my Stacia. For a reyuul, you're better looking than I expected."

"Trade secret." She began pacing in a circle around him. "A lot has happened since you arrived in Dael. I guess I'll answer some questions."

His mind raced. He didn't trust Stacia, but she was here for a reason; Stacia was here for him. She had been recommended to him by one of his contacts from Shaorn and had been in his network for two years. A reyuul in his service for two years? She must have an agenda. Geraul quickly reviewed the plan they'd made. She was supposed to have told Anvil to grab the girl. "What did you tell Anvil?"

"I told him to get the girl."

Geraul must have shown his disbelief. Stacia added, "Don't believe me. I guess you could ask Anvil. Oh, wait. He's dead."

"Of course I don't believe you. A reyuul? In Cordiae? Anvil was a two-copper ruffian. The only way he would have taken that kind of risk was if someone dumped a pile of money in his lap. You were the one person responsible for communicating with him, and you're a reyuul. I might die at the hand of the king's executioner, but I have more evidence against your lie than the king does against me."

"Says the man who got outclassed by a kid." Stacia stepped closer. She really was beautiful. How was she a reyuul?

"There is so much about this situation that you didn't know about," she said.

He silently conceded that point. Still, there was no way he could trust her.

Stacia said, "I don't know who else was involved or how someone got to Anvil. What I do know is I've put too much time into you to let you die."

Geraul narrowed his eyes. "What? What do you want?"

She looked him in the eye. "Wrong question. The right question is: what do you want? Your title, holdings, and reputation are gone. Everything you have is gone. What will you do, Geraul? Just sit here and wait to die?"

No, not that. "I want to go back to Ulloa and pretend this never happened."

She laughed, and an eerie inflection echoed in that laugh. "Not going to happen. You want to live, Geraul. You also want what your father would never take."

Geraul knew bargaining when he heard it. "Is that right?"

He dropped to the ground in a heap. Every contusion on his body rang out in a unified scream of pain.

Stacia stood over him. "You have a choice, Geraul. Me or death. With me, there are risks but also some benefits. With death, there's only certainty. Think about it. The king's representative won't be here for months."

"What would you have me do?" He groaned as he pushed himself to a sitting position.

She leaned over him. "Become a reyuul. I know it's heretical to even think of it. Cordiaens are strange like that. But you have nothing to lose." She sauntered a few steps away. "As I said, think on it." When she lifted her hand, two drops hit the puddle, and Geraul flinched.

Stacia mouthed a few words and disappeared.

A moment later, heavy steps preceded a fist pounding on the door. "Keep it down or I'll shut you up," a guard commanded.

Geraul eased back to the wall and rested against it. Yes, he had a lot to think about.

CHAPTER 8

"Even Vroshen, the legend, wore diapers as a babe. All Cordiaen commanders start as grunts so they can appreciate the value of a grunt."

–Cleric Joern. Advanced Cordiaen Military Tactics, Volume 2.

Stefan scanned the inner bailey for any other family members beyond his parents, Cyprian, and Adeel. After the humiliating dinner, his other siblings had taken turns berating him before leaving with "things to do." His older brothers had shown Father their support, but once again, Stefan had proven disappointing. On top of that, this peasant had graciously received credit never offered to Stefan. Yes, Stefan may have stepped over a line, and yes, the peasant prevented the situation from being worse, but to sit at their table in public and talk with his sister? As an added insult, Stefan had to spend a week traveling to some forgotten village near a forest with the peasant and his father's chamberlain, Hiuken.

As ire built in his heart, he consoled himself with his plans, his only hope of survival. Servants loaded his two trunks onto the red-painted travel carriage, and Stefan took a deep breath. He could endure things until the right time. Until then, Stefan did his best to ignore the peasant and the entourage who had arrived to see him off. A line of QuonGuards, peasant children, merchants, and what appeared to be family members had come up to hug him, shake the young man's hand, or salute him with words of encouragement.

Stefan should have received that kind of send-off. Only Cyprian had helped him pack, and his father had already said his peace at the dinner.

Stefan could not help but overhear the cobbler tell his son, "Your grandfather would be proud of you right now."

The peasant did not respond, and Stefan picked up on the tension. Well, they had that in common.

"If things don't work out, you'll always have a place here, Pol."

The QuonGuard uncle added, "Pol, give everything. Once you've done that, give more. That's what our father told me when I left." He handed the peasant a letter. "Read this when you have a moment."

Potential leverage?

"Yes, sir." The peasant pocketed the letter and gave his family, including his father, another hug.

The jealousy slid up a notch.

Stefan had further difficulty restraining his ire as his sister stepped up to the peasant and said something inaudible. Stefan could handle the hero's attention from others, but his sister's infatuation was another matter.

After a few moments, the quon cleared his throat, and Adeel returned to her father's side. At least Father had some sense. The quon said, "We wish you both safe travels. Stefan, learn well from the soldier who will teach you. I will send letters, and I hope your return in two years will have opened your heart."

Stefan bowed as required. Two years in a garbage village would not do that, but he continued to play the part. With tears streaming down her face, his mother presented her hand, and Stefan kissed it. Her discomfort upset him more than the ridiculous dinner had.

The chamberlain flew out of the keep, bowed to the quon, and waved the boys into the carriage.

Stefan did not even bother saying farewell, but the peasant waved as the carriage bounced toward the gate. Trying to find comfort on the padded bench seat, Stefan repositioned the small blue travel pillow behind his back.

A temporary bump in the road.

⁓〰⁓

The carriage jolted, and Pol instinctively lifted his hand to avoid hitting his head against the cab ceiling. Unfazed, he settled back onto the brown cushioned carriage bench for the hundredth time that day but avoided the perpetual wet spot to his left. The sudden carriage movement released another drip from the ceiling to his left, creating a plop sound against the plush cloth bench. Pol avoided the spot, though his hand had landed there a few times over the last week.

It was a privilege to ride inside a carriage and not on a horse for seven days, and he chose not to complain. Besides, there were no other options. Stefan and a middle-aged chamberlain occupied the bench seat across from Pol.

Stefan had mostly been quiet, but throughout each day, a range of emotions played over his face, sometimes anger and frustration, sometimes smug contentment. The emotions must have boiled inside like water in a teakettle, as the lordling had been subject to occasional outbursts. He had even erupted about the "noisy drip" next to Pol, but repairs would not be made until the carriage returned to Dael.

Pol avoided looking at the disgraced qual, who intermittently glanced at Pol with accusing eyes in between constantly adjusting his flattened blue travel pillow after each bump. Pol did not mind as long as Stefan did not talk, and he appreciated the hardship the young noble faced in being forced to leave his home. But it was Stefan's fault. Adeel had said so.

The middle-aged chamberlain, thankfully, had kept the qual in line. Dressed in a thick red doublet with white sleeves, the chamberlain did not behave like many other nobles Pol had met, as he appeared to enjoy talking to a commoner.

"I'm still confused, dear boy," Chamberlain Hiuken said to Pol, continuing their conversation. "I've considered what you've told me, but I still don't understand what made you choose to intervene. Surely you recognized a dangerous situation."

The man was so polite; Pol had to remind himself that he was speaking with a noble. "Honestly, Chamberlain Hiuken, after I got knocked down, my legs moved on their own. Didn't realize how dangerous it was until I started fighting."

"My, my. Sounds heroic, but the event could have turned out differently."

Pol's parents and uncle had thoroughly educated him on how many ways he could have died in that encounter. "Yes, sir. I credit my uncle's training."

Stefan scoffed, but one glance from the chamberlain kept the young man silent.

"Yes, yes. You've explained your training in great detail. The quon was proud to recommend you for the King's Army."

"The quon was very…generous." Pol hesitated, glancing at Stefan. Pol had learned the warning signs which signaled an impending outburst. Sure enough, Stefan's right index finger twitched, his jawline tensed, and he focused on his shoes. Pol wasn't concerned about himself. He was just tired of the yelling.

Chamberlain Hiuken gave Pol a sympathetic look. "Right, right. The quon is very generous. Stefan here just does not understand how generous."

"Qual! I am a qual. You will use it when addressing or referring to me." The young noble's fists clenched. Pol didn't react. Any movement would be interpreted as a slight against the lordling, and Pol would have preferred to sit under the drip than endure another tirade.

"Lower your voice, Stefan," the chamberlain replied.

Stefan glanced to the carriage window where a mounted guard pulled up, peering into the cab. Pol held back a smile. A few days before, three guards had yanked Stefan from his seat and made him walk behind the carriage when he had lost control of his mouth.

The chamberlain didn't skip a beat. "Pol, have you by chance discovered an answer to my question from yesterday?"

Pol had found his answer, though he hesitated to share something so bold. Yet, his situation was different now, and he had to remind himself of that. He wasn't a noble, but Quon Daoringer had called him a hero.

"What do I want to accomplish in ten years?" His head started dropping, but Pol stopped himself. He lifted his face and held the chamberlain's gaze. "I'm going to be a fall commander. I'm going to move my family from above my father's cobbler shop to a large home in southern Dael. I'm going to find a nice young lady and get married."

"Excellent! Capital, I say! A fall commander? That's just two steps away from a general. Quite ambitious, I must say, and how thoughtful of you to consider your family. What a testament to your parents and your uncle. But tell me, do you have a young lady in mind?"

Pol locked eyes with Stefan, who thinned his lips. Pol had to fight the urge to look away, to counter years of avoiding noble ire. "I recently met someone who left a strong impression."

The chamberlain replied, "Oh my. Wouldn't be the young Quel Adeel whom you recently saved, would it?"

The only female noble Pol had met who acted like a human. "Yes, sir," Pol replied.

Stefan launched from his seat. In the past, Pol would have to sit back and take whatever abuse might occur at the hands of such a deluded brat.

Not anymore.

As the lording flung himself at Pol, the carriage hit another bump, and Pol shot his left hand up to the ceiling to brace himself while grabbing the lordling's tunic with his right hand. Stefan had stumbled from the carriage jolt, and Pol deftly turned and angled him to the wet spot on the bench. Pol landed with his right forearm pinned to Stefan's neck, his right knee in Stefan's stomach, and his left hand holding the lordling's free arm.

Stefan yelled through gritted teeth with spittle flying, "Never talk about my sister, peasant!"

At six foot four, Pol was easily in control over the thin, wiry, and shorter noble. He didn't even bother answering.

In a calm tone, the chamberlain replied, "Hmm. Thank you, Pol. That will be enough. Stefan will need to release some steam outside for a bit."

As the carriage slowed to a jerky stop, Pol slowly eased up and prepared for retaliation but received a burning glare instead as Stefan got to his feet. A guard opened the door and escorted the disgraced noble outside. Pol smirked at the wet spot on Stefan's backside as the door shut but held back the outright laughter.

The chamberlain laid back against his seat and sighed. "Well, then. We were scheduled to arrive before lunch, but it appears as if it'll be afternoon when we enter Gaodis. Stefan walks slow on purpose, and I can't shackle him to the carriage."

"Fine by me, sir. As long as I get there," Pol replied.

"My, my. Excited to train under Grunt Granite?"

"Yes, sir. My uncle told me a few stories about him before we left."

"Capital, I say. That's the spirit. I'll tell you, though. He is a legend in the King's Army. You're quite lucky."

"Blessed, sir, not lucky. Could you explain why he's stationed in such a small village if he's so legendary?"

"Ahh. Yes, that's a story. I could, but I won't. If he wants to reveal that, I'll leave it to him."

Disappointed, Pol accepted the chamberlain's answer and tucked the question back into his brain for later.

The carriage slowed to a stop, and Pol wondered if Stefan had collapsed, but a guard opened the door and handed the chamberlain a scroll. Chamberlain Hiuken received the missive and said, "Excuse me."

Pol nodded, amazed at how the official still received daily missives from Dael as they journeyed. Sure, the chamberlain was the right hand of Quon Daoringer and he was responsible for overseeing Stefan's deposit into Gaodis, but did the man ever rest?

"Well, well. That's interesting. Maybe it's good that we'll be delayed. I have to write an addendum to a letter. Please excuse me."

Pol wouldn't be rude and ask about the contents. The chamberlain had already mentioned how he received intel reports from the national spy network, the Pulse. Pol was instead reminded of the letter Uncle Eash handed him. He hadn't wanted to read it in front of Stefan, and now was the perfect opportunity. Pulling it out of his pack, Pol angled the parchment to catch the daylight.

> *Pol,*
>
> *Even with all the mornings we trained, I thought we would have more time before you left, but Lohem's way is not ours.*
>
> *Your father gave me permission to explain this part of our Vroshen heritage. This isn't secret but practice keeping the information hidden. Some would use it against you.*
>
> *You described the sensation as a "fire within," which is the best description I've heard. For me, it was more like a rumbling in my belly, and your father described it as a surge when he breathed. Everyone reports it differently.*
>
> *Our ancestor, Aola, called it soulfire, the gift given to our line, though there are reports that others have it as well. We don't know much about it, but I do know a few things.*
>
> *Soulfire responds differently to emotions and intentions. Emotion generates a burst of power, but*

it's unpredictable. On the battlefield, I lost control a few times and placed friends in danger. Deliberate intention is the key. Focusing on helping others guided me.

For many reasons, I'm not an expert in using soulfire, and I'm sure you have questions, but we'll save that conversation for when you return.

Proud of you, and stay out of trouble,

Eash

Pol reread the letter a few times and leaned back against the cushioned bench seat.

Soulfire.

He had always visualized embers burning within, ready to ignite when needed, and the conviction settled in his heart: the flames often developed in response to anger. His uncle was right.

Looking at the letter, Pol focused on a few details. There were others not in his family who had soulfire. How did they receive the power? Why wasn't his uncle an expert? Why hadn't his father told him?

So many questions, but as Pol glanced up at the chamberlain receiving Pulse intelligence reports in a moving carriage, Pol was concerned that a return letter might fall into prying hands. He would just have to wait to talk to his uncle. In the meantime, Pol had to understand his anger. Where did it come from? Simple. Years of nobles beating him.

Just the thought stirred the coals in his soul.

No. That wouldn't work.

His uncle wrote about helping others, and Pol took the hint. His father had forbidden Pol from drawing attention to his skills—for the family. Pol had heard story after story about relatives being used, abducted, or killed by fellow Cordiaens for their own purposes. He had obeyed his father in Dael. Now, his uncle was giving him the freedom. Pol would show this Granite—and everyone—he could be an asset to the family, the army, and his country.

When a farmhouse rolled into view, the carriage slowed to a stop, permitting Stefan to climb inside. Sweaty and flushed, he calmly resumed his seat. The chamberlain did not look up and continued working, scratching on a piece of parchment.

The carriage jumped forward, and more homesteads rolled into view. Villagers emerged from their wooden farmhouses, watching the carriage, pointing, and chatting with each other. Kids ran around, with some children running ahead of the carriage.

Chamberlain Hiuken placed his quill in a small metal travel base next to him and broke the silence. "Stefan, this is your one reminder. Your father has commanded this course of action for you. Do nothing that would embarrass him. We are in the Shaorn Protectorate now under Quon Huem. Your father cannot bail you out of trouble here."

Stefan turned away to look out his window.

The chamberlain continued, "Pol. Thank you for being a pleasant companion on the journey."

"Thank you for allowing me to ride in the carriage."

"Nonsense, my boy. I wouldn't imagine having you do this on horseback. We've almost arrived. I'm obliged to stop at Judge Fead's residence first and then the village garrison."

Deeper within the village, they passed more farms, houses, and barns. The accompanying acrid odors of fertilizer and manure entered the carriage and made Pol sneeze. The road widened, and a well-maintained wooden fort with multiple buildings and a spiked wooden wall came into view. Pol leaned toward the window, trying to gain a better perspective of the garrison as they passed.

"You'll be there soon," Chamberlain Hiuken said in a kind voice.

The carriage stopped before an old but clean three-story wooden building with a red roof, which reminded Pol of a noble's office building in Dael.

Chamberlain Hiuken pushed past a rigid Stefan and exited the carriage, with Pol following. A bald man wearing a smile across his face and a white sash across his half-blue and red surcoat waited with a pleasant, though curious, expression.

"Judge Fead, it's a pleasure to meet you," the chamberlain said.

"Chamberlain Hiuken, is it? Not much for formality here, but I have some excellent local silver juice and refreshments. Come inside, and let's talk."

Silver juice? Pol had heard of it but had never had any, as it was usually expensive. No, he wanted to get to the garrison as soon as possible.

Hiuken gave a head bow. "I would be honored, Judge, except that I'm on a severe schedule and must beg your pardon to permit me to complete my mission and depart." Hiuken waved Stefan out of the carriage.

The judge eyed the boys with curiosity. "I understand. So, what brings the honored Chamberlain for Quon Daoringer to our tiny village? I'm sure it was a long journey."

"Ah, quite refreshing to see the country, but I bear an urgent message from the quon regarding his son." Hiuken passed over a small pale-yellow envelope from a small stack in his hand.

The judge broke the seal and, after holding the parchment at arm's length, he began reading. With eyebrows raised, Judge Fead paused from reading to glance at Stefan, Pol, and the chamberlain before finishing. "Well, um, I don't see a problem, but I don't know this Granite. Are you sure he's here?"

Hiuken replied, "We have confirmed the location of the gentleman and will stop by the garrison next."

Judge Fead folded the letter. "If I may accompany you to ensure there's no misunderstanding. This is not something that I want to leave unattended."

"Of course, Judge Fead."

Pol thought the comment about Granite odd but fell in with the group, avoiding Stefan and restraining himself from running ahead.

The judge accompanied them down the main road to the garrison. As they neared the fortified compound, villagers approached and observed from the roadside. The sight must have been a novelty to them.

The guards at the entrance snapped to attention upon seeing the judge and the chamberlain, and the party passed through the gate to the courtyard. It wasn't as impressive as entering Dael Keep, but it meant more. The tidy dirt courtyard looked like it could accommodate over a thousand soldiers and was surrounded by two-story wood buildings of uniform size. A sturdy walkway wrapped around the upper inner wall, and dutiful soldiers patrolled in pairs.

The clack of wooden swords sounded across the courtyard as a dozen sweaty male and female soldiers practiced sword drills. To his left, two more soldiers stood close together conversing, and Pol recognized the tunic pattern of a captain with half-crimson and half-black colors separated diagonally, and the other had a white-and-black tunic signifying a grunt. Uncle Eash had made him memorize the different ranked patterns, and Pol had spent the week of travel wondering which one he would start with. He didn't know what was going to happen, but Pol smiled as he looked around. This was where he was supposed to be.

Judge Fead called out, "Captain Dreint, just the man I need. A word, please."

The captain promptly disengaged from the grunt to approach while eyeing the chamberlain, Stefan, and Pol. "Yes, Judge. What can I do for you?"

"Captain, this is the Chamberlain to Quon Daoringer of Dael, and he's looking for someone that I've never heard of."

The grunt slowly approached until he stood a step behind the captain. Dirt covered his black-and-white tunic and boots, and dark rings hung below his eyes. This man had been traveling. Olive skin and a salt-and-pepper cropped haircut with a balding pattern gave the grunt a more serious look, and Pol believed him to be in his early forties, with an intense gaze that took in everything. His appearance, the way he wore his uniform, and the way he held his equipment reminded Pol of Uncle Eash. The grunt lowered a travel pack to the ground and also eyed the chamberlain with interest.

Captain Dreint replied, "Yes, Judge. Chamberlain, how may I be of service to His Grace?"

Hiuken pulled out another pale-yellow envelope and presented it to the captain. "I have a missive for Grunt Granite. The Pulse has confirmed his location here in Gaodis. May I please deliver this to him?"

The grunt standing next to the captain grimaced and folded his arms. The captain took the envelope and skimmed it. He turned his head to the grunt. "Stone, it was good while it lasted."

The grunt replied in a gruff voice, "It was a matter of time." The man called Stone held out his hand, and Chamberlain Hiuken handed him the letter. The soldier examined the chamberlain. "You serve Quon Daoringer?"

"Yes." Hiuken pulled out a gold necklace with a medallion from under his shirt. Pol recognized the imprinted ship representing the quon's crest. He wondered why the chamberlain had hidden the badge while they traveled.

"I see," replied the grunt. He caught Pol's confused glance. "Most chamberlains hide their badge of office outside their city."

"Are you Grunt Granite?" Hiuken asked.

"Only for Quon Daoringer of Dael."

Pol frowned. Just the quon? Granite opened the envelope and read it but scowled halfway through. He frowned after he finished. "I admit I owe Quon Daoringer, and I don't say that about everyone, but this is too much. We just lost a family yesterday—went missing from their farm, and I just returned from Miraden Forest searching for them. I don't have time for this." He held up the letter. "Even if I did, I don't have the authority necessary to do what the quon requests. I would need to be over the captain here to fulfill these orders. Thanks be to Lohem, I am a grunt in the King's Army now, subject to my captain, and quite content, I might add."

Hiuken pulled out another envelope, but this was a red envelope with gold markings.

Granite's face fell as he received and opened the second envelope. "From the king?"

Chamberlain Hiuken announced, "Orders to promote you to the rank of fall commander from King Sraung. The king wanted to ease you into returning to a general, Fall Commander. The quon insists."

Pol's mouth dropped.

Granite passed the orders to Captain Dreint, who took them like he was taking a snake and read. "This places you under General Croaga over the northern armies." The captain saluted Granite. "Fall Commander Granite." He turned to the gate and yelled, "Company, report!"

Before Granite could reply, a bell rang out on the gate, and soldiers quickly streamed out of the surrounding buildings, forming into multiple neat columns. Still shocked, Pol appreciated the discipline.

Captain Dreint took his place at the front, and Granite followed with his head hanging. He appeared dutiful, though resigned to his fate. Captain Dreint addressed the soldiers who assembled quickly. "Attention, company! I've just been informed that King Sraung and General Croaga have promoted Grunt Stone to Fall Commander. From now on, you will address him as F. C. Granite. Papers are official. The king himself commands it. Understood?"

A resounding "Yes, Captain" reverberated around the courtyard.

Granite looked up at the ranks of soldiers. Conflict crossed his face for a few seconds before resignation settled. The fall commander let out a slow breath and fixed his gaze on the men and women before him. "I have enjoyed serving with you for these past six years, and I had dearly hoped to remain as a grunt for years to come. The king has requested my service as an officer again. Thank you for your understanding, Captain."

Captain Dreint saluted him and turned to the soldiers. "Corporal Creyd, transfer the fall commander's belongings to the officer's quarters next to mine. Company dismissed!"

The company saluted and then dispersed as pockets of conversations erupted. Granite returned to the chamberlain, still holding the paperwork. "Tell Quon Daoringer I will keep my word." He pointed to Stefan and Pol. "Tell him, 'These kids are mine.'"

Pol smiled.

The chamberlain gave a small bow. "I shall tell him. Thank you, Fall Commander. I shall get back on the road immediately."

The driver had guided the carriage to the garrison gate and deposited two fancy trunks in the courtyard, along with Pol's small brown travel bag.

For the first time since arriving at the garrison, Pol paid attention to Stefan. Panic had gripped the lordling's face. "Wait, Hiuken. Here? With him?" He pointed to the fall commander. "He was a grunt two minutes ago."

The chamberlain grinned. "Fair warning: don't underestimate him. Obey your father. Farewell." He entered the carriage as the driver climbed to his perch, and Stefan sputtered. Pol smirked as the carriage bounced over every bump until it passed beyond the gates.

Fall Commander Granite said, "Captain, I was trying to explain that Gossama wasn't available yet. I need someone to watch for her message."

"Goors will take care of it, Stone—I mean, Fall Commander. You have your hands full."

Fall Commander Granite turned and approached Stefan and Pol, stepping right up to Stefan. "So you're the reason they've reinstated me. I knew it was a matter of time, but I didn't consider this." He held up the yellow parchment from Quon Daoringer. "You were partially responsible for the assassination attempt on your father and the attempted kidnapping of your sister. Kid, as far as I'm concerned, you're not even a grunt. Quon Daoringer chose to have mercy on you but stripped you of your title, everything. You hear that? You're not Qual Stefan. You're mine."

The warning signs started. Probably unwise for Stefan to be aggressive here.

Granite turned to Pol. "And you. Says you're the hero who saved the quon and his daughter. Also says you come from a special family. You know what that means?"

Pol instantly doubted himself. "I think so, sir."

"No, you don't. I can tell. Says you asked to be here as a reward. How old are you?"

"Sixteen, sir."

"Not even old enough to enlist. Ha! I commanded kids younger than you during the Jetean War. You'll have to tell me the story about the assassin sometime, but you're not in the King's Army yet either. Boys, I don't know why Lohem decided to drop you in my lap right now, but it's not for me to question. We'll make the best of it. Grab your things and follow me. You'll be sleeping in the barracks tonight."

Stefan didn't move. "No."

Granite's fist flew so fast, Pol barely saw it. Stefan collapsed backward with a hand to his cheek.

Granite stood over him. "It's dangerous when I have to repeat myself: you are not a qual, you are not important, but you will follow the same rules as my soldiers. Don't say another word or the other cheek will get it. I've got too many important things to worry about. Get up, get your stuff, and follow Corporal Reid to the barracks."

Stefan spat blood as he rolled over and pushed himself up. His little finger still twitched, but he obeyed and squatted down, gripping the ornate iron handles on his trunks. He tried to keep his face flat as he strained to drag the trunks.

Pol picked up his cloth traveling bag and gave the lordling a wide berth as he followed the corporal. Whatever it took, he was ready.

CHAPTER 9

"When a creature loses everything, their soul is laid bare. I'd rather have a grunt, who's risen from nothing, fighting next to me, than a general who has everything."

–Cleric Joern. Advanced Cordiaen Military Tactics, Volume 2.

Stefan moved inch by inch through a dinner line in the garrison mess hall. Burned cooking oil and musky sweat assaulted his nostrils as he held a coarse wooden trencher. Stefan ignored the looks from the soldiers in line and seated at wooden tables in the "mess hall."

The UnderRealm sounded appealing compared to this.

Stefan tongued his right cheek, which continued to throb. He had reached his limit. It was not enough that he'd had to endure his father's humiliation at the dinner before all the Dael nobility, but Stefan also had to suffer the peasant. Talking with his sister, sharing his table, sharing his carriage, quartered beside him, and standing right before him in line, the peasant had enjoyed noble privileges.

It was sacrilege to Stefan.

Cordiaen nobility stemmed from ancient families with bloodlines that traced back through the centuries. King Septiot I had bestowed the noble rank upon those who had assisted him in reclaiming the country four hundred years prior. Handpicked men and women who had helped win victory over the Ampestrian and Sperunese invasions had received the reward for their sacrifice and loyalty. There was distinction and purpose to the nobility, and his ancestors had passed down those benefits, those blessings. Over the centuries, peasants had always tried to wrestle more power for themselves, and that was all this peasant was trying to do.

The peasant had saved his father and sister? Good for him. Stefan's father should have given him a pat on the head, a loaf of bread, and sent him on his way. Now, the peasant was trying to usurp privileges not designed for his superiors. Others had been beaten for less.

The worst part for Stefan was the lack of control over the peasant, or anything, for that matter. Corporal Creyd, who had been assigned to watch his every breath, shook his head as Stefan was about to refuse the base dinner consisting of stale bread, dry chicken, watered-down leek soup, and uncut strawberries. After taking a seat, Stefan's jaw ached from Granite's hit and having to work so hard to chew the food. The stable horses at Dael Keep ate better.

The corporal and peasant chose to sit at the same table, and the corporal had the nerve to say, "Eat it all. We don't waste anything here." Stefan's hunger overruled his taste, and he finished most of the bland meal. In between bites, his chipped wooden fork stopped. The possible future dawned upon him. The imprisonment in the keep, the dinner, and the journey had been horrendous but fleeting. Sitting in the cramped mess hall and eating the overcooked, tasteless food, the cold reality hit him. His father meant for him to endure this humiliation for years.

The peasant ate everything and returned for another helping. Probably had not seen so much food in one meal. When Stefan couldn't stomach any more, the corporal escorted them across the dirt courtyard to the barracks, his supposed home until he "graduated from officer training."

Corporal Creyd commanded, "Unpack and go to sleep." He pointed at Stefan. "Don't leave this building. Fall Commander says your training begins in the morning."

A qual, a prisoner, but not for long.

The peasant replied with a "Yes, sir" and emptied his pitifully small sack into the three-foot-wide wooden chest at the foot of his bed.

Stefan turned his back on the corporal, pushed the small chest away from his bed, and replaced it with one of his large trunks. He consolidated his belongings and pushed the extra chest against the wall.

Lying on his flimsy cot, Stefan absorbed the buzzing conversations he overheard regarding F. C. Granite's advancement. He wanted to disregard the man previously known as Stone, but he had seen a hardness in the man's eyes. Stefan had enough experience with business partners and could weed out weaklings in a heartbeat. Often, it simply came down to looking a man or woman in the eyes.

F. C. Granite should not be underestimated, and Stefan recalled hearing that name before from his military history texts, but he could not place it.

The candles were extinguished, dropping darkness onto the barracks. In that quiet moment, tantalizing hope and brewing fear fought in his heart. The fear of losing his freedom and being subject to his father's whim warred with the hope of a sign, a small omen that he could be free.

Soon.

Granite's actions reminded Stefan of his father. It was Quon Daoringer's decision to send Stefan here, and every fiber in Stefan's body fought against the decision. Stefan's intelligence and talent were destined for something greater than the military. He believed this. While he would never be quon as the fifth son, Stefan had plans to ensure that he would never depend on anyone. How was the military going to help him?

Distant shouts broke through the quiet darkness. Soldiers rustled in their cots, and some got to their feet. A command from the corporal sent them to their feet. "Riot on the main street. Line up in the courtyard!"

Riot in a village? *Now that was an omen.* Stefan permitted himself a small chuckle.

The bald corporal was big enough to intimidate a dragon. He stormed down the aisle to Stefan's and Pol's cots. "You two stay here." He pointed to Stefan. "I've got a guard out front just to babysit you."

As the corporal stomped off, Stefan laid back and felt shivers run down his spine.

The plan had started.

When all the soldiers cleared the room, Stefan sat up and checked to make sure no one remained. Satisfied, he rose from his cot, still wearing his travel clothes from earlier.

Stefan stormed up to the peasant's cot. "I'm leaving, peasant. Don't say a word, or I can make your life even more miserable, and I will not stop until your family feels the same pain."

The peasant calmly regarded Stefan. After a second, he leapt from the cot and stepped up to Stefan's face, standing four inches taller. Stefan's pride prevented him from stepping back, but he remembered how their scuffle from earlier had ended.

The peasant said, "I don't care what you do or say to me, but if you ever threaten my family again, I will finish what F. C. Granite started."

Stefan took a step back.

The peasant returned to his cot. "For the record, I'd be glad if you left, but I recommend you get back in bed. This is a good thing, considering what you've done," he said.

Stefan silently conceded the peasant had scared him for a second. While Stefan appreciated how the peasant might have taken down an assassin, Stefan was not about to let the peasant have the last word.

"You think this is good because you have nothing. I already have what I need, and I'm not giving it up."

Stefan pulled a small satchel from his trunk. The rest of it had been for show.

With one last look to make sure the peasant was not interfering, Stefan went to the rear of the room and opened the exit. The night was darker than expected, but no guards patrolled the garrison's back wall. He took a deep breath, stepped out onto the walkway, and closed the door.

Once on the wall, he stayed low and confirmed that one guard remained in the courtyard patrolling the front gate. If Stefan had been in charge, he would not have left the garrison so defenseless.

Stefan pulled rope out of the satchel and fastened it to a pointed stake on the wall. After tossing the rope over, he secured the satchel across his chest.

A quick look over the wall fueled his resolve, and he pulled himself over, carefully avoiding the sharp stakes. Climbing down took more effort than expected, and the rope started burning his palms with each placement. Stefan bit his lip to prevent grunting from the effort and pain, then jumped down the last few feet, placing a hand on the wall to steady himself. He reluctantly admitted that his physical conditioning could use some work.

Leaving the rope, Stefan hugged the wall and examined the street. Half a mile down, villagers with torches yelled outside the judge's house. Stefan did not hesitate as he sprinted away and along the road toward the southeast. He needed to make it a mile out of the city, and as expected, he did not pass a soul on the streets.

Professional diversions were effective but not cheap.

His heart raced as he focused on the ground to prevent tripping or losing his footing in the dark. After what took ten minutes but felt like an hour, he breathed hard but found the expected horse tied to a tree near the road. So far, everything was going to plan.

Stefan approached the horse cautiously. No movement registered in his scan of the surrounding woods as he slowly engaged the animal. He could take his time. The horse was well-trained and remained calm as Stefan reached for the reins. He trusted that his team had stocked the saddlebags and prepped the mount well. Stefan was determined to commend Illiat for his consistent attention to detail.

With an easy mount and another quick scan of the area, Stefan set off down the road at a light canter. He flicked the reins and urged speed, growing more confident with each minute.

The wind whipped his face, and Stefan smiled and flicked the reins harder. His father would have a difficult time finding him. Jetea in southwest Cordiae was large enough to hide him while he picked up the scattered pieces of his company. If his father caught wind of his location in Jetea, Stefan could slip into foreign lands if necessary.

Stefan calculated his next contact should be another five miles southeast of the village. With a sigh of relief, he pushed the horse to go faster and reveled in the cathartic pace. Freedom tasted much better than the awful dinner.

On cue, a shout from the left side of the road directed him, and he pulled up on the reins, slowing his ride.

"Qual Stefan." A tall, bald, middle-aged man approached on his own horse.

Stefan kept his distance. "What happened to Illiat? Who are you?"

"I'm Rion. I assisted at the Eagle's Nest." He looked around and pulled his horse closer. "Illiat couldn't shake the Pulse. So he sent word: everything is ready, and we're to skirt the forest edge and head south for Jetea."

"Pulse, huh? My father really didn't trust me. We need to go." He flicked the reins and set off at a gallop.

The sense of freedom had dissipated. Stefan was glad Illiat had set in motion the additional backup plan, but too many people knew the details if it had gone into effect. After a few miles, they approached the eastern edge of Miraden Forest, and Stefan breathed a little easier. He could quickly slip into the forest and wait out any problems that arose.

He still had a chance. A fugitive's life would be challenging but much better than what his father wanted.

When a group of five riders broke out from the forest, he cursed. They wore King's Army uniforms and began galloping toward him.

No!

With a whip of the reins, Stefan leaned forward and pushed his horse into a full gallop. Rion's horse fell behind, but Stefan did not care. He was not going back.

An arrow flew wide to his right. When Stefan looked back, one of the five soldiers had another arrow nocked, but Stefan did not slow. Failure was not an option.

Stefan considered attempting the forest, but he could not guarantee his odds, and he was confident he would never make it to Jetea if his horse got injured in the woods. He winced as another arrow buzzed near his head and realized that if he could not outrun the soldiers, he would not escape. He made his choice and pushed the horse even harder, confident the arrows were intended to deter him and not hit him, as placing an arrow in a qual's back would be hard to explain to his father.

But the soldiers' horses were fresh and unburdened.

Fear strengthened his arm as he whipped the reins and leaned forward, but Stefan's shoulders slumped as two soldiers flanked him. When a soldier grabbed his reins, Stefan considered fighting but knew the probability of winning was laughable.

Once they halted his horse, they grabbed his wrists, preventing escape. An approaching soldier in the all-black tunic of a corporal called out, "Stefan, drop any weapons and dismount."

Stefan chafed at the lack of his title. One soldier had an arrow nocked and trained on him. Cursing, Stefan dismounted with his hands on his head.

The corporal bound Stefan's hands with rope. "I'm Corporal Rield. Fall Commander Granite sends his greetings. He made me memorize his response. 'I told you, boy. You're mine.' "

Stefan cursed again as the corporal tied a rope around his feet. Two grunts hoisted Stefan facedown over a horse's saddle. Stefan could not avoid a mouthful of the horse's putrid flank and could not even scratch his nose. The position and the jostling irritated Stefan's stomach, and he threw up the rest of the pathetic dinner. The hour ride back to the garrison was worse than the week in the stupid carriage from Dael as he contemplated his failure. The plan had been flawless. Someone must have snitched. There was no way he could have made a mistake. Frustration mounted. "I'm a qual. You can't do this!"

No one responded. Stefan thrashed, but a quick smack from a sword hilt to his back deflated his effort. He could do nothing.

Back in the village, the mob had been dispersed, and Granite stood waiting in the courtyard. Corporal Rield pushed Stefan off the horse, and he landed on his bound feet but then fell backward onto his rear with hands still tied behind his back.

Granite stood over him again. "You're smart, I'll give you that. But I'm experienced. Good job having your cronies incite a riot with talk of monsters in the forest. After yesterday's kidnapping, it was enough. These people have plenty to worry about without you causing trouble." The fall commander pointed toward the village center.

"Since you're a deserter, you'll sleep in the stocks tonight. I'll see you in the morning."

He walked away but stopped after a few steps. "Just so you know, I made sure to leave only one guard at the gate. You see, the chamberlain provided details of your intended escapade, and I wanted to see what you would do. The Pulse had caught wind of your plans days ago and informed him. I didn't think you could pull it off. Enjoy your evening."

———

Stefan had not slept. His wrists burned and bled, though the wood did not constrict his skin. He had fought. He had resisted. A qual. A leader. No one knew what he had built in a few years. People did what he ordered.

"I did not desert! I was never in the army!"

No one answered. The King's Army guard to his left had not engaged or responded to anything he had said all night. No one cared.

Defeated, Stefan was about to rest his head again when movement in the dark street caught his attention. Was someone watching his misery? A glance at the guard showed he had not seen it, though he was not facing the same direction. Stefan squinted but could not make out more than a dark figure.

The King's Army guard snapped to attention as Granite approached the stocks. Stefan turned his head to find the fall commander approaching. When Stefan looked back across the street, the figure was gone.

Granite stopped right before Stefan and looked him over. Stefan did not hate the man. He barely knew him. Stefan hated the limits the officer represented, but he poured that hatred into his stare.

"How did he fare, Wrues?" Granite questioned the guard.

"Sir, the prisoner hasn't slept. He thrashed about for a while. Thought he was going to cut his wrists. I beg your pardon, Fall Commander, but he has a mouth on him."

Not all my friends are noble.

"I'll bet he does." Granite chuckled. "Stefan, if I release you and you try to run again, you'll spend two nights in that thing. I'll double it every time."

"Triple it. I do not care."

Granite knelt on his left knee with his head tilted closer. "You can't leave. I think you should read the letter your father sent me."

Granite opened up the letter and held it for Stefan to read. Stefan continued to hold Granite's gaze, but Granite never looked away. After a minute, Stefan looked at the letter.

Lohem's Greetings, Granite,

It is time, my friend. General Croaga has been bothering me for years to reinstate you, but I've delayed, as I understood your situation.

I need your help.

My seventeen-year-old son, Stefan, is the mastermind behind an organization in Dael that is borderline criminal. Last week, he crossed the line and attempted to ruin a certain noble who retaliated by attempting to kidnap my daughter and assassinate me.

I owe my life and my daughter's safety to the other young man who accompanies Hiuken, Pol Vroshen. He defeated the assassin, and as a reward, he requested

As he read, Stefan's body sagged. When he dropped his head, Granite turned the page, and Stefan eventually lifted his head to finish.

"There is nothing left. Everything I built. There is nothing."

"Yes, the quon is thorough, if nothing else. Hiuken wrote an addendum that your father dissolved the business but paid out the employees. Apparently, that was something important to you." He stood. "This Illiat will keep his restaurant, but he will refrain from having any part in your work." He paused. "So, what's it going to be?"

Stefan gave a weak laugh. "You are asking me while I'm still in this device? My answer will determine if you let me out?"

Granite nodded.

"You can take your training and shove it up your… nose."

"I see. I have missing villagers to find, and you have a village to appease. They need to see who was responsible for the commotion yesterday. I'll be back this evening." He leaned over to Wrues. "Let him have one meal at noon."

"Yes, sir."

"Granite! Don't you leave me in here!"

No response. Stefan cursed.

<hr>

Stefan tilted his head and shook off the latest ripe tomato. The movement renewed the spasms in his neck, back, and legs from an entire day on his knees and leaning forward. The more he cursed, the more rotten fruit got thrown. As the sun set, most of the villagers had dispersed, but an old man, who squinted his left eye, limped up and down the street and would not leave. The old man's hand reached into a bucket filled with tomatoes, some rotten and some ripe. Those tomatoes were evil; they never missed his face.

Stefan had received a verbal dissertation from the old villager about how many extra crops the village had due to changes in trading routes. How did the old man put it? "Now we have a use for these." If Stefan was quiet and he did not roll his eyes, he was safe.

Then, something strange happened.

A jagged line, like a tear in a doublet, cut across the air. Stefan shook his head when he saw it, wondering if he had taken one too many tomatoes to the head or maybe the stress and sleep deprivation had finally caught up to him. The luminescent lavender line grew larger and opened into an oval. Lavender light flickered within the oval, and a small creature floated out.

Stefan looked around, but the old man did not seem upset or concerned. The otherworldly creature was small and resembled a flying salamander with glistening, light-pink skin. Dark-blue lightning bolts streaked across the creature's body, and the legs were smaller than a salamander's and floated beneath the creature, which measured about two hand widths. Three thin appendages outlined with fine electric blue hairlike tendrils protruded a few inches from either side of the creature's neck, and the tapered tail waved as the creature zipped around before Stefan.

Having trouble concentrating, Stefan rifled through his catalog of knowledge and came up with theories but became increasingly concerned that he was hallucinating.

In a soft, sonorous high-pitched voice, the creature spoke, [Ah, MidRealm.] It swam lazily through the air and stopped right below Stefan's head, protruding through the stocks. [Hmm. All humans are ugly, but you are particularly awful to look at.]

Stefan did not know how to respond.

[By the by, the DreadKing acts more civilized than you. I've been observing you since last night, and I don't know what half of those words mean, but I'm sure they are inappropriate.]

A mental breakdown. Stefan could not explain it except for a mental breakdown. "What in the UnderRealm is going on?"

A tomato slammed into his forehead. The creature laughed and rolled through the air. The old man pointed at Stefan. "I said watch your mouth, boy."

Stefan understood. The villager did not see or hear the creature. He shook the ripe tomato remnants off his sore face, and in a quiet voice out of the side of his mouth, he said, "What are you?"

[I am justice.] The creature produced a high-pitched laugh. [I've always wanted to say that. Truthfully, I'm a concerned citizen. You see, a few days ago, our home was invaded by a hostile. Nothing but chaos cleaning up after they left. But *you* were responsible for the village uproar last night. Anger, fear, and yelling. Do you not understand what kind of effect that has on my community?]

Stefan was trying to keep up. "Citizen of what?"

[Gaodis, of course.]

"You live here?"

[I didn't know you were dumb. I'll try to slow down. Yes, I live here, on the other side of the Veil, though we call our home something grander, but I won't tell you.]

Many things clicked into place. Memories of reading history books and religion lessons merged with bedtime stories. "You're from the FeyRealm." An entire world that lived on the same plane but hidden behind the Veil placed by Lohem.

[Oh, maybe you're not as dumb as you look.] The creature floated around his head. [No, if you were smart, you would have understood what happened last night.]

Stefan glanced at the old man hefting a tomato. Fey were rumored to have the ability to veil themselves. This one had come just for him. He whispered, "What happened? Who are you?" [Human, when violence occurs here, it affects us across the Veil. I'm in charge of managing emergencies, and the storms you created with that stunt kept me up all night! Though it wasn't as terrifying as the evil from a few days ago. Now, listen here. You Cordiaens can ruin your major cities, but here, where we can live, you have no right to stir up trouble.] With a flick of its tail, the creature added, [I am Quig, the Gaodis PeaceKeeper.]

Stefan's brain filtered the limited knowledge he had. "How did you cross the Veil?"

[I have connections.] Rolling through the air, Quig laughed. [My request to cross the Veil was promptly managed by our excellent tenedrae, Pascal.]

Tenedrae. The fey shepherd. More concepts clicked into place. "Still, fey haven't been seen in Cordiae in centuries—"

[That you know of, which doesn't sound like much.]

Stefan was having a rough day, but he was having trouble getting mad at a flying pink and blue salamander. "A few angry villagers caused a storm in the FeyRealm? If that's true, you must get storms all the time. Was this one that bad?"

[The worst we've seen in Gaodis. Listen up, Trouble. This village is a refuge for my community. We rarely see storms or have any problems. It was hard to find and even harder to keep hidden. I'm a nice fey elemental. I do my job, keep the storms quiet, and pay my essence quota. I don't need trouble. I've crossed the Veil to squash any reason for my community to uproot and move. Following? Do you understand the problem here? Are you going to cause me more trouble?] Electricity flickered down the fey's body to its tapered tail.

"As you can see, I cannot do much. In fact, I cannot do anything." It had been a brutal day.

[Good. Someone was wise enough to punish you. I cannot stay long as my community is holding the Veil open for me, but don't think this is the last you've seen of me, human—]

"Stefan."

[Whatever. I'm watching...] Waves of translucent light washed over the fey as it faded before Stefan could respond.

The old man was giving him confused looks, but Stefan ignored him, trying to assimilate what had just happened. The fey were different from neraida, who were tasked with maintaining certain biomes in the MidRealm, like the Dasari in Miraden Forest. Fey had been tasked by Lohem with tending to the FeyRealm, and there were reportedly too many species to name. Stefan could not remember every bedtime story his mother had read about them.

Crossing the Veil was unheard of except in dire situations, as told from his history lessons. Stefan could not think beyond that. Maybe it had been a hallucination. The back spasms, sore wrists, knee pain, and the crushing weight of having everything ripped away diverted his attention back to normalcy and to the menacing old villager who kept vigil.

As the sun began to set, Granite sauntered up the main street and up to the old man. "Fuiger, having fun?"

"Got a mouth on him, Stone. Got so bad the cleric had to excuse himself earlier. Just practicing my aim is all. I think he's tired. Been acting funny and talking to himself for the last bit." He looked Granite up and down. "No word yet, huh?"

"Nothing. Almost all the patrols have come up empty. Nothing on Boud's family."

"You sure this dung heap had nothing to do with it?" Fuiger said, pointing at Stefan.

"Pretty sure." Granite approached Stefan. "Well?"

Stefan was still trying to understand what happened with the fey but changed his line of thinking back to the newly instated fall commander. "Can I talk?"

Fuiger squinted both eyes. "Mind your tongue."

Stefan closed his eyes and allowed the insults to play out in his mind. After the silent tirade ended, he said, "I won't run."

"That's a start," Granite replied. "I hear you like deals."

Stefan's eyebrows flew up.

Granite said, "Your father wants you to become an officer, and I have a family to find. If you promise to submit to the training, I'll get you out of the stocks, and Judge Fead will allow you to get off with some community service. If you refuse, I must send you to Quon Huem in Shaorn."

"That's not a deal. Community service? What are you going to have me do? Scrub chamber pots?"

Fuiger piped up. "You're going to help find this missing family. It's better than a week in the stocks, if you ask me."

"I didn't."

Another tomato plowed into his cheek and mouth.

Granite turned away, obviously holding back a laugh.

Stefan spit out the tomato juices. He did not have a choice, and he could not stay in the stocks any longer, but he could not hold back. "I ended up here after offering a similar deal."

"Cal Geraul didn't deserve what you did to him. This is a step up for you. I've got things to do. Last chance."

Stefan recalculated. The results were dismal but better than remaining in the stocks. "Fine."

"You'll come right back here if you act up again."

"Yes, yes." Stefan rolled his eyes. Another tomato clobbered his chin. He could not even shout or he would get another one.

"You'll have to use correct titles as well," Granite added.

Stefan eyed the tomato in Fuiger's hand, cocked and ready. "Yes, sir."

Granite said, "Wrues, release him."

The guard fiddled with the keys at his belt, keyed the locks, and the two locks unhinged with small groans. Stefan fell backward, and when his soiled pants came into view, Granite said, "Let's go get you cleaned up. You have a busy evening."

"Wait. I'm not going to rest?"

Granite shook his head. "You had all day to rest. Latrine needs cleaning."

Stefan stopped, but Granite did not move. After a glance at Fuiger, Stefan kept moving.

"Good choice," Granite said.

CHAPTER 10

"A Cordiaen soldier serves the crown by serving the people of Cordiae. Neglecting the citizens is treason."
–Cleric Joern. Advanced Cordiaen Military Tactics,
Volume 2.

In the early morning darkness, Pol's face hit the dirt courtyard. As a small cloud of dirt floated in the air around his face, he smiled. Pol's arms wouldn't respond to his brain after the third round of one hundred push-ups. His chest ached, shoulders burned, and abdomen spasmed with subtle movement, but Pol loved every ounce of pain, every drop of sweat.

Quon Daoringer had handed him the opportunity, but Pol had to make it happen. He would work hard as Uncle Eash had taught him and show his father the fruit of his training and dedication to the family. Wincing from the spasms, Pol mustered the strength to push himself up from the dirt to a seated position.

Stefan was having a tough morning. He remained facedown, drenched in sweat, with Corporal Creyd screaming in his ear to finish his set of twenty push-ups. The lordling had spent the day before in the stocks, and it appeared Stefan was going to have another rough day. Every so often, Stefan would speak out loud to himself and wave his hand in the air before him, but Pol attributed the strange behavior to the lordling's lack of sleep and stress.

Pol caught movement in his periphery. Granite trudged toward them, rubbing his eyes. With weak arms, Pol did his best to snap to attention. Creyd lightly kicked Stefan, but the wilted lordling didn't salute.

Granite barely opened his eyes as he stretched and yawned.

"Fall Commander," Pol spoke up, unsure if it was appropriate. "You okay?"

"Yes, Pol. I have trouble falling asleep, and I have to take medicine at night. Voanya, our herbalist, makes it. I sleep better, but then I have trouble waking up, so I also take a different medicine to counter the night medicine. It takes a while to kick in."

Stefan perked up. "Why do you have trouble sleeping?"

"Because I have to deal with young men who don't know right from wrong."

Stefan rolled his eyes.

"Maybe we should have Fuiger join us," Granite said, yawning again.

Stefan covered his head and looked around. Pol wondered what had happened the day before with this Fuiger.

"Enough chatting. We have a meeting at sunrise on the south side of the village. Corporal Creyd, Captain Dreint assigned you to us, right?"

The burly corporal saluted. "Yes, Fall Commander. Your horse is ready."

"Mount up as well. Thank you for your help." After a quick salute, the corporal sprinted to get another horse, but only one. That meant that—

"You boys will be running. Stefan, the corporal will *assist* you. We're heading for Boud's farm. Pol, take the main road until it ends. Oh, and this beautiful steed is Copper. She loves me."

Pol set off after the fall commander's mount at a full run. After he passed under the gates, he settled into a strong pace and marveled at not being in a city. The dew on the morning grass, the pine scents, and open woods were foreign but beautiful. The early morning darkness slowly retreated before a light-blue dawn. Among the trees, birds flitted past, chirping to each other and singing tunes Pol had never heard in the city. He was a long way from home.

As he passed homesteads, roosters crowed, chickens pecked at feed scattered by children, and villagers waved to Granite as his horse's hooves clopped down the road. The same villagers nodded to Pol, but he didn't expect more. He was new.

After five miles, Pol slowed down to a walk near the last farm on the road. Burgeoning silverberry bushes that needed plucking waited for the daylight in long fields south of a farmhouse. Flat, open grassland spread for a half mile beyond the silverberry fields up to a forest tree line. Between the forest and the field, a single wooden pole stood, though Pol thought it odd. As he was about to walk around Copper to get a better look, Granite said, "Stop."

Pol halted.

Granite dismounted and tied Copper to a post with familiarity, as if it were his own home. "Look at the road and tell me what you see."

Pol examined the dirt road. He could see some footprints but nothing more. No insects, objects, or anything extraordinary. The quiet became noticeable after a moment. Where other homes on the way had signs of life, families waking up, and villagers doing chores, nothing moved here. "Sorry, Fall Commander. Nothing but some prints on the ground. Where's the family?"

"I wish I knew. Follow me." Granite went through the front door, and Pol followed him into the one-room farmhouse. The clean floor, well-made bed, and clear table spoke of a responsible family, but unusual things jumped out at Pol. Dirty dishes on the counter, a soiled spot on the bed comforter, and an overturned chair did not fit.

"Something happened here," Pol said.

"Yes, the family is missing. Tell me what you see."

"I guess the family left quickly, and they left after a meal." Pol was beginning to understand Granite's concern.

Outside, Corporal Creyd could be heard yelling, "Three stops! That's three extra hours of work! We've got children who run better! Move it, *boy*."

Granite stepped out and waved Stefan inside. "Thank you, Corporal. Get in here, Stefan." The lordling paused, clenching his fists. Pol held back a smirk. Stefan was about to get thrown into the stocks again. Granite just waited.

After a moment, Stefan released his fists and trudged inside, throwing scowls at Creyd and at surrounding air. Once inside, Stefan looked around for a moment, lifted an eyebrow, and then returned to his annoyed affect before glaring at Granite. "What?"

"Just because you lost your title doesn't mean everyone else has. Try that again," Granite said.

Pol bristled at Stefan's lack of respect for his superior officer.

Stefan halted an eye roll. "Don't tell the old man." He drew himself up. "How can I help you, Fall Commander?" he said with perfect false concern.

"Excellent." Granite gestured to the room. "Tell me what you see."

Pol didn't know if Stefan had an eye for such things, but he might at least have a different perspective.

Stefan pointed to the fields out the window. "The boring farm family is industrious and has too many crops and not enough workers."

"In here," Granite said with tension in his voice.

Stefan gestured to the table and kitchen area. "They had just finished eating dinner and left the home willingly, though unexpectedly." He pointed to the fallen chair. "Someone was upset before they left willingly."

Pol opened his mouth, but Granite held up a hand. "Continue, Stefan."

Stefan lifted an eyebrow at Pol. "There's no sign of a struggle beyond the chair. Nothing. The family left because they wanted to." He pointed to the bed. "For some reason, an infant was left on the bed, and it stayed long enough to soil the covers. I don't have an idea where the infant is now, but its diapers are still on the bedside table."

Pol checked his anger. He did not need to let the lordling get under his skin.

Granite said, "What about the footprints outside?" Stefan frowned and stepped out the door with everyone following. He examined the footprints for a moment.

"The family came out here, but…"

"Speak your thoughts," Granite commanded with a firm tone.

"It stops here." Stefan pointed to the middle of the street. "And there's another set of prints. Uneven, deformed prints." Stefan looked up at Granite. "I have theories, but they're weak."

Pol could see the signs clearly now that Stefan had pointed them out. Pol fought back jealousy at having missed something so simple.

Granite said, "Go ahead."

Stefan paced beside the footprints from the steps to the middle of the street. "The point of entry and exit for the deformed prints come from here," he said, pointing to the middle of the street. "The point of exit for the family is also there. No sign of a carriage, horse, or other mode of normal transportation. Given the quality of concealment, the obvious guess would be the Dasari and their rangers, especially with the forest so close."

Pol was floored. The Dasari, neraida with extended lifespans, had inhabited Miraden Forest since its creation, per his uncle. Having lived and trained for centuries, a Dasari ranger could have easily done this. Pol quickly realized Stefan's perception and knowledge were on another level.

"And the not so obvious guess?" Granite prompted Stefan.

"History lessons and scary stories parents tell their kids to make them obey." Stefan looked pointedly into the air. Pol examined the area and could see nothing. A second later, Stefan continued pacing. "To be completely objective, one should consider unnatural means of transportation. Flying or teleportation, if you believe the military history texts."

Flying? Teleportation?

"What kid your age knows about military history? What texts?" Granite asked.

Stefan snapped, "Does it matter?"

"Titles, Stefan. Yes," Granite said with a flat affect. "Not all textbooks are created equal."

"In trying to take on the world, I recognized the Cordiaen army was the easiest way to make a name for myself, so I focused on the only military history writer who had a firsthand account of the last four centuries. The rest is trash." He paused, staring at Granite.

Pol had no clue what they were talking about, and even though no one knew of his ignorance, the humiliation was real, triggering his anger.

Stefan threw up his arms. "I'm already in trouble, so it doesn't matter…Master Joern. Go ahead and get mad, but my father knows. Even the king knows; I had to get special permission."

Granite regarded Stefan quietly, and Pol let out a whistle. Everyone in Cordiae knew that name. Master Joern was a reformed traitor. Legend had it, Joern left Cordiae as a boy, became a reyuul, terrorized his homeland, and eventually repented and returned. Many still questioned whether he was actually reformed. Stefan was reading his work?

Granite nodded. "I'm not mad. I'm impressed, and for the first time since you arrived, we agree on something. Master Joern is a genius. So, who else might have taken the family?"

Stefan said, "A reyuul. The deformed tracks support the hypothesis."

Creyd guffawed. "Reyuul! Fall Commander, the kid took one too many tomatoes to the head."

Pol blinked a few times. Reyuul. But they were powerless in Coridae. Everyone knew that. And why would a reyuul want to kidnap a family?

Granite said, "Their power deforms their body. Your explanation has merit, or someone could have altered the tracks to make us think it was a reyuul. Either way, someone dangerous is involved."

"Either way, you need more evidence. Have fun with it," Stefan added.

"Not interested in helping find the villagers?"

"Not interested in fighting a reyuul, but I hope nothing bad happens to the family." He pointed out to the fields. "Besides, someone needs to work those fields. Profit is going to waste."

Pol couldn't believe what he was hearing. "A family is lost and all you can think about is profit?"

"That's me, but I already said I hope nothing bad happens to the family."

Granite shook his head. "We'll find the family. Thanks to you, we have a good start. You're pretty quick."

"I'm a genius."

Angry fire erupted in Pol's heart.

"If you were so smart, how did you end up here?" Granite asked. Pol wondered if Granite was running thin on patience.

Stefan shrugged. "Two reasons. First, it was Lohem's will. No one else could outplay me. Second, the Pulse were more established than my network."

The fire roared. Pol couldn't believe the arrogance.

Granite replied, "Could be true, but that doesn't justify your disregard for authority or the welfare of others."

"I'll own my lack of authority because most 'leaders' are idiots, but you do not know me. You cannot say I do not care about others…Fall Commander."

Pol couldn't stop his mouth. "What?"

Granite frowned. "Considering the danger you created for your family and the reports of business sabotage, I find that hard to believe."

Stefan looked up into the air as if annoyed by something. "I'm telling you, I care about…people. I might have made mistakes. What? You haven't?"

Granite replied, "So you care about others? Even Pol?"

Stefan glared. "He's different. He's trying to be something he's not."

The flames in his soul burst wide open. Red started creeping over Pol's vision.

Granite folded his arms. "Is that so? Corporal, give him and Pol the training swords and let's see how Pol feels about that."

Pol's head swiveled. Granite was going to let them fight?

Stefan said, "You have evidence for a reyuul or a political attack from the Dasari. You've got bigger problems than me. Maybe you should send me back home."

Granite chuckled. "Weak salesmanship doesn't work on me—"

"But good salesmanship does? Excellent," Stefan said.

"Never interrupt anyone, especially an officer. I assume you have some sword experience. You were a noble."

Stefan snorted. "Cheap shot, Fall Commander. I can assure you I have more experience than the peasant here. I'm a qual, not some rural cal. Father prides himself as a fighter."

As Pol received the training sword, he saw his uncle in his mind's eye wagging a finger at him as the flame threatened to consume his mind. Nobles in Cordiae were required to have some self-defense training as part of the nation's bloody heritage, and Stefan was bound to have some background in weapon use. It was an unfair advantage for nobles compared to the average citizen.

During their trip to Gaodis, Pol endured a lot from Stefan, hoping he wouldn't have to deal with Stefan much after they arrived, but Granite seemed to have other ideas. Stefan's intellect might be impressive, and he might have the bravado to be impudent to Granite, but Pol was done. He needed to make an impression here, one no one would forget.

"For someone who claims to be a genius, you really don't have a clue, do you?" Granite asked. He turned to Pol and frowned. "Pol."

"Yes, sir," Pol replied absently, ignoring the warnings in his heart. His uncle would have restrained him by now.

"Don't kill him."

Pol loosened up his shoulders. "Yes, sir."

Stefan received his sword and dropped his smile. "Kill me? Feeling good about yourself because you get to face a qual, huh?"

Inside his head, his uncle's voice said, *He's baiting you, boy. He knows you're better, and he's trying to get the advantage. Don't give it to him.*

Pol didn't reply. He had a lot of friends who would give everything they had for an opportunity like this, a chance to thrash a noble, and Stefan was the worst of the lot.

When Pol charged, Stefan's eyes opened wide.

Creyd and Granite tackled Pol before his wooden sword got close. Pol slammed into the ground and tried to roll away, but Creyd had a solid lock on his leg.

Granite yelled, "Pol, stop!" as Pol yelled and strained, throwing Granite off and trying to disengage from Creyd. Granite smacked Pol's face and then grabbed his dark-brown hair on both sides, forcing Pol to look him in the eyes. "Control yourself. Don't waste anything on him."

That hit. Pol went slack. The lordling wasn't worth the trouble. Granite and Creyd let go, both breathing hard.

Stefan hadn't moved.

Granite pointed to the fields. "Go, Stefan. You said someone needed to work those fields. Get out there and work off some of your stupidity. Creyd, I'll take Pol back and keep looking for the family."

Stefan sucked his teeth and strolled out into the field.

"Corporal, please," Granite said.

"Yes, Fall Commander. I got him. Good thing this guy calmed down." Creyd smacked Pol on the back before taking off after Stefan.

Granite held out a hand and helped Pol stand. Pol felt a touch embarrassed as the inner fire slowly died down. His uncle would have whooped him for something like that. It was exactly the thing he wasn't supposed to do.

"Be honest. Felt a bit jealous that he picked up on the little things?"

"Yes, sir." Pol sighed. "Sorry."

"You might have killed him. Had a hard time with nobles in Dael?"

Pol snorted. "Something like that." Granite acted like his uncle, but Pol did not want to reveal too much.

"Yet, you saved the quon and his daughter?"

"They were in trouble. Someone had to do it."

"No, Pol. Not everyone steps up. But I'm glad you did. Ah, here's my appointment now."

Embarrassment crept up on Pol even more from Granite's praise. He didn't deserve it, especially after what just happened.

As if Lohem, the deity of Cordiae, were listening and wanting to make a point, a cleric strolled up the dirt road and waved to Granite as he approached. A tan surcoat hung over white robes reaching to the cleric's ankles. Wrinkles in the dark-brown skin creased the edges of the cleric's smile. Outside of two worn leather pouches hanging from his belt, the cleric carried nothing except for observant eyes and a deep voice. "How's the legendary, majestic, and infallible Fall Commander Granite this fine morning?"

"Be nice. Aren't you supposed to be a good example?" Granite asked.

"Hmm, weren't you?"

"Ouch. Too soon. Cleric Bruit, meet Pol. He's from Dael, training to be an officer."

Pol bowed his head and provided the traditional greeting to a cleric of Lohem. "Lohem's blessing, Master Bruit."

"This is not the foul mouth I saw in the stocks yesterday," Cleric Bruit said.

Pol gave a slight shake of his head and pointed to the fields.

"Ah, yes. Excellent, let him work it out."

Granite replied, "Yes, but he did confirm my fears about a reyuul. I asked you here to place the protection wards on the other frontier houses. You can even take the foul mouth over there if you need a hand. Corporal Creyd will keep him in line for you. I need to bring Pol back to the garrison."

"Of course. I'll get started on this road and cut over." The cleric gave Granite a pointed look. "You could have asked me back in the village. Why else did you come out here?" Cleric Bruit asked.

Granite pointed to the wooden beam sticking up beyond the fields. "Checking for Gossama's reply. I need her help."

"You're a big shot now. Need to leave little things to the little soldiers."

"No one is little in my book. Pol, keep up, we're heading back. Hopefully, someone has found something."

Pol glanced at Stefan and the wooden pole. Did Granite know a Dasari?

CHAPTER 11

"If you only understood the value of a cleric. Any strategy that neglects the cleric in battle is doomed to fail."

—Cleric Joern. Advanced Cordiaen Military Tactics, Volume 2.

Stefan's lower back spasmed as he stooped to pluck pyramid-shaped silverberries from their bushes. The spasms, which had started during the early morning push-ups and worsened during the torturous running, shot lightning across his lower back with every movement. Any time he tried to stand, Creyd used a thin switch on his back until he resumed picking.

Stefan vowed never to forget Creyd's abuse. One day. One day…

The frustration consumed him, but he could do nothing about it. Normally, to calm his nerves, he would take a stroll around the battlements of his family's keep, swipe a delectable snack from the kitchen, or review his profit margin from his multiple businesses. All gone.

On top of everything, the fey creature would not leave him alone, and it had not revealed itself to anyone else.

Stefan was stuck in some rural hell with a crazy floating salamander, a madman torturing him to pick fruit, and a lower back rebelling against him. He could not even stand up. Why? Because some idiot had tried to assassinate his father.

Deep beneath his father's keep in Dael, the idiot rotted in jail, which brought a small amount of comfort, but why had Geraul felt so insecure, so threatened, that he had to take that step?

Another spasm cut across his back, and Stefan wanted to curse but refrained out of reflex from the day before. Flying tomatoes scared him.

But Pol had scared him more. It was to be expected, of course. That peasant had gone from having nothing to what he surely believed to be equal standing. It only made sense that all his pent-up frustration against his lot in life would be released in that situation.

But the peasant was strong.

Sure, Stefan had provoked him slightly to tip him over into anger—a natural gift Stefan utilized from time to time to unbalance opponents—and the peasant seemed easily manipulated (information stored for future use.) Still, Stefan had grossly underestimated the peasant's strength as two powerful soldiers struggled to restrain the teen. Stefan could now appreciate how the peasant could have overwhelmed a single assassin.

Quig floated above him, lidless dark eyes boring into Stefan. [I must repeat. This is all very good. I can see the evil grip peeling off of you like scales from a dragon.]

"Don't. I have enough issues. I don't need your mouth."

Creyd's switch stung his lower back, and Stefan flinched. "I know you're tired and not yourself, but don't talk to a superior like that."

Stefan had had enough. He whipped around and pointed to Quig. "You cannot see it, but there's a flying pink salamander from the FeyRealm who's making fun of me, and I'm tired of it. I'm not talking to you."

[I'm not a salamander. I'm more of an axolotl but much better.]

Corporal Creyd's lower lip twitched for an instant before he burst out laughing. "I was right. You did take one too many tomatoes to the head. Talk to your salamander all you want!" The corporal bent over, laughing. "Just keep picking."

Stefan turned back to the fey creature. "Why? Why only me?"

[You're the problem. You're the reason we were invaded. You're the one who caused the storm the other day.]

"Pol is also new. How do you know it's not him?"

A pleasant smile formed on the floating fey. [Not him. Not the blessed one. You said there were stories about us you heard as a child. Well, we have stories about him.]

Stefan fumed as he continued picking the silverberries. "He's nothing."

[Yes, you're wrong. Very wrong, but I can't say anymore. We fey take pride in maintaining the balance Lohem created. I would not dare disrupt the path of a blessed one. But you're different. You're a mess. I've come to prevent you from causing any more trouble.]

The peasant? "I don't believe it."

[Did you believe in flying axolotls before yesterday? There's a lot you don't know, most of which you can't see.]

Stefan's back spasmed again. "How do I get rid of you?"

Quig produced a villainous cackle. [Never! Or at least not until I know you won't cause me trouble. I have my own community to worry about. We've lived here for centuries, and we're not moving because of you.]

"I don't care."

[Not true. I can see your soul. You're not evil; you're just hurt.] The fey whipped around as if something alarmed it. [We'll chat later. The village Master is coming. He is revered among my community, but I am not permitted to reveal myself to him, yet. Behave, Trouble.] Quig faded away.

The approaching cleric entered the field from the tiny village lane. Could the cleric see fey?

In a gruff voice, the cleric said, "Excuse me, Corporal. Fall Commander Granite has asked me to bless the frontier homes. While I hate to interrupt the maturation of a young mind, I was hoping to steal you and the young man to accompany me."

Creyd returned and gave the cleric a bow of his head. "Honored to be of service, Master Bruit. I warn you, he's been acting funny." He pointed the switch at Stefan. "Greet the cleric, genius."

Stefan gave a shallow courtly bow and hoped the cleric would not be offended with his restricted movements. "Master Cleric, Lohem's blessing upon you."

"I'm Cleric Bruit, and you are Quon Daoringer's boy, I see. I know Daoringer. You didn't get that mouth from him."

Stefan had a quick mouth, but not even he would disrespect a cleric. "I have been influenced by the company I kept in Dael. I apologize for my words yesterday."

"Hmm. Daoringer has a deep respect for Lohem, maybe some of that rubbed off."

Stefan had received extensive training under the resident cleric, Master Rian, at his family's keep. His father had made it clear, brutally clear, that all clerics received the same treatment a quon would receive. "Doubtful, Master Bruit."

"Ha! The honesty is appreciated, but do not think you're as bad as you assume. Come, let's travel west along the village border."

Stefan obeyed, simply grateful to stand and rub his lower back. He did not relish walking all day, but it was better than listening to a crazy fey and picking silverberries, no matter how rare they were.

Creyd trailed behind as Stefan fell into pace next to the cleric, who took his time as they skirted the farm's edge. Miraden Forest lay to the south, his left, and small knolls interrupted the wide fields covered in various grass and weeds. A lone hawk floated above them on a warm, late summer breeze, which did little to prevent sweat from drenching his shirt. Stefan could not understand how clerics tolerated the weather or the activity in their robes.

"You act much better now that you're not in the stocks, Stefan."

Stefan glanced at the corporal, who shook his head. He had to watch his tongue.

Master Bruit glanced at Stefan. "With that mouth and your assignment here, I have to ask, do you believe in Lohem?"

"Yes, Cleric Bruit." Stefan could answer that easily enough. Stefan was as close to the God of Cordiae as he was to his father, which was to say not at all. Stefan mentally prepared the requisite proofs of faith taught to him by Cleric Rian in Dael.

Cleric Bruit said, "Son of a quon. You probably know more about Lohem and the faith than anyone here besides me."

Stefan agreed but kept his mouth shut.

"Silence is agreement," the cleric said. "But knowledge is one thing. Belief, another."

They approached the next home, just as banal as the rest. Cleric Bruit stood before it as Stefan and Creyd stood back.

The cleric raised both hands toward the home and recited secret prayers in a poetic cadence. Golden light flowed from his hands like mist from a waterfall toward the home.

Stefan's jaw dropped. He had only seen the Jeitoh, the visible effects of prayer, at the annual Cordiaen Festival from the king. It was rumored only those clerics deeply connected to Lohem could produce such a sign. To think such a miracle would happen here in this village for such a mundane task? Creyd seemed unaffected. The golden mist settled on to the structure until it covered the entire home and then disappeared as the cleric finished his prayer.

"Like to see a reyuul get through that," Cleric Bruit said.

"How? I mean, I know how, but how?" Stefan said.

The cleric smirked. "Granite said you were smart. You should know."

"The Jeitoh, for a house blessing? In the middle of nowhere?"

"I don't have control over it, but Lohem seems to think this is important. What are we protecting?"

Stefan considered Quig and the FeyRealm. "A small community?"

"Small? For someone as intellectually adept as Granite said you are, you have a lot to learn about what is valuable. Excuse me. I have to go inside and pay my respects." The cleric spent a few moments inside with the family.

Was Master Bruit the reason the fey wanted to live here? Did he make it safe for them? Safe against what?

"Surprised?" Creyd prompted.

"Maybe." Stefan collected himself.

"That's our cleric for you."

Master Bruit rejoined Stefan and Creyd, gesturing that they continue to the next home.

Stefan understood what he had witnessed but had trouble believing it. Was he seeing things? "Given what just happened, I have a question for you, Master Bruit." Stefan looked around for Quig. "Do you believe in the fey?"

"Of course. The tenedrae texts are very explicit about them. I place protections around the village for any fey who live here as well."

Stefan imagined Quig would be nodding. "Well then. I have a confession, Master."

"He's going to tell you about his salamander friend. He's been talking to it all morning," Creyd offered.

"I might be crazy, but I believe I've seen and talked with a fey, a flying one. It said it couldn't be around you. Do you think I'm crazy?"

"I heard your mouth yesterday. Emotionally unstable, maybe. Crazy, I don't think so. But for a fey to cross the Veil, something important must be happening. Maybe a reyuul *has* come to Gaodis."

Stefan looked around again, waiting for Quig to appear. "It said so, and that I was connected somehow.

Master Bruit, I've never met a reyuul. I don't have any connection."

"Peace, son. I believe you, but it's not wise to ignore the fey."

Creyd asked, "Cleric Bruit, you think he's telling the truth?"

"I'm saying we should always take the fey seriously. Stefan, the next time you speak with the fey, ask it to talk with me."

"Yes, Master Bruit, but I don't know if Quig will listen to me."

Creyd said, "Quig? You named it."

"No. That's its name."

Creyd did not hold back his laughter.

The cleric held up his hand to quiet the corporal. "I can hear more about the fey another time. Maybe you should tell me more about yourself. How did you get to the 'middle of nowhere'?"

Stefan did not want to relive the last few weeks. "Master Bruit, not to be rude, but you're asking delicate questions."

"Spoken like a qual. That won't do. I'm not here to judge you. I just want to understand."

Stefan had no desire to delve into what happened, but the cleric could provide an unbiased perspective. "Let's make a deal. I'll play along, but I want your observation as to why things happened the way they did."

"Ha. Granite said you liked deals. Excellent. It'll be good to hear the story as I make my rounds."

"Fine. I'll start with the morning I met Geraul." Stefan did his best to relate the details from the entire day. Given the audience, he chose not to omit any details.

By the time he finished, Cleric Bruit had stopped with his arms folded before the next farmhouse.

"You're kidding me. How do you not understand why that was bad?"

"It was business," Stefan replied.

"Stefan, you declared war on this Geraul after you hamstrung him."

"It was business."

Cleric Bruit took a step closer to the home, shaking his head as he launched into the blessing. Stefan once again marveled at the golden luminescence flowing from the cleric, but it still did not alter his opinion.

It *was* business. Geraul should have accepted defeat, but he had not. He had ruined himself in the attempted attack on Stefan's sister and father, but it did not add up.

When Cleric Bruit finished, he started for the next home. "We'll get a few more houses in before heading back. Stefan, I can understand your confusion. Even if you terribly insulted Geraul, I don't understand why he would throw his livelihood away. Even if he had assassinated the quon, he'd be a fugitive. Doesn't sound like he was ready to give up. Either way, your culpability is obvious. One day, I hope you can understand it."

"I don't believe I crossed a line, but I'm glad you see a puzzle with a piece missing. That missing piece ruined me."

Pol jogged through the garrison gates, and Granite waited for him in the courtyard's center with two Cordiaen shields and wooden swords at his feet.

"C'mon, if you're anything like me, there's nothing better than working out frustration with a sword and shield."

The fatigue ebbed away. That was something Uncle Eash would say.

Pol hustled over and armed himself. The wooden shield weighed less than its QuonGuard training counterpart and fit snug on his arm. Pol tested the shield straps and whirled his sword around a few times to loosen his shoulders.

"You're sixteen, but you wear those like a war vet. This should be interesting." The fall commander stepped forward and lashed out with his shield. Pol took the hit with his shield and met Granite's sword, mentally adjusting for the lighter weight and faster speed. As his uncle taught him, Pol patiently probed and observed, learning Granite's attack pattern but not foolish enough to believe the officer was showing him everything.

Swords battered shields and swords flew, but no one landed a hit. After ten minutes, Pol's left shoulder tightened from the push-ups earlier, and he couldn't catch Granite's sword slipping through to his left chest.

Granite was breathing hard. "We'll have to do this when you haven't tried to do over two hundred push-ups."

"If I may, can I please use a second sword instead of a shield? It's what I'm used to." Pol hoped he didn't sound presumptuous.

"Dual-wield? Be my guest."

A small crowd of soldiers had gathered to watch them fight, and a grunt offered Pol the extra sword and received his shield. Pol thanked him and noted the difference in weight immediately. His attack style preferred the double sword, and Uncle Eash had recommended it.

"Let's see what you've got," Granite said.

Pol changed his strategy and unleashed a flurry of blows, forcing Granite back but not piercing his defense. Uncle Eash had been trained in the King's Army, and Granite's defense mirrored Eash's style.

Pol used his speed to outpace Granite and landed a tap to Granite's upper arm. Winded, Granite chuckled and stepped back. "You've been trained by a Crimson Corp member. I'd know that style anywhere. I was actually quite familiar with the Corp." Granite's shoulders relaxed. "Those were some good men and women, very reliable." He sized up Pol. "Hiuken mentioned your uncle trained you. Who is your uncle?"

Pol paused. Uncle Eash wasn't ashamed of revealing the family information, but his father would be wary. Pol pushed back against the habitual silence that had suffocated him for years. If he wasn't going to trust Granite, he wasn't going to get very far. "Eash Vroshen. He left the King's Army and joined the QuonGuard in Dael."

Granite nodded. "Six years ago, after the Jetean War. I knew him. Quiet man. Your uncle is a great warrior, loyal, and dependable. Saved many lives." He approached the weapons rack outside the armory and replaced his shield and sword.

Pol couldn't believe Granite knew his uncle. "Yes, Uncle said the King's Army had changed by the war's end. Didn't like that change." Pol whispered, "Said it was the king's fault."

Granite nodded gravely. "Pol, be careful who you mention that to, but your uncle and I saw eye to eye." He started toward a shaded bench against the courtyard's far wall. "Hearing about Eash, I'm not surprised by how you handled the assassin. Care to share the story with me? I've got a few moments before Captain Dreint comes looking for me to do paperwork."

Pol sat down beside the fall commander. He wouldn't tell the story to just anyone because he felt self conscious from the attention he'd received in Dael, but he felt comfortable Granite would receive it well. "I haven't told many people, Fall Commander, but I figure you should know."

Pol related the entire incident as it occurred without embellishment, and when finished, he smiled. He had done a good thing.

"Pol, why didn't you tell me you had a leg wound?" Granite asked.

"Because, sir, it's mostly healed."

Granite shook his head. "You are something else. Is the army something your uncle put in your head?"

"No, sir. I'm a Vroshen. Grandfather told me stories when I was young, and I always wanted to be in the army. Wanted to become an officer when I started training with my uncle. Father said I could in honor of my grandfather."

"Was your father a soldier?"

Pol clamped his lips. He didn't trust his mouth to not say anything dishonorable.

"I see. Your uncle taught you. Well, I'm proud you jumped in to save the quon and that young lady. If you had hesitated, the quon might be dead. Takes a cool head, but it seems you have a sore spot with nobles. Is that why you lost your temper with Stefan today?"

Pol lowered his head. "Maybe. Had many rough encounters with noblemen and women. Selfish lot. Stefan is just like them." Pol folded his arms. "He provoked me. Won't let it happen again, sir." Pol even questioned whether he should apologize to Stefan, but he was not sure he had done anything wrong.

"Pol, not all nobles are selfish, and nobles are important to Cordiae. Believe it or not, they were created to protect the country from evil. At the most basic level, they support the King's Army. If you're going to be an officer in this army, you're going to have to remember that."

Considering the one noble he had the most interaction with was Stefan, Pol was looking at an uphill battle. But if that was what he had to do to become an officer, so be it. "Yes, sir."

"You come by it honestly with the Vroshen line. Vroshen himself turned down the offer of nobility, but the country wouldn't be here without him, without your family. Wars avoided. Kings saved. Being a general, I learned some stories, things they don't tell everyone."

"Haven't heard them all. Maybe you could tell me one sometime?"

"The Vroshen have been heroes and victims of Cordiae," Granite replied.

"You would think more Cordiaens would be grateful."

"Your line definitely has a temper and caused some problems along the way. Your great-grandmother was particularly difficult."

Aola Vroshen. Almost single-handedly repelled the Sperunese army during the Second Invasion. When the Sperunese had finally retreated across the Aeldren River, Pol's ancestor again renounced a noble rank and publicly shamed the nobility before the king.

"Yes, sir. That's one reason why I'm here. Someone's got to make up for it."

"Have you experienced the Jeitoh yet?"

Pol glanced sharply at Granite. "The what?"

"Your uncle hasn't told you everything, huh? Then, it's not for me to say."

Pol had underestimated how much Granite knew about their family. Uncle Eash never mentioned anything about a "Jeitoh." "He said in a letter he never had a chance."

"It's a blessing. Aola was rumored to have received it." When Pol gave him a confused look, Granite added, "The Jeitoh is not something you control or something you earn, Pol. It's a blessing."

"Is it like the prayers of the clerics and voltai?"

"Yes and no. It is a blessing by Lohem given to those he chooses. It is common among the more virtuous, but anyone can receive it, but especially Vroshen."

Pol replied, "Not something my father shared with me."

"I hear resentment in your voice."

This guy saw too much. Pol needed to stop talking.

"I get it. Not my business. You shouldn't underestimate yourself or your father."

"It's a sore spot, sir."

"Fathers usually are, but not always." He gave Pol a sympathetic glance. "I have to review reports on scouting patrols. Get cleaned up and meet me in the office in an hour. We still have a family to find."

Pol watched the fall commander leave. That was two men, both of whom he respected, who had advocated for his father. But they hadn't had Laor as a father either.

CHAPTER 12

"I've lived many lifetimes, and I've known many reyuul. Never underestimate their power, especially on the battlefield. But never underestimate Lohem either."

–Cleric Joern. Advanced Cordiaen Military Tactics, Volume 1.

The guard dropped the wooden food bowl on the cold stone, splashing the watered-down gruel over the sides. The harsh clatter, loss of food, and disrespect did not faze Geraul anymore. This one, with a deformed nose that must have broken many times, was just looking for a response—anything—to justify a beating. Often, Broken Nose did not even need justification.

After hawking spittle on Geraul's tattered pant leg, the guard exited the cell, slamming the door. Sighing in relief, Geraul slipped his hands from the shackles. Four weeks in the dungeon on stale bread, water, and a few rotting vegetables once a day had shriveled his muscular arms.

He slipped the shackles onto his wrists only when the guards entered but otherwise had spent his time devising his little project, a small device to direct the droplets.

Geraul had pried rotting wood from support beams to create his miniature scaffolding structure, which guided droplets into a small rivulet between stones. The resulting puddle had grown over the last few weeks, and Geraul basked in the silence.

He had control over something.

Hiding farther back in the dark cell, the small contraption had yet to be discovered, as the guards never conversed with him, nor did they remain after delivering the "meal." Geraul had not talked with anyone since Stacia's first visit. The king's representative might take months or even years to take up his case.

Having developed a routine, Geraul finished his meager meal and paced around the large cell, repeating his argument to accept mandra. Increased power fit his goals, his newfound dreams. Being a cal meant an inferior existence to all other nobles who had forced him to make deals any way possible. So many times, Geraul had to give up on transactions or advancement to accommodate a higher-ranking noble. He would not have to do that with mandra.

Geraul had to dispense of years of Cordiaen upbringing, which espoused automatic repulsion at using mandra. He had paid little attention during formation, but he could recite dogma as well as any noble. Allowing a demon to penetrate his soul was the only concern, but he would be exiled or dead anyway, so what did it matter?

Keys jingled outside his door, and Geraul retreated to his spot on the floor and slid his hands back through the manacles. He grimaced at the thought of Broken Nose returning to satisfy his need for dominance. Stacia would not need to enter that way.

The cell door creaked open, and a guard who looked like he spent too much time in the training yard entered, closing the door behind him. In his hand, he held a trencher. Geraul frowned. A random, strong guard was bringing a prisoner food. *There is no way this ends well for me.*

The guard placed the tray before Geraul and stepped back. Chicken, blue tubers, and silverberries sat before him. Geraul blinked to verify he was not hallucinating. His stomach involuntarily responded with a growl, but Geraul knew better than to rush. Why? Was it poisoned? What was the price?

"Eat."

Geraul had not spoken in weeks, and his first attempt to speak failed. He cleared his throat and coughed. "What do you want?"

"Nothing. You need to eat."

Geraul did not have much strength or patience. "What do you want?"

The guard looked at him with pity, which angered Geraul.

"I told you. I want you to eat."

Geraul kicked the plate away, scattering the food. "I don't trust you."

The guard frowned at the scattered food. "I'm Doral. Call if you need anything." The bulky guard left and locked the door with a loud metallic click.

As the steps faded up the hallway, Geraul could not understand what had just happened. He removed his arms from the shackles and crawled forward to the food. It smelled like food. He took a piece of chicken; it felt like cooked meat with clear juices running from the morsel.

For a moment, Geraul wished the food was poisoned. That would be an easy way out. Geraul took a bite. The savory chicken melted in his mouth. He had had nothing remotely close to real food in weeks, and he almost cried as he chewed, savoring the taste for a long time. After he swallowed, Geraul scrambled to pick up the rest of the meal.

He sat against the wall and must have taken an hour to eat the small portion. No horrible retching or other symptoms occurred, and Geraul assumed it had not been poisoned. Geraul did not understand, and he probably would suffer for it, but he was grateful. He wondered why the guard had brought the meal and what it might cost him later.

The generous act did not change the fact that his life was over, and he was still considering Stacia's offer, but it had to be the best meal of his life.

✶

As dusk succumbed to night, the deformed figure scanned the farmhouse. Unlike most beings, Fenric's vision penetrated the night, but the feeble moonlight aided him as well. He had spent the afternoon observing this Cordiaen family, who had diligently worked the fields and then retired as the sun set. Patience was always his ally.

Under the cover of darkness, Fenric limped toward the home. His mission required more villagers, and he had a timeline to consider. The first foray had been fruitful, and this one appeared promising as well.

Traces of protection lingered on the property but not enough to concern him, weak as they were. The cleric hadn't renewed these defenses. Slacker.

Advancing as silently as his deformed body would permit, Fenric crept up to the window. Warm candlelight illuminated the interior, and Fenric edged quietly closer to the house and peered inside.

On the solitary bed sat an old man with a sea of crinkles across his face. He fondly looked over a small trio of teenage boys and a young girl seated on the ground before him. A stout man sat at the dining table next to a woman, holding hands. The lot appeared strong, excluding the old man who started talking. Fenric could clearly hear the firm, though aged, voice.

"The storm was so bad as they crossed the Warrian Sea, the waves threatened to carry Ariel off more than once. Cor tore a rusted chain off a railing of the ship and bound their wrists together. He wasn't about to lose his precious wife, his gift from Lohem."

Fenric cringed in pain at the Name. The story was well-known even in Ampestria, but he had never heard it from a Cordiaen.

The old man paused as he nodded to the couple seated at the table. "Just a moment later, a wave carried Cor off his feet and to the railing. Ariel caught the railing with one hand and yanked on the chain. Cor dangled over the side for a second, bound by that chain. Ariel prayed out loud for strength and kept her husband from falling into the depths. Using his other arm, Cor hauled himself up, and he staggered back to the helm and grasped the wheel, relying on Ariel's guidance with her good arm."

The young female said, "Huh?"

The old man said, "You see, her other arm had been taken out of its socket when Cor had gone overboard. When he realized it, he corrected the ship's path and turned to her.

" 'Let me help you,' Cor said.

"With a hand on her shoulder and another holding her wrist, Cor rotated her arm, and Ariel cried out when her shoulder popped into its normal position.

" 'Thank you for saving me,' Cor said.

" 'Thank you for saving us,' she told him."

Fenric disregarded his nauseous reaction. He had listened enough. Muttering the incantation, Fenric concentrated on the humans inside. Once he finished, Fenric ambled up the porch but heard an unexpected voice.

"Genti? Touten? Are you okay?"

Fenric cursed and flung the front door open. The old man turned to him but didn't make any threatening gestures.

"Only in Cordiae would there be someone I couldn't turn," Fenric said to the old man. The others had fallen prey to his influence, motionless, with eyes glazed over. Cordiaens had natural protection against his power, but those who had been purified many times by the FireGate were especially resistant. Fenric wasn't a novice, which is why the High Council had selected him for this mission.

The old man narrowed his eyes at Fenric. "I know your kind." He brought his old and withered hands together and folded his fingers, except his index fingers, which pointed up. "Lohem, most glorious—"

Fenric growled and short ported, or teleported a short distance, from the door to right next to the old man and plunged his dagger in between the Cordiaen's ribs. The prayer died on the old man's lips as he tried to inhale.

"Not the Name, old man." Fenric pushed the weapon deeper. "I acknowledge your sanctity. Now die."

The old man fell forward, grabbing Fenric's arm before he toppled to the ground. He grunted as Fenric extracted the dagger with a sucking sound. Lying on his side, the old man silently mouthed words that Fenric assumed were the completion of the prayer.

"Your god didn't save you. He won't save them." When the old man stopped breathing, Fenric turned to the remaining family members with vacant stares. The drain on his power was more noticeable. The deformed man involuntarily shuddered, not surprised at his power's limitations inside the house. With a practiced concentration, Fenric redirected his thoughts, and the family stood as one and began filing outside. Fenric took one look back at the old man with a pool of blood forming before his chest. The experience was a staunch reminder of the risks he faced in this land, but he would not fail his mission. Fenric exited the house behind the family and followed them to the road.

CHAPTER 13

"Hone your observational skills as if your life depends upon it because thousands of Cordiaens might perish if you miss even one detail in battle."

–Cleric Joern. Advanced Cordiaen Military Tactics, Volume 2.

Stefan had not slept. Sitting on his cot and leaning forward with elbows on his knees, his mind ran through the events of that fateful morning in the Eagle's Nest. When he had learned Chain years before, he had experienced similar insomnia until his brain could fathom the strategies that would secure wins. When he had returned from accompanying Cleric Bruit the day before, he had flopped onto his cot, exhausted, but his brain would not shut off.

The missing piece. The cleric had even agreed something was not right. Stefan should be able to understand the problem, but no matter how many ways he attacked the question, he still could not reach the buried answer. More intel. He needed more. In Dael with his cubs, information flowed like a river, and you took what you needed and mentally filed the rest away. Intel gathering in the garrison was near impossible, and Stefan was concerned a Pulse operative was monitoring him.

But not knowing was killing him. He had failed many times at various initiatives, but he had always learned from each failure.

The peasant stirred. So many strategies floated through his mind regarding the peasant, escaping, the missing piece, flying fey, holy clerics, and even finding the stupid villagers. Stefan could not turn his brain off, he could not enact any of his ideas, and the inactivity agitated him. Stefan had not built an empire by sitting around stewing about what he could not do. He just did it.

But maybe he could do something.

The cleric seemed interested in his plight, and Granite had a vested interest in seeing Stefan advance. He would have to employ patience and take advantage of opportunities. But make no mistake, he would not remain here for years.

The garrison bell burst into an alarm. Creyd's voice shouted above the din of waking soldiers, "Form up in the courtyard! Let's go!"

Stefan had not bothered changing out of the gray tunic and pants issued to him the day before. He followed the mass of soldiers out the door and into the courtyard. Creyd found him and pushed him to the formation's rear with the peasant.

Granite took his position before the hundred soldiers and lifted his voice. "Just received word that another family has gone missing. Touten's family on the southern border, and there's a casualty. Same teams, same locations, but this time, *find* something. Officers will confirm your assignments. May Lohem guide us."

Creyd ushered them to the gate where Granite mounted Copper and said, "You boys meet me at the farm. Pol stays with Stefan. Corporal Creyd, guide them to Touten's." Granite kicked his chestnut stallion forward.

A tirade of curses floated through his brain, but Stefan clamped his mouth as he started at a steady pace. His arms hurt, and his stiff legs made jogging a chore, but he had no choice, for now. His mind was always on the lookout for opportunities. He would find a way out of this mess.

The peasant was not breathing hard and had to slow his pace multiple times to stay with Stefan, who ignored him and the pain. He did notice Creyd was leading them to a part of the village Cleric Bruit had not reached the day before.

Looked around, Stefan realized he had not seen Quig since yesterday. While he was not complaining, the absence was unusual. Maybe something had happened in the FeyRealm as well.

As dawn crept over the sky, Creyd finally pulled the reins, stopping his horse at a farm. Stefan let the others proceed as he leaned forward with his hands on his knees, sucking wind into his lungs. He accepted the torture as a necessary, though temporary, evil.

As he slowly approached the home, the inconsistencies of the farm jumped out at him—and they were similar to the day before. The same pattern of tracks was present on the road leading to the house. No broken windows or other signs of attack. The farmhouse was in excellent condition, even if it was ugly.

Inside, Stefan found Granite squatting next to a deceased old man with a trail of blood creeping away from a chest wound. Lying on his side, his hands were folded in the traditional Cordiaen manner, and his face was peaceful. Of all the details, the old man's pose struck

Stefan as odd. Even in the throes of death, especially a traumatic one, the old man had kept praying. Why?

Stefan scanned the room. One chair was overturned by the table. After calculating the possibilities, only one made sense, and the implications took his breath away.

Granite pointed to the corpse. "This was Roephis, Touten's father. Wise man and never failed to speak his mind. Pol, what do you see?"

"Died while praying. Assaulted with a sharp object, like a knife." The peasant glanced at Stefan. "Maybe there was an initial scuffle with the overturned chair, but no other signs of resistance."

"Good," Granite replied, standing, and Stefan heard Granite's foot grate on the wood planks. "Stefan?"

For a brief second, Stefan considered restraining his report so as not to provoke Pol, but the scene concerned him enough not to disregard any care about how the peasant might take his evaluation.

"There was resistance. The assailant approached from the door and subdued everyone in the room except for this old man. Whoever was in the chair recognized the danger and stood, knocking it over, but then fell prey to the assailant. The old man had no recourse except to pray; he resisted in the only way he knew how." Stefan stepped over the blood next to the body, confirming the granular material sliding under his boot. "The assailant either couldn't subdue him like the rest or did not need him, like the infant. The assailant did not intend to physically attack anyone." He bent over and swept a finger over the granules. Fine yellow particles covered the tip of his finger. "This isn't dirt. The old man must have recognized the danger; he recognized a reyuul, and I'll bet this material is something a reyuul uses."

Granite said, "Hmm. Corporal Creyd, get a sample of that. I know someone who can verify what I think it is."

The peasant looked down. Stefan understood Pol had inferior intelligence, but Stefan could not comprehend the humbled reaction. Pol had the superior strength and anger, which should have been the appropriate response to a threat. Was it the peasant's upbringing? Stefan disregarded the foreign idea and followed Granite outside when it registered they would be traveling again, which meant running.

Halfway there, Stefan nearly toppled to the ground when Quig appeared by his head. [Maybe you're not so dumb. It was a mandrate who invaded. The village is in danger, human.]

"We call them reyuul."

Pol glanced at Stefan and frowned.

[Irrelevant. What's important is the effect. Missing villagers creates fear, sorrow, tension and brews chaos. The mandrate's presence is destructive.]

"Was there another storm?" Stefan asked through forced breaths.

Pol replied, "No. Weather's been fine. You all right?"

Stefan grumbled. "Go on ahead. I'll be there soon."

Pol looked ahead and then back. "We're almost there. Don't take too long." He took off running.

[Goodbye, blessed one. Soon.] The axolotl whipped around to Stefan. [Another storm? Yes, and it took a long time to conquer. I am concerned about what these storms might attract.]

"Quig, mandrates can control fey, can't they?"

[Influence is a better word. Like Cordiaens, we have some protection. This mandrate who invaded, twice now, is powerful. I would not stand a chance against it.]

Still winded, but catching his breath, Stefan continued at a light jog. The second family's abduction and the death shook him. The fey's words rang true: this was a powerful reyuul.

"If your world is in so much trouble, why are you here? Shouldn't you be protecting your realm?"

[You're trouble. I've told you this. Why do I have to repeat myself? If harassing you will save my realm, my home, here I am.]

"The first family was kidnapped before I arrived. That wasn't my fault."

[Beings wiser than you have made it clear that your presence here is connected to the mandrate.]

"That's not possible."

[How are humans so slow to believe what is true?]

Stefan stopped short. "You expect me to take everything you say at face value? As far as I can tell, you are a flying pink figment of my imagination who insults me."

[Truth exists beyond what you can see or feel, little human. There are many fey who are angry at me for crossing the Veil, but I believe that humans can learn, reach beyond their senses, and see the truth…with some proper help, of course. If your cleric can do this, any human can. Even you.] Quig fluttered its tail. [Speaking of which, the Master is close, so this figment of your imagination must leave.]

"He wants you to show yourself to him."

Ripples of electric blue flowed through the fey's long pink body. [I do not have permission yet. It's just you and me. Aren't you happy you get all of me to yourself?] Quig faded away, and Stefan snorted at the thought.

Stefan walked the remainder of the way to the smithy. The stone building had one wooden wall with open barn doors leading out to the yard. Stefan frowned when he recognized the smith who wore a leather apron, held a hammer, and chatted with Granite. It was the same guy who had made use of a bucket of tomatoes a few days before. Fuiger.

Granite pointed at Stefan as he held up the parchment containing the granules he had just discovered, and Stefan tensed as the smith looked at him. "That foul-mouthed degenerate said all that?" He motioned to Stefan. "Get over here, boy. You look like you're about to get into trouble without something to do."

Granite waved him over, and Stefan again released a tirade of profanity in his head. Pol eyed him with concern as Stefan approached the smithy, wincing from the heat pouring from the fire.

"Stefan, you remember Fuiger?" Granite asked with a grin.

"Yes." Stefan rubbed his face.

Fuiger cackled. "Good. Now put your hands on the bellows and start pumping." Fuiger pointed at the peasant. "You, the strong-looking one, come refill my barrel from the well on the front side of the house." The peasant received a bucket and promptly obeyed.

"Stone, thanks for bringing the help."

What was the deal with everyone calling Granite "Stone"?

Granite replied, "Anytime. You can pay me in expertise. Tell me what this is." Granite poured some of the granules into Fuiger's hand.

Fuiger retrieved an eyepiece off a nearby wooden workbench. He peered at the substance in his hand but stopped and looked up at Stefan. "Don't you stop or I'll get the tomatoes." Stefan thinned his lips but kept pumping and shook the sweat off his face.

Fuiger said, "This ain't sand, wood, dirt, or anything I've seen. It looks like granules of salt or sand encased in amber."

"I think I've seen it before," Granite said. "As the kid said, I think it came from a reyuul. He makes a good case for it."

"Sorry for the delay," Cleric Bruit announced, entering the smithy yard. "Granite, I heard the bells and went to Touten's house, but your soldiers told me to find you here. Any word on the family?"

Everyone halted and bowed to the cleric. Stefan also bowed, relieved to give his shoulders a break.

"Master Bruit, I was discussing the matter with Fuiger here. The bottom line: I think we're dealing with a reyuul, and I think we have enough evidence to push forward."

The peasant came around the corner and dumped two buckets of water in the barrel. Then he bowed to the cleric.

Cleric Bruit asked, "A reyuul? Like you mentioned yesterday? I never made it to Touten's house, and I can't remember the last time I blessed it. Makes sense that a reyuul would choose it over the others."

Fuiger wagged a finger at the cleric. "Don't you dare. A village cleric willing to go house to house for protection? They don't make them like you anymore."

"That's not true, but a reyuul? So what are we to do, Fall Commander? Been years since combat training."

Granite said, "I'm sending for the one person who knows about them more than I do."

Stefan and Cleric Bruit both replied, "Master Joern."

Fuiger whipped his head around to Stefan. "Pump, boy." Stefan involuntarily ducked and obeyed.

Granite said, "I'm going to assume the worst and guess the patrols will return empty-handed, but I had to give them a chance. I'm also going to talk with Judge Fead about searching the village, home by home, just to be sure."

Fuiger said, "Now, you're gonna piss off a lot of villagers like that. Foul mouth over here already set off one riot."

Stefan stopped himself from rolling his eyes. It was only one riot.

"Better believe I got more tomatoes, boy."

Stefan put his head down and pumped. Changing habits was annoying.

"The villagers can get upset, but I have to be certain. My bet on the missing villagers is Miraden," Granite replied.

"Why can't we go there now?" the peasant asked.

"It's a separate country, even though it's just a forest. I can't bring soldiers across a nation's border without permission. I'm waiting on my Dasari contact, but if she doesn't answer in the next few days, I may just risk it."

Having multiple businesses—having had multiple businesses—Stefan had received reports on Dasari trade relations and how a few mistakes from Cordiaens had increased tensions. One farmer had hunted in the forest, which was outlawed, and poachers had slipped past the Cordiaen border into South Miraden and kidnapped a few Dasari for the neraida slave trade. Granite would have to be careful.

Still, the pieces were starting to fit together, but there were a few still missing. One thing concerned Stefan the most: the evidence suggested the reyuul would not stop attacking.

Fuiger rotated the crossbow he had been repairing. "Keep pumping."

Cleric Bruit pointed at Stefan. "Granite, are you farming him out? I'd like some help in the Point if I could."

Granite said, "My pleasure. Take him when Fuiger is done. I'll send Creyd along to make sure he behaves."

Stefan groaned.

⸺⁓⸺

The skin on his knees had become numb. In the small Point, Stefan had spent hours scrubbing the stone floor, and his knees had burned at first from all the kneeling, but now they just tingled. Thankfully, the rural Point was small, the same size as the quon's private chapel in Dael, but Stefan still had blisters on his hands from just a few hours of using the horsehair brush. Corporal Creyd knelt on the stone floor in the middle of the nave, as there were no chairs or furniture except in the sanctuary. He had been praying for hours while Stefan worked. It was impressive.

Stefan took a break and examined the sanctuary, which, like all Points in Cordiae, had a waist-high stone partition on the ground separating it from the rest of the space. Only clerics or voltai, ordained warriors, were allowed in the sanctuary, and Stefan would not have to clean it. On the far wall behind the white stone altar hung a traditional mural of the Cordiaen founders, Cord and his wife, Ariel. The details of the mural, found in every Point, depended upon the local artist, but they all depicted some variation of the voyage across the sea. This particular version was typical, with Cord at the helm of a small cog and Ariel at his side. A heavy chain with silver links connected them at the wrist, and an anchor laid against Cord's left leg. White sunlight shone on the couple with a pelican flying above.

Stefan could prattle off the symbolism found in the images, but the facial details always drew his attention as they varied with each location. This mural depicted Cord with a fierce determination while Ariel remained peaceful amid the storm.

"Keep scrubbing," came out of the side of Creyd's mouth.

Stefan dipped the brush in the soapy bucket and reapplied it to the stone. Blisters were better than beatings.

"Let him have a break, Corporal," said Cleric Bruit with his bushy white beard and bald brown head as he bounced out of the sanctuary door. "I want to ask the boy a few questions."

The corporal stood. "Not a problem, Master Bruit. Get up, Stefan."

Stefan tossed the brush into the bucket and stretched his back. He could put up with the cleric if it meant taking a break.

Cleric Bruit pointed to the mural. "Noticed you admiring the sanctuary. We get a few pilgrims each year who travel from Point to Point and praise our art. Question for you: why do you think they crossed the Warrian Sea?"

To Stefan, answering was a reflex. "To escape the terrors of a reyuul-controlled world and to obey the will of Lohem."

"Textbook." Cleric Bruit stepped up to the sanctuary railing. "Did he love her?"

"Excuse me?"

Cleric Bruit pointed to the mural again. "Did he love her?"

"I don't know."

"Don't know or don't care?"

Stefan bit his tongue again with a glance at the corporal.

Cleric Bruit held up a hand. "No, that won't do. Corporal, let him speak freely."

"Sure, but mind your tongue, Stefan."

Stefan halted another eye roll. Stupid tomatoes.

Cleric Bruit said, "The Rueda says Cord had fallen over the side, and Ariel had saved him from drowning with the chains around their wrists. Seems like she loved him if she saved him. Many of the murals either show her at peace or looking lovingly at Cord. But did he love her?"

Stefan felt baited. The determination in Cord's face did not show concern for his wife standing next to him. His hands were on the wheel, and there did not seem to be any gesture of love. Stefan was too tired and in pain to care. "I do not know. They were married. He brought her along. I guess that means he cared."

"He brought her across the sea, over the mountains, and to Eleftheria out of obedience to Lohem, but do we know if he loved her?"

Stefan finally rolled his eyes. "I do not like being led to answers. Get to the point. I do not know if he loved her."

Cleric Bruit stepped closer. "Excellent. It's not spelled out in a textbook."

"Why should I care?" Stefan asked.

"I'll make you a deal. I know you like deals. I'll talk to the fall commander so that you won't have to do any manual labor tomorrow if you can answer the question."

Stefan doubted he could receive such a reprieve, but the idea sounded good. "I do not believe Granite will agree. He's bent on breaking me."

"Son, breaking you is not the goal. He wants you to understand the truth of your situation. Sometimes we have to die to ourselves to make progress. So, about that answer—do we have a deal?"

If there was a chance he could avoid work, it was worth it. "Deal."

Stefan considered the mural. He was not sure if this was the answer the cleric was looking for. "The chain around their arms signifies his love for Ariel. He did not want to lose her, and he was determined to keep her safe, which is why he took her with him across the sea."

"Very good," Cleric Bruit said. "Now we're getting somewhere. Yes, there are many ways Cord showed his love for Ariel, but simply not wanting to lose his wife to the sea points to a deeper truth."

Stefan was in too much pain to think about deeper truths, but if this got him out of work, he would concentrate. "Cor wanted to save his wife from the reyuul and their influence."

"Correct. He wanted the best for her; that is love."

"Okay, do I get out of work tomorrow?"

"One last question."

Stefan groaned.

"Did Cor enslave Ariel or himself with that chain?"

Stefan was out of patience. "As I said, he put the chain on their wrists out of love."

"Exactly. Now, I want you to take that answer and apply it to yourself. Do you feel your father enslaved you by sending you here?"

"Of course," Stefan said, feeling like he had walked into a trap.

"What if he was trying to help you by placing chains on you so you wouldn't be lost? Chains that prevent you from 'falling off the boat.' Would you still feel enslaved?"

Stefan kept his mouth shut as his brain filtered the logic and applied his situation. His father wanted the best for him? That was supposedly love. He was exiled to this village and forced to slave under an officer because his father cared? No. Stefan could not believe that. His father had made it clear that Stefan had failed, and he was to be punished.

Stefan shook his head. "He made it clear. This was punishment."

The cleric added, "Quon Daoringer loves you, Stefan, and you have two ways to look at your circumstances: enslavement or freedom from self-destruction."

Stefan rubbed his sore knees. "Feels like enslavement. Master Bruit, I give you credit for trying, but there is a lot you don't know."

"It's always complicated, Stefan. I will honor my part of the deal and will talk with the fall commander."

Stefan dropped the brush.

Creyd pointed to the ground. "Tomorrow. Not today."

Stefan almost let some choice words slip, but he pressed his lips together. He picked up the brush and got back on his knees. Sharp pains spiked through his legs, and his sore fingers barely held the brush in line. Still felt like punishment.

CHAPTER 14

"Great commanders inspire obedience. Aola Vroshen conquered the Sperunese under Lord General Raken's example and guidance, not his whip."

—Cleric Joern. Advanced Cordiaen Military Tactics, Volume 2.

A few days later, Pol sat alone in Granite's garrison office, waiting for his afternoon academic session and wondering if he would have a similar office one day. The small room could accommodate five or six people with Granite's maple wood desk in a corner, a smaller round matching table where Pol sat in the middle, and two tall cabinets against a wall.

Maps of Gaodis, the nearby Miraden Forest, and Cordiae lined the wall, and Pol studied these in great detail. Miraden Forest was enormous with its northern border almost touching Gaodis and its southern border ending close to the southern Cordiaen border against Ampestria. The forest had its back against the hill country ,which ran along the Andren Mountain range. The Silver River flowed from the mountain peaks through the hill country and into the forest. The river turned silver as it coursed through the forest, supposedly from the towering silverwood trees found only in Miraden. Pol hoped

Granite would take them there at least once during their time in Gaodis.

On the opposite wall, a portrait of King Sraung of Cordiae hung above the regional ruler, Quon Huem. The king had been captured with a firm expression, as was custom given the militaristic history of the country, but Pol wondered if the king was as severe as his portrait depicted. In contrast, Quon Huem had a pleasant smile, and Pol hoped he would have a chance to meet him. Pol's encounter with Quon Daoringer had instilled hope that there might be other kind nobles in the country.

The office door opened and Granite swept into the office holding letters. He tossed one of the letters in Pol's lap as he headed toward his desk. Pol flipped over the parchment, heart fluttering that Adeel might have written him already, but instead, he found elaborate handwriting that could not have been the quel's.

"Master Joern doesn't waste any time in responding when it comes to reyuul." Granite sat at his desk and pointed at the letter Pol held up. "I made a special request for you. Master Joern is the best historian in the country, and I requested information about the Vroshen for you. Go ahead."

Pol was so dumbfounded, he couldn't find his voice to say thank you as he quickly unfolded the letter, discovering multiple pages. He had to shake dust off the parchment and wondered what kind of environment the infamous cleric worked in.

Fall Commander,

I'm delighted that you found an interested descendant of the Vroshen line. So many have lost their way, but given the circumstances, it's to be expected. I had access to this copy of a journal entry from Aola Vroshen, which may address your concerns about development of the ancestral potential. I look forward to hearing more about this young man who's found his way into your care.

Cleric Joern

Pol's hands shook as he laid the cleric's letter down and held the copy of the journal entry. The handwriting may not have been Aola's, but the words would be. Uncle Eash didn't have access to something like this. Aola Vroshen had gone missing not long after the Sperunese War, and her belongings had been scattered to the various branches of the family, but Pol's grandfather had never acquired any.

Pol held a treasure in his hands.

Justi, 324, (After Expulsion)

Our battalion had become separated from the main force with our single cleric and voltai to support us. The Sperunese had pinched off our force, which is the only credit I'll give those spineless vermin for the entire conflict.

But it was exactly my opinion of the enemy that cost lives.

Half of our battalion died at the hands of the enemy because I couldn't use the gift. Even with my knowledge, training, sacrifice, and desire, I failed them. I had survived the Trials, but it wasn't enough.

As I faced the enemy, I called upon the soulfire but received nothing. At first, I believed Lohem had abandoned me, but now I know the truth: my contempt had condemned me. My anger, derived from my pride, at having been trapped by humans who I had thought were nothing more than animals, shackled the blessing. Our cleric, Master Oari, was wise enough to point it out to me.

I couldn't fight like I wanted, and we lost soldiers because of my failure. For a time, I deluded myself into believing my anger was righteous, but Lohem knew my heart.

I may have saved half of our battalion, but I lost the other half. If I had been virtuous that day, the Sperunese might have retreated before the Vroshen blessing.

Aola Vroshen

Pol reread the words, allowing them to sink into his memory. Uncle Eash, who had not even read the journal, had warned Pol. Humiliation washed over him, and he looked up to find Granite waiting.

"Well?"

"It hurts. It's so true."

"The first step is understanding, but the harder step is accepting responsibility. Reflect on it, but let's get to work." Granite placed a scroll before Pol. "How's your Dasari?"

"I can read a bit."

Granite responded in Dasari, and Pol grimaced, only recognizing a single word about swords but otherwise had no clue what the officer had said.

"You didn't catch that at all, huh?" Granite asked.

"Maybe a few words—one word."

Granite pointed to the scroll and the letter. "An officer has to think, strategize, and make quick decisions. Most important, you have to learn to communicate well. You're going to have to catch up on your education."

For the first time since arriving in Gaodis, Pol questioned his talent to become an officer. Compared to Stefan's intellect, he felt like he was no more than a child, but he responded, "Yes, sir."

"Good. I have more to read from Master Joern. The man is thorough."

"What did he say about the reyuul?" Pol asked, intrigued by having an infamous cleric involved. Everyone got to see Master Joern at the annual Cordiaen Festival outside of Ariel, but it was one thing to see the former reyuul from afar and another to know he was corresponding with Granite.

"Based on the information I sent, he confirmed a reyuul is involved. He will address the problem with the Lourshen. A reyuul hasn't traveled past the Cordiaen borders in centuries that we're aware of. This will shake the country all the way to the king."

A reyuul. What was such a villain of legend doing in Gaodis?

A knock at the office door brought in Stefan, who eased himself down into a wooden chair at the table next to Pol. He glanced around the room once and occasionally into the air around his head but did not speak to himself like the day before.

Granite stood, rounded their table, and lightly smacked Stefan on the side of the head. "If you're going to learn how to be an officer, you will salute your superior officer and use titles when you enter a room."

Stefan stood and saluted with a weak "Fall Commander."

"Good. Pol, rewrite the scroll and sound out the words as you go."

"Yes, sir." Pol rewrote the words following the instructions.

"Stefan, I will not waste your time with the officer aptitude test given how many businesses you owned, but I am interested in how far you made it in Cordiaen military history."

Pol's head shot up. "Business owner?"

Granite said, "Oh yes. Stefan here had at least five businesses—that we know of—and had holdings equivalent to a couv."

Pol could not believe it.

"I take offense. My holdings matched the average daum—before they were taken away."

Granite wouldn't lie. How? How had a kid acquired so much? Quals did not have access to that amount of money.

Stefan smirked at Pol and said, "I told you. I'm a genius."

The flame ignited, but Pol closed his eyes. He could not be a slave to his emotions. The flame in his soul remained but did not grow. This was no different from sword training.

Granite pointed at Pol's scroll. "Keep working." He looked at Stefan and said, "Like I asked, Cordiaen military history—how far?"

Stefan replied, "I completed that two years ago. Everything through the last Ampestrian War six years ago."

"Is that right?"

"Yes—Fall Commander."

"I was in that war. What did you think?"

The revelation broke Pol away from his studies. Uncle Eash had been in that war.

Stefan shrugged. "The king was stupid for forcing the general to resign before losing a quarter of forty thousand troops just to make himself feel better."

Granite's face drained of color. "While I share your sentiment, Stefan, you shouldn't talk like that about the king."

"You just said you were in the war; you know how stupid it was. General Bernau knew. I read the firsthand account of their conversation from Master Joern's texts. The king publicly apologized, but the general never came out of retirement even though he was only thirty-two."

"I was thirty-one. I've got to talk to Master Joern about fixing that in his textbook."

Pol and Stefan echoed the same response. "What?"

"I was that general who told King Surtian not to invade Ampestria." He looked like he wanted to say more but didn't.

"Granite?" Stefan asked.

"That's what the troops called me, General Granite, but my real name is Bernau."

Stefan's mouth hung open.

Pol had heard of the Jetean War, but to have the general who commanded the Cordiaen forces here talking to him—it was a lot to absorb. "What? Why are you here? Why were you a grunt?"

"It's complicated, Pol, but the simple answer is, I chose to be here. War can do funny things to you. When King Surtian demanded we annihilate the Ampestrian forces, I told him I didn't believe that's what Lohem or our founding father, Cor, would have wanted. He insisted, and I stepped down. With the help of some friends, I chose this village for my sabbatical."

Pol recovered before Stefan. "Why didn't you go back?"

Granite ran a hand through his hair. "Because I started hallucinating. It's…it's difficult to share, but Cleric Bruit said it's important. I have nightmares and waking visions of walking through battlefields. Even when we won, we lost. I see them, the men and women who didn't make it." He stood and looked out the office window at the courtyard. "Eight years of the Jetean War on the southwest coast, which doesn't include the skirmishes before that. I know death better than I know myself."

Pol said, "That's why you take that medicine to make you sleep at night."

Stefan added, "That's why you're groggy in the mornings."

"Voanya, the herbalist here, provides me with both medicines. One to sleep and one to wake up. They help, but the visions are still there."

"Must be tough to train us, knowing we might die one day like the soldiers in your dreams."

Granite slowly turned around to Pol. "Son, you are wise beyond your years, but that's why I'm going to train you both so well; I won't have to worry about that." He pointed to the Dasari scroll. "Get to work."

"Yes, sir." Pol did his best to obey, but the excitement of unveiling Granite as a living legend made it difficult.

"Stefan, how's your Dasari?" Granite asked.

"I mastered it about five years ago."

Pol blurted, "Five years ago?"

Granite said, "That is unusual, even for a noble."

"I was curious one day," Stefan said.

Granite said, "Curious? Any other languages?"

"I am fluent in Sperunese, Harena, Ampestrian, and I can get by with Ghael."

Granite pursed his lips. "Hmm. Let's work on the Dasari while Pol finishes his assignment."

"Why?"

Granite stared at him.

"…Fall Commander."

"Because valuing neraida, like the Dasari, as an asset is a forgotten concept in our culture. As our neighbors, the Dasari, in particular, should receive special consideration."

"I bet they don't teach this at the Officer Academy."

Granite snorted. "They don't teach much of anything there except politics."

"You went there?" Pol asked, looking up from the scroll.

"I did. So much time wasted on procedures. Not enough time spent on real learning. Speaking of which, let's get to work."

Stefan spoke the Dasari language without hesitation and with a better accent than Granite. Pol could not believe what he heard. Was Stefan that smart, or was a noble education that good? Stefan and Granite continued to have a conversation, and Pol only understood a word here and there.

A bit later, the Dasari conversation broke into Cordiaen when Stefan shouted, "I don't care if he defeats an entire army; he's still a peasant! Don't give me that trash about what makes a noble. Heritage is our culture. Most noble families can trace their roots at least three hundred to four hundred years. My family goes back eight hundred."

Pol restrained himself from standing and throwing the scroll at Stefan by gripping the desk as hard as he could.

Granite said, "Our faith is a part of our culture, and any cleric will teach you that treating any living being, but especially humans, with respect no matter what their station, is what our country was founded upon."

"Faith? Are you serious? Politics among clerics is just as bad as nobles. Spare me."

Now the lordling was insulting clerics.

Granite shook his finger. "Clerics are far from perfect, but the Cordiaen faith is time-tested." The fall commander took a deep breath. "This is not about politics. This is about recognizing dignity in every living being, regardless of their heritage. Being a jerk to Pol just because he can't trace his family as far back as you shows what kind of person you are."

"Yeah, a noble one." Stefan glared at the older man.

The wood groaned under Pol's grip. Thinking of Aola's words, he took slow breaths to stifle the inner flames from raging out of control.

He had to think this through. What was the truth? Stefan was a genius and a noble. Pol wasn't. Stefan stated he was better simply because of his heritage, but Pol knew it wasn't true. Pol couldn't change Stefan so he had to find a way to deal with it.

Granite folded his arms. "Pol, may I?"

"Go ahead." This would be fun.

"What?" Stefan asked.

"Stefan, do you know about General Vroshen?" Granite probed.

"He led King Septiot's armies about five hundred years ago to reclaim the country after the Expulsion. Fought side by side with Uriah, the first voltai. Blessed by King Septiot on his deathbed, Lohem granted Vroshen's descendants with insane physical abilities, if developed.

The descendants repeatedly rejected the nobility and claimed that nobles had given up their God-given duty to protect the country from reyuul, who hadn't set foot in Cordiae since the Second Invasion. This caused the entire country to hate the Vroshen line, which disappeared into obscurity." Stefan folded his arms. "That's an easy one."

"Pol is a Vroshen."

Stefan's face paled.

A corner of Pol's mouth tilted up.

Granite stood from his desk. "Stefan, you will always have your family, but your father has stripped your rank. Here, Pol is your equal no matter what you think. The sooner you understand that, the easier your life will be, but let me take it a step further since you brought it up." He pointed to a small map of the village on the wall. "Judge Fead is the only noble in this village. Every other person here is your equal, and they are all special to me. In the King's Army, soldiers take an oath to serve and protect Cordiae, and these villagers are your country. If you want to survive your time here, you'll have to come to terms with that."

Stefan still didn't respond.

"Now do you understand why we held Pol back the other day?" Granite picked up Cleric Joern's letter. "I need to share this report with Captain Dreint. Both of you, out to the courtyard and grab sparring equipment. Don't start until I get there. I'll be there in a minute."

Pol stood and saluted, but Stefan stood and immediately left. Pol followed him out with a wary eye.

Stefan immediately picked out a shield and sword by the armory while Pol grabbed two wooden training swords. With a burning glint in his eyes, Stefan took a few practice swings.

Holding the weapons must have given him some confidence as the lordling growled and launched into an attack. Stefan's approach was predictable, weak, and outdated, but Pol did not waver. Uncle Eash had taught him never to underestimate an opponent.

With a few strong swings, Pol battered Stefan's weapons away and kicked the noble in the chest. Stefan flew backward, rolling over, face up in the dirt. A few nearby soldiers stopped what they were doing to watch. Pol assumed Stefan got the hint, but the rage in Stefan's eyes said otherwise. The lordling picked up his sword and shield and crouched into a traditional Cordiaen stance.

"You dare strike me?" He turned to his left and yelled, "Shut up!" to no one. Who was he talking to?

Silent, Stefan attacked again, but Pol easily weaved his own defense, quickly adapting to Stefan's attack pattern. The swings were clumsy and slow, and Stefan had trouble managing the heavy wooden training shield. He was obviously out of shape and most likely recognized the difference in ability.

As Pol easily thwarted Stefan's defenses, he refused to be complacent, and the vigilance paid off as Stefan pivoted and initiated a swift series of thrusts, many aimed at Pol's unprotected head. That was poor sportsmanship.

Finally frustrated, Pol kicked Stefan's shield away and smashed a wooden sword into Stefan's unprotected side. Pol pulled the hit or would have broken ribs, but Stefan still fell to the ground, sucking wind.

A small cheer went up from the gathering soldiers, and for a moment, victory swelled in Pol's heart. That hit was a long time coming.

Pol did what his uncle had taught and offered his hand to his opponent. Stefan ignored Pol's hand as he rose, guarding his side, and making his way to the nearby bench.

Granite called out as he approached with Captain Dreint, "Stefan, you all right? You two were supposed to wait for me."

Pol pointed his sword at Stefan. "He wanted to fight."

Granite gave Pol a withered look. "Good thing you were here to keep him from getting hurt."

Shame washed over Pol. "Could have hit him harder."

Before Granite could respond, a shout went up from the front gate, and soldiers were yelling to each other to open the gate. As the steel-reinforced gates opened inward, a horse-drawn wagon with a determined-looking man pulled inside.

Pol noticed a haphazard array of women, men, and kids crowding the wagon. The villagers were shouting and pointing as soldiers assisted them to the ground.

Granite and Dreint jogged up, and Granite raised his voice. "Quiet everyone! Raig, what happened?"

The man who drove removed his hat. "Stone, we just came from my house. My girl, Saenna, had been watching for her older brother out the front window when she screamed." He waved Saenna over. "Come here, girl. Tell Stone what you saw."

A young girl about eleven years old with brown overalls over a blue tunic slowly walked over. She leaned against her father. "Mr. Stone, I was looking for Joim to come in from the fields when I saw him."

"Who, dear?"

"A man wearing black, Mr. Stone. A green-and-purple circle appeared in the air. A man with a black hood over his head came out of it. As soon as I saw him, I screamed 'cause everyone's talking about bad things happening to families."

Raig hugged her. "Well, I looked out the window and saw the man, and I got everyone out the back door. Stormy was already hitched up from bringing supplies in from the trade store. The rest o' my family jumped in as we came down the road." He wiped his forehead. "Stone, when I saw that man…well, he didn't look like a normal man. His shoulders and arms looked funny."

Granite nodded. "Thanks, Raig. You did right by getting out of there. Your quick thinking saved your family."

Raig nodded, and Granite turned to Dreint. "I want two-quarters out the gate now. This reyuul may have retreated, but we need to try. Send someone for the cleric now."

Dreint turned to the formation and shouted orders with soldiers running. Granite put a hand on Raig's shoulder. "Why don't you take the family to get something to eat in the mess hall? I'm going to your house and will make sure everything's okay."

"Thank you, Stone." Raig looked him up and down. "You get a promotion or something?"

"Something. You folks go on ahead." He motioned Creyd over. "Bring the boys to Raig's house. Don't give Stefan a hard time. He just got injured. Pol?"

"Yes, sir."

"Go get a real sword and shield from the armory. You may need it."

CHAPTER 15

"When I was a boy, five hundred years ago, King Sieryan opened Cordiae's borders to reyuul and the seeds of the country's downfall were sown. Never underestimate the power of a single decision."

–Cleric Joern. Advanced Cordiaen Military Tactics, Volume 2.

Stefan winced as he followed the peasant to the garrison gate. A Vroshen? Stefan had read accounts of other Cordiaens who had similar abilities, heroes from ages past, but the Vroshen were the most notorious. Their inherited skill had to be developed, and Pol had obviously been training, evidenced by defeating an assassin. While Granite probably felt Stefan needed a demonstration, the humiliation only stoked his anger at Pol.

Stefan paused. Did his father know? If Granite knew, then the quon surely knew, and if the quon knew, then he had a plan for Pol. Quon Daoringer was a hard man, but he was renowned for paying his debts and rewarding those loyal to him. Stefan proudly and willingly took after his father in that regard, but as a traditional Vroshen, Pol would have turned down money and rank.

Idiot.

But the quon would have taken that into consideration, which meant that sending Pol to Granite was important. His father must have thought very well of Granite. Maybe Stefan had underestimated the general. Maybe Granite had known that Stefan would come to this conclusion if he fought Pol.

Granite already knew him well.

[You're an idiot.]

Stefan ignored the elemental fey who had berated him throughout the fight.

[Oh, still not talking to me, huh? Look what it got you?]

Stefan favored his ribs and refused to acknowledge the fey's existence. Flashes and small ropes of blue electricity fluttered over the flying fey's skin.

Outside the gate, a group of villagers had gathered with the King's Army guards barring their entrance.

An elderly woman shook her fist at the guard. "We're not safe! More families will go missing. When is it going to stop?"

Granite rode Copper out the garrison gate with Corporal Creyd at his side. The small crowd backed away as Granite addressed the villagers from his horse. "We are going to investigate now. Please go back home and allow the soldiers to patrol the area."

"We want to be safe, Stone!" yelled a villager.

"That's right, Stone. Our homes aren't safe! You all haven't found the other families yet," added a man.

Granite's jaw clenched. "There may be a reyuul in the village right now." Gasps. "Evacuate to the garrison. Let us search for the reyuul."

The crowd parted, but questions about the reyuul rang out from the villagers. "Creyd, you're with me." Granite pointed at Pol and Stefan. "Boys, we're going ahead. Meet us at Raig's farm on the western edge of the village. Just follow the road." Kicking his horse, Granite led the mounted men down the main street.

Pol took off. "Let's go."

"I heard him." Stefan followed at a pace that was bearable for his side. In his mind, he envisioned the top-down layout of the village he had seen from the wall map in Granite's office. The farm would usually be a fifteen-minute run, but with his injury, it might take a half hour. Stefan couldn't keep up with the taller boy, and it only took Pol a minute before he realized he had left Stefan behind. Stefan did not want his pity. "Leave me."

Concern flashed over Pol's face for a second before he said, "Don't take too long," and surged ahead.

Stefan fought back frustration, allowing his side pain to derail the rage. The peasant's presence was irritating, but leaving Stefan behind with barely a thought was also annoying.

If Stefan's older brother Cyprian had seen Stefan at that moment, he would have laughed at his younger brother's frustration and berated him.

After another mile, Stefan caught a flicker in his peripheral vision. He came to a stop as a green-and-purple ellipsoid shimmer appeared off the road. As it coalesced, darkness consumed the interior, morphing into a pure black void. A large humanoid figure stepped out.

[It's him. Beware, human!]

Even with a black cowl over his head, the deformed shoulders, arms, and legs could not be hidden. Stefan froze, not sure what to do. He was not a cleric, and there was nowhere to hide.

"Stefan, son of Daoringer."

Stefan forced his breathing to slow. This was not a time to lose his head. *Is this the reyuul Granite had been talking about? How does he know my name?* He regained focus. The reyuul did not seem to notice Quig. Stefan took stock of any advantage. "Who are you?"

"I'm Fenric, and I've been waiting for you."

"Why? What do you want from me?"

Fenric smiled, showing his rotting teeth. "No, the question is: what do you want from me?"

Stefan frowned. "Why would I want anything from you?"

Fenric took a step forward. He appeared eager to talk. "I know what you've lost, and I know what you seek. I'm offering to help."

Even without the fey screaming in his ear, Stefan recognized the warnings. Still, why was the reyuul targeting him? "Why would you want to help me? What do you get out of it?"

The responding smile unnerved Stefan. "They said you were smart. To answer your question: the more powerful you become, the more powerful I become. Few are worthy, very few. I want to offer you power, a chance to reclaim what was lost."

Stefan knew he should run away. Years of education and conditioning screamed at him to reject anything the reyuul offered, but as Stefan favored his side, he found himself considering the reyuul's words.

[You are a fool, human.]

Fenric said, "I knew you'd be interested." He looked down the road behind him. "I must leave, but we'll meet again…in the forest. Think on it."

Stefan turned toward the sound of the oncoming soldiers.

Fenric stepped through the void, dust trailing to the ground as he left. Once his deformed body had disappeared, the gate winked out of existence.

Stefan yelped as a shock of electricity hit his right shoulder.

[Don't you get it? This is why I'm here! Use that stupid melon sitting on your shoulders. I told you: you are connected to the trouble!]

Stefan finally acknowledged the fey. "Listen. You've belittled me ever since you arrived. Everyone has abused me, talked down to me, ignored me, or humiliated me since I left Dael. I don't like reyuul, but he is offering me an opportunity of something better than—this. You don't think I'm going to listen?"

Quig furiously swam around the air, tail twitching. [You are blind. You had made so much progress in shedding the grasp of evil since arriving, but you cannot see beyond the boundaries you place around yourself. You're willing to put your soul in danger because a mandrate talked nice to you? What about the Master, the blessed one, and the general?]

"I'll give you the cleric, but the others?" He massaged his side and remembered Granite's hit to his face.

[The mandrate's presence will have raised another storm in my realm. I must return to my village, but mark my words, human, we are not done. The tenedrae did not grant me permission to cross the Veil to fail here. I have too many who depend on me. You don't realize how many depend on you.]

Quig disappeared. Stefan doubted he had anyone who depended upon him.

A King's Army quarter, a unit of twenty-five soldiers, jogged into view a moment later. Corporal Rield led his fist, a smaller unit of five soldiers, and asked, "Stefan, you okay?"

"I'm fine. Just injured and tired from training. Pol went on ahead. I'm trying to catch up."

"Get a move on. We'll head south from here. Be careful, Stefan. If you see anything, yell and take cover."

"I understand." The patrol jogged south. After a moment to ensure they were gone, Stefan examined the ground where the portal had opened. Nothing. Whatever Fenric had dropped was gone.

Stefan turned west and continued at a light jog. *Waiting for you…what do you want from me?* Stefan berated himself. He should have asked better questions. How did Fenric know so much about him? What future could a reyuul offer?

Did Quig have a point? Stefan considered throwing the idea of Fenric out of his head immediately and reporting it to Granite. With his education, he knew the consequences of using mandra, the power Fenric referred to. Using mandra not only produced physical deformity, but the books spoke of a deformity of the soul as well.

Still, the books had never prepared him for what he had just witnessed. That was power. In the absence of what he had lost, that power attracted him. Stefan allowed the seed to remain in his thoughts.

After arriving at Raig's farm, he found Granite's horse tethered to a rail fence and soldiers milled about. Pol listened to Granite as the fall commander pointed out the footprints leading up to the house.

Granite noticed Stefan approaching. "Stefan, come here."

Stefan took his time with a hand on his side.

"You all right? Sure we don't need the cleric to take a look?"

Stefan tensed at the mention of the cleric. "No. I'll be fine, Fall Commander."

"Come, look at these prints." Granite pointed to where the prints began. "Same as before. The reyuul must have teleported right here."

Stefan thought about what he had seen earlier. "What about the dust as a mandra component?"

"Good question. Master Joern wrote that components integrate with the spells that use them. What we found at Touten's house must have fallen by accident."

Stefan turned to the house. "Anything inside?"

"No. Raig got his family out in time. It doesn't appear that the reyuul went inside." Granite looked up at the blue sky. "One thing concerns me. First, this house is nowhere near the other two on the south end of the village. Second, the attack came in the afternoon instead of the evening."

Stefan filtered his thoughts. "Is he bold, stupid, or did he have another objective?"

Granite said, "Advanced reyuul have to be intelligent and resourceful to master their art, so I don't think it was stupidity. We still haven't figured out why families are being targeted, so I can't understand if it's bold. As for another target, no one has reported another sighting, so I don't think it was a diversion." He checked the sun's position. "It's getting late. We should get back and check in with the other patrols." He eyed Stefan. "Do you need to ride with me?"

"No, I'd like time to process what you've said." He had a lot to consider.

"See you then. Pol, stay with him."

"Yes, Fall Commander."

Stefan walked back and ruminated on what had happened. He had been the real target, but that still left the question of why the families would be involved. Sure, they would be easy targets, but why? Teleportation was a valuable tool, but once on the ground, how vulnerable was the reyuul? Fenric had left quickly at just a hint of the soldiers. Stefan ran through all the interactions multiple times before he and Pol returned to the garrison. Pol had kept his distance and remained quiet.

Once back at the garrison, most of the soldiers had returned, and Granite and Captain Dreint conversed together.

Dreint nodded. "No casualties. That's very good. I'll send an update to—Fall Commander, I'm sorry. Did you want to update General Croaga?"

"Yes, and send word to Judge Fead to spread the news to the villagers as well. People are scared and need good news," Granite said.

Raig's family, the one that sought refuge from Fenric's latest attack, huddled against the rear wall of the courtyard. Guilt sank into Stefan's stomach. Families had suffered, villagers had died, and he had had a conversation with the reyuul. He swallowed the guilt and pushed it away. He had done nothing wrong.

A winded grunt—Goors was his name—raced up to Granite, panting.

"Fall Commander, I pulled it from the post just now."

Goors presented a Dasari arrow with a parchment wrapped around it.

Granite unwrapped the scroll and read aloud,

"OakenRoot gives permission to enter the forest. Be careful. More lost ones in the north. Meeting place. One day.

Peace,

G"

Granite told the captain, "Assemble the officers. I will lead a small party to Miraden at first light tomorrow."

He looked at Pol and then Stefan, and a grin crept across his face. "Well, boys, I'll be too busy to handle you if I'm guiding troops in the forest. Listen up."

Concern blossomed in Stefan's heart.

"Pol, you want to be an officer? Show me you can work with him." Granite pointed at Stefan.

Pol opened his mouth a few times but finally said, "Yes, sir."

Stefan held back laughter; he finally had leverage.

Granite turned on Stefan. "You want out of here? Same deal. Show me you can work with Pol."

"Not going to happen. Maybe another peasant, but not him."

"It's him or no one."

Stefan felt that one more than the sword to the ribs.

"Get to the barracks. Make your decision. If you're willing to do what I'm asking, show up at the gate at dawn. Make sure your pack includes extra rations." Granite's grin grew wider. "Tomorrow, I'll take you to your new instructor. She's not as forgiving as I am."

CHAPTER 16

"Neraida were created by Lohem to sculpt the world and maintain his creation. Never underestimate Lohem's Sculptors. The saddest evolution of current Cordiae military education is the negligence of neraida."

—Cleric Joern. Advanced Cordiaen Military Tactics, Volume 2.

The excitement of meeting a new instructor quickly cleared Pol's morning fogginess as he hustled across the garrison courtyard. A fist of soldiers, consisting of four grunts and Corporal Rield, waited at the gate with Granite as Pol approached.

Granite said, "You're committed, then?"

"Yes, sir." Pol was going to become an officer. All he had to do was learn how to put up with Stefan. He had doubts, but he wasn't going to give up now. "I trust your judgment."

"You'll see. Ah, here he comes."

Stefan approached with his pack almost bursting and an expression that fluctuated between irritated and pensive. When he approached, Granite gave the lopsided rucksack a frown but said, "Coming?"

"You are going to take us to a forest with a reyuul. I don't think my father would appreciate that."

Pol had also considered that, but again, he trusted Granite.

"Actually, I'm placing you with the most capable person I know when it comes to reyuul. There's nowhere safer from reyuul than by her side."

That was high praise coming from Granite. Stefan grunted in response.

"Boys, you know Corporal Rield, but this is Thielda, Wrues, Sounder, and Geanna. Once we drop you off with Gossama, I will train them to lead other fists to search for the villagers. Let's get going."

As they traveled the familiar road, villagers stopped their morning chores and saluted as they passed. "Stone, find them for us!"

Guilt washed over Pol. He should have been more considerate of the missing villagers rather than focusing on his own ambitions. One reason he had wanted to enter the army was to defend those who couldn't defend themselves. As they passed Boud's farm, he remembered a baby was in the village without a mother or family. If he was going to be an officer, helping Granite should be more important than his own advancement.

"Fall Commander, if you need help finding the villagers, I'll do it."

"Pol, I appreciate that. I know you mean well, but Miraden is brutal, and I can't watch you while I'm searching for them. I need you to learn to work with this guy," Granite said, nodding to Stefan. Stefan glanced up. He was already struggling under the weight of his pack, and Pol wondered if he would have to help him carry it.

They passed Boud's farm again and crossed through the ripe silverberry fields and past the open land beyond. Between the fields and the forest, a six-foot-tall wooden beam with multiple notches stood like a sentry.

"What's that?" Pol asked.

"That's how I communicate with my contact. This Dasari is not easily accessible and doesn't prefer to leave the forest." The forest's edge was a quarter-mile away, and the notches were all near the top of the post. "They can hit this from the tree line?"

"Oh, yes. That's nothing."

"Amazing." Pol wondered about such accuracy as the group arrived at the tree line. He took a deep breath as he approached Miraden Forest. Uncle Eash had taken him to Elsakien Forest, south of Dael, but it was a tame forest compared to what he had heard of Miraden. The massive tree line towered before him like a living wall.

Granite repositioned his pack and adjusted his weapons. "Follow my lead. Don't stray." Pol and the other soldiers followed his example. Miraden Forest must not grant mercy to the unprepared.

Pol followed Granite into the trees and realized he had stepped into a different world. The forest ceiling soared above them, with slender shafts of light piercing through the thick canopy. Thick branches snaked above, and some appeared to have a silver sheen. Could those be from silverwoods? A narrow trail led through the massive trunks and underbrush.

Granite swept away fallen branches in the path. "Sorry, I haven't cleared this in months."

As Pol followed, stepping over roots, he asked, "If I may, who is this contact, Fall Commander?"

"Her name is Gossama, and she's the one who's going to continue your training."

"What does a Dasari know of the Cordiaen military?"

Granite pushed a low-hanging branch out of the way. "To be honest, not much. But among the Dasari, Gossama is legendary."

Pol held back the same branch as he passed. Legendary?

Granite continued, "Thankfully, she speaks Cordiaen."

"Why is she willing to train us if she's so legendary?"

"She owes me a favor."

Pol asked, "What did you do for her?"

Granite stopped in the middle of the trail. "While Gossama is legendary among her people, she's also an outcast. It is rude to discuss her past without her permission, but I can tell you how I met her." He resumed hiking up a small hill. "I had been making frequent trips to the forest when I first transferred to Gaodis. At the time, humans were permitted entrance, and Captain Dreint had ordered basic training in the forest. I really enjoyed it. Not long after I arrived, I disobeyed orders to only enter with Dasari permission." Granite paused at the top of the hill. "I didn't know Gossama had been following me almost every time I entered. She's very good at being aware of intruders. She's even better at moving without being seen, but she never interfered with my hikes. On one of those visits, Gossama discovered I was about to come into contact with a small group of Dasari warriors from RainCrest, a northern Dasari town. She intervened before I made contact, and they attacked her."

"Why?" Pol asked.

"I told you, she'll have to explain that. I knew little about Dasari, but I didn't like a group of males attacking one female."

"What could you do against a group of Dasari warriors?" Stefan blurted.

"I'm not *that* old. I engaged the group long enough to allow Gossama to escape. They were so surprised to see a human that they laughed more than they fought me. I didn't seriously injure anyone, and with some correspondence from the judge to Leader OakenRoot, we avoided anything bigger."

Pol stepped next to Granite. "She must have been grateful."

"Actually, she was angry. Gossama is totally self-reliant. She hates feeling like she owes anyone, especially humans. She also argued that if I hadn't been in the forest, then she wouldn't have had to get involved. I told her we were even, but she always reminds me she owes me."

"Thank you, sir, for using your favor on us," Pol said.

"Pol, don't thank me yet. Training with Gossama may be the worst experience of your life. She's not really a 'people person.' But I trust her, and you boys need it."

He stopped for a moment, and Pol tensed.

Stefan said, "What? What is it?"

"Be quiet," Granite replied. He closed his eyes and placed a hand on the bark of a nearby fir tree. Pol slowed his breathing and listened for what Granite might be hearing. Rustling leaves, soldiers breathing, and Stefan shuffling behind him were the only things he caught.

Granite intoned something in Dasari, and then he opened his eyes and spoke Cordiaen.

"Permit me to grow, O sovereign one.

"My roots grow because of your sun.

"Turn my face to where you shine.

"Grant me hope. Make it mine.

"I bow to your will;

"My heart, be still.

"Listen well;

"Thoughts quell.

"Wait."

Pol said, "What were you doing?"

"Gossama called it 'sinking into the forest.' She said I couldn't do it like a Dasari, but it was important to try so you can listen to the forest. You'll get your chance." He didn't wait for a reply and continued on the path.

Pol followed, wondering why anyone would want to sink into the ground.

As they continued through the day, Pol noticed a few skittish squirrels and snakes but no larger animals. While he didn't expect to meet a panther, bear, or boar at every turn, Pol didn't see any large tracks, either.

Granite stopped the group for a break, finding wild hinkleberries once and nibbling on dried fruit the second time.

Pol's jaw dropped when he realized Granite sat at the base of a silver tree. The bark, leaves, and vines gleamed a metallic silver. When Pol placed his hand against the surface, he half expected it to be metal, but his fingertips brushed the smooth bark. Above him, dozens of large branches wove through the canopy, with small rays of sunlight glinting off the leaves in the faint breeze.

"Silverwood," Granite said, "only found in Miraden. No fruit, at least not this year. Legend tells of a special fruit that blooms once every few hundred years. These trees are responsible for the silver water found in streams and the great river which flows through the forest."

"That's amazing," Pol said, unable to take his eyes off the sight until he heard someone collapse. Stefan had dropped his pack, and Pol saw the warning signs and backed away.

"It's your fault for bringing all that," Granite said.

"I didn't say anything—Fall Commander. Just need a moment." Stefan plopped next to his bag.

"No. We're on a timeline." Granite led the way, and Stefan groaned as he stood and followed.

After miles in the surreal forest, the fall commander brought them to a white limestone outcropping on a hillside. The irregular formation did not reach as high as the forest canopy, and the white limestone glittered in the intermittent shafts of midday sunlight.

Granite climbed the outcropping almost to the top and smiled as he looked over the forest. "Gather a mix of kindling, dry leaves, and green leaves."

The soldiers and Pol scattered to obey while Stefan sat down next to his pack. Granite set up a small fire, placing some wet green leaves into the flames. The smoke billowed, and he blew into the flames, increasing the yield.

Granite chuckled to himself as he erased his tracks around the camp. "Hurry, follow me. This is a game I play with Gossama every time I visit."

He led them backward, wiping away the evidence of their presence and directing them to an oak tree fifty yards away. With ease, he made it up to a high, fat limb and settled down.

"Pick a branch and don't make a sound. Boys, join me up here."

Pol gripped the lowest branch and pulled himself up, climbing until he reached Granite's limb. Being that high up surprised and excited him.

Stefan's grunts turned Pol's attention to the forest floor, and without hesitation, he lowered himself down to the first branch and offered his hand. Stefan smacked it away and scooted behind a bush and sat down. Pol frowned and returned to Granite's side.

"Lay flat and be quiet."

Pol obeyed and focused on the smoke near the rock outcropping. He regulated his breathing and focused on the leaves rustling in the canopy. The air carried myriad oak, pine, and birch.

A rapid staccato of deep vibrations reverberated through the trees. Pol sank lower over the branch, concerned for what the fire had attracted. No animal made such a racket, and Pol could only imagine what crashed through the trees.

An earsplitting roar broke through the canopy as a lichen-covered, dark-brown tree hurled itself at the fire. Standing twelve feet tall and four feet wide, it had distorted humanoid appendages, bark-like skin rippled and shed at the furious movement. Red glowing eyes lined with black glowered at the offending fire. Pol winced with every stomp of the creature's leg, and when the fire had been pulverized, the creature whirled in every direction as if searching for the creator.

Pol hugged the branch tighter and couldn't remember ever having seen such a creature.

After failing to find prey, the giant turned its rage to the stone outcropping. With each punch, limestone boulders exploded into pulverized bits. The raw power sent vibrations to his branch with each hit. After a few minutes, the creature's movements slowed, and a majority of the rock formation lay in rubble at the giant rootlike feet. The movements continued to slow. Where the extremities had moved with ease, breaking off pieces of bark, the arms slowed to a crawl, and the last swing took three seconds to complete.

To get a better look, Pol lifted his head, but he met resistance. A hand kept him from moving. A young Dasari female gave a small shake of her head and slowly laid down on the branch next to him as she eyed the creature.

Was this Gossama? She looked like she could be in her early twenties. On her exposed hand and wrist, light-green leaf shapes covered her bronzed skin. She wore a dark-brown mud-splattered cloak with the hood pulled up.

Pol turned his attention back to the gigantic creature, who continued to stomp near the outcropping. The creature had lost all speed and moved in slow circles without purpose.

A tug on Pol's arm brought him to his feet, and he followed the Dasari to the forest floor. She jumped from branch to branch while he eased himself down the trunk with Granite. When he reached the ground, Granite gave the group a salute and pointed to the Dasari. This was Gossama.

Stefan pulled himself up, shaking the bush and earning a scowl from Gossama and Granite. When the fist of soldiers gathered, Gossama put a finger over her lips and pointed southwest. She burst into a sprint, leaving everyone standing for a second before they followed. Leaving the scene, Pol was grateful to put distance between himself and the monster tree.

Gossama flitted through the forest like a butterfly, but it seemed like the short Dasari was holding back. After a quarter hour, she stopped short at a birch.

Pol caught his breath and noted Stefan wasn't with them. He should have been paying attention, but after a few minutes, the young man appeared with a wild look, toting his large rucksack.

In halting Cordiaen, she said, "You slow."

Granite replied, "You sound like you've been living under a rock."

Her lower lip pushed forward. "I live under a rock, Granite. It's been four moon cycles since I speak."

"I'm proud of you. That's better than four rotations of the seasons."

"Not funny. Follow me."

Gossama led them to the other side of the tree, where an eight-foot panther lay dead. Three gashes had ripped open the dark-green flesh from the neck down the flank. The edges of the wounds were swollen with green drainage and mixed with blood.

Granite grimaced at the smell. "What did this? It wasn't what we just saw back there. I don't even know what that thing was."

"No. A vrent did this. Poisonous claws."

"A vrent? A lost one?"

"Lost one, yes."

Surely, she couldn't mean a real lost one? Uncle Eash had told stories of fighting monsters but that was south in Jetea.

Granite squatted down next to her. "You had told me stories about the lost ones from the forest. Is that what that big tree-looking thing was?"

"Barkbeast. Not just stories."

"How can this be? The SilverGate is closed. That is the only way for them to get out, right?"

Gossama replied, "No. That is the main gate. Not the only way. Vrent and barkbeast have come a different way."

"What do you mean SilverGate is not the only way?"

Gossama stood. "Two ways. First, lost ones can escape. Second, reyuul opens the way for them."

That was a real one.

Gossama pointed at the dead panther. "First time I've seen signs of a vrent in a long time. Why are you surprised? You fought lost ones when you were a Big Soldier."

"Yes, but those were different. Few humans have seen lost ones from the forest. I know I haven't."

Gossama picked up a wooden shovel tucked behind the oak. "These were once Dasari. All lost ones made a choice." She planted her shovel into the ground. "We bury this panther." She pointed to Pol. "They help."

Granite dropped his pack and unfastened a small shovel from the bottom. "Pull your shovels. Dasari usually won't mess with dead animals, but this one will be a priority to prevent anything from eating its contaminated flesh."

Everyone complied. Stefan balked but eventually pulled off his shovel and assisted.

Gossama nodded. "Hmm. Good help." She attacked the dirt with the shovel and asked, "Find the human family?"

"No. Two families are now missing, and a third was almost taken yesterday. We think a reyuul teleported another family into the forest."

"Teleported? Another family?"

"Yes."

Gossama scanned the trees. "A reyuul that teleports can open a gate for lost ones."

"All patrols failed to find the families. The forest is the only place we haven't checked."

"Reyuul. Yes. There's one here in the forest. Can't find him."

How could she know?

Granite asked, "How is that possible? You're Gossama. How can you not locate the reyuul?"

"There are some reyuul who can hide their presence, but it is difficult for them. Help me."

"Granite, how can Gossama know there's a reyuul in the forest?" Pol couldn't help himself.

"I have a gift," she replied solemnly.

Granite gave him a look that said, *Don't ask anything else.*

When the hole was completed, everyone except Stefan helped drag the carcass to the hole and refill it. Pol wondered if Gossama would have buried the panther by herself if they hadn't been there. She seemed quite capable of surviving on her own. Once they filled the hole, Gossama knelt for a moment with eyes closed. Granite joined her, and Pol didn't know what to do, so he bowed his head.

Gossama stood. "Thank you. I hunted more lost ones. Many west of here near RainCrest. No villagers, but RainCrest warriors wouldn't let me past the town."

"Nothing has changed, then," Granite replied.

"No. They hunted me. I must lie low for some time. It's your turn to hunt."

"Thank you for asking OakenRoot. He is kind."

"It was good he found out. Will you bring more little soldiers?" she asked.

"Yes. I'll teach them, and we'll patrol near the border."

Gossama folded her arms. "I cannot watch so many humans. I do not promise safety."

"I understand. I will guide them and approach from the north," Granite said. "I need another favor, Gossama."

"I'm already doing a favor looking for your lost humans; I hate favors."

Granite stepped back from the Dasari and pointed to Stefan and Pol. "I need you to train these young ones. I need them to learn from you as I did."

"Right now?" Gossama said, pointing to the trees. "With lost ones and reyuul?"

"Lie low for a few days. They need the forest. They need you. I'll make it up to you."

Gossama's star eyes narrowed. "Shovel, axe, and… sweets?"

Pol placed a hand over his mouth to keep from laughing out loud. She was bargaining?

"Wood?" Granite asked.

"Metal." With a flash in her eyes, Gossama added, "And I want chocolate."

"Do you know how hard it is to get chocolate?" Granite asked.

"Very busy…"

"Deal."

"Hmm. You really want this." She looked Pol and Stefan up and down. "Skinny and young. Can they run? Can they fight?"

Granite pointed to Pol. "He can keep up with you, but his Dasari is not very good." He pointed to Stefan. "He is slow and fat, but his mind is quick…very quick. You will need to keep an eye on him."

Stefan did not respond.

"I see." She held Stefan's eyes and studied him. "You understand?" she asked him in Dasari.

"Yes." He looked uncomfortable for the first time since Pol had met him.

Gossama returned to Cordiaen. "Yes, Granite. He is a shrewd one. I can see it in the eyes, and I can see mandra connected to all of you, but especially him." She turned to Pol and sized him up. "This one is strong. Do you understand me?"

"Little. Sorry," Pol said.

She returned to Cordiaen. "They will help each other. I understand why you want this, Granite. I accept."

"Thank you, Gossama. One week."

"Sure. If I need you, I will send a message."

"Understood. Thank you for taking the young ones. Try not to let them die, please."

"No promises. Forest is forest."

"Forest is forest," he replied.

Granite addressed the boys. "She is your instructor. If you want to live, do what she says and do it quickly. You'll both have challenges. Help each other."

"Yes, sir." Pol saluted.

As Granite left with the soldiers, Stefan replied, "Want to live?"

CHAPTER 17

"Fey and neraida are inherently different. The neraida were created to sculpt MidRealm. Lohem created fey to shepherd the FeyRealm beyond the Veil. Both are dangerous enemies and valuable allies."

–Cleric Joern. Advanced Cordiaen Military Tactics, Volume 2.

Stefan had trouble processing everything that had just happened. Lost ones? The forest was already an alien environment with silver trees, snagging roots, and a dark canopy, but the exhaustion, the running, the demanding Dasari, and the monster tree almost pushed him to the edge.

"Leaving home is a scary adventure, isn't it, human?" The sonorous high-pitched voice made Stefan's head snap around. It was not inside his head.

Gossama and Pol also whipped around to find the pink fey floating before them. Pol pointed, and with a confused expression, said, "Is that a lost one, too?"

"If you weren't Pol, the Conqueror, I would take offense, but no, I'm not a lost one," Quig replied.

Conqueror? Pol hadn't conquered anything.

Gossama said, "Youngling, it's a fey. I've seen some before, but this one is not familiar."

"Dragon's Bane, Scourge of Mandrates, Savior of the Hill Towns, Wielder of the Orange Arrow. Gossama of the Dasari, it is an honor," Quig said, dipping its head.

Gossama dipped her head in return. "They fey watch beyond the Veil."

Pol whispered. "A fey? From beyond the Veil?"

Stefan could not understand what was happening. "Quig, what's going on? How can they hear you?"

"Because I revealed myself. You're supposed to be intelligent." Quig swam around Gossama once. "Beware of that one, Dasari. He has secrets. I had to fix my village, but now I've returned to keep an eye on him."

The fey was not going to reveal his encounter with Fenric?

Gossama gave Stefan a side glance. "A fey PeaceKeeper left its home, crossed the Veil, and is determined to watch you?" She cocked her head. "Granite was right."

Stefan maybe had underestimated the fey.

Gossama's eyes smiled even though her mouth did not as she gave Stefan a firm stare. "When I run, you run. I stop, you stop. I give order, do it. Now, take packs off and roll on the ground."

Pol shot her and the fey a bewildered look, but he dropped his pack and began rolling on the ground.

Stefan shook his head. "You're just doing this to get us to obey."

"Yep. He's that stubborn," Quig added.

"I'm not going to make you." She pointed to Pol. "You. Stop. Get up."

Pol picked up his pack and secured it.

"Run." She took off at a sprint. Pol flew after her. Alarmed, Stefan threw on his heavy pack and ran. A tinge of anxiety sparked when he realized how much faster they were.

"This will be good for you," the fey said.

Stefan did not have the breath to argue as he sprinted. Gossama got farther away and then turned right into the trees, Pol following a second after and disappearing into the trees. When Stefan finally reached where he thought they had turned, he skidded to a stop. He couldn't see them. Concerned, Stefan scanned the trees and the brush. Where did they go?

Something hard hit his head from above. Quig laughed. A silver seedpod fell to the ground at his feet. Looking up, Stefan found a disappointed-looking Gossama.

"You are fat and slow. Climb now."

"Why?"

Quig produced a high-pitched vicious laugh, and Pol's lower jaw dropped. Gossama pointed behind Stefan.

A huge brown bear was barreling toward him. The enormous paws beat the ground, and a row of spikes formed a studded line down his head and back. Stefan panicked, ran to the nearest tree, and tried to climb. He could not reach the lower limb.

"Too bad you can't fly," Quig quipped.

Stefan ran to another tree, which did not have any limbs. He kept running and then turning as he heard the bear's paws galloping behind him. Maybe if he turned enough around trees, he could lose the bear.

He stepped around a large trunk to come face-to-face with the bear. The horrific maw snapped shut, removing a small chunk of his uplifted left forearm.

The hovering fey remarked, "That's going to hurt."

Screaming, Stefan pulled his arm back and fell backward. As the bear chomped on its morsel, Stefan dropped his pack and scrambled back to his feet, grabbing his bleeding arm. He raced to a nearby tree with a limb low enough to grab. Sheer terror provided the strength needed to haul himself onto the limb. Finding other limbs, he continued climbing and forcing his breath to be silent at about ten feet up.

"I see you."

Stefan was quite done with the flying axolotl.

The bear padded its way to his tree, sniffing as he went. It stood up on its legs, and with deft movements, the bear climbed the tree. Stefan looked around and spotted a nearby tree he could transfer to.

"Gonna try flying?"

With fear overriding reason, he walked along the tree limb, which dipped precariously before he jumped to the next tree. He missed the intended limb, but his hands caught another a few feet down. His hands seared from the unaccustomed weight, and he felt skin tear on his palms. The momentum flung his body into the trunk, with his pelvis taking the brunt of the impact, and then he landed on his back. With tears in his eyes, he hefted himself up.

"Not going to make it as a fey, I tell you."

The bear roared and attempted to walk out on its limb, but the branch dipped down, and the beast backed up. After climbing down, the bear padded around the base of Stefan's tree. Just before the bear began climbing again, a hand-sized leather pouch burst open as it hit the bear's face.

A small cloud of orange dust mushroomed from the pouch, and the bear pawed at its face and whined. After a few more swipes at its own face, it roared again and ran away, moaning. Gossama dropped onto the branch next to Stefan, whipped out a small green bandage, and quickly wrapped his arm.

"Obey and you will live. Next time roll on the ground. You do not smell like the forest. Mandra clings to you. The bear thinks you are the enemy. It guards the forest. Good jumping, though." She looked down the trunk. "Follow."

She jumped to a lower branch and then grabbed the lowest with her hands as she swung down. In his leather boots, Stefan doubted he could jump to the next branch, but the thought of using his hands to climb down made him groan. When he jumped to the next lower branch, his feet slipped, his butt hit the branch, and he tumbled backward. His stomach slammed into the lowest branch before he flipped to the ground and landed on his back. With the wind knocked out of him, he fought for his breath.

"And that is why humans should not climb trees," Quig announced.

Holding Stefan's pack, Pol gave the fey a confused look before assisting Stefan to his feet. "We have to keep up. Come on."

All Stefan could do was nod.

Pol half carried him for what felt like hours. On the way, they hid in bushes, climbed trees, and sprinted whenever Gossama commanded. She finally stopped at a large formation of boulders, stepped around the rocks, and then disappeared. Stefan hobbled to follow and found a hole between boulders.

"Come down," he heard Gossama command.

Taking a deep breath, he slid down the hole.

A short and rapid descent dropped him into darkness on his rear. The landing jarred his injuries to a new level of pain. Gossama tore something that sounded like fabric in the dark. After a moment, a faint light-blue glow emanated from a small bowl that hung from the low ceiling. Gossama continued to rub a blue-and-green plant together and place them in a fresh bowl. She hung the bowls on hooks anchored in the ceiling. Stefan could barely see, but with each minute, he could discern more and found himself in a small cave.

"Now this is more like it," the fey said, appearing near Stefan. "All the amenities you could ask for. What a great vacation spot."

"You are welcome anytime," Gossama said.

"Coming down!" Pol called out.

Stefan scooted his exhausted body along the floor, away from the entrance. Each movement shot pain through his ribs, and he could not take a deep breath without shooting pain. Between the throbbing pain in his stomach and the spasms in his lower back, Stefan could not find a comfortable position. Blood seeped from his right forearm bandage, and he recognized hunger, but fatigue and pain outweighed any other bodily concerns.

Pol slid down next to him and examined the surroundings upon landing.

Gossama pushed Pol out of the way and forcibly examined Stefan, who winced and held back cries as she poked and prodded. "Ribs broken. Must land on both feet." She mercilessly unwrapped the bandage over his forearm. "Just flesh, no muscle."

Gossama grabbed his wrist and hauled him over to the wall. How a small neraida had the strength to move a larger human made him wonder. A small rivulet of water, tinted blue and green from the cavern light, ran down the stone wall and through an embedded stone canal. The canal drained into a small pool but did not overflow.

Gossama took some unknown plants and a handful of water, crushing them. She mashed the wet mass together before slapping it on his forearm. Stefan bit his lower lip but did not cry out. She repeated the steps and slapped the poultice to his lacerated hands and bruised ribs before wrapping a bandage over each.

"Drink."

Stefan scooped the cool water into his mouth, allowing it to run down his chin. He could not believe it tasted so good.

Gossama pointed to the ground. "Lay down. Rest. Don't die."

He eased himself to the ground, wincing with every movement.

"Shrewd One, forest is forest. Has many dangers. You must learn quickly."

He wanted to cry.

Gossama glanced at Quig. "Yes, he deserves it, but don't push too hard."

Quig appeared chastised. "I understand, Dragon's Bane."

"Fey, neraida, and lost ones. This is another world," Pol said.

"No, this is home," Gossama said.

A painful home. Stefan attempted to get comfortable on the ground without success.

"I remember bedtime stories about the fey, but where do lost ones come from?" Pol asked.

Gossama said, "Lost ones are reyuul that could not ascend."

"Abominations," Quig added.

Pol gave Gossama a strange look. Gossama explained, "When reyuul reach a certain point, they must transform.

Must have strength and will to ascend. Ascend to their ultimate form. For some, a dragon. But dragon is not the only ultimate form. If reyuul don't have what they need to ascend, they descend into a lost one. Dasari lost ones descend to vrent, barkbeasts, and iveys."

Even through the haze of fatigue and pain, Stefan absorbed her answer, which was actually a useful confirmation of something he had read.

"Jonta…do they still have their minds?" Pol asked.

"No, minds fail. They become wild. Serve reyuul."

"They don't have a choice?" Stefan asked, ignoring the pain.

"No. Mandra transforms the reyuul. Deformed inside and out."

Quig said, "Mmm-hmm," while swimming above Stefan, looking down at him.

Stefan ignored the fey, but the truth in her words hit hard.

Pol rubbed his hands together. "How do you kill them?"

Gossama tilted her head at Pol. "Were your ancestors Dasari?"

Pol answered, "No. Vroshen. Why?"

"Ahhh. Sleep now. Tomorrow, learn to climb trees—without falling. I leave for a while. Quig, you watch?"

"Of course."

"Stay." She scurried back up the tunnel entrance.

The pain made Stefan want to cry, but it hurt to do anything.

Pol knelt down next to him and said, "Maybe you should do what she says next time."

Stefan's anger flared for a moment and he allowed it to show in his eyes before drowning in the pain from his arm, side, back, and stomach. Pol retreated to the far end of the cave.

"The Conqueror is right. The correct path lies within obedience, human."

Stefan ignored the fey and lay still in agony, doubting he would sleep. As he lay there staring at the cavern ceiling, bathed in a strange luminescent green glow, it finally hit.

He had lost it. He had completely lost any control he had over his life, and he could not do anything about it.

The horrible forest had removed him from any semblance of civilization—or anything—he knew. At least the garrison had a cot instead of an uneven stone floor that exacerbated his injuries. Tears threatened to form, but Stefan refused to cry. Weaklings cried.

Instead, his thoughts returned to Fenric.

Master Joern was a controversial author in Cordiae as a cleric discussing reyuul powers in his texts, but he claimed that if strategists did not take the enemies' powers into account, how could they effectively counter them? Having read those texts, Stefan had learned of the reyuul. Elemental powers, teleportation, enchantment, telekinesis, barrier, and other types were mentioned and did not even include the possibilities of combining certain disciplines. He could have teleported away from the bear, enchanted the bear, or even used the elemental disciplines to attack or kill the bear.

A cough to clear his throat wracked his body with pain.

But Cordiaen education had drilled the consequences into his head for years. To use their power, reyuul channeled mandra, which corrupted their souls and deformed their bodies, but the power they wielded…

What would happen when he met Fenric again? The reyuul had said they would meet again in the forest, which had intrigued Stefan enough to come. As he had done many times, Stefan considered what kind of future he wanted. His father had made it clear that he would not allow his children to freeload. Other quons provided their children with economic opportunities, but Quon Daoringer insisted his children make opportunities for themselves. His brothers had taken positions as merchants, landlords, or worked for their father in some capacity.

Stefan had always dreamed of leaving Dael and becoming independent of his father. Mercantilism was his passion, but the King's Army could also give him independence. But mandra? What Gossama said confirmed what he had read. Mandra had its costs. Were the costs worth it? Would he end up a mindless monster or a raging dragon? He worried about both ends until fatigue overruled his brain, and he fell asleep.

CHAPTER 18

"Leverage: Find it. Exploit it."

*– ArchMandrate Koen, Ampestria. Journal of
Mandrate Recruitment, Volume 1873, Issue 10.*

Geraul could not stand after Broken Nose's last beating a few hours before. There had been no reason. He laid on his back, staring at the cell ceiling, and taking solace in the muted drops managed by his wooden device.

Even with Dural providing an actual meal every day, Geraul was so weak he couldn't move. Dural would not arrive till later, and he would likely treat Geraul's wounds as he had done before. The kind guard had never asked for anything, but the attention confused Geraul, who had stopped rejecting the guard's considerate service.

No one could do anything for him now. He couldn't even cough for fear of the pain from the beating. Helpless, Geraul's anger quickly welled up again. The injustice of his situation haunted him and weighed upon him. The brat, Stefan, should be in here receiving beatings, not him. The anger, the beatings, and the hopelessness had firmly drowned the concerns regarding his soul. All the Cordiaen teachings of Lohem could not save him, protect him, or free him. Not even Duval's kind acts could detract from the oppressive despair consuming his heart. Mandra was the only means of salvation.

"My life here no longer has meaning. I will create meaning with power."

"I've been waiting to hear you say that," Stacia responded as she materialized near the door.

He turned to look at her. "I might have said it sooner if I had known that you'd be back sooner." Her light-brown skin, mistaken for a commoner's complexion, shone on her lower legs and arms. Geraul found Stacia very attractive. That reminded him. "I've thought about it, and I can't understand why you are not deformed by the power you use. Why do you look so good?"

"I can show you one day if you'd like."

Geraul returned to looking up at the familiar ceiling. "I'd like that, but I'd like it better if I could get out of this cell."

"You can get out of the cell whenever you want. You just have to get yourself out," she said.

"Now, how do I go about doing something like that?"

Stacia held a slip of paper over his face. The writing was Ampestrian.

Geraul frowned. "I don't speak Ampestrian."

"You will learn. Cordiaen has anti-mandra properties weaved throughout the language. You must use Ampestrian if you want to do anything worthwhile. If you want to leave, you will learn here in secret and away from the influence of the Point."

Geraul stared at her. "What do you want in return? What do you want of me?"

"An Ampestrian noble willing to learn mandra. I have needs, and that's all you need to know. If you progress, then we will talk. Until then, shall we begin the lesson?"

Geraul glanced at the ceiling and then back at the slip of paper. This was his ticket to freedom and surpassing the nobles. He would pay the price.

"Yes. Teach me."

⁓⁓⁓

Immersed in the black night, Fenric used his elemental mandra, attuned to the teresan, or ground, to monitor the surrounding forest, scanning with enhanced senses and registering minute changes through the ground. The forest held enough dangers, but the expected Dasari were to be feared for many reasons. He couldn't be sure they would not lay a trap for him.

A mandrate, a user of mandra, had not made contact with the Dasari in over a century. With tensions still present between the forest neraida and Cordiae, his superiors desired a connection with the neraida nation.

Fenric pulled his cowl further over his head as a reflex, attempting to hide his deformed features. In the absence of light, the useless gesture still made him feel better. Dasari tended to be more hostile to mandra users than Cordiaens, and he didn't want to provoke a hostile reaction. The Ampestrian High Council, his country's governing body, made it quite clear that he should establish a rapport with the neraida and not alienate them.

When ten Dasari suddenly appeared in a circle around him, Fenric snickered. The forest neraida had no qualms about alienating him.

"I know you're there. I am called Fenric," he said in coarse Dasari. RainCrest, the northernmost Dasari city, was over ten miles to the west, and he wasn't worried about other non-mandrates spying on them. After examining the surrounding Dasari with his senses, Fenric mentally reviewed his numerous escape plans if negotiations deteriorated.

Before him, a bluish-green glow blossomed from a pouch held by a Dasari. Fenric couldn't discern the Dasari's skin color in the blue light, but an intense, though patient, face reflected the faint light.

The neraida wasn't an elder, but he still had the look of experience. "There hasn't been a reyuul in the forest for many cycles. Many here would reject your presence, but Leader MistFall was intrigued by your offer."

"I'm pleased to have something to offer the leader and your community."

"How do you see us, reyuul?"

"Ah, I have ways. Is Leader MistFall here? Who are you?"

"You do not need to know our names, nor would we willingly hand over such power to one such as you." The group stepped in closer as one. "I speak for Leader MistFall. I will hear your words."

Fenric snorted. "Such as me? I simply offer assistance." He pointed to a woven basket on the ground before him, which held fruits and baked bread. "This gift is for your leader. I can provide more once I talk with him. I must discuss an important matter with him. I'm well aware of the difficulties your community faces."

A deeper voice with accustomed authority spoke from behind him. "Speak, then. How do you know our difficulties?"

Fenric turned to face the speaker, who lit his own pouch and tilted up his chin.

"Leader MistFall." He made a small bow. "Pleasure to meet you. To answer your question: a mandrate has many gifts to learn about the world. What's important is that your people are starving, and it's not your fault. Ampestria seeks to help Miraden."

"I see that you've not gone to OakenRoot," the leader said.

"Of course not. This is the first step in altering Dasari perception of mandrates. I hide nothing. OakenRoot has a strong dislike for my kind."

Leader MistFall grunted. "What do you want in return for this gift of food?"

"I'd like to finish some…research…in your forest. I'd appreciate it if your warriors gave me time and distance to do my work. That's all."

Leader MistFall paused, and Fenric cautiously prepared to fight if necessary, holding on to his invisible mandra.

"We've had sightings of lost ones around the city. Would you be responsible for them?"

"Lost one's escape in Miraden regularly, Leader. It's not fair to blame me for natural occurrences. I expected your question, but it's not polite."

Leader MistFall folded his arms. "I see." Another Dasari spoke, but the leader cut him off with a barking command. Seems not everyone was open to a mandrate's assistance. "I agree to your terms."

Fenric smiled under his cowl. "Tomorrow morning, you will find the first shipment in your storage building."

"You will not be permitted inside the city, reyuul." The finality in his voice confirmed the leader's true opinion, and Fenric silently chuckled again because leaders still had to feed their flock. "I will not need to be there. The supplies will appear without me."

"We shall see."

Fenric said, "One more thing, Leader. The Tainted One must also be kept away. That one cannot be reasoned with."

Leader MistFall replied, "If you deliver, I will ensure the Tainted One is barred from the area. If you lie, then I will find you."

The ring of Dasari closed a step closer, and Fenric short ported outside of the circle right behind the leader. "I'm here to help you, Leader. No need for threats." With a series of short portations, Fenric put a mile between him and the Dasari. That went better than expected, and he confirmed the Tainted One roamed the forest. While he used a technique to specifically hide from her, he would need to be careful.

CHAPTER 19

"Pride is the impenetrable barrier to victory for a Cordiaen Commander."

–Cleric Joern, Advanced Cordiaen Military Tactics, Volume 2.

Five days after arriving in Miraden, exhilaration overruled fear as Pol leapt from one silver branch to another. Silverwood…more firm than oak branches. The arms of the silver trees flowed in undulating patterns, providing a highway through the canopy. The freedom of jumping and running from one branch to the next overrode the fear of arcing high over the forest floor.

Pol couldn't keep pace with Gossama and had to stop frequently to catch his breath, but his smile never faded. Even after two falls where Gossama had either caught him or guided his crash, Pol's excitement about the forest canopy would not be diminished. Each day he grew in confidence and found that he could leap a little farther with a single stride, but he silently admitted that he relished the adrenaline rush, wondering if he would stick the landing and maintain his footing.

Gossama appeared and matched his stride as he traveled through the canopy. She ran everywhere. When asked, she had said, "A ranger should be faster than the forest." Pol admitted to himself that he was a little enamored with the female Dasari. Her skill with weapons, survival ability, and honesty, coupled with her blue eyes and star-shaped pupils, made Gossama attractive. He even appreciated the beauty of her leaf-patterns covering her brown skin that glistened like bronze. The red dragon claw mark on her left neck intrigued him as it looked more like a tattoo, but he didn't feel comfortable or confident enough to ask about it. Pol didn't mind that she was almost two feet shorter, but the two-hundred-year age difference made him think of his grandmother, and he couldn't get past that. Besides, he still had hope for Adeel.

Pol couldn't help contrasting the Dasari to Adeel. Even though Gossama might not have ridden in a carriage, she would have destroyed the assassin, Anvil, in Dael. It probably wasn't fair to compare a fifteen-year-old noblewoman to a two-hundred-and fifty-year-old Dasari ranger, but Adeel's genteel behavior, noble heritage, and perfect brown complexion were almost as foreign to him as the Dasari's features.

As they leapt from branch to branch, Gossama called out to him, "You are strange, youngling. Humans don't learn to travel the canopy as quickly as you. And the smile?"

Breathing hard, Pol stopped at the next tree and placed a hand on a silver trunk. He instinctively examined his palm, always wondering if any silver would rub off, but it never did.

"Never claimed to be normal," he replied between breaths. He wasn't sure how he sounded to Gossama in his broken Dasari, but she never belittled him. Pol did not think he needed to explain his heritage to Gossama, but he wasn't surprised how she recognized his abilities.

"I see. Let us wait for Shrewd One."

Pol experienced a twinge of regret at the other boy, who wore a slightly panicked expression whenever he fell behind. Stefan held his ribs as he jogged into view a few moments later with the elemental fey in tow. The disgraced qual refused to travel through the canopy since his first day, doing his best on the ground and constantly vigilant for any animals.

The fey, which followed Stefan, was a complete mystery to Pol. Quig, as it called itself, had not spoken much to Pol, but it had been very pleasant. Of course, the fey was cute, swimming around with its light-pink tail, little legs, and electric blue, fluffy appendages around its head. Pol especially liked the blue lightning, which occasionally flowed along the axolotl's body. Gossama had treated the visitor from across the Veil with familiarity but had made it clear that the fey's presence spoke of ominous events. Of course, Pol couldn't help but laugh as the fey berated Stefan for lagging behind, but Stefan must be in serious trouble for the alien fey to accompany him.

Gossama called down, "Come up, Shrewd One."

Pol estimated they were ten miles away from Gossama's cave, which took them a little farther than the day before. Gossama was pushing their endurance each day.

Stefan slowly climbed the silver tree, grunting and cursing under his breath, which Pol could easily hear. Stefan had become better at climbing, but his injuries were significant enough that Pol felt a little compassionate for him. A little.

Sweating, hunched over, and flushed, Stefan said, "Why did you call me up here? Is there trouble?"

"Only you," Quig interjected as it swam around the branches.

"Good job obeying. No danger. It's time to learn," Gossama replied.

Stefan groaned. "We've spent days learning about gardening, herbs, iveys, barkbeasts, vrents, other lost ones, and even sewing. What now?"

"Simple training." She removed her bow and quiver and hung them on a branch. Pol noticed some arrows differed from the others, larger with blue fletching.

"Gossama, why are those arrows blue?" Pol asked.

Gossama reached into her quiver and removed one arrow. The wooden shaft ended in a sharp head with a blue metallic sheen reflecting the daylight.

"Bluesteel," Gossama said.

"Bluesteel?" Pol asked.

"Yes. Only found in Miraden."

Stefan said, "It's very rare."

"Yes, very rare. I received the arrows from Petra. Special mission." Petra were neraida from the mountains.

Stefan said, "Must have been a really special mission."

"Shrewd One, don't push."

"What's special about bluesteel?" Pol asked. He wondered if it was similar to whitesteel. He knew little about whitesteel except that the voltai, or Cordiaen holy warriors, wore plate armor made from the white metal.

"Bluesteel works against reyuul. Mandra won't affect it." She returned the arrow back to her quiver. "Very good at killing reyuul."

Stefan said, "That's why voltai wear whitesteel armor. Mandra has no effect on it, but the whitesteel armor also has an area of effect."

Gossama nodded. "Bluesteel only works on what it touches. Always reliable."

Quig had been hopping around as if wanting to speak and finally said, "It's one of the few metals that can kill fey—I mean dark fey. I know you wouldn't kill me."

Gossama nodded. "Yes, ancient Dasari used bluesteel weapons to drive the dark fey back beyond the Veil." She looked up at Quig. "Still don't get many fey here."

"Wouldn't be here without good reason and special permission." Quig looked pointedly at Stefan. "But Miraden Forest has been a bastion of strength against the DreadKing." The fey tilted toward Pol and said, "That's why our little community lives close to Miraden. We're allies."

"This DreadKing sounds like a problem," Pol said.

"See, Stefan. He cares. Yes, the DreadKing and his minions feed off humanity's depravity. Gaodis is small, and the humans are virtuous but not perfect. As long as we don't attract attention, the dark fey won't be interested, but with a mandrate invasion and this human's troublemaking, storms have erupted. We hope the DreadKing hasn't noticed."

"A tenedrae wouldn't lift the Veil for something small. This is bigger than us," Gossama said.

Pol glanced at Stefan, who said, "We never see Pascal, the Cordiaen tenedrae, except at Festival. If this is so important, why isn't he here?"

Gossama replied, "You could not understand the responsibility he has. There are very few tenedrae and thousands of problems throughout Cordiae and Miraden. We have to do our best."

Pol took the hint, but what about Stefan? How was he involved that required Quig's presence?

Gossama didn't look like she wanted more conversation. "Let's begin." She pulled a pack of silver leaves from beneath her muddy brown cloak and removed them one by one, slapping three leaves on Pol's tunic in various spots and three more on Stefan. She placed two leaves on her tunic over her abdomen and handed another leaf to Pol. "Hold the stem and place it on my back."

She turned around, and Pol placed it on her cloak. When he finished, he rubbed his fingers together, noting a sticky substance. He sniffed it. "Honey?"

Gossama's lopsided grin made it clear she didn't use that facial expression often. "Yes, nails would hurt." She pointed to his leaves. "Let's play. Take my leaves, and I try to take yours. You can run, hide, and fight, but no weapons."

"Oh, can I play too?" Quig asked.

Gossama gave the fey a withered look.

Stefan examined the leaves. "We have to take all three?"

"No. Take one of mine. I will take all three from you."

"This isn't fair," Stefan said. "Why are we doing this?"

"Because Granite said you need to learn to work together. So work together."

"When do we start?" Pol asked.

Gossama gave her irregular lopsided smile and walked into the silver tree. She didn't stop, and the tree didn't open. To Pol, it seemed like she had melted into the tree. Stefan pointed, speechless. Quig laughed at their reactions. Pol blinked a few times but remembered they were training. "How do you want to do this?" he asked Stefan.

Stefan drew himself up and pointed away from the tree. "Run that way."

Pol hesitated against the command, intentionally fighting back the angry flames that sprung up in his soul. He was going to be the bait while Stefan took the leaves, but Gossama was too fast for Stefan. Everything in his head screamed to not let the ungrateful noble have his way, but his goals were more important.

Resigned, Pol bolted along the thick branch away from the trunk and just before he leapt to the next branch, Gossama rose from the silverwood before him. Pol couldn't change his trajectory, and she sidestepped, picking a leaf from him. Pol launched himself and landed on the next tree branch and continued running. Again, before he could react, Gossama rose from the branch. This time, Pol tried to block, but she stole the remaining leaves with quick hands.

"You lose," she said before turning back to Stefan. When she sank into the silverwood, Pol shook his head and blinked again. Stefan hadn't moved, but his eyes had narrowed in Pol's direction.

Stefan had been observing.

"You have no chance," Quig said lazily floating above their heads.

Stefan crouched slightly and closed his eyes. Pol wondered if Stefan had given up, but when Gossama stepped out of the trunk behind him, he already whirled on her with a wild fist, but she dodged and stole one of his leaves from his shirt. Gossama dropped back into the branch, but Stefan didn't run. Instead, he spread his legs farther apart, crouched, and closed his eyes again. Pol didn't understand Stefan's strategy, but he assumed Stefan didn't feel comfortable moving around the canopy and remained still.

From his angle, Pol watched as Gossama shot up from the branch behind Stefan, who sprang into action as if anticipating Gossama's presence. Stefan swept his leg backward, but Gossama leapt over his leg.

In midair, Gossama snatched another leaf from his back, but Stefan had rotated after his leg sweep and faced Gossama. She pushed his hand away, attempting to grab a leaf, but in midair it turned her around. Stefan almost snatched the leaf on her back before she landed but missed.

Gossama snatched his last leaf.

"You tried. I'll give you that," Quig commented.

Gossama clicked her tongue. "Not bad, Shrewd One."

Pol called out, "How did you do that, Stefan?"

Stefan looked frustrated. "I wasn't going to run, and I couldn't fight a legend, but I could tell when she was moving through the wood."

Pol leapt back to the branch they were on, and he asked, "How could you tell?"

"The wood vibrates slightly. I had to be quiet, but I could feel it."

Gossama said, "You swept your leg, but you knew I would jump and block your attack."

Stefan nodded. "I planned out the movements."

Pol couldn't believe it. "But that means you would have had to plan four movements ahead. How?"

Stefan was about to say something and stopped himself. Instead, he replied, "I practice."

Pol said, "You were going to say 'I'm a genius.' "

Stefan turned to find Quig right in front of his face. He fell backward, surprised. "So, you *can* do the right thing."

Stefan rolled his eyes and caught himself from falling off the limb.

Gossama said, "Hmm. Controlling your mouth is good, but you sacrificed Youngling to save yourself. Youngling served Shrewd One and obeyed."

Stefan stood. "I needed information. I didn't know your capabilities."

"That is fine, but Youngling is not wood to burn. He is your sword. Don't throw away your sword." She faced Pol. "Youngling, your fire went out."

"What are you talking about?" Pol asked, wondering if she could see inside his soul.

"The fire in your eyes. You squashed it."

Pol looked down at the limb. "Oh. I'm trying to control my anger."

"That fire is not your anger. It responds to your anger. That fire within you is something else. When else do you have it?"

Pol closed his eyes and reflected. There were many times when he had noticed the fire in his soul. "When I fight, when Adeel was in trouble, and sometimes when I'm at the Point, but most of all when I'm angry."

Quig's little feet rubbed together. "I can't believe I get to see this. The others will be so jealous."

Gossama ignored the fey. "Hmm. What is justice, Youngling?"

Pol strained to remember his lessons. " 'To give each and all what belongs to them.' "

"Excellent. This is the core, the heart, of your fire, not anger. Whether you protect, serve, or—what is the word?—avenge, yes. When you do these things, let the fire build. The fire is a gift."

Her words made sense to him as if a sword locked perfectly into a scabbard made for it. "How do you know this?"

"Because she's Gossama, the Dasari," Quig intoned.

"No. Youngling, I had the same problem. Had to learn I'm not evil. Had to learn to use my gift."

"You are not evil," Pol said.

"I know. At one time, I doubted. Lohem—Dasari call him DarVida—guided me." She folded her arms. "Go ahead. Try it."

Pol closed his eyes and focused on the always-present embers within his soul.

Crimson embers burned. Thoughts of Stefan flared the red coals. Pol suppressed Stefan's image and replaced it with villagers. *I want to serve Cordiae.* The crimson embers burned brighter. That's not what he wanted. *I want to protect the villagers.* He focused on protection. The crimson faded, and so did the embers. "I'm not sure I understand. The fire went out."

"Not based on feelings. Emotions rise and fall like the breeze through the forest. Commitment should not waver. Link the fire to the things you said."

Pol nodded. That was in line with Uncle Eash's letter. Intention was more consistent than feelings. That made sense.

Light-blue electricity flared around Quig, with ripples of dark pink flowing across the fey's skin. "I want to fight now. Let me fight."

Stefan stood, remaining silent.

Gossama replaced the leaves on Stefan and Pol. "Again."

They spent the rest of the afternoon failing repeatedly, with Pol still following Stefan's directions at a distance, but Pol couldn't beat Gossama one-to-one. Every time Pol had been taken out, Stefan fell soon after. Pol improved his reaction speed and maintained the whisper of a flame, but Gossama was too quick. Pol also was forced to admit how adept Stefan was. The young man adapted quickly and could easily predict Gossama, but he could do nothing about it.

Finally, after Gossama disappeared the twentieth time, Pol said, "Put your back against mine and tell me where and when."

Stefan didn't respond.

"Being far away is not working."

Stefan said, "I'm just tired and injured."

"Then, let me do it."

Quig watched them from behind a branch.

"Fine." Stefan placed his back against Pol's, and they waited. With Stefan right there, willing to cooperate, and needing "protection," the embers in his soul flickered with a pale light instead of red. Pol tensed, ready to act.

"Above."

Pol pushed Stefan back as Gossama dropped, grabbing one of Pol's front leaves as she landed on the branch below them. She melded out of sight, and Pol readied himself again.

"Here," Stefan said.

Pol whipped around with an arm around Stefan's waist, swinging him out of Gossama's reach as she popped out of the branch. Gossama snagged the second leaf from Pol's back and disappeared again. They resumed their back-to-back stance.

"Duck."

Instead of crouching, Pol threw himself backward, forcing Stefan down as Gossama leapt over them. Pol snagged a leaf from her cloak before Stefan shifted, throwing Pol off the branch. Pol easily caught another branch just below them and hefted himself back up.

Quig snorted. "Finally. Only took you forever."

Gossama retrieved her equipment hanging from the tree. "The fey is correct. Could have done that quicker, but progress is progress."

The pale embers doused, but Pol was proud and spent. That had been hard. While Pol didn't appreciate being thrown from the limb, he said, "Good job, Stefan."

"Okay."

That seemed like all Pol was going to get.

Stefan turned to Gossama. "How do you do it? Enter the tree? You said you could sense mandra. Do you use mandra?"

Gossama regarded Stefan for a moment. "You are not Dasari. I forgive the question. Not mandra. I am neraida, created by Lohem from the beginning. Shrewd One should know our history."

Stefan responded in a practiced tone, as if reciting a lesson. " 'Made from the beginning, the first neraida were the assistants to form and shape the world.' "

Gossama bowed her head. "From the holy text. Ancestors helped Lohem shape the forests. I do not have that power. Leader OakenRoot does, but Dasari can meld with trees." Stefan had a thoughtful look, and Gossama studied his face. "Humans cannot meld with the tree. You did well to be quiet. This is the Dasari way, but you don't do it well."

"I'm not Dasari."

"No, but some Dasari think they are better than others. This is not true, and it hurts the community. They need each other." She pointed back and forth between Stefan and Pol. "You need him."

"I need him like I need another bear biting my arm."

Gossama shook her head slowly. "Quig, this is hard."

"Like regrowing a tail, but it has to be done," the fey replied. The fey and the Dasari understood something that Pol did not.

Stefan sat down on the branch, sulking.

Pol sighed. He could see the potential, but he could also see the obstacles that no one but Stefan could remove. Pol's uncle and father had counseled Pol many times to consider other people's circumstances before passing judgment. He remembered how everything had been stripped from Stefan and how Granite had asked him to help Stefan. Again, he held his tongue.

Instead, since Gossama had shared so much, he decided to try his luck. "Gossama, I want to ask…something." Pol hesitated. "Do other Dasari have a mark on their neck?"

Gossama turned on Pol. "Youngling, that's a human question. I forget you're human."

Pol flinched, but she took a deep breath and exhaled slowly. "Difficult to relive the past, but important to share." She leaned against the tree trunk. "My father was a reyuul."

What?

Gossama nodded. "Yes, a reyuul. Like Cordiaens, becoming reyuul is a death sentence among Dasari. My mother did not know at the time, as he hid his powers. She loved him and bore him a child. Neraida differ from humans. Consequences of his choice passed to me. Children of Dasari reyuul bear the mark." She put a hand to her neck and pointed to the red dragon claw visible on the left of her neck. "My soul is corrupted."

"Corrupted?" Pol blurted.

"Don't interrupt or I stop."

Pol sucked in his lips. Even Quig stopped cold.

Gossama explained, "My soul hungers for mandra. I always have. I smell mandra, and I feel it if I'm close. Mandra leaves a taste in my mouth too."

"Other Dasari judge you for the mark?" Stefan ventured.

"Yes, Shrewd One. A few years after I was born, my mother died. My father was nowhere to be found. I was raised by Petra, the giant neraida, in the mountains. No Dasari would take me." She paused, touching the mark. "I am not welcome by Dasari."

Inhaling, she continued, "The Petran leader paid Dasari to train me, and I received an education like the children of the Petran leader. I miss those mountains." Gossama narrowed her eyes. "About fifty years ago, my father left hiding. He had become a dragon. He hurt many Petra. I helped Petra drive him away. We wounded him but didn't kill him."

She held up her hand to Stefan, who had opened his mouth. He slowly closed it.

"Petran leader told the Dasari leader what I did. Leader OakenRoot welcomed me to SilverGate. Did not matter. No one wanted a marked Dasari in the city. Didn't matter if the marked Dasari had been brave." She lowered her eyes. "Leader needed help in the woods. I became a ranger. I love the forest very much, and I live here. That is that."

"Why don't you just hide your mark?" Stefan asked.

"Shrewd One, you don't know how Dasari feels the mark like I feel mandra."

"I see."

"No, you don't." She gave Stefan a direct look. "There are many Dasari who don't like me because of what my father did, but I have saved this forest many times. That is truth." She jabbed another finger into Stefan's chest. "You think of Youngling as less than you, but he submits to you, which makes him greater."

"Submission is weakness."

"Spoken like a reyuul."

Pol's eyes opened wide. Gossama didn't play.

Stefan sputtered for a moment. "I'm not a reyuul!"

Quig looked like he was going to burst but remained silent.

"You talk like one. I've met many reyuul, and all want to be the boss." She pointed at Pol. "Heroes serve others in little ways and big ways."

Gossama sounded like Uncle Eash.

"But heroes do it without hesitation." She wagged her finger at Pol.

Chastised, Pol knew Uncle Eash would say the same. Pol still had work to do, and Gossama's example would be good for him to control his inner fire and work with Stefan. It would take time.

As for now, Pol couldn't believe what she had revealed about her past. A child of a reyuul! She must have kept much to herself, but Pol was grateful for what she had shared and refrained from asking more questions. He could only imagine what she had endured.

CHAPTER 20

–Cleric Joern. Advanced Cordiaen Military Tactics, Volume 2.

*S*weat rolled down Fenric's black-scaled face as he focused mandra into carving a deeper hole. While the soil in Miraden was mostly dirt, the forest's proximity to the Andren Mountain range meant he had to excavate rocks as well. The deeper the hole, the easier it would be to extract the descended. The deep rumble halted once Fenric was satisfied with the depth.

The mission would be much easier with another mandrate, but the Ampestrian High Council demanded the threat level be as minimal as possible. Raising five vrent and a barkbeast had taken a month and forced him to wait days in between to recover. Fenric shuddered at the effort required to raise the barkbeast. He would not do that again.

With the extra descended, or lost ones as the Dasari preferred, Fenric feared arousing the tenedrae. The Realm Guardians did not wander the forest without a reason, but he knew it would be a matter of time. Fenric could handle the Tainted One, but a tenedrae, with their otherworldly power, could single-handedly ruin his entire plan. Thankfully, he had thus far escaped notice.

RainCrest continued to protect his small area of the forest, and he ensured they continued receiving food. Not enough to solve their problems, but enough to keep them wanting more. So many pieces to juggle, but the payoff wasn't far away. Soon, he wouldn't have to work so hard to raise the descended.

Fenric stood before the deep hole he had created and started forming intricate movements with his hands, his confidence having improved with previous success, as this feat could only be accomplished in an environment connected to the UnderRealm.

Drawing in mandra from his source, known as a well, Fenric funneled the power through his body with the prescribed patterns and into the hole and surrounding ground. Three hundred years of training in the teleportation arts had strengthened, though deformed, his body as massive torrents of power funneled through him. After a few minutes of cycling through the required ritual, sigils burst through the ground around the hole in luminescent red and orange outlines. Red light burst forth from the hole, and Fenric stepped back, physically drained but able to stand.

Slowly, a glowing and pulsating red mass of light ascended from the hole. White pinpoints of light coursed through the amorphous mass, with two orange slits appearing and then opening. The red mass thinned and swirled, condensing again and again until it formed a diamond shape. The ruby-red light became blinding for a second before the diamond-shaped light floated to the ground. How could anyone condemn such beauty?

Cordiaens were fools. Once the jewel touched the ground, the dirt, rocks, and nearby twigs coalesced into a short humanoid rising from the teresan.

Among the mandrates of Ampestria, no one had seen a lost ivey in centuries, as they were native to Miraden Dasari who had descended. The red diamond had centered itself in the chest, and the lost ivey opened its glowing orange eyes.

Fenric extended a thin tether of mandra to command the descended. "Come, we have a lordling to catch."

⌇

Between the residual pain and the stone floor, Stefan did not sleep well. He opened his eyes to the dwindling green luminescent light in the cave. For the last week, since they had arrived, Gossama's poultices had been doing a miraculous job, and his external wounds were almost healed.

His ribs concerned him. Each breath still induced soreness, and he worried some ribs had broken on his left side. Whenever Gossama changed the poultice, he breathed easier and could tell the difference. The bruises and soreness in his arms and legs had improved each day.

Suppressing a groan, Stefan sat up and winced. The others had not stirred. Quig produced a faint high-pitched snore and curled up next to a sleeping Pol. In the far corner, Gossama also slept, lying on her side facing them. The opportunity was too good to pass up.

Stefan stood but had to bend his neck under the low ceiling. Pol had to bend over, but Gossama, at five feet tall, could move freely in her home. Stefan crept as quietly as possible to the back of the cave to Gossama's quiver where he pulled out arrows and examined the heads. The third arrow he pulled had the color he searched for: a blue metallic sheen reflecting in the low light. The arrow felt lighter than the others.

Bluesteel. Created to fight reyuul, lost ones, and dark fairies, bluesteel-made weapons had forged the way for Dasari to retake Miraden Forest, according to his history texts. The fact that weapons had been created to fight reyuul meant the mandra users had weaknesses.

Stefan glanced at the sleeping Gossama. She had kept a close eye on him since his arrival, but she had not pressed him for information. Still, her accusation from their training stung.

Stefan returned the arrow and took a sip of water from the natural source on the wall. He conceded he had never tasted such pure water. Something so simple, so common, but so refined that the water at the King's Palace in Ariel would be inferior confounded Stefan.

Standing within the silent dark cave, he could not help but compare the pure cavern water to Pol, who also held refined qualities that should only be found in a fellow noble. Yet, as an elite Cordiaen, Stefan lacked similar quality in comparison.

Pol had been patient with him and had always offered to assist. Stefan wanted to be angry with Pol and his lack of stature, but his weak excuses did not hold up. Stefan still had plenty of reasons for being jealous of Pol's physical strength, height, abilities, and adaptability in the forest. Most of all, Hiuken, Granite, and Quon Daoringer had praised and acknowledged Pol. They had never done that for Stefan. Even the fey proclaimed Pol to be a hero, but for Stefan, nothing.

"So loud, Shrewd One." Gossama sat up and brushed her dark hair back with her hand. "I taught you how to be quiet." She got up and washed her face.

Pol sat up, flailing his arms for a second before rubbing his eyes. Quig just rolled over and continued with a light snore.

Stefan grimaced at her remark. Everyone always criticized him, but he did not want to reveal his thoughts and attempted redirection. "Just thinking about the reyuul. Any progress on his location?" Stefan hoped they all assumed Fenric was male. He did not want to give away any information.

"Almost. I'm finding patterns. How often he moves and where. Granite and his soldiers will investigate the north for me. I cannot go near RainCrest without good reason right now." When she saw Stefan's questioning glance, she said, "Leader MistFall does not like me," and pointed to the mark on her neck.

She really was an outcast.

"I hope the villagers are safe," Pol said.

"We will find them. Grab your packs. Big day." She rolled the elemental fey over with her soft leather boot. Quig's appendages flexed before the fey slowly rose from the ground. "It's illegal to wake a fey."

"No, it isn't," Gossama replied.

"It should be."

Gossama snorted and climbed up the cave tunnel to the surface.

Gossama expected Stefan to keep pace even with injuries. After six days, Stefan climbed out of the underground residence easier but still in pain. Once they were all out, Gossama started running. She ran everywhere. It was depressing.

After a quick stop to pluck hinkleberries, pecans, and silverberries, Gossama led them southeast. Stefan's growling stomach constantly reminded him he was not eating the quantity found in Dael Keep, but Pol seemed to relish whatever they found.

Pol and Gossama took to the canopy, and Stefan fumed at his own weakness. His conditioning had improved since leaving Dael, but he still feared jumping from branch to branch. The consequences of failure were too real. Keeping an eye on the two, who never ran too far ahead, Stefan maintained a steady pace for the next hour and a half.

Quig floated next to him. "Why haven't you told them about Fenric?"

"Do I have to? Would it make a difference?"

"Just concerned."

Stefan gave the fey a small amount of credit, as the creature had not snitched. "What? I'm nowhere near your home. I'm not causing trouble."

Waves of dark blue and pink flowed down the axolotl's body. "Maybe I'm concerned about you."

"Doubt that. You love Gossama and Pol."

"Jealous? They are special, but I did not leave my home for them. There is a cost to my being here. Very few in my community can manage emergencies."

"Then maybe you should go back if your community needs you so bad."

"You need me more! Don't you get it?" The fey's voice sounded sonorous even when raised.

Stefan slowed to a stop. "What are you talking about? I told you. I'm not looking for any trouble."

"Trouble comes looking for you! I'm here to help. Many fey have told me I'm crazy for talking to humans, and many more are worried that I've crossed the Veil."

"I didn't ask you to be here. Go back."

"Listen! When humans make bad decisions, it doesn't just affect this realm. Innocent fey suffer those consequences, but this time, this one time, I have permission to help. If keeping you out of trouble means saving my realm, why wouldn't I try?"

"So, you admit that you're doing this for yourself. You only care about me as long as it helps you." Stefan remembered Cyprian saying that to him.

"For someone so smart, your pride makes you stupid. I don't want you to fall or fail. I want you to fulfill your dreams. I just don't want you to lose yourself, and I'm not the only one."

Stefan wanted to believe the fey, but doubts clouded his heart. Without a good reply, he continued running. Did others care about him? Maybe, but where were they when he had needed help in the past? His mind roamed enough that he did not realize he had caught up to Gossama, who had returned to the forest floor, waiting.

"Where's Pol?"

"Practicing scouting," she replied.

Stefan caught movement amidst the leaves and found Pol returning and bounding from limb to limb through the canopy. Stefan didn't hear him make a sound except for some mild leaf rustling, which could have been mistaken for wind. Twenty-five yards away, Pol squatted on a branch.

Gossama asked in Dasari, "He is human, yes?"

"Of course." Stefan allowed the jealousy to boil. Pol always received the attention and the praise.

Wait.

Pol did not get all the attention. Fenric, the reyuul, had spoken to Stefan, not Pol. *I know what you want. I'm offering to help.* Stefan allowed himself to imagine what mandra might do for him here. With that kind of power, Stefan could teleport. He could do things that would make Pol's success seem like a child's. Stefan could ignore his father, leave the forest, and humiliate Pol. He would not have to be humiliated or weak.

Maybe mandra would not be so bad if it did not have all the consequences, but he really should learn how to move through the trees without hurting himself.

"Up the tree. Time to make the jump," Gossama said, as if reading his thoughts.

"Fine." He followed her up a tree, easier than a week before, but his side still ached.

Twenty feet up, she stopped, and he followed her onto a branch. She pointed to another one four feet away. "Don't die."

The cold reality of his injuries made him disregard any fantasy of flying to that branch, but he had a deep-seated fear of the height and the ground below. Still, he was resolved to do this. With a deep breath, he bent his knees and leapt. He landed on the branch and immediately flung his arm out to the trunk to steady himself. He needed to improve his balance, but it was progress.

"Like watching a bunny take its first hop," Quig said from over his shoulder.

Gossama and Pol joined him on the large silver branch. She patted him on the back. "Fat and slow and loud. Better at obeying, though."

Pol reported, "Good job, Stefan. Gossama, no lost ones or large animals nearby."

"Good. It's time to give you boys a chance to work together without me. You will stay in the forest tonight. Sleep in a tree. I go check on Granite. Tomorrow, return to the cave alive. I will meet you there in two days. Do not die. Quig, you're in charge."

"Excellent. I will make them suffer in your honor," the fey replied.

Without waiting, Gossama leapt from the branch and ran along a lower one before moving from one tree to the next like a squirrel.

It took Stefan a second to process what she had just said. A night in the forest? He looked down at the branch he sat upon. He imagined trying to lie down on it and then falling to the ground.

No.

Pol said, "I think we should find a better tree. Let me know when you're ready."

Stefan whirled on him. "Are you joking? Do you think I can sleep in a tree?"

"Why not?"

"Because I'm not falling to my death." Stefan stood. "I can't believe that I'd prefer to sleep on a cave floor."

"Cave floors are comfy," Quig said.

Pol cleared his throat to hide his laughter. "Sleeping on the forest floor is a death sentence with the bears, wolves, and panthers. We have rope to secure us onto a limb. It could be fun."

Stefan shot Pol a death glare. "I concede it might be safer in a tree, but that doesn't mean I want to."

"Let's find a better tree. We can head back west toward the cave."

Stefan grumbled but followed Pol down the trunk to the ground, and once on the ground, Pol took off running. Stefan threw up his arms. "Why are we running?"

Pol stopped. "It's what Gossama would want. What if she's watching?"

"She can watch me walk. If I have to sleep in a tree, I don't have to run."

Stefan heard Quig say to Pol, "Don't get angry. Get even. Walk real slow."

Stefan walked past them and kept going, not wanting an argument, but after a moment, he heard something drop.

Turning around, Stefan found Pol collapsed on the ground with Quig swimming anxiously above him.

"Pol?" Quig asked.

Above, an angry red line ripped through the air, and a gnarled purple hand shot out and seized Quig, who squealed as the hand dragged the fey through the Veil, which closed afterward.

Stefan cried out, "Quig!"

Before he could take a step, six clumps of grass, dirt, twigs, and vines rose from the ground between them, forming short humanoid figures. Gaping mouths with no other facial features greeted Stefan, though the farthest one had a glowing red diamond in its chest with bright-orange eyes.

As Stefan stepped back, a wavering tenor voice called out from behind a silverwood. "Ah. I wouldn't move, Stefan. Lost iveys and their brood are temperamental. They will paralyze you and then suck you into the ground to feast on you for the next week."

Stefan examined Pol, noting his chest rising and falling. His senses heightened, and he focused on details as Fenric continued, "That boy will be fine. He's just sleeping. The fey was interfering too much. I would like to talk with you now that Gossama has left, and I don't want you paralyzed."

Stefan was concerned about Pol and Quig but recognized he could do nothing for them now and had to play the game. "Let's talk."

The iveys in front backed away as Fenric approached. "I'm sorry I can't show you my home city of Caragal. The inner city is beautiful, with gleaming gold spires rising to the sky and surrounded by a wide river. I've seen your militaristic keeps; you would appreciate our breathtaking architecture."

Fenric pulled back his cowl. Large black scales had formed in patches over his face and hands. Bony protrusions were associated with the black scaly skin, resulting in a hideously deformed face. Gray skin immediately surrounded the black scales, but pale white skin framing blue-green eyes confirmed his Ampestrian heritage. His smile unnerved Stefan.

Stefan was curious. "Why can't we go to your city?"

"An inquisitive mind. So appealing. This particular forest is protected from outside teleportation, as is Cordiae. I had to travel here on foot. Quite tedious."

That means he had to travel south by Jetea or north around the Andren Mountains. Either way was a long trip. He had a purpose for being here. "But you can teleport within the forest?"

"Yes, yes. The barrier is only on the outside. Stop trying to interrogate me. I'm here for you."

A sales pitch. Stefan could handle that. "I'm listening."

"As I've said, I'm here to offer you a chance at something amazing. I would have visited sooner, but you keep dangerous company."

"Gossama?"

"Oh, yes. Her and the general. We've been keeping a close watch on those two. Quite dangerous. Gossama, daughter of Malvos, has been particularly lethal to reyuul, and the general ruined several orchestrated attacks on Jetea over the last two decades. But...I'm not here for them."

A teresan chair formed from the ground. Stefan tried to keep his eyes from widening, but he stepped back. Fenric sat down slowly. "Excuse me. When you're five hundred, you tend to move a little more carefully."

That caught Stefan off guard. "Five hundred? How's that possible? You're not Dasari."

"Mandra can do anything, Stefan. Anything. I'm so sorry that you don't know that. In Ampestria, children are taught to respect mandrates from a young age."

"What's your interest in me?"

"So impatient. It's all about what you want from me. I'm here on a dual mission. One goal was to talk with you."

There was another goal, but Stefan needed to tread cautiously. "You must have been in the forest before I arrived. How did you know I would end up here?"

"You definitely fit the mold. Good questions and quick mind." Fenric leaned back, trying to get comfortable. "The Ampestrian High Council can divine the future. It's not like fey or your Cordiaen prophecies. We can pull visions from the future. What we found was that you would probably make a legendary mandrate."

So he knew Stefan would arrive in Miraden. Could Fenric have played a part in the attempted assassination of his father? Was Fenric the missing piece to explain what happened? No. He could not have teleported to Dael, but maybe he knew more. "So it is already decided? I end up becoming a reyuul?"

"Such a nasty word. We prefer 'mandrate.' Our divinations are not perfect. There was no guarantee you would take up the mantle of mandrate. I'm here to make the offer. The Divination Corp decided this particular time in your life had the best chance of success."

"So, what is the offer?"

Fenric laughed. "Are we bargaining?"

"I always like to hear the deal."

Fenric smiled. "You help me with my other goal, and I will get you what you want. Power, funding, and freedom. I will bring you back to Ampestria, and we will take it from there."

"But I would end up looking like you, right? No way of getting out of that."

Fenric spread his arms. "There are…temporary loopholes, but all power has its costs. Eventually, you would look like this or worse. But, Stefan…Stefan, the power is more than you can imagine, and it's also a journey to something better."

Fenric spoke an incantation, and a blue circle coalesced to their right. Images of gold, jewels, and castles faded to reyuul calling down fireballs on armies. A reyuul healed a comrade's wound, which faded to another mandrate flying up to a castle tower when the hovering blue circle faded.

Stefan's eyes widened. That was impressive. "Got to admit, that was better than most sales pitches. You're telling me I could do that? And I will be 'legendary'?"

"Yes, yes, that's what I've been told. I personally can only divine very short distances into the future."

Stefan looked down at his feet. The possibilities Fenric showed him lined up with his imagination, but the cost still concerned him. "I have to think about it some more."

"Understandable, but I will not remain in the forest forever. Can you speak Ampestrian?"

"Yes. It's one language my father ensured I knew because of the Jetean War."

"Excellent. Do you know the word for 'push'?"

Stefan frowned. "Yes."

"Permit me, then." He disappeared. "I'm up here." Stefan looked up, finding Fenric on a branch above him. The reyuul had transferred without the black portal or delay.

"When I push down against the ground, I can slow my descent. All I need to do is say 'push.' " He stepped off and floated to the ground, landing gracefully on his feet.

Stefan stared in disbelief. "All I have to do is say the word?"

"You need to draw in mandra, which grants you the power I just showed you, and that takes practice."

He pulled out a dagger from his black robes and handed the weapon to Stefan, handle first. Stefan hesitated in taking it.

"Consider it a gift. It will teach you how to draw in mandra."

Intrigued, Stefan took the dagger, and as soon as it entered his hand, power coursed through his arm, and he immediately noticed the increased strength. His entire body tingled.

"You should feel the mandra, but you have to choose to draw the power into yourself to do what I can do." Fenric stepped back and scattered what appeared to be sand from his hand as a black void with green-and-purple twisting ropes materialized next to him. The iveys fell apart into piles of debris while the lost ivey with the red diamond approached and entered the void.

Fenric waved. "Think on it. We'll meet again." He stepped through the void, and it winked out of existence.

Stefan opened his pack and immediately dropped the dagger inside. The weapon scared him more than anything else, but he had to admit it tempted him. The power in the dagger, which must have been enchanted, was real and dangerous. Stefan understood enough about sales tactics to see through Fenric's plan. All Stefan had to do was hold the dagger long enough and using mandra would become easy. Stefan also figured out that he had been watched because how else would Fenric have known that floating to the ground would be the one thing he would find useful enough to use mandra.

The tactics were subtle yet effective. But the consequences…Stefan needed time to process, but the whole interaction had thrown his mindset off course.

What was more disturbing was how the reyuul had handled Pol and Quig. Quig had been abducted by something hostile, and Stefan hoped that if the fey could manage storms, it could handle being kidnapped. Pol remained unconscious on the ground, and Stefan tried to wake him, but Pol slept regardless of how many times Stefan slapped his face.

A growl made Stefan whip around to find a gigantic bear twenty feet away with studs running down its head. It had to be the same bear that had attacked him on his first day.

Stefan glanced at the unconscious Pol and back at the bear, who continued padding toward him.

He couldn't move Pol, and he could not kill the bear. Or could he?

CHAPTER 21

"In your darkest moment, when you believe you are alone, you might find yourself closer to Lohem's light than ever before.

—Lourshen Elaunt. Cleric Novitiate Manual.

Pol awoke to Stefan yelling his name. The sun had not set, but it wasn't morning any longer in the silverwood forest. Pol shook his head, feeling groggy. How had he fallen asleep?

Clawing noises and growling cleared the head fog, and Pol discovered an enormous bear climbing an oak tree that did not have any connecting branches, and Stefan was at the end of one branch. Pol registered the danger and briefly wondered if the animal was the same one that had attacked before. Had it remembered Stefan's scent? And where was the fey?

With the bear quickly climbing, Stefan had less than a minute with nowhere else to run. Stefan kept reaching for his rucksack and looking down at the ground, making Pol wonder if he was considering jumping. But after a few seconds, Stefan jerked his hand away from the rucksack and took a defensive position against the climbing bear.

Looking down, Pol found a limestone rock the size of his hand and hurled the stone, hitting the bear's flank. The bear roared but kept climbing. Pol hurled another rock, striking the bear in the head and ultimately convincing the animal to switch targets and slide down the tree. Pol waited just a moment for the bear to mark him, and then he took off into the forest hoping to draw the bear away from Stefan.

He sprinted north. The crashing sounds in the brush behind him spurred his legs to pump faster, but he only had to get the bear away from Stefan. To the left, he spotted a low branch of a silverwood. With a quick push off the trunk and using his momentum, Pol flung himself upward and continued climbing until he found a solid branch with an escape option. Thankfully, the bear took the bait and followed. The bear's climbing speed surprised him, but Pol was ready as he crouched, patiently waiting.

Pol opened the leather pouch of herbs Gossama gave him, and as the bear crested the branch underneath, Pol flung the pouch at the bear's face before leaping to another tree with a good network of branches to traverse.

Pol didn't look back as he jumped to the lower branches and then hit the ground with a roll. After a moment, he confirmed the absence of pursuit and returned to Stefan's position.

Breathing hard, Pol found Stefan clinging to the trunk of the oak fifteen feet up. "C'mon, we have to move before it regains your scent."

Stefan didn't move for a moment, staring at Pol. His hand reached toward his rucksack, then halted. With a deep breath, Stefan climbed down.

Pol waited patiently for Stefan to descend. "Let's head back toward Gossama's cave." When Stefan nodded, Pol broke into a run without complaints from Stefan, and as he led them through the forest, Pol tried to piece the situation together. He remembered Gossama telling them to find a tree and sleep in the forest, but then everything went blank from there.

His body seemed rested, and he didn't register any injuries, but why did he pass out? Maybe something was wrong with him, but other than some residual grogginess, he didn't feel sick.

A little later, Pol stopped at a few blackberry bushes and scanned the canopy and the ground for any lurking dangers. Waiting for Stefan to catch up, he filled up his berry pouch that Gossama had helped him make from large silverwood leaves.

When Stefan arrived, Pol said, "Fill up your berry pouch. I don't know if we'll find another one before tomorrow." Stefan paused a moment but then complied, remaining quiet. Pol didn't push for information; the guy was having a hard time.

"I remember a large silverwood a few miles ahead. Let's stop there." He wanted to ask if Stefan knew why he fell asleep, but Stefan wasn't volunteering the information, and they needed to move.

Pol secured his berry pouch and raced to the west. He used all Gossama's training and scanned, listened, and quieted his heart and mind. He needed to protect Stefan.

The embers in his soul flared to life, half orange and half white. Experimenting, Pol focused on protecting Stefan, and the white coals overtook the orange. The strength filled his body, and he missed flying through the canopy, but he had to watch Stefan and keep him safe. That was usually Quig's job, but he still didn't know what had happened to the fey.

They arrived at the large silverwood without further incident, and Pol climbed up twenty feet, finding a wide branch that forked from the trunk and would easily hold them through the night. He reached his hand down to assist Stefan, who paused, but after a second, took the hand and hauled himself up to the branch. Pol didn't know what to say; it was the first time Stefan hadn't knocked his hand away.

Stefan leaned against the trunk of the tree, breathing hard and sweating. Pol examined him for any wounds. "You all right?"

Stefan still breathed hard. "Why? Why did you help me?"

"Because you were in trouble?" Pol was confused. Was Stefan angry that he had been saved?

Stefan took a deep breath, and Pol thought he was going to yell, but Stefan clamped his jaw and exhaled through his teeth. "But why?"

Why was he questioning Pol's protection? The soul flame lit a deep orange. "Because you needed it."

Stefan's cheeks flushed. "You had every right to let that bear eat me."

The fire burned red. "Why would you say that? Why would you think I would let that happen?"

"Because I'm not worth saving." Stefan paused. "I'm not like you. I keep failing. Even now, I'm failing."

The guy didn't understand why someone would risk themselves to help another? Pol took a deep breath and focused on releasing his anger through the breaths. As he did, the flame returned to orange. "You're not that bad," Pol tried.

"Of all people, you can't say that. You know better."

Pol decided to hold back. A little. "You're not perfect… okay, you're a prideful pain in my side, but I think you're trying."

"Trying? Look at my life; everything's gone. I'm nothing but a problem to you and everyone, so why you would save me?"

Pol just let it out. "Because even if you're a pain, and I can't stand you sometimes, and if you keep making mistakes, your life is valuable or Lohem would not have created you. I'm not perfect. I've made plenty of mistakes. Just ask my father and my uncle, but we have to keep trying to do the right thing."

Stefan narrowed his eyes. "The right thing? Maybe you rescued me because you want to be an officer. You need to prove to Granite you can work with me."

Pol held back the reactive answer and took deep breaths as a shield against the anger within. He considered why Stefan would say these things, and the best answer was that the former qual must be used to relying on himself. "That's not how I was raised." Pol took a deep breath. "Because I know what it's like to not be in control…to be hurt and beaten and wish someone would have helped me. Because it's what my father and my uncle taught me to do." He looked at Stefan. "I could also say 'because I learned it at Point,' but the truth is the two strongest men I know would have been disappointed if I hadn't."

Stefan folded his arms. "It's funny that you talk about your father like that. Didn't seem like you thought well of him when we left Dael."

That hit harder than a training sword to the gut. "Yeah, maybe I don't give him the credit he deserves."

"I'm not one to talk. My father banished me here." Stefan sighed. "So, you're telling me you don't want anything in return?"

"No. I told you. It was the right thing to do." Pol pulled out some blackberries and ate them as he gazed out over the canopy. When Stefan didn't reply, Pol considered Stefan's observation. Pol hadn't left on great terms with his father, the man who had never defended him—rarely defended him. Pol gazed out over the forest. Maybe his father had given him more than he realized? Pol wouldn't be here without his father, but…his father also had allowed nobles to beat him and always claimed that he was looking out for the family, but what about his son? Maybe he felt Pol could take it? That's not how Pol would live his life. Pol made a promise to himself: *I will defend those who can't defend themselves.*

His inner soulfire blazed orange and white again. Taking deep breaths, Pol concentrated on the forest, allowing the anger to siphon out. He needed to distract himself. "What happened when I got knocked out?"

Stefan gave him a pained glance. "I can't tell you." He put his face in his hands. "I don't know what to do. I don't have a plan, and I'm not in control." He rubbed his hands through his short, black hair.

Pol found himself pitying the young man. "Uncle Eash always said, 'Control is an illusion.' Said Lohem was in control, and that was good enough for him. I'm still working on that." He held some blackberries out to Stefan, who ignored the offer and remained silent.

Pol didn't push it. His soulfire had calmed back to embers, and he focused on what would bring him peace. Sparring with his uncle had always worked, but Dael was far away. He couldn't wait to share the stories of everything that had happened with Uncle Eash, but his father would be interested too, right? Maybe he could share the stories with Adeel?

Pol wanted to ask Stefan questions about Adeel but decided now might not be the best time. Looking over,

Pol found Stefan staring at his rucksack. Something had really shaken this guy. "You're not going to tell me what happened?"

Stefan tensed again. "A lost ivey, a lost one. They sedate their victims, but it did not affect me, and it eventually left."

"Wow. Left? How did it leave?"

"It's complicated, and I don't want to talk about it. You're safe."

Once again, Pol had to restrain his anger, so he redirected. "What happened to Quig?"

"When the ivey attacked, the Veil opened, and Quig was taken by something. I swear I could not do anything. I do not know what happened."

That concerned Pol, but he didn't know how much trouble the fey was in. "Maybe it was the DreadKing it keeps talking about. I hope Quig can take care of himself, right?"

"It's my fault. Quig kept saying that I bring trouble, but I cannot do anything about it right now."

"I don't know what you're talking about unless you tell me everything."

Stefan balled his hands into fists. "I can't. Just leave it alone." Stefan folded his arms and closed his eyes.

Pol felt helpless but recognized Stefan needed time. Instead, he leaned back against the tree and closed his eyes for a while as the questions about his father repeated in his head.

The vibrations began softly. The steady rhythm continued and progressed until the sound of boulders hitting the ground echoed through the trees. Remaining stone-still, Pol watched the spiky branches jutting upward and brushing just below the canopy. The jagged vertical branches advanced with each boom, shaking the tree.

Pol leaned an inch to the side as the pounding reached its peak.

A barkbeast. The barklike skin rippled with each movement, and red eyes lined with black scanned the ground.

Pol slid lower on his back. His heart pounded, and shivers ran down his body. Why so afraid? As the barkbeast plodded below the tree, Pol returned his gaze to the hulking giant, unwilling to allow his feelings to paralyze him. He didn't like feeling fear.

His uncle once said to him, *It's not wrong to be afraid; it's wrong to let that fear paralyze you from acting.* Sitting up, Pol locked his gaze on the departing lost one.

I need to fight it.

He formulated strategies against an opponent so large with several ideas he wanted to try. He brought his feet underneath when a hand grabbed his wrist.

Stefan had fierce eyes. "What are you doing?"

"I'm going to destroy that thing."

"No. No you will not." Stefan's strained voice was firm.

"Why not?"

"What do you mean, why not?" Stefan asked as he laid low over his branch.

The barkbeast continued past. Pol narrowed his eyes and kept his voice low. "I don't like being afraid." He sat back and took a deep breath. "Besides, it feels wrong; it feels evil. The bear that attacked you was dangerous, but the animals belong here. That thing doesn't."

"So what? You can't fight it by yourself."

"Jonta, you don't know that?" Pol kept his eyes on the barkbeast. If he did attack, Stefan might get hurt, and Pol should have calculated that. Stefan must be protected.

Pol sat back down on the branch and laid his head against the trunk.

They just had to make it to the morning and to the cave. Gossama would return and put everything in order. Something had happened to Stefan, which shook him, and Pol was willing to bet Stefan had something in his rucksack that was a part of it. Stefan said he had chased off a lost one, but there seemed to be more. Pol shook his head; suspicion would eat at him, at them. Yet, as he watched the lost one stomp out of sight, Pol wondered: would Stefan have rescued him if he was in trouble?

～～～

Stefan woke. The pitch-black night hid everything. Pol's steady breathing from the next branch reassured him a little. Stefan had been tired enough to sleep earlier after strapping himself to the tree with a rope. Three not-so-small spiders had viciously attacked his arms and chest. After fighting them off with his bare hands, Stefan had trouble falling asleep as he swatted at any perceived movement on his body. The chirps, cries, howls, and growls did not help. Packed taverns in Dael were quieter than the forest. Even at this hour, the insects and animals continued their chatter.

Stefan's thoughts were louder than the forest. He could have used that dagger against the bear earlier, but he did not. He feared it, feared the cost. He was not stupid. He recognized the dagger for what it was, but he also feared having to rely on Pol.

He hated not being in control.

Stefan wanted to sulk and believe that no one else was going to take care of him, but many had. His father, his mother, Illiat, and most recently, Granite, Gossama, and

Pol. He wanted to believe that he could do everything on his own, but obviously he could not.

He hated it.

Using the dagger would have gotten him out of that situation with the bear, and he could have either harmed the bear or escaped, but then what? He always considered everything in light of five steps later, and either way would have led to more trouble.

Besides, Gossama would have been able to sense that he had used mandra, and he was not ready to explain himself to her. He respected her, which was why he could not understand how someone like Gossama, who lived in a cave, had fought monsters and reyuul, could be rejected by her people.

Stefan considered Gossama a genuine hero like Uriah, the first Cordiaen voltai, or Jeitoh, the first cleric and first to receive the golden light named after him.

She had fought off a dragon!

Gossama lived under the norms of Dasari society, which, like Cordiaen culture, tolerated nothing related to reyuul. If other Dasari could sense her mark, she would never be allowed to live freely in their communities. Living in the forest made sense, but it must have been lonely. Would he really want to be associated with reyuul and face the same solitude?

Cord had founded Cordiae as a direct result of fleeing a country dominated by reyuul. Cordiae was the first country void of any mandra use. Mandra was so incompatible with his Cordiaen upbringing that Stefan should have rejected it outright. Why didn't he?

As he stared at the stars winking through the canopy, Stefan said, "I was desperate. I am desperate." He had lost everything he had built for himself, and he was open to anything that would allow him to take control.

Then, Pol saved him. Pol had saved his sister as well. Stefan could not remember anyone *not* in his family who had done something for him without expecting anything in return. Stefan wanted to hate him for that. He wanted to hate him because he wanted to be like him, and nobles should not want to be like commonfolk.

Dael was a large, unforgiving city where only the cutthroats made profits. Kindness, faith, and integrity made little money. Stefan berated himself. He was smart enough to figure it out.

His foot brushed his pack. The dagger weighed little, but he could feel its power through the leather. He felt ashamed for considering what he could do with mandra, but he could not restrain his analytical mind from the possibilities and solutions available to him. All decisions had consequences; he recalled textbook after textbook that warned of the reyuul and what happened to those who rebelled against Lohem.

Stefan recognized he had to address his relationship with Lohem. The God of Cordiae had dealt Stefan a rough hand through the quon, his father. From a purely financial and influential perspective, taking Fenric's offer would provide him the power he would need to regain his wealth by force. So by taking Fenric's offer, he would defy his father and Lohem. The texts were explicit in describing what awaits the soul after death for those who reject Lohem. Unending torture. Some theorized that the reyuul's souls were torn and broken down into mandra, but that was speculation.

Stefan had not given the concept of the afterlife much consideration, as money meant more to him, but now that he faced the decision, he could not ignore the possibility. Logically, his brain considered whether he gave credence to the consequence. Did he actually believe that Lohem existed?

Yes. He had been to Festival and seen King Sraung call down the FireGate, the purifying wall of fire that cleansed Cordiaens of their sins. He had passed through the FireGate. He had seen clerics heal and voltai defend in their glowing pearl armor. Those were the things he had witnessed with his eyes, but they had only so much meaning for him. There were moments, very few, where he felt like Lohem had been present, and one of those moments was at the dinner where his father announced his exile into the army.

His well-developed and executed plans had been destroyed so completely that no one on this planet, except the God of Cordiae, could have done such a thorough job. After his father and Cyprian had scolded him for being rude to Pol, Stefan had no choice but to face the consequences, and he had to give Lohem the credit. No one else could have bested him in such a manner.

So if he believed Lohem was real, did he believe that defying him would result in eternal torture?

Stefan could not see it. He had not experienced it. All he had were textbooks, sermons, PointDays, and word of mouth that described it.

That required faith to believe something without seeing it. But he *had* seen and endured the last three weeks. His father, Cleric Bruit, and Granite had warned him that what he had done in Dael had been wrong, and if he believed Lohem had unraveled his plans with consequences from his actions, then there could be more devastating consequences for defying Lohem and using mandra later.

It was enough to prevent him from using the dagger.

As the sky lightened with the predawn, Stefan unwrapped himself from the branch as quietly as he could.

Pol stirred and woke, twitching at first, then calming. After a moment, he started untying the ropes securing him to the tree. "We need to get back to the cave now. We need to tell Gossama about what happened."

Maybe when Gossama returned to the cave, they could do something about Quig. The fey had been right. Fenric had come for Stefan, and Quig paid the price. Stefan did not like feeling guilty, and he really hoped the fey and the villagers were not hurt.

"Okay." Stefan eased himself down to the next branch. His leather boots had been traded out for light leather shoes, which had a better grip on wood. Gossama had little leather, but she had said, "I'm tired of watching you fall."

When they hit the ground, Pol took off running. Stefan's side ached a little when he ran, but Pol had set a good pace that Stefan could maintain.

Magnanimous jerk.

Pol threaded their route amidst the trees and kept to the shadows as much as possible. The cave was a good five miles west, but Pol stopped them a half mile into the journey. He kept his hand on a trunk and visibly calmed his breathing. After a moment, he motioned downward. "Hide." They quickly scampered into brush near a birch. Stefan lay on his stomach and forced his own breathing to calm as he focused on hearing.

Leaf-patterned legs in leather shoes appeared in front of them. The skin color ranged from bright green to dark yellow.

In a light voice, one of the Dasari announced, "Come out. Now."

Pol looked at Stefan, who nodded. There would be no point in trying to hide, and they emerged from the brush and stood. Four Dasari males stood before them. Two had arrows trained on the boys.

"You understand us?" the Dasari with yellow leaves asked in a foreign Dasari accent.

"Yes," Stefan replied.

"Good. You reek of the Tainted One. Why are you with her?"

Stefan considered his options. "She is our teacher. We've only been with her for a few weeks."

The four quietly conversed, and the yellow-skinned Dasari replied, "Take us to where she lives."

"No. We don't have permission."

A sword point pressed against his chest. "I give you permission."

Stefan held the warrior's gaze. She may have let his arm get chomped by a bear, but he was not a snitch, though had to spin the response in her favor. "I fear Gossama more than I fear you."

The yellow-skinned warrior's eyes became deadly. "Never mention that name again. It is a curse." He lowered the sword. "Scared humans. Young ones, too. You'll come with us. Leader MistFall will decide your fate."

Pol's hand moved to his sword hilt. The Dasari followed the movement. "We do not need you to remove your weapons, but if you try to use them, we will kill you."

Pol removed his hand.

Stefan sighed. They were going to RainCrest.

CHAPTER 22

"Even when the odds are stacked against you, a capable commander can turn the tide."

—Cleric Joern, Advanced Cordiaen Military Tactics, Volume 2.

Apparently, RainCrest warriors did not run through the forest like Gossama. RainCrest must hold a different culture among the Dasari. As for how they treated Stefan and Pol, there were no blindfolds and no aggression. Stefan assumed they thought poorly of humans. They even interacted with the forest differently. Whenever a forest beast threatened, the four would either bare steel or nock arrows and chase the beast away. Stefan absorbed every detail.

He realized he had an opportunity to obtain a different perspective. "Are RainCrest Dasari different from those of SilverGate?"

The four warriors snorted and grunted at the question. The yellow-skinned warrior replied, "Humans. All you need to know is that RainCrest is superior. Leader MistFall broke away from SilverGate fifty years ago to bring the Dasari back to the glory of our ancestors."

Fifty years? That's what Gossama had said. "This happened because of Gossama."

A Dasari saber edge pressed against Stefan's throat. "You have been warned. The Tainted One's curse is real. It's fallen on our people. Leader MistFall freed us away from her influence, her corruption. You would do well to heed his advice when you meet him."

Information was leverage. Stefan wanted more to find an option for escape but could sense now was not the time. Seemed the RainCrest community blamed Gossama for whatever might be convenient.

Given what he knew about Dasari in the forest, there was no point in trying to run. Instead, he considered his options. Since his normal options were limited, he wondered what he could do if he had mandra. Dasari did not have a natural defense against reyuul, and Cordiaen history taught that the forest nation had relied upon Cordiaen assistance to drive out lost ones, reyuul, and dark fey from the forest.

The RainCrest warriors would then be at *his* mercy. He stopped himself as his mind plowed steps ahead: the consequences…

After hours of trudging through the forest, they came upon a steep hill with limestone boulders jutting out of the grassy forest floor. At the top, a crude stone wall, twenty feet high, flanked a large, irregular stone gate. Ten RainCrest warriors held positions atop the gate. They waved the patrol through with curious glances at the young humans.

Stefan had never been inside a Dasari city before, and while the towers and homes appeared to have grown from the ground in a natural beauty, the Dasari inhabitants struck him as unnatural. The warriors that escorted them appeared in decent health like Gossama, but the Dasari lining the streets were thin with hollowed cheeks. Fatigue lined their features, and the younger ones clung to their parents with dark eyes. Stefan had seen the same signs in the poor quarter of Dael; these Dasari were hungry.

Down the dirt road from the gate, the warriors brought them to a one-story silverwood building with smooth corners; the building appeared to have been "grown" from the ground. The RainCrest guards escorted them down a short ramp and through a maze of wooden hallways to a row of cells with wooden bars. The guards opened the doors and gestured the young humans inside.

Sweat had beaded on Pol's forehead, and the young man finally spoke. "What are we going to do?"

"Worried?"

Pol wiped his forehead. "Maybe. We are in a Dasari jail."

"Almost getting mauled by a bear when I'm supposed to be protected by a ranger has put things into perspective. The guards have been courteous, if not careless. I think we're more of an anomaly than a threat."

Pol frowned. "At least we can count on Gossama to get us out."

"I don't think she's allowed inside the city. There's no way she could get us out without possibly hurting a lot of Dasari. She would not do that."

Pol sat down. "Why are we even here? The Dasari leader gave us permission to be in the forest."

"Politics. The SilverGate leader said we could. This is RainCrest. But something's wrong here. Those neraida out there are about to fall over from hunger, but the guards look healthy. When you sacrifice the populace to keep your warriors fed, you are afraid of being invaded."

"So whoever is in charge here might be at odds with that leader, OakenRoot?"

"Yes." Stefan glanced at Pol. "Wait. Is this your first time in a jail cell?"

"Of course! You've been in jail?"

"My father thought dungeons were a great way for me to learn life lessons. I picked up a few things during those wonderfully boring days with convicted felons."

"Quiet! Do not disturb the other prisoners." A Dasari guard rapped his sword hilt onto the bars. "We are waiting for Leader MistFall. Do not be difficult or we will be difficult."

Stefan stepped back and sat down near Pol.

"Good younglings." Walking away, Stefan heard one of them say, "See how fat those humans are?"

Stefan closed his eyes. He had an idea.

"What will this leader do?" Pol asked.

"Shut up. I'm thinking."

"Don't have to be mean about it." Pol folded his arms and took slow breaths.

Stefan could tell Pol was suppressing his anger. He was right; Stefan did not have to say that. Even if Stefan needed to concentrate, his lack of consideration for others separated him from Pol. This was hard. "Sorry. Please let me think."

Pol's eyes widened, but he did not reply.

An hour later, the two Dasari warriors returned and opened the door to their cell. "Come with us. The leader is ready." Stefan and Pol were guided upstairs to an open-air court at the apex of another hill in the city's rear. From their vantage point, Stefan could see the layout of the entire city.

A thin male Dasari with wrinkles and red leaf-patterned skin spotted with black dots stood talking with other Dasari, who had various shades of brown, yellow, and red skin. They deferred to the one with red leaves, and Stefan assumed he was Leader MistFall, a proud-looking Dasari with a perpetual furrow in his eyebrows.

The leader stopped his conversation when Pol and Stefan arrived, examining them. In Dasari, he said, "Two ragged human younglings who bear the scent of the curse mark have come before me. Why do I feel that this will be the start of trouble?"

The rest of the Dasari turned to face the boys. One with brown skin the color of dried leaves said, "They have spent time with the Tainted One. Why are they here?"

Their guard answered, "Leader MistFall, the little one speaks our language."

Little one? The tallest Dasari was a little over five feet.

The leader narrowed his eyes at Stefan. "Answer me."

This Dasari was the leader, and these were his council. It didn't seem like he and Pol were in trouble, but if he spoke wrong here, it would be bad. Stefan waited quietly, withholding emotion from his face as he considered his options.

"Good afternoon, Leader of RainCrest. I am Stefan, son of Quon Daoringer of Dael. This is Pol. We are citizens of Cordiae. We recently began training for the King's Army a few moons ago. Our teacher, Fall Commander Granite, brought us to the forest two weeks ago. We are currently under the tutelage of Gossama. She left us so she could monitor the activity of what she calls 'lost ones.' "

At Granite's name, murmurs passed between the council members. Leader MistFall sat down with his legs folded. "I appreciate you took your time to answer. Patience is not something we attribute to humans. Why would the Tainted One agree to teach you?"

"She owed Granite a favor."

"This Granite…does he have brown skin, black-and-silver hair, and is strong? Has he been in the forest before?"

"Yes."

"I see. You are weak, and this Granite wants you to train and learn from one who is strong. You are not a threat, and it is to the Tainted One's credit that you are still alive. The Tainted One does not belong in the city, but we know she has been tracking lost ones. Many lost ones around the city."

The council nodded in agreement. Stefan had to bite his tongue to keep from ruining the conversation. Weak? Really?

Leader MistFall continued, "Your father is a quon? A leader? We do not wish to offend the human leaders or their king, but we are wary of outsiders. There are lots of dangers in the forest. Humans must have a reason to be in the forest."

Stefan saw an opportunity. There were risks, but the payoff would be amazing. He glanced at Pol, who seemed lost in the Dasari conversation.

"Leader MistFall, the Dasari are strong. How is it you do not have enough food when you have an entire forest to take from?"

"Who told you we do not have enough food?"

Stefan grimaced. "I may be human, but I'm not stupid. I saw your people; they are starving."

The council was dead quiet, looking at Leader MistFall. Stefan had struck a chord.

The leader paused for a moment. "I will use this opportunity to teach you, youngling. We eat what we grow in our city and keep safe within our walls. Our food stores caught fire in the dry season this year, and we lost almost everything."

"What about other Dasari communities?"

MistFall appeared uncomfortable. "Our position is complicated with our Dasari brethren."

Stefan tried not to be excited. "May I suggest a proposition?"

The leader folded his arms and chuckled. "What would you say, little human?"

"The village that I have been living in, Gaodis, has an excess of crops. I wonder if you would trade with humans?"

Loud comments amongst the Dasari council broke out. Some stood and shook their hands, while others remained calm and seated. Without turning, the leader spoke quietly to them, and they stopped talking.

"This is not a small thing to suggest. What authority do you have to say such a thing? You are a human youngling."

"I have made such negotiations in the past. It is easy to make such a thing happen. The question stands: will you trade with humans?"

The leader's raised hand quelled even more commotion. He gave them a death glare before returning his thoughtful gaze to Stefan. "I may not trust humans, youngling, but I do not fear them." His face remained passive, but he did not continue. Stefan knew better than to press. He had struck a nerve but did not know all the details complicating the situation.

"As I said, this is not a small thing. If I can get more food for my people, then I will negotiate, but you would have to deliver first and soon. What do you want in return?"

Stefan suppressed his excitement. The hard part was over. Now, he was just haggling.

"Three things. First, we would trade for your medical herbs." Stefan removed the bandage from his arm. "Your medicines are better than ours, and our cleric cannot be everywhere at once. Second, we would take some lumber. It doesn't matter if the tree is dead, old, or young."

Murmurs of approval came from the council.

"What is the third thing?" Leader MistFall asked.

"Allow Gossama, the Tainted One, to enter the city. She helps to protect your city and can bring you the slaughtered animals for trading. She is also in need of supplies."

The council blew up. Dasari stood and began yelling and shaking their fists. Leader MistFall allowed them. Stefan didn't realize how much of a stigma Gossama was to these people. He had wanted room to negotiate, but if they could budge a little, Gossama would benefit.

Pol tugged on Stefan's tunic. "What's happening? What did you do?"

"I asked them to accept Gossama."

"That's like asking them to accept a dragon into their city."

"She's alone; she needs it."

Pol shook his head. "Sure you're not doing this for yourself?"

"For pure profit, I would have left Gossama out of it."

Leader MistFall stood. "Food would be good. Medicine and fallen trees are easy to obtain and are good trades. The

Tainted One, though…not in the city. I know OakenRoot has accepted her, but he does not speak for RainCrest." He paused. "If our trade happens, and we receive food, we might allow her to trade at the gate. Depending upon how much food you provide, I will add a special benefit your country has received in the past." The council quieted.

"What's that, Leader?"

"We will give you some silverwood. This wood is useful for your voltai. They need it to make their special armor."

Stefan could hear imaginary coins jingling. "You are most kind, Leader."

The leader leaned forward. "So, shrewd youngling, what kind of food does your village grow?"

Stefan grinned as he handled their concerns. After the negotiations, the leader escorted them down to the city gate. A crowd gathered behind them. At the gate, a tense Gossama waited with eyes darting to all the residents and guards.

The leader pointed to her. "Go to her."

Stefan and Pol passed through the gates and stood next to Gossama.

"Shrewd One, what did you do?"

Leader MistFall held up his arms. "Hear me: the Tainted One will be allowed at the gates. We will trade with her, but she will not be allowed in the city."

Gossama grabbed Stefan's shirt and lifted the taller human off the ground. "Trade?"

Leader MistFall said, "This is a trade agreement, Tainted One. The Shrewd One spoke for you. Do you accept?"

Gossama threw Stefan to the side. "I accept."

Leader MistFall replied, "Good. Shrewd One, we await the food. Do not take long."

Stefan stood and brushed himself off. "Yes, Leader. You'll see."

Gossama turned and ran into the forest. Pol and Stefan followed her. Stefan smiled for the first time in weeks, and a thought hit him. As a reyuul, he would have used his powers to escape. Today, he used what Lohem had given him. The results would have been different. Was it enough?

CHAPTER 23

"Make no mistake, even with my knowledge and Lohem's guidance, I still walked the way of the enemy, the path of a reyuul. I stand humbled by the grunt who remained loyal to Cordiae when I had not."

–Cleric Joern, Advanced Cordiaen Military Tactics, Volume 2.

Pol couldn't believe Stefan had pulled it off. He'd saved them from being prisoners with his mouth. Pol had only caught a few words in Dasari, but as they jogged away from RainCrest, Pol was dying to know how Stefan did it.

A mile south of the city, they met Granite and his weary fist of soldiers, squatting by a silverwood. "You found them," Granite said with relief.

Gossama ignored the fall commander. "I don't know what to do with you!" she said to Stefan.

Pol had never seen the Dasari ranger so flustered.

Granite chuckled. "It's only been a few weeks."

Stefan rolled his eyes at Granite and sat on the ground, resting against the silverwood trunk. "What? We were captured. I saw an opportunity, and I tried to make everyone happy. Gossama needed food, tools, and supplies. Now she can trade. How is this a bad thing?"

"Tell me everything. MistFall is not to be trusted," Gossama replied with an edge to her voice.

Pol lifted his eyebrows at that. "Why?"

Gossama gave their surrounding area a quick scan. "MistFall was once an elder on the SilverGate Council, an advisor to Leader OakenRoot. All I can say is MistFall did not value my life, and he was removed from the council. He fled SilverGate and took control of RainCrest, making himself a leader here."

"OakenRoot permitted it?" Pol asked.

"A previous group of Dasari had left SilverGate, but they had left Miraden for another forest. MistFall left SilverGate and slithered into RainCrest because he hated me. OakenRoot didn't want to risk a civil war. RainCrest is small with few resources." She turned on Stefan. "You are causing trouble."

"No, I'm feeding starving Dasari. "

"What?" Granite said. "What did you do?"

"I merely suggested a trade with Leader MistFall."

Granite pointed at Gossama. "This happens when you don't watch him." Granite dropped his arms at his side. "How? How did you get to a position to even talk with the leader of a Dasari city?"

Stefan shrugged. "It must have been Lohem's will."

Pol could see the laughter in Stefan's eyes.

"What did you agree to?" Granite asked.

"Just that we would transport food from Gaodis to RainCrest in return for medical supplies, silverwood, and privileges for Gossama."

Granite and Pol both shouted, "What?"

"What food? How will you get it here?"

Gossama added, "What about beasts? Lost ones? Shrewd One, if you do not deliver, it is bad for Granite's village and SilverGate."

Stefan placed his arms behind his head as he reclined against the tree trunk and occasionally glanced at his rucksack next to him. "I thought about it. The beasts of the forest dislike large numbers. Give villagers jobs clearing a trail. A caravan carrying food…with guards. We can do this. Gossama, the village could use the trade and medical supplies. They would help, especially if it meant getting rid of their excess crops. And Granite, this is a chance to establish diplomacy with RainCrest and maybe even SilverGate."

"That's not for you to decide!" Granite exclaimed.

"Shrewd One. You did not ask me. This is not the Dasari way."

"I was in a jail cell. I used my resources. We're out. It'll be okay."

Gossama tsked. "Your mouth gets you in trouble."

"It already has. That's why I'm here."

Pol had one question. "Why doesn't OakenRoot help RainCrest?"

"He tried. MistFall rejected it," Gossama replied.

Pol said, "He'd let Dasari starve because of pride?"

Gossama said, "You don't know MistFall, but maybe this is good that MistFall is working with foreigners. Maybe this *is* Lohem's will."

"Maybe the first step toward building peace?" Stefan said.

Pol chuckled, and Gossama sighed, and folded her arms. "Difficult to be around…my people." She folded her arms. "I do not like owing people, especially shrewd younglings."

Granite had folded his arms. "I hate to say it, but there's a chance it will work out as he's suggesting."

"See?" Stefan said.

Granite added, "With the appropriate supervision."

Pol still couldn't believe it. Stefan really made the best of their situation and took others into consideration.

Gossama whipped around. "Where's Quig?"

"Who?" Granite asked.

"A fey from across the Veil. It showed up right after you left us," Pol replied.

Stefan said, "We were attacked by a lost ivey, and Quig was kidnapped back through the Veil. We haven't seen the fey since."

Gossama and Granite shared a look, and Pol knew Stefan wasn't going to get away with that. "Fall Commander, how did you get here? Did you find the villagers?" Pol asked.

The surrounding soldiers grumbled. Still eyeing Stefan, Granite said, "No. We were stopped five miles north of here by a RainCrest scouting party. Gossama found us and prevented trouble, but I understand how you were taken. They wouldn't let us go farther."

"Are they hiding something? Surely not the villagers? Right? The reyuul?" Pol asked.

Stefan said, "I'm actually impressed, Pol, that you considered that. If MistFall is willing to work with foreigners, why not reyuul?"

Granite said, "When you're desperate, you're willing to lower your standards."

Gossama said, "This is not a simple thing, a simple accusation, but I could see the mandra around MistFall." She gave Stefan a pointed look. "Granite, would you have your soldiers scout the area?"

Granite said, "Sure. Corporal Rield, quarter-mile perimeter. Report back in ten."

The corporal saluted and dispatched the soldiers.

Pol stepped back. Gossama looked serious, and she was eyeing Stefan. Something else had happened when he had blacked out.

Gossama pointed at Stefan's rucksack. "Shrewd One, why are you trying to hide it? You reek of mandra. What's in your pack?"

Stefan swallowed. "What are you talking about?"

Granite gripped Stefan's tunic from the back.

"Okay, okay. I may have met the reyuul, and he may have given me something."

Pol's mouth dropped.

"It's strong mandra. I give you credit for resisting this long, but without help, you cannot last. Shrewd One, reyuul destroyed my life. I cannot make a choice for you, but you cannot return to my home until you make a choice."

Stefan didn't look up at her. "You don't understand."

Granite said, "Stefan—"

Gossama threw dirt at Stefan. "I have not gone a day without mandra tempting me. Do not talk to me about understanding! I am cursed. *You* do not understand. I choose Lohem every day, and still Dasari reject me. I have done nothing wrong." She poked his forehead. "Use your smart brain, but I will not have mandra come into my home," she said, pointing to the rucksack.

A soldier's scream, followed by a screech, erupted from the south. Gossama said through gritted teeth, "Don't move." She melded into the silverwood behind him and reappeared a second later on the branches above with her bow drawn and an arrow nocked.

"What was that?" Pol asked.

Granite pulled his sword. "Vrent. Don't move!" He bounded after Gossama, and more screeches could be heard.

Stefan stood, picking up his pack and slinging it around his shoulders.

Pol felt tired all of a sudden. His vision became hazy as he placed his hand on a tree, fearful he may topple over from the dizziness.

He wanted to shake his head to clear the blurred vision, but his head wouldn't move. Pol panicked. His body wouldn't respond.

Then, it moved on its own.

He felt like his mind was pushed back and something or someone else controlled his movements. Pol watched himself plod up to Stefan.

"What?" Stefan asked. "Pol?"

Pol's inner voice yelled, but his mouth did not reply, and as he got closer, Stefan furrowed his brow. "Pol, are you okay?"

Stefan didn't expect Pol's fist to connect with his left temple. The blow sent the young man to the ground, and Pol couldn't do a thing about it. Pol watched himself pick up Stefan's body and turn toward a black oval floating in the air.

Pol fought against his body. He reactively started praying to Lohem, which made his body stall, but an overwhelming force pushed his legs, and slowly he entered the portal.

⁓⁓⁓

Two months after his breakfast with the brat, Geraul could read and speak basic Ampestrian. He would stick out if he ever visited Ampestria, but he could get by with common words found in spells. As he waited for his dinner, he examined his pale arms. A few small black scales had erupted on his forearms. They were merely single scales that might be mistaken for moles, with some larger than others. His wrists still easily slid out of the shackles, but he kept his arms chained. This was the last time he had to play the part.

Dural entered on schedule with the tray, and Geraul nodded upon his arrival. The guard placed the tray down, and Geraul said, "Thank you."

Dural's surprise showed in his voice. This was the first time Geraul had thanked him. "You're welcome."

While practicing mandra in his cell, there were many moments when he questioned himself, but none more than when he interacted with Dural. Geraul gave the God of Cordiae credit. He had tried, but not even the deity could save Geraul now. "You remind me of my father. I will never forget your kindness."

Dural said, "All for Lohem. Prisoners are still citizens."

The Name made Geraul wince from pain shooting across his head and heart. He had already crossed the line, and there was no return.

Geraul simply responded, "Thank you."

The guard said, "I'll see you tomorrow."

The door closed.

Geraul slipped his hands from the shackles. He walked over to the wooden contraption that guided water droplets from the ceiling to the small puddle. As he had practiced, Geraul recited the Ampestrian phrase for strength. His eyes rolled back with the exhilaration of the mandra coursing through his blood. Stacia said it wouldn't always feel as good once his body grew accustomed to the power.

He pushed his hand forward and released the spell. The small wooden structure burst into wet splinters away from him. The minor explosion was quieter than he expected.

This was power. This was control.

Geraul braced himself. He had practiced enough to prevent losing consciousness, unlike his initial successful attempts. The wave of fatigue rushed upon him, and he regulated his breathing. Stacia had required him to perform a minor spell in the cell before his escape to ensure he was prepared to handle the effects of the transportation spell. As the weakness passed, he smiled. "I can do this."

Geraul stepped to the door and looked to the side. No one heard. He gathered his concentration and mentally rehearsed the other spell he had mastered. Practicing in the dark had been one thing. Mistakes could still be deadly, but if he failed, the consequences were minimal. With his hands trembling, he envisioned the hall outside his cell and recited the phrase for "space." With a deep breath, he released the spell. As before, a black void rushed forward and engulfed him. For a fraction of a second, he floated in the void. He bent his knees slightly and braced for the landing, which occurred in the hall outside his cell door.

Geraul shook his head once and backed against the cold stone wall outside his cell. He steeled himself again, allowing the wave of fatigue to pass.

No yelling, which meant no guards in the hall. He crept down the hall to the only exit, vengeance burning in his heart. A group of QuonGuard playing dice could be heard through the small grate near the top. This was a guardroom for the block of cells.

After all the abuse he had received, this was his moment to take back what these fools had taken from him. They should be grateful; their deaths would be quick. He slowly inched his face to the door grate and peeked. Another door lay on the opposite wall of the guard's room.

"Dural, I swear you baby that traitor more than you should," a guard intoned.

"My job is to protect those who can't protect themselves. Leave it be."

Geraul swallowed. The others deserved death, but in that instant, Geraul knew he couldn't do it. He would not allow harm to come to that man, someone he vowed to never forget. But he didn't have any further time to waste.

Geraul focused on the far side of the other door and recited the spell once more. He released. When he landed, he almost fell to the floor but threw a hand to the wall and caught himself. With a greater distance, the fatigue almost dropped him. With ragged breaths, the former cal leaned against the wall to support himself down the hallway. He strained his ears as he panted. Even with his mandra conditioning in the cell for the last month, he could only use two more spells before he became worthless.

With the keep layout memorized from Stacia's verbal report, Geraul staggered as quickly as possible down hallways and into a small closet just outside the dungeon. He stripped off the ragged, dirty gray prison tunic and pants. He donned the anticipated purple pants and clean white tunic. Last, he covered his arms and head with a cowled green robe. Satisfied, Geraul lifted his chin, left the closet, and strode through the hall. He turned one corner and came face-to-face with Broken Nose.

Without hesitation, he released the strength spell against the guard, who flew backward into a wall and slumped to the ground. Geraul placed a hand on the wall to steady himself and shook his head as his vision darkened. Broken Nose lifted his head. Blood oozed from his lips. Geraul kicked the man's head, repeatedly, and the movement ceased.

He could not linger or he would not make it. Revenge tasted sweeter than the mandra in his blood.

With small steps, Geraul scurried down the hall to a heavy oak door, which he slowly opened. Careful that no one noticed him emerging from the small exit, he slipped into the wider public hallway. With a casual stride which belied his racing heart, he made it to the foyer.

Keeping his head down, he passed servants and nobles. No one stopped him as he exited the foyer into the bailey. With a sharp left turn away from the gate with more guards, Geraul aimed for the bailey wall. The statue of Jeitoh, the first Cordiaen cleric, served as the reference point against the wall.

As he reached out to his "well," he found it distant. Stacia mentioned that the closer he was to a Point, the harder it would be to use the mandra. The other risk entailed not knowing what may be on the other side of the wall. Last, the fatigue threatened to drop him to his knees. All the preparations had gone well, but Geraul fought to draw the mandra, creating spots in his vision. Focusing as hard as he could beyond the wall, Geraul whispered the phrase for "space" and released.

He stumbled forward into the arms of an awaiting Stacia. She flung him into a carriage, and he sprawled onto the floor as she climbed onto the bench seat. As consciousness slipped away, he heard, "Well done, Geraul."

CHAPTER 24

"To be a mandrate is to embrace sacrifice. As a new life begins, another life must be spent. Only through death can you be reborn into something greater."

–ArchMandrate Koen. Journal of Mandrate Recruitment, Volume 1873, issue 3.

Stefan opened his eyes to a sharp pain in his left temple. Wooden manacles with chains bound his wrists. To his left, Pol lay on his stomach, unconscious and bound by similar manacles behind his back. Both he and Pol were on a smooth birch platform with three curved walls and an arched ceiling. The missing fourth wall revealed an open view of the forest canopy and illuminated the space with afternoon light. The smooth wood structure appeared to be formed from a single piece extending from the tree, and while he couldn't see the ground, he could hear movement and talking below. The voices sounded like Cordiaens.

Stefan remembered Gossama going after a vrent and then Pol hitting him, but he could not tell where he was.

A very faint hum started. A green-and-purple portal materialized to his right. From the black center, the deformed reyuul stepped onto the smooth wood floor as the portal remained open. Fenric pulled back his cowl. Stefan resisted the natural desire to recoil from the deformities.

Fenric ignored Pol and strode directly to Stefan's pack. After retrieving the dagger, he said, "Sorry for the use of force, but my time is running short, and there are some recent developments. I see you haven't used my gift."

Stefan's mind calculated the appropriate response and strategies. "I have reservations."

Fenric nodded. "Cordiaen upbringing. Its efficacy is notorious among mandrates."

A large chair grew from the smooth wood floor, and Stefan's eyes widened at the use of power. Fenric sat down slowly and laid the dagger on the right armrest. The reyuul slowly brought his hands together and folded them. "It's very simple. Have you ever seen Lohem?"

"No."

Fenric spread his hands. "What proof do you have that he exists? If you can't see him or touch him, then how can you prove he is real?"

"Only by what I have experienced. My small empire was toppled in a day. Only Lohem could have allowed it. You also cannot disregard cleric powers, the FireGate, and voltai."

Fenric tensed at the Name but then rubbed his hands together. "Easy. Your clerics, voltai, and king don't rely on this so-called deity. They use their own power, which is just a variation of mandra. There's no god, just mortals fighting one another using their own power."

Stefan had already memorized the proofs against such an argument, but he refrained from denying it out loud, wondering what other arguments Fenric had.

The reyuul continued, "As for toppling your little empire, I think you're prideful. You can attribute that to your failure with Cal Geraul."

"Sure." Stefan internally froze at the name but tried to appear unfazed.

The mandrate said, "So if you can't prove Lohem's existence, how can you prove Lohem's retribution? You can't. There are few risks to mandra, and most of those can be mitigated with the right skill and path. Your country, your Point, and your faith: everything you've known, is false. Mandrates and Ampestria have existed long before Cordiae."

The argument had many holes. This reyuul was rushing. "That's a lot to take in, but if you can remove the objections, then all that's left to consider is the benefits, the power."

Fenric smacked the chair with his hand. "Exactly."

"And I'm supposed to be legendary, right?"

"The Ampestrian High Council believes it and is prepared to offer you everything you need to advance, and I'm prepared to send you through a portal to Caragal."

Stefan hesitated. "You can do that?"

"I can't teleport in, but I can teleport home with enough mandra. I can't afford to leave now, but I can ensure you get there."

He needed more information. "Can you tell me what you're doing here? It's not all about me."

Fenric cackled. "I've been waiting to tell someone." He whispered, "I'm opening a gate, a special gate." He rose from his chair. "I've been preparing for over a hundred years, and when I'm done, the High Council will allow me to succeed my master, but more important,"—he leaned toward Stefan—"I will unleash a plague on Cordiae and

Miraden that none have ever seen, another reason to take my offer to leave now."

Stefan looked down at his feet to give himself time to recalculate. This guy was going to destroy Cordiae. The chaos and carnage would also destroy the FeyRealm. "I have to think about it some more."

"It's a life-changing decision, but I can only give you an hour." He unlocked Stefan's arms with a wave of his hand, and the wooden manacles dropped to the floor. "I need to take care of a developing situation. It's like that Cordiaen game you play, Chain is it? I have to take out key pieces to win." He opened a portal and glanced at Stefan. "Make your decision, but mandra is not something you can be half sure about. To demonstrate your resolve and begin developing your own will, you will need to make a commitment to the decision." He pointed to the dagger on the armrest of the chair. "If you would become a mandrate, kill that one." Fenric pointed to Pol. "I've seen the divination reports on him. He's a Vroshen. He rebuffed my control after a few minutes and is a threat to Ampestria. His death will save many mandrates. I leave it to you to safeguard our future."

Fenric slowly stood and entered the green-and-purple portal without flourish. When the gate winked away, Stefan rubbed his wrists and stared at the dagger. He sat down in the newly created chair and folded his arms.

The weight of everything that had happened over the last few months crashed against him. Stefan closed his eyes and waded through the torrent of his memories. Faces of his father, Granite, Cleric Bruit, Gossama, and Pol surfaced. What would they say? He could imagine Quig saying, "What are you thinking?"

Remembering the cleric brought a sense of shame to his heart as Stefan recalled the image of Cor and Ariel with the cleric's questions of love and enslavement. Stefan considered Gossama's desire for community and Granite's sadness at having lost soldiers, but he frowned when he remembered Pol punching his face before coming here.

In the end, there was only one decision he could make with everything that had happened.

Stefan picked up the dagger. Strength flowed into his arm. The power made his arm tingle. Reversing the dagger's grip, he stood and knelt down by Pol's neck.

He hesitated for a moment.

Stefan raised his arm and brought the knife down, slashing the wooden manacles. The dagger cut through with little effort. Stefan rolled Pol onto his back and fell backward when he saw Pol's open eyes.

Stefan dropped the dagger. "How long have you been awake?"

"Long enough to hear everything." Pol stood. "Does this mean you won't join him?"

Stefan recovered quickly. "No, I know a terrible deal when I hear one."

Pol sat up. "What about control? What about your future?"

" 'Control is an illusion.' I'm working on it."

Pol rubbed his head. "You thought about it, though. You sat there thinking about it. Worried I was dead."

If Pol had heard everything, then Stefan did not have anything to lose. "I've been considering joining Fenric for days. These last few months have been brutal, but they've shown me what I really am. A weak kid, but I figured that if I could be a legendary reyuul, then maybe I could be great at something else. But, really, the final tipping point was you. I don't have faith like you, but I've seen you act like Cor. When I think of everything I've learned about our faith, you do it. You do it well." Stefan sighed. "The reason I do not like you is that I want to be like you. You are better than me, and I'm supposed to be better than you, but I am not."

Pol said nothing for a moment, and Stefan held his breath. He had never been so vulnerable.

"It's not about who is 'better.' We're different. You've got gifts I don't have." Pol folded his arms. "Still don't understand why you would even consider becoming a reyuul."

"I've got issues. That's why my father sent me here. I do not think he will believe what has happened, but if this reyuul had come to me in Dael, I do not know if I would have said no. Now, I think there might be better options for my future." Stefan smirked. "Besides, I do not want to look that ugly."

They both jumped when something dropped to the edge of the platform. Black gore covered Gossama's cloak, and she breathed hard. "I cannot leave you two alone. This is too much. Granite will be angry when he hears." She narrowed her eyes at Stefan, and she gave a slight bow. "Much respect, Shrewd One, for not following that path. It is miserable."

Stefan asked, "How long have you been watching?"

"I could not fight the reyuul here." She sighed. "I also needed to see if I had to kill you." She removed the poison-laden cloak onto the platform. "So, you don't believe the reyuul?"

"No. He was lying to close the deal. He knew about Geraul, and I had never mentioned him. I think Fenric had something to do with Geraul in Dael, and even if

I had my doubts about faith, I do not do business with people who lie to me."

Gossama tilted her head and gave him a strange look. "You chose well."

"I knew he would," Quig said, materializing next to Gossama.

"Quig!" Stefan and Pol cried out together.

The fey swam around and between them, pink waves undulating across its body. Stefan noted a new purple wound across its tail. "Yes, yes, my little humans. Did you worry about me?" The fey tsked. "No, no. That won't do. I can handle a few dark fey. This mandrate made a mistake thinking a few of his dark minions could take me."

"I'm sorry, Quig," Stefan said.

The fey floated to a stop before Stefan. "It wasn't your fault, Stefan. I'm proud of you."

That meant a lot. "Thanks for keeping an eye on me."

Gossama said, "Yes, yes, but the reyuul will return soon. We need to leave, but let me show you."

Stefan stepped up to the wooden platform's edge and looked down at the forest floor. Human men, women, and children were pushing stones and logs on the ground. Though not finished, from their vantage point, the structure was a circle with five points. A fifth of the circle had not been completed, and there was a large hole in the middle. The diameter must have been twenty-five yards. These were the families from the village. This was what they were building. Fenric had called it a gate.

Gossama shifted her belt. "I tried to get them to leave. They are under some spell and won't even look at me. When I got in their way, the men became aggressive."

Pol scanned the forest floor. "We can't just leave them here."

"Pol, Gossama is right; we need help to rescue them. We need to report this to Granite and get Cleric Bruit."

Gossama finished securing her gear without the cloak. "We go. I killed vrent, but there are other lost ones around. The reyuul is up to something."

Electricity flared around Quig. "Let's go. That mandrate won't catch me off guard again."

Gossama jumped down onto a branch, and Pol followed. Stefan turned back to the chair and the dagger on the ground. He hadn't used mandra, but he had felt the taste of power. After a moment's pause, he left the dagger. He would trust his future to Lohem.

⸻

Fenric completed the prescribed markings around the hole with his dagger. He hated leaving Stefan alone, but the general had found him sooner than expected, which meant the tenedrae would not be far behind. He needed more time, and he needed to strike now.

Standing to the side of his newly made hole, he began the enchantment and observed the glowing sigils in the dirt. Completing the crescendo of intonations, Fenric thrust his hands out and upward.

The soil darkened in a circle around the hole and cracked just before a claw emerged. Four more black claws with green veins erupted, grabbing the edges, followed by a screeching maw. The vrent burst from the hole and thrashed, its glowing yellow eyes finding Fenric, and the creature hissed but dipped its oblong head toward the reyuul.

"I have a mission for you; be quick and kill this one." Fenric implanted an image of the human into the vrent's mind. "Do not displease me."

The vrent cowered. Opening the UnderRealm gate had sapped most of Fenric's mandra, but with his remaining strength, he opened a portal.

Straining, the reyuul commanded, "Go."

With a screech, the vrent jumped through the black portal. The High Council had been clear: if the descended didn't kill its target, his mission success deteriorated significantly.

Weak and barely able to stand, he calculated risks versus benefits of supervising the vrent completing the mission without him. He would have to trust the descended to do its job. He had to return to Stefan.

CHAPTER 25

"I cannot repeat this enough: protect the cleric. Everything depends upon this. In MidRealm, Lohem heals and protects through the cleric. The commander who loses his cleric loses the battle and a precious treasure."

—Cleric Joern, Advanced Cordiaen Military Tactics, Volume 2.

I could have died. Pol shivered as they ran through the woods. He had been totally vulnerable and completely in Stefan's hands. Lohem had delivered him from death through Stefan.

Pol was dumbfounded. That was the second time Stefan had saved him today. No matter the actual intentions— and Pol still had every reason to be suspicious—Stefan had delivered. Pol could picture his uncle shaking his head at the turn of events. *He might be a mess, but he's done the right thing.*

Pol realized they were heading northeast, back toward the village. "Gossama, where's Granite?"

"He started for the village to get reinforcements." She abruptly halted, and Pol almost ran into her on a branch. "Shh." She motioned for them to get down as she pulled her bow. Quig flopped down next to Pol.

Further ahead, a hum preceded a black portal opening, and Fenric staggered out onto a tree branch. "General!"

Granite's voice could be heard through the woods. "I'm not a general. Who are you?"

"Fenric, disciple of Jenter and mandrate of Ampestria, and you should be the Lord General but are playing soldier out here. Mental breakdown over yet? Or do you still weep at night for the souls you lost?" Fenric's evil laugh echoed among the trees. "I have a message from the Ampestrian Council: your death will be a glorious victory for Ampestria. Retribution for countless lives lost. Now, where's the boy?"

The soul embers flared white. *No one's going to kill Granite.*

"What do you want with Stefan?" Granite asked.

Pol perked his ears.

"He's going to be Cordiae's downfall, my greatest masterpiece."

In their hiding spot, Quig whispered, "Not anymore."

"He's too smart for you, reyuul," Granite replied.

"No. He's seen through Cordiae's lies. He's ripe for the picking, General. Cordiae has grown soft, throwing talent like him to the side."

"You underestimate Cordiae. Your kind always has. Seems as if you were expecting the boy to be here. Did you have a hand in that?"

"Ah. Wouldn't you like to know? You've lost your edge. A step behind, always worried about those you are meant to protect but cannot. Too bad you continue to fail."

No flame, but the embers flared brighter.

Gossama let a bluesteel arrow fly, but when Pol expected the arrow to land, it passed right through where the reyuul's heart would have been. Fenric had disappeared from his branch to appear ten feet away on the other side of the tree.

"Tainted One. Not even you can stop me. Try. I'll be waiting." He didn't wait for a reply as he ducked into a newly formed portal.

Gossama grunted and led them to Granite. "Slow and fat, Granite."

"Really?"

Gossama scanned the canopy. "Dangerous here, but he looked tired like he just used a lot of mandra and will need to rest." She melded down to the forest floor while Pol swung down. The accompanying soldiers let out shouts of astonishment at her emergence from the tree. "I found the villagers, but they're under a spell. Building something. Don't know what it is."

Stefan finally caught up and leaned forward, hands on his knees. "Gate—It's a gate. Don't know more, except Fenric said he was going to open a plague on Cordiae."

"The UnderRealm," Gossama said.

Quig added, "A gate for lost ones."

Granite pointed at Quig. "What is that?"

"An awesome being at your service," the flying elemental fey replied.

Pol said, "It's a fey from across the Veil. He's been keeping an eye on Stefan. His name is Quig." Soldiers pointed, and Quig preened at the attention.

The fall commander said, "Fey. If beings from across the Veil are involved—"

"Yes. This is bigger than us. Tenedrae are involved," Gossama said.

Pol understood enough to be concerned. An army of barkbeasts, vrent, iveys, or other lost ones would decimate Gaodis and the country.

Granite said, "Right now, I'm more concerned about what he said about protecting. We need reinforcements, and we need to retake the advantage. Gossama, we need OakenRoot's help. How soon can you get reinforcements?"

"Noon, tomorrow, if I leave now."

"I'll take it. I'll return to get our troops and Cleric Bruit. He'll be the key for shutting this Fenric down."

Gossama shrugged. "I make no promises."

"Thank you. And thank you for taking care of the boys."

"They did not die." Gossama grinned. "Shrewd One has much to tell you. I trust him. The youngling is more than you hoped for. If you want to succeed, bring them tomorrow."

Pol lifted his eyebrows. That was high praise.

Granite didn't look convinced. "Bring them? Isn't that playing into Fenric's hands?"

"For humans, they understand the forest better than your soldiers," Gossama replied.

Quig swam before Granite. "You don't know me, but I agree with the Dasari. As far as humans go, I say those two are a good bet."

"I see. Noon, tomorrow." Granite saluted Gossama.

"Noon." She looked to the floating fey. "Coming or going?"

"Sadly, I cannot bless you all with my presence tonight. If this reyuul has enlisted dark fey, then you'll need a bit more help than a few competent humans. I must secure my village. See you tomorrow." Quig's voice echoed as he faded from sight.

Granite motioned for the rest to follow as he took off at a jog. Gossama slipped Stefan something into his hand.

"Don't die," she said. To Pol, she said, "Protect him." She bounded off into the forest.

Stefan opened up his hand and examined something inscribed on a leaf. Pol half expected Stefan to complain or make a smart remark. Instead, he looked up at Pol, his expression serious, before following Granite.

What did the leaf say?

"Move out!" Granite commanded.

The forest edge was an hour away at a steady pace, and Pol stayed with Stefan but said nothing. The serious expression never left Stefan's face. He must be thinking.

More than anything, Pol felt he had a better understanding of Stefan as compared to when they had entered Miraden. The young man had not exhibited his "warning signs" in weeks, and he had demonstrated resolve to do the right thing today. Stefan was far from perfect, but Pol appreciated him more.

Pol had a deeper appreciation of many things since coming to Miraden but especially from his near-death experience in Fenric's lair. The threat of death made him realize there were things he needed to do and resolve. First, he wanted to spend time with Adeel and get to know her. The letter he had sent prior to leaving for the forest had hopefully made it to her. Would she respond? Did she really mean the things she had said in Dael? He wanted to know.

Second, Pol didn't want to die being angry at his father. The man had made mistakes, and Pol had gotten hurt, but lying on his belly with his arms shackled, he regretted the rift between them. Pol realized he would have to forgive his father, and Pol didn't know if he could do that, but he respected his father for allowing him to make his own decisions, which had led Pol to Miraden. Now that Pol could take care of himself and not have to endure abuse at the hands of nobles or anyone, Pol would use that respect as a bridge to heal the relationship with his father.

Thinking about it, Pol realized that anger at his father was probably the true source of the angry red flames in his heart. Redirecting his thoughts to protect others was good, but he couldn't ignore the damage in his heart.

When they reached the forest edge, Granite halted the group. A ragged, eerie screech pierced the air. There was no mistaking the sound, but it wasn't from the forest. It came from the village.

Color drained from Granite's face as cold determination overtook his features. "That's what the reyuul meant." He tightened the straps of his pack and walked over to Stefan, placing his face a few inches away. "This is a strategic attack against the village and a diversion. I can't leave you unprotected, but every second you delay me, another person may die." He tightened his pack. "Corporal, your fist protects Stefan. Go." He broke into a run.

Pol tore Stefan's pack off his back and pushed him forward. He mimicked Granite and scanned every direction as they ran up the road toward the village. Not having to jump across branches or watch for roots made running easier, and Stefan thankfully kept pace. They didn't encounter any obstacles over the few miles to the village center, but Stefan cursed a few times, his face flushed, and Pol had to catch him twice from falling.

When they arrived, Pol almost repeated Stefan's curses.

A slimy black monster with bright-green veins coursing down its body prowled before the Point. The eight-foot-long creature released a screech that sounded like metal raking against stone as it stalked back and forth before the holy structure.

Granite pulled up to the two lines of soldiers facing the vrent. The forward line held spears, with men and women pale and visibly shaking. Archers formed the rear line.

Captain Dreint turned as murmurs started when Granite reached the rear line.

Granite gave a salute. "Report."

Dreint shook his head. "We found it like this. It keeps screeching at the Point, but it won't go inside. There's blood on the steps, and we think the cleric is inside, but we can't get past it. Cleric Bruit was heading home from the garrison after having asked about you."

Pol saw the bright-red blood smears. A small red flame ignited over the embers deep in his soul. He focused on the cleric. *Protect them.* The red drained away, leaving brilliant white embers.

Granite asked, "Arrows?"

"If they stick, nothing. The few crossbows we have hit harder, but then it gets angry." He pointed to the group of soldiers, including Corporal Creyd, tending wounded in front of Judge Fead's residence. "We need to get to the cleric, but it won't leave."

"That evil abomination can't enter the Point, but the cleric is probably the target," Granite replied.

The damned creature couldn't enter holy ground. Pol dropped the packs. "Fall Commander, I'll fight it."

Granite glanced back at him. "Captain, get the kid a sword and shield, and someone find Fuiger."

"You're late, Stone." Fuiger limped forward with a huge crossbow. He locked in a bolt and said, "We need to get to Bruit, now."

Pol received the standard issue one-handed midsword and shield from a shaky grunt. Granite received another set and said, "Dreint, split the lines and have them flank the beast. Advance on my mark. Don't let it escape."

The captain stepped away and called out orders, forming the lines into two groups.

"Fuiger, don't kill us."

"Ask your boy about how good my aim was with the tomatoes."

"Pol, aim for the neck but don't let it scratch you. There's poison on the talons. Stay by my side."

The vrent growled in their direction. Pol heard his uncle's voice through the rushing noise in his ears. *Calm your breathing. Never underestimate a lost one and never show it mercy.*

Granite raised a hand up and brought it down in a chopping motion toward the monster.

Pol followed Granite in a dead sprint. The first bolt hummed between them, hitting the vrent in the shoulder. Fuiger had timed it well as the monster reared from the shot while Granite and Pol sliced both flanks. Green ichor oozed from the open flesh, blasting putrid odor.

Pol jumped over the lashing tail and hacked downward as it passed. The chomping maw latched onto Granite's shield, and he held it while another crossbow bolt lodged into the monster's flank. Pol reversed his grip and plunged his sword down toward the vrent's haunch, but the monster bucked, and the sword tip slid off the scales.

Granite landed another blow to the top of the neck, and the vrent took off, trying to escape the two attackers. The line of soldiers faltered, and the vrent tore through as it launched itself onto the tavern.

"Reform the lines! Keep it between you!" Granite yelled. "Rield! Find the cleric. Bring Stefan." He nodded at Pol. "Don't touch your blade. Protect the Point."

The vrent clambered over the roof and leapt to the tailor's roof before finding purchase atop the judge's residence.

Pol followed Corporal Rield and the grunts into the Point, and, surprisingly, Stefan joined them. They slowed down to avoid slipping in the blood on the steps. Past the foyer, the cleric lay on the ground, pale and sweating, with blood-soaked tan robes.

Corporal Rield shook the cleric. "Master Bruit!"

The pale eyelids fluttered open. "I'm here," he said weakly.

"How long have you been here?"

"A while."

Flustered, Pol didn't know where to begin, but Rield had the experience. "Lift his legs. Goors, apply pressure to his side." The soldier knelt in a pool of blood and used the cleric's robes to press against his side.

Stefan dropped his pack, pulled out green leaves, and tore them up. He poured water from his pouch onto the mass and pushed his way toward the cleric. He applied the poultice to the cleric's side. Master Bruit groaned for a moment.

Pol was about to help when the main doors burst open. The vrent barreled through, covered in white flames, with cross bolts and a sword embedded at various angles. The inner embers burst into white soulfire, and Pol raised his shield and plowed into the vrent, ramming it into the wall.

Roaring, Pol repeatedly drove his sword into the beast as it twitched. The vrent collapsed on its side but continued to claw its way toward the cleric and Stefan.

"No you will not!" Pol stood and, with two hands, brought the sword point down into the neck. Once embedded, Pol wrenched the sword ninety degrees, and the vrent finally collapsed, twitching and burning with white flames. After a moment, the vrent started disintegrating, with small pieces peeling off and disappearing.

Granite, Captain Dreint, and more soldiers burst into the Point, taking in the situation. Pol left the sword and dropped the shield, breathing hard.

Granite knelt down by Bruit. "Master Bruit, can you heal yourself?"

The cleric barely opened his eyes. "I've tried."

"Dreint, set up a temporary infirmary here. We'll need supplies. Have the command center ready as well. I want all officers there in one hour."

Dreint saluted and started barking orders.

"Don't die, Bruit," Granite said.

"Lohem decides." The cleric closed his eyes. Granite had another soldier replace Stefan, who still held pressure, and he escorted the boys outside. Pol felt shaky, but the embers remained strong and white.

"Excellent work. Pol, you really are a Vroshen. Stefan, thank you for helping the cleric. Wash up and meet me in the command center. Pol, don't leave his side."

Pol saluted and followed Stefan out. Gratitude. Pol felt so grateful to have helped and even more proud that he had killed the lost one. Uncle Eash would be proud.

Outside the Point, the buildings along the main street had significant damage to their roofs. Clumps of soldiers assisted the wounded onto litters to bring to the garrison infirmary.

"I understand now," Stefan whispered.

"What?"

"It's who you are. You were made to help others, to save others. It's natural, isn't it?" Stefan said.

Pol couldn't say much at first. "I just try to do the right thing."

"I'm not used to it."

"Have to start somewhere," Pol said.

Inside the garrison, villagers huddled with their families throughout the courtyard. Children clung to their parents. Fathers stood before their families with farm tools in hand. Pol led Stefan to the barracks, and he went directly to the washroom. Vrent saliva and gore did not wash off easily. Pol found his face was a little thinner in the mirror after a few weeks in the forest.

After getting cleaned up, he returned to his cot. There was an unopened letter sitting there. At first, he thought it might be from his family, but the beautiful penmanship and the quality of the paper led him to hope otherwise.

"She answered my letter." Heart racing and still only wearing his towel, he carefully opened the envelope without tearing it. Pol sat on the bed, dumbfounded.

Dear Pol,

I was so glad to hear from you. I haven't heard anything from my brother. I hope he hasn't been giving you a hard time.

I have so many questions. What's it like there in the village? Have you been to the forest? Is the training going well?

I must admit it's rather dull here. I am biased now, considering everything I have been through. I don't need that kind of excitement again. Can't wait to hear from you.

Thinking of you,

Adeel

Pol grinned at the letter. He read it again. This girl was not like other nobles. Her brother—Pol looked up to find Stefan standing in front of him.

"That's my sister's handwriting."

Pol slowly put the letter behind him, hoping Stefan might forget about it.

"What are you doing? I know it's still there."

Words had trouble forming in his mouth.

Stefan's face went through a wave of reactions. It ended with a deep breath.

"I know you just killed a vrent, but I can't approve. She's the daughter of a quon. She is Cordiaen nobility, and there are responsibilities that come with that. Do you understand? I'm saying that for both her sake and yours."

Pol held Stefan's eyes and squashed the small hint of anger that arose. "You may have guessed, but I don't like nobles. That someone could be 'better' than me just because they were born in a different family is insanity. That anyone can hurt my family just because they feel like it really angers me." He stood. "I want to believe that she is different. I want to believe that you are different. What happened today with you and that morning in Dael with the carriage made me realize nobles are people too and that some, very few—like, five—might be good people."

Stefan backed up a step. "I can't say that I'm different from other nobles. Being here has changed some things for me, but I know that a few weeks of getting my butt whooped and almost dying won't change everything. You may be a Vroshen, but you're still a commoner. I've never known a commoner, but you're not…horrible."

Pol said, "That's a start. So, can I write back to her? That's okay with you?"

"As long as you heed my warning, I...I won't get in the way."

Pol was surprised. "Thanks, Stefan."

"No. You haven't seen her throw a tantrum. Don't thank me."

<hr>

The command center was nothing more than a large room with spartan furnishings next to Captain Dreint's office, and Stefan considered what changes he would make if he ever had such an office. He sat on a tall wooden stool, glancing around and waiting for the meeting to begin. Maps of the village and surrounding area, including Miraden, hung on the walls. Granite sat at a desk, reviewing fresh reports. Stefan caught sight of parchments with the Pulse's designation, King's Army scrolls, and courtesan letters.

Granite sifted through everything in a matter of minutes. A general would have to assimilate a mountain of information, creating a plan in an instant on the battlefield, and Granite had been one of the most successful generals in Cordiaen history. Stefan should feel comfortable following such a man into battle.

But should he go into battle?

Nearby, Pol lounged in his chair with bags under his eyes. He really was a warrior. Stefan finally accepted it. A Blessed One, a Vroshen. Gossama was right. They would need Pol tomorrow.

Did they really need Stefan?

Yes. He could prevent deaths, and Gossama's message on the leaf confirmed it. Pol had strength. Stefan had knowledge. Granite had been trying to show him, and

Stefan finally agreed: they had to work together to defeat Fenric.

But the reyuul disturbed him. Fenric must have been handpicked by his superiors to enter the forest, evade Gossama, lure Stefan, and open a gate to unleash terror on the country. But why?

If someone else was pulling the strings, why? The strategic answer was for testing purposes. Fenric was a scout. They must have deployed him to see what trouble he could cause and pull him back if necessary. Fenric had a high chance of success, statistically speaking, with lost ones, mind-controlled villagers, and teleportation, but their Cordiaen force had fewer resources and no cleric to fight.

Fenric had a good plan, and the persistent, lurking concern in the back of Stefan's brain was the unknown factor that led to Stefan's arrival in Gaodis. Fenric knew about Geraul, which meant he knew about the attempted assassination, but who else was working with Fenric in Dael? Stefan may never find out…unless he asked his father.

Until then, Stefan had to focus on the battle. Stefan could see various solutions to the problems Fenric presented, and he could even develop contingency plans, assuming he wanted to place his life at risk.

The last time he failed to engage, people almost died. His family almost died. The consequences of his failure had been real. Stefan closed his eyes and reflected on the consequences of those decisions.

This fight was the right thing to do. It's what Pol was going to do. "Granite," Stefan said, "I want to fight Fenric, but I don't want to die."

Granite gave Stefan a side glance and said, "Did I ever tell you how I came to Gaodis?"

"You told the King of Cordiae he was wrong…to his face."

Granite leaned back in his seat. "I mentioned that I was the general responsible for the southwestern legions in Jetea. We had fought against Ampestrian raids for years, and this constituted much of the war. We had just repelled one of the largest and most brutal invasion forces while being stationed at Fort Cherrien. We won and fought them back across the river and routed them back to BladeHeight. King Sraung's father, King Surtian, wanted us to take the stronghold, but I thought it was strategically unnecessary and would waste lives."

"We've talked about this," Stefan replied.

"Not all of it. I argued with the king for hours that night. I told him that if he was going to fight at BladeHeight, then he would do it without me because I could not justify leading the men and women who trusted me to their imminent deaths." Granite sighed. "I handed him my resignation. He appointed Commander Iota to become the new general. I returned to Jetea by morning, picked up my things, and headed straight for your father in Dael. Know what I'm known for?"

"Lowest mortality of any general in the history of Cordiae," Stefan said.

"Believe it. If we come up with the right plan, we can avoid a lot of deaths, including yours. So use that big brain of yours."

Stefan could fight for that. "Father really helped you, huh?"

Granite smiled. "When I left Jetea, Daoringer welcomed me and was going to advocate for me to have a position as a general for the northern armies, but I told him no. I loved this country, and I loved the King's Army, but I wanted to sit back and let someone else lead for a while. I came to Gaodis to serve these people, and I couldn't have done it without your father."

"He never mentioned it," Stefan said.

"I had spent years corresponding with and counseling him about the Sperunese, and I learned that Daoringer can be rough around the edges, but when it counted, the man cared about his people and his country. He also cared about his family. Looking at you, he saw what you had done, and he knew sending you to Gaodis would help you like it helped me."

Stefan wanted to curse. "I'm not saying you're wrong. It just sucked." It was the toughest thing Stefan had ever done, but he did not want to dwell on it. He needed to focus on the battle. "I'm really sorry about Cleric Bruit. He's a good cleric."

"He's not gone yet, and he is a great cleric, one who saw a young man who needed Lohem."

Stefan needed to thank the cleric. "Yes, sir. Still, losing a cleric is tough for our situation."

Granite cleared his throat. "Reyuul always target the clerics. I underestimated the reyuul, and I failed Bruit today."

"Will you fail us? Can you function for this fight?" Stefan asked.

Pol said, "Stefan!"

"No, it's a fair question," Granite said. "I'm struggling, but I have hope. Bruit taught me that. Hope that we'll get those families. Hope that we'll protect the village. Hope that no one will die, but I know I can't protect everyone, especially without a cleric. But I can't hide. I'm needed. I'll deal with it the best I can, day by day, hour by hour." Granite smiled. "Enough about me. Ready to fight, huh?"

"I think so," Stefan replied.

"I am," said Pol.

"We know that," Granite said. "You just have to keep your head about you."

"Yes, sir."

Captain Dreint, Judge Fead, HQs Tontia, Veroaniss, Jieggs, and Reamy entered and took their seats in the circle of chairs facing Granite's desk.

Granite said, "Welcome, Captain. Report."

"Fall Commander, we lost one soldier in the attack; Grunt Geanna didn't survive."

Granite's jaw tensed.

Captain Dreint continued, "Sorry about that, Fall Commander. Another four soldiers were injured. Two civilians died. A small fire in the judge's house was extinguished. No word on reinforcements, but civilian messengers have been sent to Ariel and General Croaga."

"Excellent. Captain, is Fuiger okay?"

"Yes, sir, but he won't leave Bruit's side."

"Thank you, Captain. Bruit's in good hands." He looked at Judge Fead. "I'm glad you and your family are safe."

"Thanks to you and the King's Army."

Granite nodded. "As for the situation, we are dealing with an experienced and skilled reyuul named Fenric. His primary ability seems to be teleportation, which is how he moved the villagers to his base of operations and how he transported the vrent to the middle of the village. Cleric Bruit's assault was intentional."

Granite looked directly at Judge Fead. "We can expect more attacks."

"We can't stand another assault like that one," Judge Fead said.

"That's why we are going to leave at first light tomorrow." He pointed to a crude map of the forest on the wall with RainCrest labeled.

"Fenric has the villagers at a site near RainCrest. They are alive but under some sort of mind control. They are building a gate to release lost ones."

"That's unbelievable," Judge Fead replied.

"We have a witness. It's big. Gossama tells us that the gate is not completed, but that's not something we can just wait for."

Captain Dreint stopped taking notes. "How do you want to attack?"

"Without reinforcements, we just have an incomplete company of ninety soldiers, which will have to divide to both defend and attack."

"Surely we don't need too many against one reyuul?" Judge Fead asked.

"Judge, I don't think you understand. This reyuul has a mental ability to control others. We may fight against more than just him. We might have to fight against the villagers."

"You can't. Those are our people."

"I understand, but it is what it is. We'll bring fifty men and leave the rest. Captain, where do you want to be?"

"I know the village better than the forest. I'll stay here and coordinate the defense."

"Fine. It may be the worst of the deal. There's a good chance you'll face more monsters, but I agree. I have some strategies to finalize, but the plan is to leave before dawn and enter the forest at first light. We'll arrive by noon."

"What about the people in the village?" Concern edged the judge's voice.

"If Fenric is to attack, he'll aim where we are most vulnerable. He'll transport the lost ones throughout the village. If we are to keep the people safe, then they should be protected in the garrison."

"Can you fit everyone in here?" Judge Fead asked.

Captain nodded. "It'll be tight, but the soldiers can sleep on the walls, and we can fit the thousand or more villagers into the compound. We have enough food and water. The barracks were designed to house a full regiment, so it shouldn't be a problem."

Granite said, "Captain, you're in charge of coordinating the villagers. I'll have you work out logistics, and then we'll bring the people tonight."

Dreint saluted. "Yes, sir. Let me get to it. HQ Elquin and Tiatol, you're with me."

Judge Fead stood. "Captain, I'm coming with you. I'll help coordinate the evacuation to the garrison."

"Thank you, Judge."

After they left, Granite said, "Pol, go with Jieggs and Reamy here and help at the armory. We need to let Fuiger know if there's any repairs."

Pol looked between Stefan and Granite but said, "Yes, sir," and left with the two HQs.

Alone with Stefan, the fall commander said, "Let's brainstorm how to hunt a reyuul. What are some of his strengths and weaknesses?"

Stefan opened up his thoughts like a catalog. "He can teleport long distances, but it takes time to create the portal. He can also teleport short distances in a flash, but he's vulnerable to physical attacks."

"What else?"

"Uh, he can command lost ones, but I don't know how many at once." Stefan closed his eyes. "Mind control or enchantment, as the books refer to it. He should be able to send the villagers against us. Directing the attacks from a distance complements his style. Melee attacks will be useless because he can evade them. We'll have to rely on long-range attacks."

"Excellent. Tell me the plans you've come up with."

Stefan balked.

"I sent everyone away so you wouldn't feel embarrassed, and I know you've already thought about it. Spill it."

Stefan had to get over the discomfort of revealing his plans, something he was not used to, but there was a decent probability of success. The plan was unorthodox, but his resources in such a village were limited.

After he finished sharing his ideas, Granite leaned back in his chair and placed his hands behind his head. "That's crazy." He glanced over to the forest map and then back at Stefan. "Let's talk about how to make it happen."

CHAPTER 26

"Preparing for war is like writing a symphony. When every element synchronizes, it's beautiful. If one instrument is off, it's a mess, and it could cost lives."

–Cleric Joern, Advanced Cordiaen Military Tactics, Volume 2.

Pol woke to Stefan shaking him. After assisting at the armory, Pol had returned to the barracks alone but had fallen asleep easily after writing a few letters, one to Adeel and one to his father. He rubbed his eyes. "Is everything okay?"

"Yes." Stefan had bags under his eyes and looked tired.

"Did you sleep?"

"I had a few hours. There were some things to prepare. Speaking of which, check your trunk."

Pol noticed his personal chest was open. Pol climbed out of the cot and stood over his trunk. The sight stole his breath.

Next to his usual white training uniform, a chain mail cuirass and standard Cordiaen helmet awaited him. His eyes widened as they found the black pants, black boots, and an official white and black grunt surcoat. A King's Army issue sword and shield with the Cordiaen crest rested next to the chest. HQ Jieggs had asked about his sizes in the armory, and Pol had allowed himself a seed of hope.

Pol glanced at Stefan. "Does this mean…"

"Yes. Granite approved. Let's get ready," Stefan said, a faint smirk playing at the corner of his mouth. Pol quickly donned the armor and new clothes, belted on the sword, and hefted the shield. He always appreciated how light the actual weapons were compared to the heavy wooden training equipment.

Stefan had put on his uniform as well; he also had a sword and a shield, and leather pouches hanging from his belt.

Pol pointed to Stefan's belt. "Last night's preparations?"

Stefan shrugged. "If I'm going to face death, I'd like to believe I am prepared."

"We're going to work together?" Pol hesitated to ask.

"Yes. That's calculated in the best chances of survival."

Pol chuckled. "That's something."

In the courtyard, Granite waited as soldiers formed up before him, grouped into fists. Each fist had a corporal as the leader, who handed out small leather pouches like the one Stefan wore.

Granite waved Stefan and Pol over and handed Pol a small leather pouch. "Attach this to your belt. Stefan, we got the final preparations done when you went to sleep. I'll say it again: it's crazy, dangerous, and unpredictable."

"Thank you, sir."

"Sir, huh? I guess that means you're ready to enter the King's Army."

"It is in my best interests, sir."

"For someone so smart, Gossama is right: you're slow."

Stefan rolled his eyes. Pol grinned at the interaction; given how Stefan had applied himself in RainCrest, if he was actually committed to action, they had a good chance against the reyuul.

"Gentlemen, you've earned the rank of grunt. Do you accept this honor?"

Pol saluted. "Yes, sir!"

Stefan looked down at his tunic and gave a hesitant salute. "Yes, sir."

Granite called out, "Attention! We've got new recruits! Welcome grunts, Pol and Stefan. They'll be assigned to Corporal Rield's fist."

The assembled company launched into singing "The Act of Valor." The chorus produced goosebumps, and Pol's hand rested on his sword hilt. He had waited a long time for this. He wasn't an officer yet, but this was a huge first step.

Granite pointed the boys to a waiting Corporal Rield. "Go join your fist."

Pol jogged over and saluted the corporal while Stefan took his time but also gave a salute.

As he passed the assembled troops, Corporal Creyd smiled and yelled, "Hustle, Grunt!"

Rield also smiled at Stefan. "I remember when I had to sling you over my saddle."

Stefan said, "Be nice to me. I might be your superior one day."

Rield laughed out loud. "You have to survive today. For now, shut up and form up."

Pol obeyed and agreed Stefan needed that.

Captain Dreint yelled, "Attention!"

Granite raised his voice from the front. "Half the battle is showing up. Even after yesterday, even after the monster tore through the village, you're here. We lost comrades, and no one takes that harder than me. But you're here, and because you're here, we've already won."

Under his breath, Stefan murmured, "I *could* go back to bed."

"No," Pol said. The young man might be committed, but that didn't mean he wasn't scared. Pol remembered Gossama's direction to protect Stefan.

"Today, we march to Miraden," Granite called out. "We will recover the lost villagers. We will destroy this reyuul who has infiltrated our lands. Trust in your officers and their instructions. Your corporals will brief you as we travel. May Lohem be with us. For King and Country!"

"For King and Country!" replied the assembled soldiers.

"For Cordiae!"

"For Cordiae!"

Pol and Stefan fell in line with Thielda and Wrues behind Rield, who held a torch. Their fist was the last to leave, and Granite traveled next to them. His new fist mates had entered Miraden with them a few weeks ago, but now Geanna had been slain, and Sounder had been injured. He and Stefan had filled their roles.

Corporal Rield said, "Fist Nine, ears up. Stefan and Pol, welcome to the fist. You've already met Thielda and Wrues. Today's primary objective is to rescue the villagers. Secondary objective is the reyuul. You will cover each other in pairs, and I'll cover you. We will most likely be fighting the villagers. Use your shields and fists if you can but defend your life. Keep your new pouch handy. You will need it."

Pol wasn't sure if he should speak, but he said, "I'm sorry for what happened yesterday. We can't replace those soldiers, but I'm glad to fight beside you today."

Thielda and Wrues gave him serious glances. Thielda said, "That Dasari ranger said you should be there. We'll get you there. You'll have to step up now that you're a grunt."

Pol would have run the entire way and destroyed the reyuul right then. "I do."

Rield added, "It's good to have you, Pol, and you, Stefan."

Giving a terse nod, Stefan looked pale and kept marching.

As they passed homesteads and farms on their way to the forest, Pol couldn't help but notice the silence. With dawn arriving, people should be out doing chores by now and working on breakfast even before the sun came out. Instead, all the villagers were housed at the garrison, waiting for an attack.

The sky lightened by the time they entered the tree line. Pol thought of Gossama. "Think Gossama will make it on time?"

Stefan shifted his chain mail cuirass. "SilverGate is miles away. She had a long way to go, but she'll be there."

Pol wanted to run and scout, growing restless. After weeks of running to go anywhere in the forest, he itched to break into a sprint.

"Patience," Granite said, falling back to their position. "Soldiers who keep their wits about them tend to do better."

"How are you so calm?"

Granite smiled. "I've had practice."

"Yes, sir." Pol kept formation as they traveled deeper into the forest. His eyes scanned everything—bushes, the canopy, and other soldiers. He expected an attack from anywhere. Surely, the reyuul knew they were coming, but other than a few small rustling bushes, which made everyone in the formation turn, nothing jumped out at them.

After an hour at a snail's pace compared to how Gossama traveled, Pol grew tired as they entered a small clearing. He shook his head and berated himself for feeling fatigued after just a few miles, even with mail armor. After a yawn, Pol yelped in surprise when Stefan slapped his face. Stefan then shoved an open leather bag up to Pol's nose. A pungent smell assaulted his nostrils.

"What are you doing?"

Stefan pulled the pouch back and pointed to a small clump of leaves forming into a two-foot-tall humanoid figure to their left. The little leaf figure had a toothless mouth with no other facial features, and vines grew around its torso, upper and lower appendages securing the debris into a solid form.

"Pol, if those iveys touch you, they will paralyze you. Keep them occupied for a moment."

Pol felt more awake but became concerned as his comrades began drooping and then collapsing to the ground. Even Granite fell. Pol drew his sword as twelve compact figures took shape from the natural debris on the ground and formed a perimeter around their force.

"What do we do?" Pol said.

"Those are the copies of a lost ivey, a lost one, and I'm looking for it."

"Were these the ones responsible for the last time I passed out?"

Stefan scanned the clearing. "Yes."

A small whip of panic lashed out inside of Pol as the little creatures ran forward, placing their "hands" on the exposed faces of the fallen soldiers. Some soldiers spasmed for a few seconds before going limp. The small monsters detached to attack other fallen soldiers. Even Creyd went down. Three of the monsters slowly approached Pol, who stood before Stefan.

Pol swallowed against the fear and said, "No," lashing out at the nearest ivey. His sword tore through the monster with minimal resistance, and it fell apart. Pol blinked and attacked the others with the same result. With a step back toward Stefan, he watched as the piles of dirt, leaves, and tendrils quivered before they reformed. As more and more of his comrades succumbed to the monsters, more iveys surrounded Pol.

"Stefan?"

"I know, I know. Go for the tree," Stefan said.

Pol slashed through another five, clearing a path to the nearest tree. The iveys didn't move fast, but they didn't need to if their prey had been immobilized.

Stefan clambered up a silverwood, grunting while Pol continued to sweep his sword and keep the iveys at bay. With a quick jump, Pol hauled himself up and followed Stefan higher.

"What are we doing?" Pol asked, blinking his eyes against the fatigue.

"I told you, I'm searching for the main ivey." Stefan shoved the pungent-smelling pouch back into Pol's face. "We have to keep moving or they'll find us, and we have to hurry."

"Why?" Pol asked as he roused.

Stefan pointed at the other King's Army soldiers. The surrounding ground had turned dark, and the soldiers were slowly sinking into the softer ground. "The iveys aren't strong, but they will devour each person they sink into the ground."

"How do you know which one is the main one?"

Stefan pointed to an ivey that was larger than the rest, with a red diamond-shaped jewel in the chest. It was watching from behind a tree.

"I've seen it before. Here, take this." Stefan inhaled with the herb pouch near his nose and then gave Pol the pouch. "You have a better chance than I do, but you'll have to use this. The closer you get, the stronger the sedation."

"What do I have to do?"

"The main ivey is weak, but the others will fiercely protect it. Get close enough and destroy the red jewel."

"How do you know this? Wait...you're a genius, right?"

"I knew of the lost iveys, but Gossama handed me the recipe for the antidote before she left. I went to the village herbalist last night. Enough questions. They need you."

Pol looked down at the soldiers slowly sinking into the ground. There wasn't much time. He observed the locations of each ivey and pushed any fear of the monsters away. With a deep breath, he focused on the soldiers in trouble, and a small white flame ignited over the embers in his soul.

Pol dropped his shield and held out his hand. "Give me your sword."

Stefan handed him the hilt and said, "Don't die."

Pol reversed his grip on the extra sword, nodded, and with a quick leap, he traversed the canopy while keeping his eyes on the red diamond. The main ivey must have sensed his approach as it retreated behind the group of incapacitated soldiers. The other iveys waddled quickly to place themselves before the main ivey. No matter how fast he could move through the canopy, Pol would have to engage some of the little monsters.

Deep inside his soul, the flame grew. He was not angry; he was determined. People were going to die if he did not do this.

With a series of leaps from branch to branch, Pol burned his nostrils with an inhalation of the herb pouch and finally hopped off a limb to a lower branch and swung himself to the ground, running and drawing both swords.

Pol cut through the iveys, but he knew it would be temporary as he plowed a path toward the main ivey, which continued to retreat around the unconscious soldiers. Pol could feel fatigue encroach upon his awareness. No other soldiers stirred, and he knew Stefan wouldn't be able to stay awake without the herbs.

If he didn't finish this, no one would.

With a burst of speed, Pol swatted two iveys away, careful not to let their appendages touch him, scared that even a brush against his skin would paralyze him.

Instinct made him jump as an ivey shot upward, concealed within the ground. Pol barely escaped the emerging ivey, but he didn't stop progressing toward his goal.

A group of six iveys formed before Pol as the main red diamond ivey stopped and glared with gleaming orange eyes.

While there were many little monsters, they weren't fast. Pol aimed left of the formation, jumping over fellow soldiers, and the main ivey moved clockwise away from him, keeping the other iveys between them. Pol made a sharp turn straight toward the defending monsters, who struggled to keep up and vaulted himself over all the iveys.

The iveys grew upward, but Pol sliced their reaching appendages as he flew over and whirled both weapons as he landed, destroying the nearest two minions. Pol's swords kept their momentum, and he lashed out at the main ivey, cleaving the monster's head in two and rolling away. The smaller iveys froze.

The orange eyes flickered, and a green gas released from its broken body. Pol backed away farther, concerned the gas was deadly. Slowly, the main ivey's head repaired itself with leaves, vines, and mud, while the red diamond glowed angrily as it reformed. The other iveys reanimated with jerky movements.

Pol understood.

Holding his breath, he charged toward the jewel with his right sword, and three smaller iveys rose before his sword tip impaling themselves upon it and locking it in place. Pol released the sword as they reached for his arm, and he lunged with the left sword and plunged it through the red diamond and twisted.

The diamond shattered.

A single, sonorous wail released from the main ivey, which slowly disintegrated into a pile of vegetation. The green cloud lingered, but the remaining iveys fell apart.

Pol backed away from the cloud, which dissipated in the gentle forest breeze, and finally took a deep breath. He whipped out the herb pouch and inhaled. Reeling from the acrid smell, he searched and verified all the little monsters had fallen.

Then, he took a deep breath and roared his exhilaration. It was a long, satisfying roar that no one heard, but it felt good to release the pent up fear in his heart. If he could take down a lost one, he could do more; he could honor his family's name.

Invigorated, Pol started reviving the other soldiers with the pouch. Some were halfway in the ground when their eyes opened, and many of them couldn't move once awakened.

Pol climbed the tree and found Stefan asleep, but he awoke easily to the herbs. When Stefan sat up and looked around and then down, he said, "I was right. You did it."

Pol considered that a tremendous compliment and handed Stefan back his sword while retrieving his own shield. "Stefan, how long will the paralysis last?"

"Don't know, but we're vulnerable right now. Let's dig them out."

Pol and Stefan found Granite with his left leg and arm stuck in the ground. When he awoke, he appeared embarrassed.

"Good job, boys. Help me out." The ground was still soft, and the fall commander emerged with their help.

Granite rested on his back, unable to sit up. "Secure as many as possible and set up a guard until we recover."

As soon as Granite finished talking, Pol heard the hum of a portal. His heart constricted as he found the portal in the trees and two vrent emerged, stalking along branches. The monsters released bellowing screeches and prowled through the canopy above them.

Pol's fingers blanched as he gripped his sword. Most of the King's Army soldiers couldn't even move, and some realized their predicament and began shouting. They were going to be slaughtered. Pol's inner white flame burst into a full fire.

His feet moved on their own as Pol followed the monster's movement and traversed the path between impaired soldiers who cringed in fear. One vrent dropped onto a fallen tree outside the group of soldiers. Pol advanced past the edge of soldiers who were shouting and trying to wield their weapons.

Pol pressed his lips together and took his battle stance. Slimy black scales with bulging green veins rippled over its monstrous form. The vrent snapped its moist maw with saliva stretching between fangs. The muscular legs crouched while the powerful tail swept back and forth. The vrent's red eyes appeared intelligent and menacing.

Pol took deep breaths through his nose. He dropped his shield and picked up a fallen sword.

The other vrent moved around their position. Pol couldn't fight two separate battles.

Behind him, Stefan said, "Pol, I'll take the other side."

Pol couldn't believe what he had just heard. Was Stefan really going to try? The disgraced qual wouldn't stand a chance against a vrent, but he seemed determined. Did he know he was going to his death? But if no one stood before the other vrent, the soldiers didn't have a hope. "Aim for their throats, if you can. Lohem's blessing."

"Thanks," Stefan replied as he left. He really was going to try. Pol needed to be quick with this one so he could help Stefan. His soulfire burned bigger and hotter.

No one was going to die. Nothing was going to get past. He roared at the vrent, raised his sword, and charged.

The monster tilted its head as if confused for a second before also charging.

When the vrent leapt, Pol used his momentum to slide underneath and pierce the vrent's underside. Black gore sluiced onto his new white-and-black tunic, and that angered him almost more than the threat to the soldiers.

The vrent had responded to his dive by bringing down its tail, but Pol crossed his swords and took the brunt with his blades digging into the writhing tail. The force slammed Pol to the ground, and he grunted and rolled to his feet. The resulting screech shook his body as the vrent whipped around and charged with its gaping maw snapping for Pol.

Pol barely slipped to the side, slicing the vrent's flank with both swords before resetting his stance and placing himself before the onlooking crowd of soldiers.

Breathing hard, Pol flicked the gore from his weapons and held them out to the sides.

When the vrent screeched again, Pol yelled in response, but the vrent didn't advance. Black gore continued to flow from its flank and underside, and it retreated a step.

No. Pol raced forward. He wasn't going to allow the vrent to escape.

The vrent whipped its body around, flinging its tail at Pol, who leapt over it and aimed his swords into the scaly flank, but this time he poured his strength into piercing the scales. The blades found purchase, but the vrent continued to whirl, and its shoulder slammed into Pol, flinging him into a tree. Thankfully, he held onto the weapons, which had released a small fountain of black-and-green gore, but he fell to a knee, pain exploding from his back and head from the hit.

The vrent was slower but took advantage of Pol's disengagement and pounced. Pol flung his swords up against a claw, and the talons raked against the steel, producing sparks and driving Pol to the side. The vrent used the opportunity to launch itself onto the tree, but Pol lunged, reversing his right sword grip and plunging the steel tips into the monster's lower half. The vrent squirmed and flung its lower body from side to side as it climbed, but the movement allowed Pol to leverage his weight and rip open more flesh as he clung to the lower half. As the vrent continued onto the lowest branch, Pol repeatedly plunged his swords into the vrent's dorsum until the vrent lost its footing and plunged ten feet to the ground. Pol rolled off, dropped a sword, and caught a limb with one hand.

The vrent collapsed to the ground and twitched. When it started to rise, Pol once again almost cursed. Stefan had been a bad influence on his mouth. Instead, he dropped from the branch and drove his remaining sword downward, skewering the vrent's neck as he landed. More gore exploded from the wound and onto Pol's surcoat.

He withdrew the sword and slashed down on the neck once, twice, three times, finally severing the head.

As the vrent dissolved, Pol staggered, catching his breath and wincing from the pain in his back, head, and shoulder.

But he did it.

⁓⁓

Stefan did not have to shake off the lingering drowsiness from the iveys. Watching the vrent jump from branch to branch as he stood before Granite and the other soldiers made his heart pound. Giving Pol the bag of herbs and having him attack the main ivey was easy. Stefan just had to trust in Pol's abilities, and having been at the wrong end of Pol's training swords, Stefan understood what the Vroshen could do.

Stefan's breathing quickened as the vrent dropped to the ground. The stalking monster's muscles rippled underneath the black and vibrant-green moist scales. The maw snapped as the vrent slowly approached, making Stefan blink.

Stefan was not Pol. He could not kill this abomination. He was going to die right here, but what else could he do? Behind him, forty-eight incapacitated soldiers lay on the ground. If he did not stand before them, no one would. He did not lie to himself; Stefan wanted to run away. But he chose not to.

Stefan widened his stance. The vrent continued to stalk toward him with twenty feet separating them. Stefan calculated his options for the best outcome, and the steps required to defeat the vrent flitted through his awareness, but it was useless. His physical ability did not match the requirements he needed to kill the monster; he was not Pol.

But Pol had not backed down when he had needed to kill the iveys.

The vrent tensed and exploded toward him. Stefan clamped his jaw.

When the vrent pounced, Stefan sidestepped the snapping jaws with the intention of plunging his sword into the beast's neck, but his strike did not penetrate the scales.

Instead, the vrent's front leg slammed into Stefan's chest and sent him flying backward, landing on his side. He lost his shield but kept the sword in his hand. Pol would have been proud that he had not lost his sword.

The vrent veered toward him, and Stefan could only watch with a hand over his hurting left side and his sword held feebly before him.

A rope of blue lightning tore through the air, accompanied by a sonorous high-pitched battle cry.

Quig had returned.

The charging slimy black-and-green monster skidded to a halt a few feet before Stefan as the blue lightning coursed through its twitching reptilian body. Then, an enormous animal plowed into the vrent's left side. It took Stefan a moment to register the brown, furry animal with large studs forming a line down the head and back.

It was the bear that had attacked Stefan twice.

The vrent had fallen on its side, and the studded bear continued to tear into the lost one's flank with its jaw and took out swathes of scaled skin with its claws. Stefan stepped back as the vrent regained its balance and knocked the bear backward. Once again, vibrant blue lightning ripped through the air, seizing the vrent. The bear returned, barreling into the vrent once again and continued its assault.

Stefan held his breath as the vrent's fangs were about to rip into the bear's midsection, knowing that any bite would be a death sentence, when the vrent's head snapped to the side with a blue arrow sticking out of its left eye.

The bear threw the stunned monster off and continued to tear the monster apart until it no longer thrashed. With fatigued movements, the bear shook its head and found Stefan.

Stefan reached for his belt to produce another small leather pouch as the bear slowly padded its way over to him. The bear growled but did not charge him, and Stefan did not know what to do. Gossama stepped up beside him, and the bear approached her, allowing her to cuff her hand along his neck.

In Dasari, she said, "Little soldier now?"

Still wary, he replied, "Yes."

"You stink of metal. Good luck running and climbing trees in that."

"Thank you for your encouragement, honored elder."

Gossama laughed, and Stefan cringed at her snorting.

"Thank you for saving me, Gossama."

"You're slow, Shrewd One. But good work."

"What about me?" Quig said with vestiges of electricity flickering around the fey.

"Thank you for saving—"

"Of course, you're welcome. See what happens when I leave you alone?"

Stefan rolled his eyes. "Did you just both get here, or were you watching us?"

"Just arrived," Gossama said.

"Me too," Quig added.

Stefan sighed, and the bear turned toward him, sniffing. Stefan was about to thrust a pouch at the bear's face when the bear pawed his chest playfully, pushing Stefan back a few steps.

Stefan winced at the pain in his left ribs, but his concern deflated. "Tell the bear I said 'thank you' as well."

"Durnah likes to have her neck scratched. I asked her to help. She knew your scent and found you quickly. She likes you."

"She attacked me and ate my arm," Stefan replied.

"She's a bear. She guards the forest. You were an outsider when she first met you, and you had a mandra weapon the second time." Gossama examined the bear's hide, and after she was satisfied, she pointed to the trees and the bear padded off.

"Thank you for not letting me die," Stefan said.

The female Dasari shrugged and headed toward the group of soldiers on the ground. "Granite would yell at me if you died, but he's not doing well either."

Granite shook his head as he propped himself up with his right arm. "I heard that. Thank you, Gossama." He looked at Stefan. "Thank you, Stefan."

"I did nothing."

"You did everything. You gave Gossama time. She was slow."

Gossama folded her arms. "I had errands." They turned to find Pol approaching them. Green-and-black gore covered his tunic and chain mail, and two swords hung limply from his hands.

Gossama said, "Youngling didn't need help."

Pol grinned. "I didn't die." He examined Stefan up and down. "You all right?"

Stefan held his left side. "I think my ribs broke again, but I'll be fine. Quig, Gossama, and a bear saved me."

Quig swam around Pol. "I see you've learned to use your soulfire, Conqueror."

"How do you know about soulfire?"

Quig whispered, "Legends...oh, the legends."

Stefan felt a small twinge of jealousy, but he squashed it. Pol probably should have legends told about him.

Granite sat up. "Gossama, I'm getting some control back, but how long will the paralysis last?"

Gossama said, "Another half hour and you can move."

"Fenric laid a smart trap," Granite said. "Attacking with an ivey almost killed us if not for Stefan's foresight, and the follow-up with the vrents should have finished the job."

"Yes. Shrewd reyuul. Do not fear. I'm here," Gossama said.

"Yes, but I thought you were bringing reinforcements."

Gossama shrugged. "They're debating. I left. May come. May not."

"Quig, any help from the fey?"

"No fey is foolish enough to cross the Veil like me. Our community banded together to eradicate a small company of dark fey. I think this mandrate was planning to bring them through, but not anymore!"

Stefan folded his arms and lowered his head. He absorbed everything, including the attacks, the plan, and Gossama's report.

Granite said, "What's on your mind, Stefan?"

"Is Fenric really that smart, or could he be watching from afar? I wonder if he didn't use divination to assist him."

"Either way, he's one step ahead," Pol said.

Granite said, "Yes, but Stefan's right. How he takes that step is important."

"If he requires that kind of preparation, then he might make mistakes if we don't give him time to prepare," Stefan said.

Granite sat up taller. "Which is what we're doing right now. Help the others get up and moving. Gossama, can you make sure we don't have any more surprises?"

"Of course." The Dasari flitted off into the forest while Stefan assisted Pol in helping soldiers out of the ground. Stefan realized how lucky it was that Gossama and Quig showed up when they did. Was it luck or divine assistance? Was Lohem aiding them? They would need his help to continue.

After a half hour, and without further attacks, the King's Army resumed their formation, with many coming to thank Pol and Stefan as word spread about what happened.

Granite called out, "You can thank them later. Let's move out. We have a reyuul to kill."

CHAPTER 27

"At some point as a commander, you must trust your troops."

–Cleric Joern, Advanced Cordiaen Military Tactics, Volume 2.

Two hours later, Pol decided that he should have been more careful to avoid vrent ichor from soaking the front of his surcoat and armor. The rancid smell was only half as bad as having to march in the sticky aftermath.

The white embers still burned within his soul, even after battling the vrent. Uncle Eash had been right; emotions destabilized soulfire, creating massive ebbs and flows like the North Sea near Dael. Having a purpose or intention generated reliable strength that didn't waste energy. They still had another battle, but Pol could fight, even with his injuries.

The Cordiaen soldiers marched through the trees, with only Pol and Stefan having taken injuries from the battle with the lost ones. A sense of accomplishment replaced the initial jitters of facing battle. Maybe they did have a chance against the reyuul.

Gossama melded from a tree right next to Granite, who pulled his dagger.

"I almost killed you. I thought you were the reyuul," Granite whispered.

"You're slow. You would have died," she whispered back. She pointed west. "It's a half mile that way."

"I see. Let me know if we're going to be in trouble before we are in trouble."

"Watch for my arrow," she said before running off into the woods and out of sight again. Granite leaned over to Head of Quarter Jieggs. "HQ Jieggs, inform the rest that we're only a mile away. Weapons out and at the ready."

"Yes, sir."

Pol surveyed the forest as they continued and tried to remain alert, not wanting to be surprised again by a subtle attack. After a few hundred feet, the leaves had more of a gray hue. More leaves lay on the ground, and the quiet was unnerving. Bird tweets, bushes rustling, and even light breezes through the canopy were absent. Pol heard the arrow cut through the air before it plunked into the tree next to Granite.

The fall commander yelled, "Halt!"

A moment later, Gossama's brown cloak flitted through the trees before dropping next to him. "The villagers wait in the clearing up ahead. They are still under Fenric's control."

Relief warred with concern in Pol's heart. They had found the villagers, but they would have to fight them.

Granite shared a look with Stefan. "I hope this works." He yelled, "First vial!"

In a calm though forced tone, Corporal Rield commanded his fist, "Listen carefully. Open your pouches." He waited for everyone to follow the instruction. "Take out the blue painted vial." Rield verified everyone had the right color and took his out as well. "Open and drink it now."

Pol pulled out his wooden blue vial and drank the thick, sweet liquid. He shivered as he gulped it down.

Granite called out, "Five fists front and five behind. Hold the line and prepare to stop at the clearing."

Gossama said, "Distract the reyuul. Quig, you're with me."

"Wouldn't it be better to have Quig with us?" Pol asked.

"So flattered you want me by your side, but I can't do much in a pitched battle. I *can* snipe," the fey said.

Granite nodded, and Gossama fled with Quig. She would have the best chance of landing a shot, and Quig could keep up with her.

The fists moved into formation with Pol and Stefan's fist in the rear line, and under the guidance of the HQs, the formation advanced the last five hundred yards to the clearing.

Inside the large clearing, the two Gaodis families, including the children, waited for them, standing stone-still. Pol swallowed hard, seeing the emaciated youths and the sunken eyes of the adults. If they had to fight the enchanted villagers, there wouldn't be much resistance.

The HQs paused the troops at the clearing's edge. The villagers turned their heads as one to the left as if listening, and then all of them broke into a run toward the soldiers.

Granite lifted his voice. "Incapacitate them. Don't kill them. First line, advance."

HQ Jieggs called out orders, and the twenty-five frontline soldiers advanced with shields raised. The villagers plowed into the shields. The children crumpled to the ground while their parents continued to throw themselves at the soldiers. Pol's heart ached at the sight, but it only lasted a moment. The attacking villagers halted their attacks and stood still with vacant stares.

A shimmer of green-and-purple translucent light appeared in the center of the clearing.

Fenric materialized behind a shield of three adult villagers, smiling. "Thank you, General, for the soldiers."

Granite frowned. "Hold your positions."

With fluid movements, Fenric's hands weaved signs above his head in addition to his incantation.

Jieggs called out. "Shields up! Be ready for an attack."

The front line of soldiers in the clearing raised their shields with swords ready. Fenric finished with a small flourish and blurred a few feet away as one of Gossama's arrows hit the ground where he had been.

Two things happened at the same time. The villagers awoke, and the men caught the women who had started collapsing as they found their children on the ground. Boud looked around, confused for a moment, but appeared reassured when he saw the King's Army soldiers. "Help us. Please, help us!"

At the same time, the forward line of soldiers lowered their shields and swords.

"Come," Fenric called.

King's Army soldiers, including HQ Jieggs, advanced past the villagers toward the reyuul and into the clearing.

Touten and Boud yelled at the advancing soldiers, but none acknowledged the villagers as they continued into the clearing's center.

Fenric cackled, "Must have an even fight, General."

Granite yelled, "Red! Red!"

Corporal Rield commanded, "Drink the red vial now!"

Pol confirmed his red vial color, removed the cork, and slammed the bitter contents of the red vial to the back of his throat.

Granite shouted, "Corporal Rield, secure the villagers! HQ Reamy, form the line, three by two. Incapacitate and hold out as long as possible."

Pol heard Fenric command, "Protect me. Kill them."

HQ Jieggs calmly lifted his sword. "Interlocking formation." The now-enemy soldiers coalesced into a single line, with swords and shields at the ready. "Advance."

Pol wasn't afraid, and he wasn't angry. He had a mission. The small white flame flared within his soul.

<hr>

After the bitter draught from the red wooden vial raced down his throat, Stefan's heart pounded. So far, events were going according to plan, but he was not prepared for how many soldiers Fenric would turn against them.

He assisted Corporal Rield, Wrues, Thielda, and Pol in moving the villagers behind Granite's position. The children were alive but unconscious, with large bloody welts on their foreheads.

Boud carried his wife, and Stefan supported his eldest son to the edge of the clearing. Touten, the other father, carried his eldest daughter with his wife trailing wearily behind. Boud said, "Thank you. Thank you so much. We prayed for someone to save us."

Stefan pointed to Granite. "The fall commander never gave up on you."

"Stone? Thank Lohem. I knew Stone wouldn't stop looking."

Stefan wanted to be that reliable. Once the villagers were safely removed to the edge of the clearing, Rield said, "We have to return. The other soldiers will outnumber them."

Stefan followed Rield back in line, where twenty-five "enemy" King's Army soldiers advanced. Their movements were smooth and appeared voluntary, complicit with Fenric's commands. Without a cleric to break the reyuul's influence, there would be no way to reverse the control; they had to incapacitate their comrades. Stefan hoped their plan continued working. How much of the reyuul's strength did it take to control twenty-five adult men and women?

Three soldiers protected Fenric with shields raised as the reyuul continued with intricate movements and words.

Starting from their heads and running down the enemy soldiers, purple streaks of light ran down the swords, shields, and armor of the approaching fists.

Granite spat on the ground. "Jonta! They're enhanced. Be careful!"

Stefan's fist of soldiers formed the middle of the line, and he stood next to Pol behind Rield, Wrues, and Thielda in the front line. The bright-purple lines winding across the skin and armor concerned Stefan, but he figured he had a better chance here than with the vrent from earlier. The plan required they hold out for a little longer.

When the first blows came from the purple glowing swords, many friendly soldiers in the front line crumpled. Cries of pain rang out as shields and swords were batted away.

The purple light must have granted the enemy increased strength, as more than five in the front line immediately fell back, holding their shields against the onslaught or collapsing to the ground. In front of Pol, Thielda retreated, grunting and favoring her shield arm. Pol stepped forward into the hole, and Stefan shifted to his left, behind Wrues, ready to fill a gap.

Pol unleashed his fury, blocking massive blows with his shield and returning a brutal assault. He hammered the flat of his blade against the ear of his opponent, who crumpled to the ground. Pol then turned to help Wrues.

A grunt to Pol's left took a shield to the face and flew backward. Stefan took a deep breath and stepped forward into the line, his shield up to face a female soldier with a purple aura. With a flat affect and vacant eyes, she charged.

Stefan braced with his shield before him and flew backward, rolling from the impact and crying out in pain as his left ribs screamed from the jolt. He kept his feet underneath him and focused on not passing out from the pain. Not wanting the advancing female soldier to get behind Pol, Stefan charged and aimed his shield down, tackling her waist.

She brought her hilt down on his right flank as he attacked, and more ribs cracked through the chain mail. The soldier fell backwards with Stefan on top.

"Stop fighting!" Stefan yelled, holding her down with his shield, but she continued to struggle and started overpowering him. Bracing against the agonizing tearing pain across his chest and back, Stefan brought his shield up and then down with a glancing blow against her head. The female soldier went limp, and Stefan hoped he had not hurt her too badly.

Looking up, he found Pol parrying a stroke meant to skewer Stefan's chest.

Pol's crumpled shield and notched sword did not stop moving. A second purple-streaked soldier attacked Pol, and then a third. Stefan scanned the defending line of soldiers, noting breaks with at least two fists down or wounded. They were now outnumbered by the "enemy" soldiers. Pol was the stopgap in the line, and while his weapons blurred as he fought off the enhanced enemies, he had taken some hard hits.

Then Stefan saw something. A faint golden hue around Pol? Wait. No, there was nothing. Stefan looked back at the villagers huddled together. If the line did not hold here, they would die. Emboldened, Stefan braced his side and ran forward to fight alongside the glowing Pol, purposefully ignoring the risk of further hits to his chest or flank.

An enhanced purple Creyd aimed a glowing purple sword at Stefan's head. He dodged the swing and remained on the defensive with his sword, parrying instead of blocking the massive blows. The problem was that with every parry, his chest screamed in pain, and it was harder to breathe.

Stefan both felt and heard a humming sound behind him. It was a portal. Creyd continued his attacks when the screeching of vrents and the howl of a barkbeast poured through the portal. Their backs were unguarded, and the villagers were vulnerable. He and Granite had assumed the lost ones might attack the village, but Fenric must have kept them as insurance against their small force here in the forest.

Unable to spare another glance as he barely defended against a ferocious Creyd, he heard multiple arrows splitting the air with resulting screeches or thuds. A dozen or more Dasari rangers in brown cloaks led by Gossama burst past their flank, releasing blue-tipped arrows into howling monsters. Blue lightning flared above them as Quig flew through the canopy with the rangers.

Stefan lost his sword to one of Creyd's attacks, but as Stefan's chest was about to burst from pain, Creyd's movements slowed noticeably. His eyelids drooped as well. With a shake of his head, Creyd brought his sword down onto Stefan's shield, throwing Stefan backward.

Stefan could not inhale from the pain. The glowing Creyd stumbled forward, unable to raise his sword, and toppled onto his face before Stefan. The purple light receded and winked out all over his body.

Stefan threw his shield to the side and rolled onto his hands and knees. His upper body protested against any movement, but Stefan did not have the luxury to rest. Once on his feet, he jogged to help Pol, who retreated from four assailants. Pol favored his right side and limped, but just like Creyd, the enemy soldiers' movements became sluggish. Pol continued to defend and back away, and one by one, the enchanted soldiers collapsed where they stood.

Pol turned to Stefan. "What happened?"

Stefan was about to answer but was tackled to the ground by a Dasari ranger. A barkbeast's fist slammed down where Stefan had just been. The Dasari hauled Stefan to his feet and pushed him away from the barkbeast, saying, "Human, I know you can't understand me, but you are slow."

Stefan vomited from the pain but scrambled to regain balance, retreating from the barkbeast, and, in perfect Dasari, responded, "Gossama tells me that every day."

The male ranger tripped over his own feet as his head whipped around. Catching himself before he fell, he replied, "Dasari? From a human?"

Stefan asked beyond the wracking pains from his chest, "Who are you? How did you come here?"

"I am FallingLeaf from SilverGate. Excuse me. Your friends on the ground are in danger."

One vrent lay twitching on the ground with half a dozen arrows sticking out of it, but the plodding barkbeast was heading straight toward the King's Army soldiers lying unconscious in the clearing. Another vrent jumped from tree to tree above them. More Dasari were following it on the ground and over branches. Stefan did not have to worry about the vrent, but he had a tree stomping toward his allies.

Stefan did not know what to do, but then Pol stood between the barkbeast and the soldiers. His golden aura flared as he picked up his battered shield and then looked up at the huge monster. Pol shook his head, threw the shield down, and once again picked up a second sword. With a furious look in his eyes, Pol rushed forward, golden aura flaring and proceeded to hack and slash at the beast.

A second vrent, impaled with arrows, fell in a twitching mass to the ground a few feet from Stefan. Surprised, he jumped back and almost dropped his sword.

Gossama appeared next to him. "It missed."

"You could have warned me," Stefan said.

"Not my problem."

FallingLeaf pointed at Pol, hacking at the barkbeast and dodging away when gigantic fists swung. "Are you sure that one is not Dasari?"

"Not sure," Gossama said.

Quig exclaimed as it observed Pol, "It's happened. He's doing it. I want to help, but I can't do anything against a creature made of wood." The fey turned to Stefan. "Good job not dying!"

"Thanks," Stefan replied with a wry tone. "Gossama, how do we kill that thing?"

Gossama shrugged. "Don't know. Never tried."

FallingLeaf nodded. "Never tried."

"I have a reyuul to hunt. You kill the barkbeast," she told FallingLeaf and then melded into a tree.

Quig said, "Keep an eye on him, Stefan," and followed Gossama.

"I'll be fine," Stefan called out.

FallingLeaf yelled at Pol, "Youngling, out of the clearing!"

Pol nodded and continued hacking away at the barkbeast, successfully leading the monster away from the unconscious soldiers in the clearing. In his gold aura, Pol successfully avoided monstrous hits, and Stefan marveled at the young man's agility even while injured. When Pol finally tripped, the barkbeast's fist almost connected, but Pol spun out of the way, losing one of his swords and ending up facing the monster's backside. He stayed behind the barkbeast, which had a difficult time turning, and climbed up the back of the monster as easily as any tree. With the speed of an elemental fey, Pol reached the barkbeast's shoulder, and with a two-handed reverse thrust, he plunged his sword into the lost one's eye. Barely avoiding the hit from the barkbeast's arm, Pol fell to the ground as the monster reared in pain.

Stefan rushed forward and pulled Pol out of the way as the barkbeast roared in agony, grabbing at the sword which would not dislodge. The barkbeast retreated, howling, but tripped over a rope secured by two trees. The barkbeast fell, and FallingLeaf and other Dasari descended upon it, hacking it with their short swords and axes.

Every other minute, an arrow would buzz overhead, and Stefan knew Gossama and Quig continued to hunt Fenric.

Pol stumbled past Stefan and limped to his fallen sword. The young man's limp was serious, and he only held one sword as his other arm hung at his side. He pointed to the clearing where Granite was organizing the remaining King's Army troops to secure unconscious soldiers in the clearing. The villagers still huddled together on the south edge of the clearing with Dasari rangers standing guard.

"We have to protect those soldiers," Pol said.

"You're done," Stefan replied.

"I'm fine." Pol limped to Granite, who was directing soldiers to move the unconscious troops on the ground.

Amazed, Stefan followed Pol and approached Granite. "Fall Commander, where is Fenric?" Stefan asked.

Granite scanned the clearing. "Somewhere scheming; he may retreat, but I don't think he'll miss an opportunity to kill more Cordiaens, especially me. I am worried that we've given him time."

"I don't know if he has more lost ones to throw at us, but with the villagers secure, he doesn't have the same leverage against us," Stefan said.

"Why doesn't he just control more soldiers?" Pol asked.

"Reyuul only have so much power in a battle. It takes effort, concentration, and time. He also has to be close to his targets," Granite replied.

Stefan agreed with the logic, but the reyuul had other dangerous tricks.

Granite pointed to a shimmer as Fenric appeared next to a wounded soldier and slammed his dagger into the soldier's chest before disappearing.

"No!" Granite sprinted forward, with Stefan close behind. Granite yelled, "To me! To me!" King's Army soldiers who could, ran in his direction. "Cover the fallen!"

Stefan ran with Granite. They ended up on the far edge of the scattered groups of unconscious soldiers.

Pol could not move as fast and ended up covering a closer group by himself. The remaining guards were scattered about the field, ready to defend their unconscious brethren. Everyone searched for Fenric with swords drawn, and the uncertainty of the attacks was more daunting than the roaming lost ones being chased by the Dasari rangers.

When Fenric appeared and stabbed another soldier in the back, everyone, including Granite, ran to assist, but Fenric disappeared with a wicked grin.

Stefan grabbed Granite's arm. "Wait. That's what he wants. Tell the troops to stand back-to-back."

The soldiers obeyed Granite's shouted orders, and most formed pairs to guard the unconscious soldiers, but there were not enough, and some defended alone.

Fenric materialized to Stefan's left and jabbed at Granite. Stefan recognized the enchanted dagger, which Granite deflected down to his leg, slicing into his thigh. Fenric disappeared as Stefan countered with his sword.

The reyuul reappeared on a nearby tree. "You cannot win, General. I can decimate everyone here." Fenric disappeared as two arrows lodged in the tree where he had just stood. Stefan began counting.

"Stand your ground!" Granite yelled out as he fell to his knee and pressed his hands to the blood gushing from his leg. "Fenric! You don't have enough strength to take on all of us."

Fenric materialized, driving his dagger into an unprotected Wrues's back. "You're losing soldiers, General. I can do this for hours." Dark-blue lightning and bluesteel arrows cut through the air as the reyuul disappeared again.

Stefan kept the count and pushed anger aside, knowing it would cloud his judgment. He calmed his breathing and attempted to "sink" into the forest with both hands on his sword hilt. Looking at the fallen Wrues, Stefan remembered finding the dead old man in the village with his hands folded.

Lohem, I need help.

Nothing. He had to think. Stefan remembered his earlier conclusion after facing the ivey and the vrent. Once Fenric did not have time to prepare, he might become predictable.

Stefan scanned the locations of the nearby soldiers and visualized the scene from a bird's-eye view. He followed the path of where Fenric had attacked and the relationship to the previous one and continued to examine.

Fenric landed another successful stab at Goors's defending arm. The soldier cried out but prevented a mortal wound. Every second was another life, but Stefan had the count and the beginnings of a pattern.

Nearby, Pol met the reyuul's sudden dagger with his sword. Fenric growled and disappeared, but Pol had somehow anticipated the reyuul.

Stefan sprinted toward Pol and stood back to back over the fallen Wrues.

Pol said, "There's a faint hum just before he attacks, like when Gossama melded."

The pieces clicked into place in Stefan's mind, and the pattern emerged. "I know you're hurt, but run to Thielda. Now!"

To his credit, Pol did not hesitate and sprinted with his limp toward his fistmate. Stefan watched with trepidation and then validation as Pol defended against another dagger thrust aimed at Thielda. Fenric cursed and disappeared before the arrow flew right where he had just been.

Stefan yelled, "To me!" as he pointed to Granite.

Pol nodded, cocked his sword, and yelled back, "Aim low!"

Stefan set his sword and charged to the kneeling Granite with his sword pointed at Granite's head. Granite appeared confused for a second, looking between Pol and Stefan before understanding overtook his features. Granite's eyes narrowed as Stefan and Pol raced toward him, and at the last second, Granite leaned backward and away from Stefan's aim.

Fenric materialized on the other side of Granite, but Pol had already swung his sword in a high arc. The reyuul ducked under Pol's swing while Stefan angled his sword past Granite, sliding the blade into Fenric's gut.

Granite grabbed the distracted reyuul's arm and redirected the dagger away from his neck, driving it into Fenric's abdomen. Fenric was already disappearing and re-materialized a few feet away, falling over. The impaled sword and dagger remained.

Two bluesteel arrows pierced Fenric's chest.

Stefan shook his head and called out, "Gossama—"

"Yes, I'm slow. Do not call me fat, Shrewd One."

Granite grabbed Stefan's tunic. "Not over. You must kill him now."

Stefan dashed over to Fenric, who was mouthing words. The wounds around the dagger and the arrows began closing. Stefan ripped the dagger from Fenric's abdomen, and the reyuul screamed in agony. The dagger's power coursed through Stefan's arm.

With blood dripping from his mouth, Fenric whispered, "You cannot escape. We will find you."

Stefan lifted his arm, but blue lightning sizzled into the reyuul and three more bluesteel arrows implanted into the reyuul's body, including his eye and neck. The reyuul exhaled and fell limp.

Stefan dropped the dagger, which landed point first in the dirt, and he realized the mistake he was about to make in using the dagger. Gossama must have understood what might have happened.

After a moment, small pieces of Fenric's body fell away like ash from a burning log. More pieces fell away until the reyuul dissolved into the air, leaving behind a single rib. Again, the myths were true. All reyuul had at least one pure bone in their body.

He felt responsible for the reyuul's items and groaned as he bent over to pick up the rib and place it with the dagger in his belt. These were not things he could leave for anyone to pick up.

Pol slowly limped over and lifted his arm to clap Stefan on the back, but Stefan said, "Don't touch me."

Stefan could not handle another jolt to his ribs. He also felt jittery from the battle, the dagger, and the antidote, and every quiver shot additional pain through his ribs.

Pol held up his hands. "Okay, okay. Good job."

"You too, Hero."

"Hero. Oh, yes," Quig said, materializing above them.

Pol looked at his arms, but the light had faded. "Thanks, but I should be dead. How did the mind-controlled soldiers just collapse?"

"They were sedated. We used up all the herbalist's sleeping draught she makes for Granite. That was in the blue vial. The red vial had the antidote."

Pol's eyes opened wide. "But the timing. How did you know?"

"I didn't. Granite did. These guys will be out for hours. Granite took a risk, but the gamble worked. We might have killed some or been killed."

"Not bad, for a human," Quig said.

Stefan grinned. "Thanks for your help today, Quig."

"Dangerous, I admit, but the fey were well represented today."

Pol favored his left arm.

"How bad are you hurt?" Stefan asked.

"My left forearm and elbow won't move, and my ankle may not ever be the same. Those shields are almost worthless. I would be dead if that sleeping potion hadn't worked."

"When you make it four times as potent, it was all a matter of time…"

Stefan trailed off as he watched Granite drag himself over to Wrues. Granite cradled the soldier, whose lifeblood poured out of the chest puncture wound. Stefan and Pol followed and stood by, watching the rattling breaths. Wrues died a moment later. Granite laid him down and closed his eyes, moving on to the next dying soldier. Stefan didn't know first aid or how to help.

Corporal Rield grabbed his arm and guided him over to Granite. "Apply pressure to the wound using this pad. Once the bleeding has stopped, wrap this bandage around tightly. You understand?"

"Yes, sir." The dagger had severed the leg muscle. Stefan did not know if it had cleaved the bone.

When he pressed, Granite gritted his teeth. "How did you know where the reyuul would show up?"

Stefan pursed his lips. "Probability, physics, and psychology. Fenric must have assumed that we would have died at the hands of our enchanted brethren if not from the lost ones. Once he ran out of options, he became predictable. I'm sorry you got hurt."

Granite lay on the ground. "Not as bad as others. Might be dead if you hadn't anticipated him."

"Was not good enough. Many died."

Granite gave him an intense look. "Death is just the next step on the journey, not the end. But don't you see? So many more would have died if we hadn't followed your plan. For years, I will mourn those who died today, but I will rejoice in those who will live. Thank you."

"Would have been better if we had a cleric."

"What's Master Joern's first rule of military strategy?"

Stefan said, "Always protect the cleric." Fenric had executed an excellent strategy by removing the cleric from the battle. Stefan would remember these tactics.

After securing the bandage on Granite's leg, someone cleared their throat behind them.

"Stone?"

"Boud, I'm so glad you're safe," Granite said. Stefan had never heard the fall commander sound so relieved.

Boud dropped to his knees and hugged the fall commander. "Thank you for saving us. It was horrible. When we could control ourselves, we were locked in wooden cages, tired and hungry. My children cried, and then we would wake up every evening more tired and hungry."

Granite nodded. "I tried, Boud."

"I know you did, Stone. Seeing all those monsters and the reyuul…I don't know how you did it."

Granite pointed to Stefan and Pol. "With their help."

"Thank you very much." Boud looked over his shoulder at Quig. "But, Stone, am I seeing things or is there a flying salamander behind you?"

"I prefer axolotl, but yes, this is all me," Quig replied.

"He's a friend," Granite said, and Boud nodded.

"See, Stefan. I'm a friend. I upgraded."

"Yes, Quig, you are a friend." He looked around at the unconscious soldiers. "Do you have a way to get these soldiers back to the village? We can't carry everyone back. We'll have to call for help."

FallingLeaf stepped up with Gossama. "We won't need to."

A group of forty Dasari appeared at the edge of the clearing. Stefan recognized their rustic RainCrest clothing. Leader Mistfall approached Stefan with members of his council.

"Leader MistFall, it's been a long time," Stefan said.

The older Dasari smirked. "Shrewd One, you are always in the middle of events."

"Yes, I am trouble."

"It was reported that you killed the reyuul. Is this true?"

"We did, Leader," he said, pointing to Pol.

MistFall appeared thoughtful as he examined Pol. "And you attacked a barkbeast and killed a vrent?"

Pol nodded. "Yes, Leader."

MistFall sighed. "You are not normal humans. RainCrest owes you a debt." He gave commands to the other Dasari, who started creating litters and assisting soldiers to be transported. "Shrewd One. You helped us. We will help you get home. I must protect my investment."

Stefan gave Leader MistFall a small bow. "Thank you for the assistance. This is my commanding officer, Fall Commander Granite."

"Ah, the soldier. Please allow us to assist with your wounded."

Granite pointed to other fallen soldiers. "There are mortally wounded that I would ask to have priority."

Leader MistFall nodded. "Of course."

Granite thinned his lips. "Leader, I'm grateful for your assistance, and I don't want to seem ungrateful, but aren't we close to RainCrest? Did you know about this reyuul?"

Stefan balked at the question.

MistFall replied, "I was only aware of the reyuul recently, but with a starving population, there were more pressing things to deal with. I apologize for any neglect. I hope this won't affect our trading."

Granite replied, "Certainly not. We will stand by the agreement, and I will convey your apology to my superiors."

MistFall nodded. "Thank you, Fall Commander."

FallingLeaf approached and said, "Forgive me for interrupting, Leader MistFall, but a half mile west of here is a gate the reyuul had been constructing. Can your people guard it for now until it can be destroyed?"

"A gate?" the Leader asked.

Gossama said, "I have seen it. A gate that was to be like the SilverGate."

The leader's face fell flat. "Tainted One. Yes, we will guard it. For now, let's care for the humans." He left to direct his warriors.

Granite eyed the leader for a moment before accepting the invitation to ride on a litter. Gossama assisted others as well.

Granite raised his voice. "Pol, I see that arm and leg. Get on a litter."

"Yes, sir." Pol eased himself onto one of the litters set up by the RainCrest warriors.

Granite said, "What about you, Stefan?"

"I don't want to be jostled around. I can walk…but I'm not carrying Pol."

CHAPTER 28

Stefan's legs could not move anymore. He had been trudging behind Pol's litter for three hours as two RainCrest Dasari carried Pol. As usual, Pol had been magnanimous and offered to walk, but the two Dasari rangers snorted at Pol, whose left ankle and arm had become bruised, swollen, and deformed.

FallingLeaf and the RainCrest Dasari had already taken Granite and the more seriously wounded ahead. When the edge of the forest finally came into view, a young man wearing pearl-plate armor trimmed in crimson approached Stefan.

"Hail citizen, I'm Deukel, Voltai of the Forge. Allow me to assist."

When the Dasari dropped the litter and walked away, Pol grunted.

Stefan said, "Thank you, Voltai Deukel." He restrained the impulse to yell, *Where were you this morning?*

Voltai Deukel pulled Pol's litter with ease toward a pavilion that had been erected near the forest. Stefan remained at the tree line, examining the open pavilion with clerics and their guardian voltai tending to the wounded soldiers. The rest of the village had gathered around the missing villagers, hugging and dancing.

An infant was placed in its mother's arms, and the thin and tired woman cried and hugged her baby while Boud hugged her. Stefan smiled. He had helped do something good.

Stefan jumped in surprise when Quig landed on his shoulder with its small paws. "That's why I'm here, Stefan. My home is safe. You did well. Real well."

"Not as good as Pol."

"It's not a competition. You two received different gifts. You know, maybe there are some fey legends about you too." The fey grinned, and its blue furry appendages quivered around its head.

Stefan snapped his eyes to Quig. "What? Why didn't—"

"Because your head was already too full of yourself and probably still is. Why do you think the tenedrae allowed me to cross the Veil? Pol would not have made it through today without you."

Gossama stood right next to Stefan. "The fey is correct, but you are still slow."

Stefan grunted, and Quig said, "I must return for now. A battle like that is sure to have caused storms across the Veil. Shhh! Don't make it awkward. I'll be back." The fey faded from his shoulder with an exaggerated cackle.

FallingLeaf arrived, shielding his eyes from the sun. The remaining rangers must have hidden further into the forest.

Gossama said, "Fearless ranger of Miraden, still scared of the sky?"

"If you remember, I have traveled beyond our forest, but not in a long time. I like my forest."

"I have many homes, but I also like my forest," Gossama replied.

"But you didn't seem to like MistFall," Stefan prodded.

Their Dasari faces fell. Gossama said, "MistFall and I have our differences."

"Granite seemed to agree," Stefan added.

"Yes. He is wise. Here he comes."

Granite limped from the pavilion to where they stood. "The clerics and voltai arrived a few hours ago from Ariel." He patted his leg. "Lohem is amazing."

FallingLeaf said, "It is an unexpected blessing. How are they here?"

"We had called for them weeks ago. As Gossama says, we're slow."

The gathered RainCrest Dasari finished bringing soldiers to the forest's edge and hovered nearby while one of their warriors approached FallingLeaf. "I am RiverSap. We have fulfilled our obligation here. We will return to guard the reyuul's work. Have the humans bring their cleric soon."

FallingLeaf said, "Your help is appreciated."

RiverSap nodded and looked at Stefan. "My people are hungry. Don't take too long, Shrewd One."

"We will be there soon."

"Till then." The RainCrest Dasari melded into trees and disappeared into the forest.

FallingLeaf glanced at Gossama. "We should return and report to OakenRoot." He pointed to Granite's leg.

"You should rest your leg. Will you remain in Gaodis for some time?"

Granite patted Stefan on the back. "Yes. I've got two officers to train." He looked over at Gossama. "You'll train them again once Pol's healed?"

"Yes, but I must go to SilverGate with FallingLeaf. Will take time, I think."

"We'll be in RainCrest by the end of the week with supplies and the cleric. Keep an eye out for us."

FallingLeaf gave Granite a small bow. "Fall Commander, I'm sorry for the men and women you lost today. Gossama tells me that losing soldiers is especially difficult for you. The victory today was not small. Between the Dasari and Cordiae, this will be remembered."

Granite pursed his lips. "Who exactly are you, FallingLeaf?"

"I am Leader OakenRoot's son and a council member." His eyes became grave. "When Gossama sent word,"—he looked down—"there was some debate as to how to assist. I led the few rangers. I'm sorry I did not come with more."

"Many would not be alive if not for your help," Granite returned with a small bow. "Thank you."

FallingLeaf reached out his hand, and Granite grabbed his forearm. FallingLeaf held his arm for a moment before turning back into the forest. The other SilverGate Dasari rangers followed from their hiding spots.

Gossama stayed. "Thank you, Granite."

"Be nice when you get to SilverGate. FallingLeaf will speak of your efforts."

"Maybe." She looked at Stefan. "This one had much exposure to mandra. He will need purging."

"Good point. We won't have time to make it to the FireGate. I will have the cleric pray over him, and some chores will help purge his soul," Granite said.

Stefan grunted, and Gossama laughed. "Good job, Shrewd One. Thank you. Tell Youngling, thank you."

"I will. We'll see you soon."

Gossama lingered for a moment, gazing at the open field with the gathered villagers before sprinting away.

Granite lightly smacked Stefan on the head before leaning on him. "Do you know how much work I'm going to have to do to make this deal of yours work out?"

Stefan rubbed his head. "I'll give you a share of the profit."

"Better be more than one percent."

"One point five sounds right," Stefan replied.

Captain Dreint met them with a brown-bearded voltai and a cleric. "You did well, Fall Commander. Nothing to report except the clerics and voltai showed up a few hours ago."

"Fall Commander, I'm Heart, Voltai of the Hall, and this is Cleric Aileb. I'm sorry we didn't arrive sooner."

"Thank you, Voltai Heart. My wounded troops will survive now that you're here. Don't apologize. We couldn't wait for fear that the reyuul might attack the village again. Speaking of which, Stefan, cough up that dagger."

Stefan pulled the sheathed dagger and the solitary rib from his belt; he could still feel the vibration of mandra in the dagger's hilt. Voltai Heart began praying, and the edges of his pearl armor glowed. The hum in Stefan's hand dissipated, and the voltai took the dagger and bone with a white linen cloth edged with Cordiaen words. He wrapped the dagger in the cloth.

"That was a nasty dagger," Granite said. He glanced back at the forest. "And there's a gate that needs further dismantling, and the clerics should consecrate the ground. We'll combine that with the trip to RainCrest."

Cleric Aileb nodded. "We'll be happy to help; things like that have a tendency to cause problems if not addressed." He eyed the rib. "Necromancy is not beyond reyuul. Voltai Heart, place those items in my quarters. I'll dispose of them properly." The voltai nodded and left for the cleric's pavilion, still murmuring prayers with his glowing pearl armor.

Granite began limping toward the pavilion and holding on to Stefan. "Excellent. Is Master Joern here?"

"He…he couldn't make it, Fall Commander. He sent his request for a very detailed report," Cleric Aileb replied.

Granite said, "I was hoping to meet him. One day. Let's coordinate getting the wounded back to the garrison."

⁓⁓⁓

Three days after the Battle of Miraden, as it became known, Stefan assisted Goors in lowering Wrues's casket into a grave. The entire village, the remaining garrison, and the visiting clerics and voltai watched as Stefan did his best not to drop the decorated pine casket. Once the wood container rested in the grave, Stefan took Goors's offered hand and climbed out. Stefan brushed off any remaining dirt and resumed his position by Pol, who stood to the side.

Cleric Aileb led his fellow clerics in a circle around the graves and began chanting the initial ritual dirge. In typical Cordiaen fashion, the clerics and voltai continued with prayers, chants, and finished with "The Hymn of Death," and the assembly joined in singing.

Once the song ended, the clerics and voltai fell in line behind Granite. In his officer's dress uniform—a collared crimson shirt with crimson pants trimmed in white—Granite stepped forward from a line of dignitaries, including Judge Fead and the assembled clerics.

He cleared his throat. "I want to thank everyone for coming here today. We're grieving for the men and women who died protecting this village and this country. Ten soldiers gave their lives fighting evil that threatened the community. Had this evil not been stopped here, untold horrors would have been unleashed on the village and beyond. Some might say that these battles were small and not like legendary wars of history, but every single soldier who died fought just as bravely as those heroes of old. Thank you for being here and honoring these men and women. Thank you for working with the soldiers to rebuild. As a community, this village will continue to prosper."

"Hear! Hear!" someone called out.

"Tell it, Stone."

Granite cleared his throat again. "I served as General for Cordiae in the Jetean War before coming to Gaodis and lost many good men and women. Coming here made a difference for me, and I thank you for that, but I especially thank Cleric Bruit, who saw that pain and pointed me to Lohem. I know Lohem is calling me to continue defending this country against the evil that would infest it. I can't hide from it, just like I couldn't hide from the pain."

"That's right, Stone."

Granite nodded. "I've learned a lot of tactics over the years leading Cordiaen armies, but the most important one is: 'Protect the cleric.' " The gathered voltai nodded along with the clerics. "I want to publicly apologize for having failed Bruit when the reyuul targeted him. Lohem helped us win the battle. It won't be easy, but I won't stop fighting until the reyuul can't threaten Cordiae. I will protect the clerics that serve us, and I will do my best to protect everyone. Thank you, again, for being here."

Granite stepped back as the voltai resumed their guard positions. The villagers formed a line and came by the casket as families to pay their respects.

Stefan absorbed every single detail and burned it into his brain. The deaths weighed upon him. If he was going to become an officer, he resolved to prevent as many deaths as possible, especially clerics.

Granite came up to Stefan and Pol and shook their hands. "Not the same since you arrived."

"Much better," Pol admitted.

"It's fine," Stefan replied.

"Just fine? I sent a glowing review of your success to your father. It's more than just fine."

"Depends on how much profit I make on the Dasari trade."

Granite snorted.

Stefan added, "The military is going to take getting used to, but I still feel like I'm meant for more."

Granite shrugged. "Have to see where it leads. You've made some good decisions recently."

"Maybe."

"What about you, Granite?" Pol asked.

"Lohem made it clear that my return to command was long overdue. I'm doing well."

Fuiger stepped up with a flushed face and eyes on the brink of losing tears. He handed Granite a wooden mug filled with beer and passed Cleric Bruit another while keeping one for himself.

"For those who left before us."

"May they travel in peace," came the response from everyone, including Stefan and Pol.

Granite emptied the contents. "Thanks, Fuiger. I'll have to wait for more when I get back."

"Oh, I figured. It'll give me time to fix more things here." He smacked Stefan on the back, and the pain erupted across his chest from his injuries. "Heard you were a big help and not a whiny baby. Granite, you should put him in the stocks more often."

"Don't you worry, Fuiger. We got plans for him. You two return to the garrison and finish preparations. We leave at first light for RainCrest."

～～～

A few days later, Pol raced through the canopy with Gossama ahead of Stefan, Granite, and FallingLeaf. They were almost to SilverGate, and Pol could not believe how much he had missed the trees after only ten days.

The trade convoy safely delivered the supplies to RainCrest, and Leader MistFall beamed as the RainCrest Dasari cheered in the streets. Gossama had remained outside the gates while FallingLeaf acted as envoy for his father.

"Leader OakenRoot sends his happiness that the citizens of RainCrest are being fed. He extends his support for food if needed," FallingLeaf reported.

"Duly noted, but surely OakenRoot can see that RainCrest can survive on its own even with setbacks," MistFall replied.

Pride tainted the leader's voice. Stefan had talked like that when Pol had first met him.

If FallingLeaf was offended, his face didn't show it. "Leader OakenRoot is grateful for your assistance with the demolition of the reyuul's attempt at the UnderRealm gate nearby."

"Ah, yes. Once the clerics have finished their part, we will work on taking the gate apart, as agreed."

Relief washed over Pol knowing that Fenric's work would be destroyed. The accompanying delegation of soldiers, clerics, and voltai left for the reyuul's gate while Stefan, Pol, Granite, Gossama, and FallingLeaf departed for SilverGate.

Unlike RainCrest, SilverGate was an ancient city that soared above the canopy. FallingLeaf had explained how his ancestors had raised the city from the ground and worked with Petra to create the structures. Silver-bordered tiered towers interspersed with enormous trees served as residences throughout the city. Streams draining from the Silver River meandered through the city and weaved under towers and through the architecture. Tradespeople and shops adorned various avenues leading up to the central tower where FallingLeaf lived.

A main stone road began at the gates and wound through the city with streams of silver water passing under the wide path. At the base of the largest tower, a large Dasari with yellow leaf-patterned skin that had a touch of orange on the edges stood with eight other Dasari of various colors.

When Pol's group approached, FallingLeaf stepped forward and bowed to the yellow Dasari. Pol assumed him to be Leader OakenRoot, who embraced his son and then purposefully stepped forward and embraced a shocked Gossama.

"Gossama, you do not visit enough. Welcome."

When he released her, Gossama dipped her head. "Don't embarrass me, Leader."

OakenRoot smiled impishly as another Dasari male, with dark-green and orange leaves adorning his skin, also hugged Gossama. "The leader is correct. You should visit your old teacher more."

"Thank you, TwoStems. I've been busy."

"Excuses, youngling."

"Good excuses."

Pol marveled at how well Gossama was treated in SilverGate as compared to RainCrest.

Using Cordiaen, Leader OakenRoot said, "Welcome, Fall Commander Granite; Stefan, son of Daoringer; and Pol, son of Laor. I am Leader OakenRoot. This is TwoStems, Head of the Council. We welcome you to SilverGate."

Granite responded in Dasari, "Thank you, Leader, for welcoming us to your home." He scooped a small pile of dirt and placed it before the leader. Stefan and Pol did the same, as previously instructed.

Leader OakenRoot shook his head. "Is it not enough that you have saved our forest, but you also speak our language and show respect like a Dasari?" The leader motioned for them to follow him inside the tower. Pol marveled at the massive silverwood that formed the core; the tower appeared to have grown from the immense tree.

OakenRoot observed him. "Wonderful, yes?"

"Yes, Leader."

The leader placed his hand into the tree, and a silver platform materialized underneath them, formed from the tree. "Do not be scared. We will move upward."

Pol felt Gossama's steadying hand on his arm when the platform rose. When he gave her a strange look, Gossama replied, "Leader is a Sculptor. Has the old power. Same as ancient neraida who fashioned the forest."

OakenRoot smiled and pointed for them to step off at the top. The elder Dasari took their spots while Leader OakenRoot assumed his chair.

OakenRoot cleared his throat. "Gossama and FallingLeaf have told me what happened with the reyuul and the gate. This is not a small thing. I also know that you all just came from providing RainCrest with food from your village. This also is not a small thing. I have sent word to your king. I am pleased that he was surprised." OakenRoot paused. "But Dasari do not like to owe favors."

Gossama gave Pol a smug smile.

"Fall Commander Granite," OakenRoot continued, "I understand these two younglings have been entrusted to your care and teaching."

"Yes, Leader. I am indebted to Quon Daoringer, who recommended them to become officers in the King's Army."

"Gossama has said as much. She values your friendship, and she is not one to speak highly of most. I had offered to train the boys as rangers, but they would not survive long enough to endure the training."

Pol was crestfallen, and OakenRoot pointed and laughed at him. "Yes, FallingLeaf, he acts like a Dasari, no?"

Gossama and FallingLeaf nodded with serious faces.

Leader OakenRoot continued, "Since I cannot make them Dasari rangers, I offer them both a gift to help with their training." He motioned for two Dasari servants to approach. One carried a matching blue sword and shield, both with silver trim, and laid them before Stefan, while the other struggled under a two-handed blue greatsword before Pol.

OakenRoot said, "These weapons will take some getting used to."

"It's bluesteel," Pol said. He received the two-handed sword with awe. Never in his dreams had he imagined such a gift.

OakenRoot said, "King Sraung gave permission for you two to receive these gifts and receive training."

Granite lifted an eyebrow. "Did he?"

"Oh yes. Your defeat of the reyuul and cleansing the forest of lost ones is now a historical event in Miraden. It will be made into song. Your actions go above and beyond the accords with Cordiae."

Granite held up a hand. "Leader, we only defended our village."

OakenRoot lifted his chin. "No, not only." FallingLeaf and Gossama lowered their heads at his tone. "You saved this forest, you aided RainCrest, and you ensured the land became sacred again with your own clerics." Granite smiled. "Your humility and your experience is known to me, Fall Commander. Will they accept my gifts?"

Granite bowed, and Stefan and Pol followed his example. "I would let them speak."

Pol rose and said, "I would be honored."

"Coming from a Vroshen, we are honored," OakenRoot replied.

Stefan picked up the weapons, and after admiring them, said, "It's strange for me to accept gifts that I cannot repay."

OakenRoot clapped his hands. "This is good. Stefan, son of Daoringer, and Pol, son of Laor, you are now citizens and students of SilverGate. This has never been done before."

"Don't mess up," Gossama whispered.

Stefan and Pol replied in unison, "Thank you, Leader OakenRoot."

"You are most welcome, but be warned. As with anything Lohem provides, these gifts come with responsibility. The metal is not like the whitesteel of your country. You must train to be accustomed to it. It will only protect the bearer of the armor and weapons and not those around you."

Gossama added, "Like my arrows, you will learn to hunt reyuul. Leader OakenRoot has big plans for you."

Pol turned to Granite. "Really?"

"Yes. Fenric was bold enough to attempt this mission. I have fought reyuul often enough to know they plan and scheme and do nothing without a reason. We've only seen the beginning."

Pol hefted the sword. The silver trim accented the burnished and gleaming blue metal. A smile crept across his face. This was more than he had hoped for. This was his chance to restore honor to his family. Then his fingers found a large ornate button on the hilt with a small flame engraved on it.

Gossama's eyes smiled. "Go ahead."

When Pol pressed the button, the greatsword glowed a bright blue and cleanly fractured into two perfectly balanced sabers. "Now that's special."

"Just like you," a high-pitched voice piped from the side of the large chamber. Quig had appeared next to a great horse with iridescent wings.

OakenRoot and the Dasari Elders stood and bowed to the fey guests. "It's true then. A fey crossed the Veil and assisted in the battle. Jord, you have not blessed our council chamber in centuries. I welcome you and your companion."

The pegasus dipped its head in a smooth, graceful movement. "The Sculptor is kind," it replied in a perfect tenor.

Pol just assumed by its majesty that it was some sort of elite creature in the FeyRealm.

"Pascal informed me that this elemental, Quig, had been granted permission to cross the Veil and assist these humans. The tenedrae is always occupied with greater dangers."

OakenRoot's face became grave, and the Council murmured at the news. Gossama leaned over. "Lohem was concerned about you two."

OakenRoot said, "Quig, is it? We thank you for your service to this realm and for Miraden."

"Pleasure was mine, Sculptor. These events wreaked havoc in our realm, but I believed we needed to take a larger role in defending our home."

Jord flexed its iridescent wings. "This battle is being discussed in our communities. This mandrate also involved our fey enemies, and we must be prepared."

His soulfire embers ignited, and Pol tightened his grip on his new swords. "Whatever you need, Quig. Just ask."

"Told you," Quig said to the pegasus. "Just learn how to wield those, Pol."

Stefan said, "Thank you, Quig. You made a difference."

Quig whipped around the air in a tight circle. "Gratitude? Oh, my." Quig bowed. "You're welcome, Stefan. I'm sorry I can't stay, but the Veil exists for a reason. Fey are not meant to remain here."

"You will be missed. Thank you," Gossama added.

Jord said, "You were right, Quig. So many heroes."

Pol glanced at Stefan. He was a hero, too, not just some noble.

Stefan examined his weapons. "This. This is more like it." He glanced at Pol. "I guess we're in this together."

Pol said, "You better keep up."

EPILOGUE

Geraul roused, opening his eyes to blinding morning light piercing the carriage window. He slowly lifted himself on the carriage bench and found Stacia sitting across from him, wearing her usual gray tunic and brown pants with her dark hair in a ponytail. He remembered escaping the keep, but when he glanced out the window, the unfamiliar buildings and streets concerned him. "Where are we?"

Stacia wore simple clothes, but she sat like a noblewoman with her hands folded atop her lap and her legs crossed. Still beautiful. "Shaorn. How are you feeling?"

He rubbed his head. "Shaorn? How long was I out?"

"Four days. You emptied your well, and that has consequences, especially for beginners."

He remembered his escape and looked out the windows. "Are we being chased?"

"Word of your escape is still behind us. It usually takes a week to travel from Dael to Shaorn; I have some friends who assisted our travels." She leaned forward. "You'll have to hide for a while. Maybe do some training?"

Geraul stared out the window at the poorly maintained buildings, beggars, and ragged clothes of the citizens. Things were going to be different, but he didn't have anywhere else to go. "Sure. I have to pick up the pieces of my life." He examined the two black scales on his right forearm. "This power gave me my freedom. I pay my debts."

Stacia smiled as the carriage came to a halt next to a two-story building. With weak legs, Geraul followed Stacia. She stopped before a closed door to what appeared to be a warehouse, and the smell reminded him of a tannery.

A horizontal wooden slot opened, and a pair of eyes examined Stacia and widened. The slot closed, and he could hear a flurry of activity with hushed warnings.

Geraul said, "What is this?"

She lifted her voice to be heard on the other side of the door, which was being unlocked. "This is my guild."

"Your guild? You run it? How? You've been working for me for two years."

"I'm a woman; I can multitask. I needed you."

The door opened, and Geraul followed Stacia into the warehouse. Stacks of skins lay near the walls as workers, sweating and dirty, lined up on either side as Stacia passed through. They kept their eyes on the ground and remained silent as she passed. Near the end of the warehouse, two workers pulled up doors. Geraul peered down, finding a dark, winding staircase. Stacia descended, and Geraul glanced around as everyone remained still, waiting for her to leave. Who was this woman?

At the bottom of the stairs, an open door led to a cellar, but Stacia paused before the cellar entrance. She lifted out a key from around her neck and pushed it forward; the end of the key disappeared as if inserted into an invisible lock. When she turned the key, the door didn't open. Instead, an elliptical black void with blue and red borders appeared. Stacia grabbed Geraul's hand and guided him through.

The sensation of passing through the void was similar to walking through an icy waterfall, and Geraul became lightheaded and slightly disoriented, similar to his short teleports, but more disconcerting.

His feet stepped on stone after passing through the void, and Geraul held his breath as he looked around. The vast hall reached so high and far. He had never seen anything like it.

A short man with one brown and one blue eye, a weathered face, gray hair, and light skin waited.

"Sienter, if you're greeting me, something's wrong," Stacia said.

"Fenric failed on all accounts, but I see you were successful."

Stacia sighed. "Fenric was a gamble. Koen won't be surprised." She gestured to Geraul. "Sienter, this is Geraul. Geraul, this is Sienter. He's very useful."

The short man gave Geraul a critical look. "So, this is the one."

Stacia replied, "Yes. Are you ready to train, Geraul?"

"The one?" Geraul asked.

Stacia nodded. "Yes, the one who will help us win Shaorn."

Geraul recognized purpose. He could manipulate it as needed, but he had a goal now.

"I'm ready."

<hr>

Quon Daoringer ignored the stuttering chamberlain and stone-still KingGuards as he stormed into the King's Council Chamber.

King Sraung sat in a gold studded leather chair at a small table with a squat-looking Cordiaen noble.

"Daoringer, you can't just do that. You're going to give my chamberlain a stroke," King Sraung said.

"They attacked my son, Your Majesty. Tell me we're at war."

"Of course we are, Daoringer, but what do you want me to do? Send an army into Ampestria? I'm not my father, and you know it. Sit down, we're waiting on a guest."

Daoringer walked around and took an open seat next to the king.

"Are you going to bring your troublemaker home?" King Sraung asked.

Daoringer held up a letter from Stefan. "No. He's a different kid. Granite's doing what I knew he could do. I don't want to pull him back, but I want him protected."

"Agreed. We've already decided to fill the garrison and support Granite." The King leaned forward, resting his arms on the table. "We are reinstituting the trade embargo against Ampestria and increasing army conscriptions, but what we need is more information about what the reyuul was doing."

With a pointed glance at Quon Daoringer, the king's chamberlain raised his voice from the entrance. "Master Joern of the Royal Point."

Daoringer had never seen the famed recluse cleric up close. The right leg and left arm were so deformed, the cleric almost dragged his leg. Black scales ran up and down his face and scalp, with patches of hair missing. Bulges from his abdomen and flank pushed against his cleric's robes. The cleric was hideous, but Daoringer knew that the appearance, while earned, was deceiving. The reyuul-turned-cleric was an unusual creature.

The cleric shuffled into the room with a small bow to the king. In a craggy voice, he said, "Forgive my inability to kneel, King Sraung."

"Don't bother. Your loyalty is not in question here." King Sraung pointed to the Head of the Pulse. "Minister Caive?"

The squat man gave Cleric Joern a serious look. "We know what happened in Gaodis and Miraden, Master Joern, but what we don't know is what the reyuul wanted with the forest and Qual Stefan. What can you tell us?"

"Quon Daoringer, I'm confident they wanted a new reyuul. Intelligent but troubled youth are classic targets, especially if they have connections. Your son must be talented."

"Don't tell him that," the quon said.

"I won't, but I would like to question him, Quon. He could provide insights I can only speculate upon."

Daoringer inwardly laughed at what his son would think of the enigma of Cleric Joern.

"I approve. Your Majesty?"

King Sraung leaned back in his chair. "Most definitely. Whatever you need."

Cleric Joern bowed his head. "Thank you, Your Majesty. Minister Caive, as for the forest, this would have been an ambitious mission for the Ampestrian Council. High risk, but high reward for them. Make no mistake. This is an act of war."

"See!" Daoringer said.

"Also, the Ampestrian High Council would not have trusted a mission like this to chance. I'm concerned Fenric was working with others who might be in the country."

Caive continued to regard the cleric seriously. "Agreed. Our intelligence supports this hypothesis."

King Sraung said, "Fine. Go to Gaodis, Master Joern, and report back to me. Caive, dig deep and root out any foreign infiltration. I feel like we're missing something. Daoringer, let's get the other quons on board. We have work to do."

〜〜

Prime Minister Koen of Ampestria noted the spatial disturbance of a portal into his private chambers before it opened. He turned over some sensitive documents as ArchMandrate Jenter stepped out of a portal before him.

"Fenric failed," Jenter reported. "Though he came close on both accounts."

"A shame," Koen replied without emotion. "A river of descended pouring out into Cordiae would have been lovely."

"What about the boy? Getting more reyuul to take such a mission would be hard. Surely the country will be on alert."

Koen floated out of his chair and landed near Jenter. "Pointless. They're too far behind. The boy must die, but we also have new targets now. If reyuul won't do it, we have other options. Send a message across the Veil. Tell him it's time."

〜〜

Laor answered the door to his home.

"Are you Laor?" A King's Army grunt held a letter.

Dear Lohem, let my son be alive. "Yes. How can I help?"

The grunt held out the letter.

Laor took a deep breath. "Is this about Pol?"

"Yes. Don't worry. He's alive."

Relief washed over the cobbler. "Forgive me, but doesn't the post usually deliver messages for the King's Army?"

"Not for someone like Pol. This is an honor."

The tone caught Laor by surprise. "I didn't catch your name."

"Goors, sir."

"Thank you."

"No. Thank you for raising him so well. You can send a reply through the Dael garrison. Pol didn't want me to wait. Excuse me."

Bewildered at the comments, Laor watched the soldier leave and closed the door. He immediately opened the letter.

Father,

I've written this letter many times since I've been here. I just came back from a battle in Miraden Forest where we defeated a reyuul.

Grandfather would have been proud. Uncle Eash would have been proud.

I did well, Father. But, the only reason I did well was that I forgave you. I forgive you. I wasn't really angry at the nobles. I was angry with you, and I'm sorry.

Don't be upset, but I almost died a few times since I've been here, and I realized how upset I would have been if I hadn't made sure you knew that I love you.

Thank you for letting me make my own decisions and supporting me. Don't tell Mother I almost died, and give my love to the girls. I will write again.

Peace,

Pol

Holding the letter, Laor slid to the ground against the door.

Lohem had answered his prayers, again.

THE END

DID YOU REALLY THINK THIS WAS THE END?

This is only the beginning:

Within the story, you will find a *game* for you! This is the *first* puzzle. Pay attention and find the password. The clues are hidden and will grant you access to the *First* Trial of the Tenedrae. You will learn the rules as you go, but you will need to follow the *letter* of the law. Yes, the *move* order is important.

Travel to www.mustardseedrealms.com/rotlopuzzle

Find the clues. Survive the Trial. Enter Mariad.

ACKNOWLEDGEMENTS

What an adventure! It takes a community to make a story come alive. With each stage of development, God sent awesome people to guide and help me reach the next level.

Thank you to my wife, Frances, who allowed me to follow my dream and sub-create the MSR universe.

Special thank you to my kids who have been so patient with their father while navigating Church, school, sports, playtime, dinner, diapers, discipline, trips, etc. You made the journey special, and I don't think I would have made the first hurdle without my first superfan. Thank you, Teresa, for reading the first draft, and all subsequent drafts. You pushed through, and that gave me the strength to continue.

To my early alpha readers, Amanda McGoff and Fr. Jonathan Torres, who took on the third draft and rewarded me with crucial feedback. Without your epic efforts, I don't know if I would have persevered beyond that stage. Thank you.

To Brittani, for providing amazing pro editing insights that helped shape the story. Thank you for being kind and brutal all at once.

A special thank you to my beta readers, Carmel, Matthew, John, Will, Nocthar, Dicing, Veronica, Cyprian, Zack G, and Martin for blessing me with their amazing perspective. Thank you for strengthening my resolve through your encouragement and critiques. Thank you for also being a part of the early discord community and supporting the vision.

To Joe for his gift of art that made the invisible, visible. Teresan took on a whole new dimension with your talent.

To all the early Mustardseed Realms discord members who put up with my GM's, followed the MSR updates, newsletter, YouTube channel, and supported me with good advice, community, and honest critiques:

Tenedrae: Souce (See below), MashinMango (master of security and puzzles who spent hours listening to a crazy old man.)

Sculptors: Pokerface, pipers.cpp, Dicing, Nocthar

Advisors: brainstorm.eth, SeizeYour, Zack G.

Council Members: Deanzy

Members: Pierre and more.

I'm grateful to all the Neo Tokyo citizens who advised on web3 and business matters, especially Seize, brainstorm (Omar), MHL, Flower83, and Prodigi. Thank you to hogsheadcheese for legal services, and special props to FireStorm.

Last, but not least, thank you to the one who never faded, never gave up, and always gave his time and blistering honest critiques day in and day out for months and months. This guy was the first in Mustardseed Realms, the one who listened to all my crazy ideas, and the one who shared his amazing art to create the foundation of MSR. Souce, sir…bro…words can't describe my gratitude except to say: this is only the beginning.

ABOUT THE AUTHOR

David raises his hand, and his family quiets. One by one, portals open behind each member, and they gleefully jump through, eager to cause trouble. As the maniacal laughter spreads throughout the capitol city of Mariad, the Mustardseed Realms team members shake their heads, wondering what insanity will occur next.

The founder, David Liberto, has put years into the project to fulfill a dream of telling stories that his mother, father, wife, kids, friends, and God would enjoy and appreciate.

David lives with his wife and five children in the United States, where he battles lawn monsters every week, occasionally teleports to work, and volunteers in Church ministries during the day. At night, David continues to craft diabolical plans to take over the world through Mustardseed Realms.

Code Key:

a b c d e f g h i j k l m n o p q r

s t u v w x y z

MUSTARDSEED REALMS

WWW.MUSTARDSEEDREALMS.COM

Come visit Mustardseed Realms on the world wide web for all your world domination needs, but especially to find good stories, podcasts, and portals to fun realms.

Sign up for the Mustardseed Realms Newsletter, the official and exclusive newsletter for David Liberto. When you sign up for the newsletter, you will be rewarded with a free short story featuring Quig!

Explore the MSR website and discover loads of content, including the video and audios version of our podcast.

SOCIAL MEDIA

Portal to current links and apps:
www.linktr.ee/mustardseedrealms

Community:
Join our community hang-out in the MSR Discord and Facebook group. Invites available on our website and in the linktr.ee directory.

CORDIAEN PULSE COMMUNICATION

It has come to our attention that you may not have the training we offer our Pulse operatives in decoding.

Do not be alarmed. I have provided the documents necessary for you to continue your mission.

Find the key. Solve the code...we won't give you everything.

-Minister Caive